Dave Margoshes

WISEMAN'S WAGER

A Novel

COTEAU BOOKS

Edited by David Homel
Front cover designed by David Drummond
Interior designed and typeset by Susan Buck
Printed and bound in Canada at Houghton Boston

Library and Archives Canada Cataloguing in Publication

Margoshes, Dave, 1941-, author
        Wiseman's wager : a novel / Dave Margoshes.

Issued in print and electronic formats.
ISBN 978-1-55050-601-3 (pbk.).--ISBN 978-1-55050-602-0 (pdf).--
ISBN 978-1-55050-809-3 (epub).--ISBN 978-1-55050-810-9 (mobi)

        I. Title.

PS8576.A647W58 2014   C813'.54   C2014-903783-X ·
                                           C2014-903784-8

COTEAU
BOOKS
2517 Victoria Avenue
Regina, Saskatchewan
Canada   S4P 0T2
www.coteaubooks.com

Available in Canada from:
Publishers Group Canada
2440 Viking Way
Richmond, British Columbia
Canada   V6V 1N2

10 9 8 7 6 5 4 3 2 1

Coteau Books gratefully acknowledges the financial support of its publishing program by: the Saskatchewan Arts Board, The Canada Council for the Arts, the Government of Canada through the Canada Book Fund, the City of Regina and the Government of Saskatchewan through Creative Saskatchewan.

*This novel was inspired by the lives of the
American novelist Henry Roth,
and my late father-in-law Ira Silbar.*

It's dedicated to Ira's memory.

PART I

A POSSIBLE BEGINNING

FOUR FORTY-FIVE. The Earth wobbles on its axis like a gyroscope beginning to run down and the motion awakens Zan, jerking him upright in the dark like a puppet. Fitzgerald was both right and wrong. It *is* always night in the soul, but not always three a.m.

But what kind of a *cockamayme* believes in the soul anyway? He was at synagogue the day before, with Abe. Some nice people there, all right, but much talk of God. Synagogue is one thing, no harm there, maybe he'll join, if they'll have him, but what kind of a *cockamayme* believes in God? Two thousand years ago, three thousand, all that Biblical spirit, maybe then. *Alter cockers* like Abraham and Moses, heavy hitters like David, okay, those guys believing in God maybe made some sense. They didn't know any better. But after the Romans, the Assyrians, the Inquisition, the pogroms, Auschwitz? Not to mention the new barbarians at Israel's gates, suicide bombers and airplane hijackers. And not a peep from on high in all that time. Who the hell could believe in a God like that? Zan gives his head a shake and burrows it back into the pillow.

"JAN. 1, 1989. A new year. Celebrated by sleeping late. No hangover – and why should there be?"

Zan makes this entry in his journal between his first cup of coffee and the second. Why, indeed? He hasn't had a drink in as many years as he's been keeping the journal, twenty-three years exactly, not since Jan. 1, 1966, almost two years after – he has to pause for a second to summon up her name – Rose, that's it, Rose told him if he went away for the weekend not to bother coming back. He'd had his first meltdown then – breakup, breakdown, then fix up, if not exactly redemption. It had led eventually to Jack, the man who, he had gradually come to acknowledge, saved his life, putting him back together piece by piece like Humpty Dumpty. "You're not really an alcoholic," Jack had said after they'd been meeting for a couple of weeks. "You don't even like to drink. You're acting out some sort of a twisted image of yourself, a false self, this macho thing, *men drink*. You don't need to prove you're a man to anyone, certainly not yourself. Just stop." He really had been that easy to read, it really had been that easy to quit what he'd thought was an addiction but was really just an obsession. One new year's resolution that really worked.

He had forgotten that, or it hadn't registered, which amounts to the same thing, Jack used to say; he was sixty years old then and already his memory was going. Neurological scar or emotional scar, it's scar tissue just the same, and almost a quarter of a century later, that tissue was *thick*. Either way, getting things down on paper seemed like a prudent course of action, a record, a way of keeping tabs on himself. So Jack had told him. Zan had to laugh: "Telling a writer to write things down!" But in those days, when Jack said something, Zan tended to listen. He was his lifeline. Not like this Zelda woman – she tells Zan things, sometimes he listens, more often not. What could she tell him he doesn't already know? Eighty-two years old, almost eighty-three – old enough to be this girl's grandfather! – he's been around the block once or twice.

And what kind of a name for a woman is Zelda anyway?

He thinks, inevitably, of Fitzgerald again, *his* Zelda, of the craziness that man had to endure, the craziness he caused. Three a.m., well, maybe so.

He has his usual breakfast, a peeled orange, toast, a cup of the yogurt he makes on the windowsill the old-fashioned way, the way his mother used to do it, except with skim milk, in Mason jars. Afterwards, on a whim, he phones for a cab and rides to the airport, the pretentiously named Calgary International, has a third cup of coffee and a sawdusty bran muffin in the coffee shop upstairs and watches, as much as he can through the glass brick windows, one arrival and one departure. He could find a pay phone, call Abe, invite him to join him, but he knows Abe would just laugh, "what *meshugener* nonsense is this? Coffee at an airport? You *farshluggineh?*" All right, no Abe then. And there's no one else.

He sits in a moulded plastic chair and dozes for a few minutes. Like the cliché of the drowning man, chunks of his life pass before his eyes in dream: snow-bound Winnipeg, his father's horse, Luna's toothy smile, the clicking of a typewriter, his grinning brothers, Goldie, Toronto, Rose, Las Vegas, Myrna, the incessant blank page…. He wakes with a start, shaking his head. Then he takes a cab back to his suite, feeling as if he has accomplished something after all. A theatrical gesture, no more than that, ritual, but he can afford a little treat now and then. What with the exchange rate, the Social Security and university pensions he inherited from Myrna, their savings and the insurance go further in Canada, and with his own Canadian pensions and the royalties – royalties! Still hard to believe – he's doing all right. Doing fine, actually.

"A new year, a new beginning," he writes in his journal. It's a brand new one, leather binding, the numbers "1989" embossed in gold, a present from Abe, ever the optimist. "Here, write something," he said. When he was in the *stalag* in Germany, he told Zan, he kept a journal of his three-year imprisonment, so he wouldn't forget, wrote something every day, even if only a word or two. Sometimes, he said, if he was being punished and had no paper or pencil, he scratched a few words with a stone on the wall. Just to leave a record, testimony that he'd been there. Once, he said, he'd scratched a word with his fingernail on the parchment-dry skin of his arm: "remember."

"You keep a journal?" Zan was incredulous. "This is the first I'm hearing of this. You sure that really happened, or you making it up? Imagining it?"

"What, you think I tell you everything?" Abe said.

"Just arrived from the airport," Zan writes now. *"I'm ready to start the rest of my life."* He winces and crosses the last phrase out, replacing it with *"the next phase."* Then, taking a deep, theatrical breath, adds: *"A new novel!!!!"*

He's been in Calgary since the middle of September, in fact, arriving just six weeks after Myrna's death, but a little self-delusion never hurt anyone, that's what Jack had told him. Twenty-three years ago – was it really that long? Jack had saved his life, more or less. That woman at Alberta Mental Health, this improbably named Zelda, didn't believe in journals, other than to write down dreams, didn't believe, he was sure, in self-deception, too much of a hard-headed realist, young and, as far as he could tell, naïve as she is. Jack had been a realist too, but with the heart of a romantic. She had a framed degree on the wall, doctor of psychology, but she was no Jack. Still, there was so much less of his life left to save.

CHAPTER I

September 17, 1988

ARRIVING AT THE AIRPORT THE FIRST TIME, more than three months earlier, he'd had one of those flashing-by out-of-body experiences, if that was the right term for it. He'd had them occasionally over the past few years, never when he was shaving or brushing his teeth or for some other reason standing square in front of a mirror gazing at himself, no, then he was always only himself – the same Zan as ever he'd been, only older, obviously, and a little the worse for wear – and that was who he would see. But sometimes, walking down a street in Las Vegas – not on the casino strip with all its crazy street life and where he was unlikely to go at any rate, but in the regular city, which was not all that different than Calgary, with stores and street corners and houses and unexpected moments of grace like a young woman smiling at him at a bus stop, the bus driver calling him "sir" – he would catch a glimpse of himself in a store's plate glass window through the corner of his eye and would be startled by the image of an old man, bent, shuffling, white-haired, sallow-faced, slightly shabby clothes hanging off him scarecrow fashion.... *Was that him?* He knew it was, knew, too, that those taken-by-surprise moments revealed more who he really was than any length of gazing fondly – hair still thick, skin still remarkably smooth – or even critically – nose too big, too bent, chin too weak, eyes too small, deficiencies in his face he'd been finding most of his conscious life – at himself in the bathroom mirror, where the face he presented to himself was the same one he'd had all his life only...*altered,* that was it, altered in some way, *matured,* he liked to think, with a self-pricking chuckle, but only himself, the one he knew so well. The glimpses of himself he caught through the corner of his eye, taken unawares, was a different Zan, the Zan he realized he was becoming, would become, and the feeling always reminded him of that shivery sensation he'd sometimes get as a boy when Abe or Saul would say, "What's the matter? Someone walking on your grave? Someone pissing in your ear?"

His brothers would always look away then, remembering Adam, and feeling the fool for having reminded him, that mention of a grave. They all missed Adam, of course, but the consensus in the family seemed to be that Zan, having lost what amounted to half of himself, missed him the most, that he needed to be sheltered from painful memories. Zan himself was not so sure; he'd already shifted his attention and affections to Abe, just one year older and enough like him to be a virtual twin.

Now here was Abe, caught not full on but in the first moment as Zan stepped off the escalator and through a doorway into the already-crowded arrival area and through the corner of his eye, just for a moment, there he was, small, shrunken really, stooped, shuffling, almost bald, gaunt...almost a dead man, that's who was here to greet him, his twin – well, his proxy twin – a dead man. The moment dissolved as quickly as it had formed, Zan lost sight of him in the hustle and bustle around the still dormant baggage carousel, the swirl of elbows and heads above the crowd, and when he saw his brother again – his only surviving brother – full on this time, Abe had reverted back into himself, a bit more stooped, a bit more shrunken, head almost bald, the glistening scalp at the top of his skull frosted with wisps of snowy hair still growing behind and just above the slightly protruding ears, but in every other way an almost-mirror image of Zan, two old men, miles closer to the end than the start. Twins not twins.

Still, Zan couldn't resist asking, as they stood at arm's length facing each other, "Who the hell are you?"

"What?"

"Who the hell are you?" he repeated, louder.

"Who am I? Just your brother for all of your life, you *putz*. You're getting senile finally?"

"My brother, no, my brother is a boy like me."

"What?"

"A boy, my brother is a boy."

"A boy!" No one could snort like Abe.

"Well, all right, a teenager. A young man maybe. Middle-aged even, maybe, in his prime. But an old man like you? How could my own twin brother be old enough to be my father, my grandfather maybe?"

Dave Margoshes

"Twin!" Abe said scornfully, as if speaking not to Zan but a passerby. "Always my *meshugener* brother lives in the twilight zone." No one Zan had ever encountered in his long, somewhat eventful life could ever quite match the sardonic tone that Abe had long ago perfected. The two of them, so alike they even talked alike, but the tone, Abe's tone always different. It came, Zan imagined, from talking to boxers and boxing managers, to cops, to prison guards, to German interrogators.

With that, the brothers had embraced, and there it was again, through the corner of Zan's eye, in the large glass wall separating the crowded arrival area from the airport lobby proper, the image of two old men caught in a bearclutch, one with a full head of white hair, the other almost bald, both bent, shrunken, shabby caricatures of the men they had once been, though even in their straight-standing prime they'd both been half a head shorter than most men. "So, you're glad to see me, *Abela*, or is that a gun in your pocket?" Zan asked, hoping to break the ice.

Abe snorted again: "Always with you the gun."

"Just a joke," Zan protested.

"Right, always with you a joke."

The two brothers eyed each other warily, like boxers in the ring taking each other's measure, then embraced each other again, so quickly it left Zan wondering later whether he had made the first move or Abe had.

"Dancing," Zan said.

"What's that?" They were struggling out of each other's embrace, gazing at each other's faces. Anyone walking by would have had no difficulty seeing the fondness in either man's eyes.

"Dancing, not walking." And, after a moment when Abe's incomprehension became clear, "On our graves. And not someone, a whole street gang."

"*Meshugener,*" Abe replied, shaking his head. "So, is that it, Pantsy, that one little bag, or you have maybe some luggage?"

They'd turned to the carousel that, at that very moment, cleared its throat and lurched into life. On a pedestal above the mouth beginning to vomit suitcases stood a dinosaur, one of those big man-eaters, a Something-or-other Rex, not life-size but big enough that the sight of it rocked Zan back on his heels, ten feet high perhaps, green with stunted front legs and a huge head with beady, menacing eyes. The rumble that Zan had been hearing, he realized, was not the baggage carousel but was emanating from this mechanical creature's moving jaws. "What the hell?"

"Oh, that's from the museum," Abe said. "There was a fire there, so they put it here for awhile, let the poor *boychic* get some air."

"To greet the other dinosaurs. And here we are, dinosaurs three, you and me and our friend. I'm relieved to hear that rumbling isn't my stomach."

"What?" Abe said. "They didn't feed you on the plane?"

THREE DAYS LATER, stuffed with roast chicken prepared much the way their mother had, and flaky-crusted apple pie and other examples of Abe's not inconsiderable skills in the kitchen, he'd found himself at the General Hospital, in Emergency, having his insides reamed out. His bowels hadn't twitched for almost a week.

"Constipation I'm used to," he told the intern who examined him first. "This is something special."

The intern placed two fingers against his swollen belly and pressed lightly. "Hurt?"

"Ouch! Hurt? You might say so. I feel like I'm dying, even without the punch in the belly. This is a hell of a way to go out...."

"I don't think you're in any danger of dying," the intern said. He had a crooked smile, bad teeth, looked no older than sixteen.

"Maybe I should just kill myself and get it over with," Zan said. "Just keep eating till I burst and go out in a blaze of glory."

A week after that, at the suggestion of a social worker at the hospital, he was at Mental Health downtown, spilling his guts again.

"We'll start with a medical history," the woman said.

"I don't really need to be here," Zan explained, for the second or third time. "They insisted at the hospital, but it's really not necessary. I'm no crazier than any other bedbug."

The woman had a pleasant enough smile. She was in her late twenties, no older than thirty, Zan was sure, and no doubt a rookie – no need to bring out a seasoned pro for a garden-variety case like him. Nice looking, just slightly overweight, thick, dark curls caught up in a

Dave Margoshes

ponytail, light milk-chocolate skin, interracial, he guessed, black and white. She wore a fitted blue suit of what he judged to be a good material and a crisp white blouse. Everything about her was professional, clinical, except her black-framed glasses, which seemed too old for her, making her look like a cartoon librarian or old-maid schoolteacher. Zan would have expected big round lenses, something to echo her round face and giving her an owlish look. "It's just standard procedure, really," she said. She glanced cursorily at the chart that had preceded him. "No one is assuming anything."

"It must be the water," he explained, in reference to the first cleansing. "It's hard, they tell me, harder than I'm used to. I didn't eat anything I don't always, just more of it. My brother inherited that much from our mother, an insistence that you eat till you're bursting. This was constipation with a capital C. The tunnel was cemented closed. They had to use jackhammers to get me open. Excuse my vulgarity, please."

The therapist eyed him warily and made a brief note. The tag on the breast of her collarless jacket read "Zelda." What an old-fashioned name, and another Z, just like him. Zan chuckled.

"Zelda, that was Fitzgerald's wife's name, F. Scott Fitzgerald," he'd exclaimed when she introduced herself. "The novelist? *The Great Gatsby?*"

"Yes, I know. My father was a fan."

"Well, me too. Smart fellow, your dad. Give him my regards."

Zan had her card in his hand but he'd already forgotten her last name. Zelda, it should be something Russian or Ukrainian maybe, but no, a regular white-bread Anglo name, Mc-something, just like Luna's, white bread despite her colour. Maybe she really was named after Zelda Fitzgerald.

He'd forgotten Jack's last name too, and long ago lost his card, which made writing to him all but impossible. He might have been able to track him down, with some effort – he'd been affiliated with the University of Toronto – but didn't know how, lacked the energy to try. Anyway, what could Jack possibly say, presuming he was even still in practice, still alive, if his phone should ring some day and it was Zan, back yet again from the almost dead. He longed for those days when his appointments would be for eleven o'clock. Monday and he and Jack would go for lunch afterwards, the seamless monologue spinning on for another hour or more. Strictly unethical, Jack always said, "but I find you irresistible."

This woman looked like she *could* resist. She was browsing through the chart on her lap. "It's not just that, though," she said. "Constipation. At the hospital you said something that made them think you might hurt yourself. There's a note here."

For a moment, Zan was nonplussed. "Me? No, I don't think so." He paused to think. "Maybe I said something like 'What's the use of living?' But suicide? No. Believe me, Miss Zelda, excuse me, Doctor Zelda, I've been in worse spots and the thought never entered my mind. When I feel down, I always remember the advice some wise man gave me years ago: 'Don't give the bastards the satisfaction.'"

The woman looked at him appraisingly. "All right, good." She made a note.

"I see you've had some heart trouble?"

"Heart attacks, I lost track of how many. Nothing too serious. It runs in the family."

She raised an eyebrow.

"Father, dead young. A brother, very young. An uncle.... And my sister – who knew women had heart attacks? But I'm still here, still among the walking-arounds."

"And bypass surgery. Single? Double?"

"Double is for kids. I had six. You should see the scars on my leg where they took the veins." Zan shook his head and closed his eyes, marshalling something. He was used to giving medical history. "All of this you can get in detail from the hospital in Las Vegas. They knew me by my first name there, I was a regular. Thank some god Myrna – that was my wife – had good insurance. I gave the particulars to the nurses at the hospital here, the General? It took an hour, almost."

"I know, but indulge me, please. Anything else?"

"No offence meant. Let's see. A stroke last year, not a big one. A bit of a slur when I talk – maybe you can hear it? That's all that's left. Arthritis, too, not so bad today." He wiggled the fingers of his right hand to demonstrate their flexibility. "Falls – last year, a broken collarbone, four months healing, it still hurts if I move my head too fast. And I almost forgot, the Big Fall, out of a tree, on my head, when I was eight or nine. I still have a lump." He reached up to stroke the back

Dave Margoshes

of his head, where there was a visible swelling in the pink scalp, though in fact it was the result of banging his head in the shower that morning, clumsy as ever. Abe's bathroom had an old-fashioned tub, with a plastic hose hooked up by wire and held in place by a jumper cable clamp, its handles still clad in red rubber.

"Also scarlet fever, then rheumatic fever, when I was ten, that's the source of the bum ticker, or maybe the bum ticker brought on the fever, I don't know. Either way, bad valves all my life. It kept me out of the war, I can tell you that. The Second World War, that is, maybe your dad mentioned it to you. Killed my career as a weightlifter and a sprinter, too. Always I was a little smaller than I should have been, the runt of the litter, except that the whole litter, all my brothers and my sister, shorties, like our dad. Oh, and St. Vitus's dance the next year, or maybe it was the same. I never did catch up on that year I lost, always a step behind somehow, in school and everything else. I don't remember that year very well." He didn't mention Adam – not out of deceit, just genuine forgetfulness. He hadn't thought of that long-dead brother, his true twin, other than in a fleeting way, in a long time.

Instead, he remembered the excruciating hours and days of boredom, lying in bed at St. Joseph's Hospital, just a few blocks from his own house but a world away from his life there, excruciating boredom broken finally by his discovery of books – Grimms' fairy tales, Greek myths, Kipling, Robert Louis Stevenson, Dickens, Conan Doyle, Jules Verne, Jack London, a whole other world revealed to him, worlds within worlds.

"I should think not," Zelda said. "Not a lot of fun for a growing boy."

"Sickness isn't a lot of fun for anybody, and I'm an authority on the subject. Oh, and did I mention macular something in my eyes...."

"Degeneration," Zelda said.

Zan frowned. "That's it, but you have to pronounce it like you're making a moral judgment? A degenerate I'm not, not yet. Going blind, that's the main thing. The main thing. The main thing is, nature's sending me a message."

"And?"

"And I'm a little hard of hearing, so I don't always hear messages the first time."

Zelda smiled.

Zan tapped his temple. "And this sort of thing."

"Mental, you mean?"

"Mental, yes. Not loony bin, exactly, but..."

"Yes?"

"A breakdown, they called it." Zan pronounced the word as if there were a sour taste in his mouth. "Twice. The first time, run-of-the-mill depression, things...not going well." He paused. "The second time, a little more dramatic. Marriage falling apart, drinking too much, a lot of things....This was all a long time ago."

"Suicide attempts?"

"Ah. They said it might have been, I said it was an accident...too many pills. To tell you the truth, I don't remember. But I don't think so."

"But you were hospitalized. And this was where? When?"

"The first time or the second? I guess it doesn't matter, both the same place. I was a regular. Toronto, Queen Street Mental Health something or other, 1950-something, then 1960-something. There was actually a nurse there the second time who remembered me from the first! *Welcome back, Mr. Wiseman*, she said. You could check with them maybe, you really want to know. And then, the second time, private therapy, something like this. A wonderful fellow. Jack...Jack something."

Zelda was scribbling furiously, reminding him of Jack, whose penmanship was unreadable. Zan shrugged. "That's the other thing, the memory doesn't work so good any more."

"Yes. That's okay." She put the pen down and looked up.

"And what brought you to Calgary, Mr. Wiseman?" It seemed like more of a bureaucratic question than a medical one.

"Death."

"Death?"

"Don't worry, not my own. For that I'm not ready yet. My...wife...died. I could have stayed where I was, but... my brother Abe, he lives here. He's the only *mishpokhe* I got. I didn't want him to have to worry."

"No children?"

Zan hesitated for a moment. "Not really. A couple miscarriages, a long time ago. Not me, my wife...excuse me, I forget...Rose. Rose." He shook his head. "That's not really a child, though, is it? A couple step-kids, children of the next wife, the one who just died. Myrna. But they were already adults when I met them, they never lived with us, so that never counted. Not really. More like friendly neighbours than children."

"No other family?"

"A few nieces and nephews, second and third cousins, nobody I was ever close to. My brother, Abe, he has a daughter, lives in Vancouver. My niece, Ana, named for our sister Annie. A son too he had, Benjy, a long time dead, still a little boy. Abe and Ana, I don't think they get on that well, but where's the surprise there? Nobody gets on with Abe. There's a picture of her in his house, all grown up, I didn't even recognize her, that's how close we are. I've been living out of the country for twenty years, hardly ever got back, just for funerals. Everybody else dead, my parents long ago, of course, my other brothers and sister, my wives...."

"You had other wives?"

"Wives, girlfriends...." He held up one hand, the fingers splayed, first one finger, then another, half bent down. "It's hard to remember how many, and which was which category. But all dead, so what's the difference?" He paused again, just for a beat, but he saw the woman put pen to paper, so she wasn't unalert. "I'm alone, and Abe is too – or might as well be." Zelda looked up. "His wife, Dolly, she's in a coma, some rare disease, I forget what – ten, twelve years now, something like that, not much change, and before that, she's an invalid for years – so he's as good as alone. My brother, he's the other pea in the pod, he can love me, he can hate me – I'm not saying he does; I can drive him crazy, and the same goes both ways, but he can't be disinterested. He looks in the mirror, he sees me; I look, it's him I see."

The therapist smiled faintly. "You're twins?"

"You got that right, Lady Doctor. But Abe, he's the older, he's the old man of the act; me, I'm the kid brother."

FROM ZAN'S JOURNAL

Sept. 27, 1988 – Been to see a shrink – a woman, no less! Fresh out of shrink school, I imagine, and gullible as a kitten. I'll have to be careful. Nice enough. Some numbskull at the hospital the other day made a connection between my anus and my brainus, so off they sent me. Poor woman, she must be lonely, or bored with her regular patients: she wants to see me once a week! Every Tuesday at two. With Jack, it was Mondays at eleven, so I guess I'm making progress! If I live long enough, I could fill a week with therapists. Not too likely! Still, maybe not such a bad idea to have someone to talk to – talk at! Talking to Abe is a little more complicated than I'd remembered. I talk, he talks, is anybody listening? We're like two freight trains roaring down the track toward each other in the middle of the night, lights blinking, whistles moaning, someone watching might think, oh, no, disaster! But it's okay, they're on parallel tracks. That's Abe and me, a lot of huffing and puffing but there's really no danger of a collision, of us even meeting.

Dave Margoshes

ABE I

So hello, Dolly, how are you today? You look good – is that a little colour I see in your cheeks? That nurse, Lorraine, she says you're doing a little better maybe, but she always says that. A regular Pollyanna, that one. Better than Miss Gloomypants on the night shift, that one will find fault when she arrives at the Golden Gate, she should be so lucky, the gate will squeak, her wings won't fit quite right. Better to be an optimist than a pessimist, don't you think, Dolly? Okay, so don't answer, I know you agree, you would have died long ago if you didn't. "I don't know what keeps her alive, Mr. Wiseman," that doctor tells me, but I know, *we* know, don't we, Dolly, darling. Oh, *Gott in himmel*, your hand is cold. Let me rub it, there, that's better.

So, guess what, Zan is here. He really came. I told you yesterday – *yesterday*, I've been telling you for weeks – I'd believe it when I saw him getting off the plane, but seeing is believing and I did, there he was, big as life, and you should have seen us, the two of us hugging, a couple of old grizzly bears doing a dance in between the suitcases. He's been threatening for weeks, since his Myrna died – a saint that woman was, the way she took care of him, the *mensch* she made of him, well, almost made of him. But, you know, I always said, why would he want to come here, especially in fall, winter just around the corner? To leave Nevada, all those artichokes and lemons sweet on the tree or whatever they grow there, it's *meshuge*, better I should go there, not that I ever would, but that at least would make sense. To leave a place like that to come to Canada – to *Calgary*, for God's sake – when you're in your eighties, that's no sense at all. Still, blood is thicker than water and I'm all he's got now. Abie and Zannie, the A to Zed Brothers, together again after all these years.

It's hard to believe we come from the same town, the same neighbourhood, let alone the same father and mother – the same womb. Hard to believe we suckled from the same mother's breasts, drank the same milk, wet our diapers with the same piss, you'll excuse me, Dolly, a little off-colour joke. Zan had his life, I had mine and all the rest is a bridge over the river, as they say. You bend the shoot, so grows the plant – is that in the Bible? I don't remember. I bent one way, Zannie bent the other, and it's not his bent nose I'm talking, or my own *peculiar* bent, heh heh. No, no, together we were in our short pants, all three of us, Abie, Zannie and Adam, the three musketeers we were, three little peas in a pod, three fingers on a hand we were that close, three little piggies on the same baby's foot, three *petselehs* when we pissed in Saul's ear, it was all three of us did it, at the same time, all three who ran away screaming, all three who had our ears boxed. The Three *Pischers*, that was us. Then Adam and Zan were sick and I wasn't. Adam died, blessed be his memory. Zan didn't. He got better. Everything was different. We moved to Toronto, we came back. I had the paper route, then Zan had the paper route, I had the bowling pins and all of a sudden we were *different!* For him, paper – reading, writing, the life of the mind. For me, bowling pins, knocking things down, putting them back up, mending. That's the way our lives went, he his way, me mine, always with Adam in the back of our minds, a ghost on our pillows.

But you know all this, Dolly – what am I telling you for? Just to hear the sound of my own voice, what else?

"I fell out of the tree, *Abela*," he reminded me this morning, sitting at breakfast, talking, remembering the way we were as kids. "It gave me a lump, shook up my brains, when they settled down I was a different person."

We're at the table and – what else – we're arguing already. Four years we haven't seen each other, not since Annie's funeral, and we're arguing, but who expected anything different? He doesn't like orange juice, don't I have apple? He doesn't like the coffee I make, it's too weak, not hot enough. He doesn't like the oatmeal, never mind that it's thirty below outside, he wants cold cereal with milk and sliced fruit. "That I eat in the summer," I tell him, "not in the winter. This isn't your fancy-schmancy Nevada."

All right, so maybe it isn't winter yet, it will be, isn't really thirty below, it's nice enough, but it could be, it will be soon enough.

"You're telling *me* it isn't Nevada," he says.

"So who told you to come? Who invited you?"

"You did," he reminds me, and it's true, I did, it isn't right that two brothers with nothing keeping them apart should live alone, especially when they have so little time left to live, but who ever thought he'd really come?

"You're right," I say, "and I'm glad you're here. But now what? Can we really live together, you bent one way, me the other?"

Zan laughs, you remember that laugh of his. He throws back his head – and this is a thin head, not the round pumpkin he used to have on his shoulders – and his whole face lights up, like someone's clicked on the bulb he's got wedged way up that battered nose of his, so light comes shining out not just the eyes but the mouth, even the hairy nostrils I bent up long ago with one mistimed punch. Duck, I told him, but did he duck? No. I wish I could look so young when I laugh – I wish I had something to laugh about.

"Live together? No," he says. "All the things I am, masochist ain't one of them, Benchy," he tells me. "I love you like a brother – you *are* my brother – but not like a lover. Live together? No. A guest I'll be happy to be for a week, maybe two, while I look around, till I get my bearings, find a place. But live together?"

Benchy, he calls me. I haven't heard that nickname in years. He can't remember his own name sometimes, that brother of mine, but Benchy he remembers.

"All right, all right already," I say. "I hear you. Stay as long as you want. You know you're welcome." I'm disappointed – I can tell you this, Dolly – but relieved too. I don't know what I had in mind, what I expected. I don't remember what he said in his calls. The house...the house is like a vacuum, it sucks me up. I sit in the living room at night, reading or watching the idiot box, and suddenly I feel this...this vacuum, pulling me into the bedroom, into Ana's room, into Benjy's room, the bathroom, the basement. What am I looking for? Not you, I know you're not there, haven't been there for a long time. You I know where to find, right here, darling Dolly. Ana? Ana I know isn't there, Ana I can call anytime I want in Vancouver, every other Sunday, six o'clock, that's best, sometimes she's there, sometimes not. Benjy, I know where he is, once a week at the cemetery I visit him. Who else could there be? Who...*what?* It's not a voice calling me, it's a...*force*, a vacuum, pulling me from one empty room to another. Someone else in the house, even Zannie, would be a blessing. But that's *meshugener*, I know as well as he we can't live together. We're not lovers, he tells me – this is news? Peter Mansbridge should be informed? Gzowski should have a panel to discuss it?

So, we'll see what happens. Already every newspaper in the house is bent, books are off the shelves, that man never puts anything back. He asks about you, he'll be here to see you soon, you should maybe get your hair done, pretty yourself up. I'm sorry, just a joke. Out of the tree he fell, ten years old, his brains shaken up, a different person. He doesn't remember the sickness he had, the sickness that killed his twin brother – no, it's falling out of the tree he remembers, that's what changed *him*. That's what he tells me. Maybe he's right, but that's not the way I remember it. Dolly, have I ever told you? Wasn't it *me* who fell out of the tree?

Dave Margoshes

CHAPTER 2

October 4, 1988

"HOW ARE YOU TODAY?" the therapist asked. He'd consulted her card – Zelda McArthur, McArthur like the general, *Dr.* Zelda McArthur. But when he'd greeted her as "Dr. McArthur" today, she corrected him, "Please, call me Zelda."

"Dr. Zelda?"

"Just Zelda, Mr. Wiseman."

"Okay, but only if you call me Zan."

"Deal." Her smile, displaying bright pink gums, was appealing.

She was wearing a yellow dress, a yellow silk scarf, amber earrings, all that yellow bringing out the lighter tones in her glossy skin. She looked festive, not as austere as he remembered from their first meeting, a week before.

"I'm Fine. Tops. *You* look good. You're going out tonight?"

The therapist flushed, just slightly. Barely a blush, but she seemed pleased by his awareness of her. "I am, actually. Meeting a friend. But this is about you, not me. How are you really?"

"You know what a *nudnik* is?"

"A *nudnik?* Someone naked? No. What is it?"

"It's a *schlemiel* who, when you ask him how are you, he tells you. Believe me, nobody likes a *nudnik.*"

"Except that in my business, when I ask, I really mean it. So humour me, be a *nudnik.*"

There was a notebook in her lap. She wrote something, then looked up.

"You were having trouble with digestion. That cleared up?"

"Digestion?"

"Yes, you were constipated, that's what brought you to me. Remember?"

"Remember? Of course. But such things a gentleman doesn't discuss with a lady."

"Ah. But all well in that department now?"

"All well. Yes. Like clockwork."

"Good." She made a note. "And the other matter...suicidal thoughts?"

"No, I told you last time, that was a misunderstanding. Maybe I made a joke.... No, no thoughts then or now."

"Good. So, tell me, what did you do for a living, Mr. Wiseman?"

"Zan. You agreed to call me Zan."

"Right, excuse me, Zan. What did you do for a living?"

"Did? Do, you mean. Not retired yet. I'm a failed novelist."

"I don't quite understand."

"Nothing could be simpler. I'm a novelist, which means I wrote one novel that got published. Without that much, you can't be in the club, can't call yourself a novelist. That was fifty years ago. Fifty! Fifty-five, actually."

"Might I have read it? What's it called?"

Zan smiled shyly. "Maybe you have, a few people have. *The Wise Men of Chelm*."

"Wise men...Chelm, where is that?"

"Chelm! You don't know Chelm? The most famous place in Poland? Where have you been all your life, Dr. Zelda?" Zan tapped his temple. "Where? Here, there and everywhere, but mostly in here. It's a mythological place, Chelm, a place where all the residents are fools, so foolish they sometimes stumble accidentally into wisdom. You know maybe *Gimpel the Fool?* Isaac Singer? Another Isaac. It's the same idea, someone so foolish he's wise. I don't say Singer stole the idea from me – maybe he did, maybe he didn't, but I had mine first. Or maybe I stole the idea from him, before he even knew he had it. That's the kind of thing can happen in a place like Chelm. A holy place, this Chelm."

"I see. And your novel is set there?"

"No, not really. It's about a boy. In Winnipeg, just like I was. He goes there, well, in his imagination, his dreams. It...wanders. Well, you go to the public library, if you want. They got it, maybe. *The Wise Men of Chelm*, easy to remember, Wiseman the author, "wise men" in the title. Don't worry, there'll only be one book called that by someone named Wiseman." He paused, put together a feeble smile. "One book. Still, there is the one, so maybe not completely failed. Wrote, finished, published, reviews, some good, even made me a few dollars. Lots of years I dined out on that book, I can tell you that, lots of years. Not another word in print since, true, terminal mental constipation, what I had the other day at the other end was nothing in comparison, terminal strangulation of the imagination, but that one – they can't take that away from me. Isn't there a song like that? Anyway, that's why I say my profession is failed novelist. You might say I made a success of failure, a whole career of it. I did lots of other things – to make a living, to keep alive, you do anything, whatever comes along, whatever you have to, teacher sometimes, beekeeper sometimes, believe it or not, mostly as a machinist, a pretty good one, too. But they don't count. Novelist, that's the noun. Failed, that's the adjective. And not just *novelist* either – failed husband, failed son, failed brother, failed friend, failed Communist.... You name it, I failed at it. *Failed*, that's the operative word."

Through this whole speech, Zelda had merely looked at him, watched, the eraser tip of her pencil against her lips in a way he thought must be only unconsciously provocative. Now she took her time writing several sentences in her notebook.

"I used to call myself a dead writer," Zan said into the silence. "*This dead writer*. But maybe there's still some life left in me."

"Very much alive, I'd say." The therapist lifted her head. "I'll look for your book, it sounds interesting. Now, why don't you tell me a little more about yourself? I don't mean what's bothering you, we'll come to that. How old did you say you were?"

"Old! You heard about Methuselah? I don't remember when I was born, I was distracted then, but my brother Abe claims it was 1906. That was the year Hannibal crossed the Alps, if you remember, and Caesar conquered all of Gaul. '*Veni, vidi, vici.*' That's what he said. 'I came, I saw, I conquered.' Man of few words, Caesar. Saw him when he came through Winnipeg. He spoke at the *shul*. The printing press was invented that year, too. Gutenberg, he was a Winnipeg boy. His father was a butcher. Not kosher, so we didn't go to him, but some of us kids used to get sausage from him, five links for a penny. Good stuff. Used to feed it to my pet dinosaur. Oh, yes, there were still dinosaurs back then. We had a little one. Smart, those things, but my mother always said not to get too close. She said it in Yiddish, so the dinosaur wouldn't understand. That smart, they weren't. There's one at the airport, you know? Not smart enough to walk away. So...1906. You subtract that from whatever year this is, multiply by two for Abe and me, the A to Zed boys, divide by two and you get how old Abe is. I'm half an hour younger. Maybe a little more."

"And you were born in Winnipeg?"

"Very good, Dr. Watson. You picked up the clues. The North End. *Mitzraim*, the Jews there used to call it, Egypt. They say Portage and Main is the centre of Winnipeg but that's a *goyisha* fabrication. You know that word, *goyisha*? Gentile." He laughed. "I've forgotten most of these Yiddish expressions, but Abe, my brother, he's full of them.

"Anyway, *Selkirk* and Main, that's the heart of Winnipeg city. It also happens to be where I sold newspapers when I was ten or eleven, but that's strictly a coincidence. Flora and Salter, 424 Flora Avenue, that's where I was born, grew up, that's where I fell out of the tree, where I became whatever I am. One year in Toronto my parents tried, but that didn't work out, so back we came to Winnipeg, the motherland. Then, except for these last twenty years, living in Las Vegas of all places – but not a croupier or a card shark, that I can assure you, nothing like that – except for those Las Vegas years, I was like a yoyo, back and forth between Toronto and Winnipeg. Winnipeg and Toronto. Sometimes I didn't know which was which. But that's your territory, Zelda, isn't it? Figuring out where I am, what I am?"

"And your name – Zan? Is that short for Alexander?"

"I say that sometimes, but the truth is, it's Isaac. But no one but my mother ever called me that, and she's been dead over twenty-five years. If I was walking down the street and someone called out, 'Isaac!' it wouldn't occur to me he was talking to me. I wouldn't even turn my head."

"And from Isaac to Zan?"

"Isaac to Zac, that part's easy. How Zac became Zan, though, I can't say. It just did. Abe, he probably remembers."

"School?"

"School, sure, school. What, I look like a dummy? Strathcona School, Aberdeen School, Talmud Torah – that's the Hebrew school. Talmud Torah and Aberdeen both on our own street, Flora Avenue – one a couple of blocks in one direction, the other a couple blocks the other way. School, they had me coming and going, you might say. Then St. John's Tech, two years at the University of Manitoba before they kicked me out. And hard knocks, Dr. Zelda, an advanced degree, a PhD, even, from the school of hard knocks. Other alumni you've probably met."

"A few. You didn't graduate from the university?"

"I didn't graduate from any of them! That used to be a badge of honour, but just now I can't remember why. Out of Strathcona when I got sick, back into Aberdeen the next year, I don't remember why – but a whole year lost, I never did catch up. Out of there when we moved to Toronto – or was that St. John's? School in Toronto, I forget the name. Then back to St. John's, out of there for sure when my father got sick and I went to work. Kicked out of Talmud Torah for being smart with the rabbi. Kicked out of university. I must have been a bad person, so much kicking out, wouldn't you say? Or just another example of failure."

"I don't know the circumstances. What would *you* say? You've already proclaimed yourself a failure, successful at it." She smiled. "But do you consider yourself a bad person?"

"You go right to the heart, Dr. Zelda, *mazel tov*. I like that. No, of course not. Does anybody? Did Eichmann consider himself a bad person? Certainly not, just following orders. Hitler? Just following a vision. This is my weakness too, perhaps."

"Following orders is what got you kicked out of university?"

"No, not exactly. I meant in a larger sense."

"Well. We'll get into that another time."

"Yes, Dr. Zelda, by all means. Another time."

FROM ZAN'S JOURNAL

Oct. 4, 1988 – At the shrink again. Nice woman to talk to. The questions she asks – did Jack ask me such things? What did you do, how old, where did you go to school? How are your bowels?

I have to laugh, though. What did I have for lunch? Who knows? What colour are my socks? Who cares? What's my address? Don't worry, I got it written down. But 424 Flora Avenue, this I remember like it was the headline in this morning's *Calgary Herald*. She asks me where I lived seventy-five years ago, that I can tell her. Strathcona School, Aberdeen School, Talmud Torah...those I can rattle off. The street where I get off the bus going back to Abe's? That's another matter entirely.

My mother's eyes I remember as clearly as if she was gazing at me when I woke up this morning. Myrna, my dear Myrna, I can't remember what colour her eyes were. Luna's eyes I remember, Rose's. And today – look – even their names I remember. A good day.

Dave Margoshes

DUET I

"Zannie, I told you, stay out of the kitchen. How many times I gotta tell you?"

"So who's in the kitchen? I'm not in your darling kitchen."

"What, I'm seeing things? I'm dreaming, hallucinating? This isn't the kitchen, *my* kitchen, the kitchen in *my* house, *my* house, the house *I* live in, the house where *you* are a guest? And this isn't me? I'm not me? You're not you?"

"Yes, yes, but what's all the fuss? I had a bite so I washed the dishes. You want a bite? I can fix you something?"

"I can see that. I'm not half blind, like you. I can see you had a bite, which I don't begrudge you. My house is your house."

"Except the kitchen."

"Except I asked you not to wash the dishes, not to touch things. How many times I gotta ask you, Zannie?"

"So what's so wrong with me washing the dishes? They're dirty, they have to be washed. Why not by me?"

"Because you're half blind."

"So?"

"So the dishes are sitting in the drainer as dirty as they were when you put them in the sink. I have to wash them all over again, plus the drainer because now *it's* dirty too."

"I *washed* them already."

"Pantsy, listen, listen to your brother, listen to your host, fucking *listen* to me: Don't wash the dishes."

"All right, I won't touch the precious dishes. But why?"

"What do you mean, why? Because I said so."

"But why? I have to have a reason."

"A reason? He has to have a reason. Because I said so, that's enough. That's all the reason you need."

"For you maybe, but not for me. I want to know why."

"Why? You want to know why? I'll tell you why. Because I say so, that's why – that's the *w*, that's the *h*, that's the fucking *y*. You got it? That's all the reason there is, and if you don't like it you can kiss my *tuchas*."

"Of kissing your *tuchas*, I've had plenty, *Abela*. I'll find an apartment in the morning."

Dave Margoshes

CHAPTER 3

October 11, 1988

"TELL ME, ZAN, HOW ARE YOU FEELING TODAY?"

Zan shifted his shoulders, his hips, settled himself, considered the question. Jack, after he'd been to see him for a few months, had begun opening their sessions with a cheery "So, I see you're still alive," a sharp-edged counterpoint to his own habitual end-of-session salute, "See you next time, God willing, if there's a God, which is unlikely." How God had gotten into the picture he didn't know, but he'd liked it when his own attempts at irony were one-upped.

"How I'm feeling today," he began slowly. "I'm alive."

"Good. And the constipation? Everything still okay?"

"You don't beat around the bush, Lady Doctor. What a thing to ask a gentleman."

"You'd rather I made small talk first? I had the impression you were a man who doesn't like small talk."

"I don't, but give a man some credit for a bit of modesty."

"Modesty? I wouldn't have taken you for a particularly modest man."

"Take me. What do you know of me? You don't know me at all."

"Admitted. That's what I'm trying to do. But constipation is what brought you here, isn't that right? That and what you've assured me was a misunderstanding. It seems like a legitimate topic of conversation."

"I don't argue that. I'm just a little shy."

"Shy?" This time she laughed. "Modest I can believe, but shy? I don't think so."

Zan smiled. "Why not? Maybe not so much any more, but I remember when I was a boy I would cross the street if I saw people coming I knew, to avoid having to talk to them."

"That *is* shy."

"At school, I'd be called on, I'd know the answer and I'd want to give it, but I was too tongue-tied. If it was something I had to read out loud, that was fine, I could keep my nose in the book or on the paper, but to have to talk in class, looking at people...no."

"So what happened?"

"Happened?"

"You're not shy any more. Or I should say, you've overcome it."

Zan laughed. "Life happened. People happened to me. Writing, acting, politics, teaching, love affairs.... Being shy wasn't allowed."

"Acting! I thought you were a writer."

"A failed writer, remember? But just an amateur actor – just an amateur at the other things too, maybe, politics, the love affairs, other things.

"Because of shyness?"

"No, I was over that long before any of those things – that's what allowed those other things to happen. I was told I had a gift in my mouth, I should make use of it."

"Ah, a gift," Zelda said, in a satisfied tone, as if she had made an important discovery. She made a note.

But where had the damned gift come from? He remembered his disbelief, that summer in Toronto when he'd been forced to go door to door raising funds for the Young Pioneers. Forced, no – he'd done it of his own volition, but that's what he was asked to do, and if he wanted to be a part, which he was pretty sure he did want, that's what he had to do.

He'd been fourteen, not quite alone but feeling that way without Abe along as he usually was – where *had* Abe been? Zan had gone with his cousin Bernie to a meeting of the Pioneers and immediately fallen in. The family had pulled up most of their stakes and made the move east a year after the General Strike crippled Winnipeg. His father, so proud to drive his horse and wagon in the predawn darkness delivering milk, had lost his job with the dairy and still had not found another. His brother Saul had disappeared somewhere out west, and there were hopes that the change in scene and crowd might keep Abe out of trouble.

After Winnipeg, Toronto had seemed enormous, and bustling, filled with returned soldiers looking for work, just as Winnipeg had been, and, also like Winnipeg, still getting back on its feet from the influenza epidemic – many of the people they met, he remembered, had lost someone. Even one of the cousins, whose already cramped apartment they had at first crowded into, had almost died. Other than those *mishpokhe*, the Wisemans knew nobody, leaving the boys even more on their own than they usually were. Both of them had wound up at the *Arbeiter Ring*, the Workmen's Circle, on Bloor Street taking improvement classes. Abe somehow finagled his way into a physical education class, and from there to a nearby gym and into the Golden Gloves – ah, that's where he'd been that day – but Zan had landed in a public speaking course taught by a woman named Annie Buller, who made her political views clear the first minute by greeting the students as "comrades."

Zan liked her – "you have my sister's name," he told her shyly when they introduced each other in the first class; "Can't we share it?" the young woman replied – and when she challenged him to do what would be hardest for him, his path was set. Through her, he got involved with the Young Pioneers, who met at the YMCA nearby. The group's full name was Young Socialist Pioneers, but it was convenient to leave out the middle word. All the talk was about changing things, the system, about revolution, but everything they thought of actually doing seemed to require money, for bus trips to a strike site or paper and ink for posters. They all were going door to door, doing little more than begging, it seemed to Zan, but he took a deep breath and agreed.

He chose carefully, picking the Jewish tenements on Bathurst Avenue just north of Bloor, not far from where his family had found a place of their own, next door to his mother's sister, Esther. At the first door, before the woman who answered could say a word, he blurted out in Yiddish that he was collecting for the Pioneers. Her eyes lit up and she rummaged through her apron pocket for coins, showering him with blessings. Dazed, he tried the same approach at the next door with the same results, raising several dollars in the first building alone.

"It took me a while before I realized they confused the Young Pioneers with the Jewish Pioneers, a Zionist group that was raising money for Israel around the same time," he told Zelda.

"So you conned them?"

"Not really. I just didn't tell them everything. That was a skill that served me well later when I was an organizer for..." He paused, considered.

"Yes?"

"Oh, I guess I can say it, the Communist Party. It's been years since the cops have had any interest in me, I don't think they'll start again. Don't look so shocked, yes I was in the big bad Communist Party. Anyway, it was for their own good, the conning."

"And it gave you some confidence."

"I still had to work up my courage each time, but it started to come easier."

He described for Zelda how, years later, as a Party activist in Winnipeg, he would set up in Market Square with a supply of cheap plastic combs he'd pick up three for a penny on Main Street.

"Hey, get your indestructible combs right here, just a penny each, seven for a nickel," he'd call. "Twist it, drop it, sit on it, put it in the fire – there isn't anything you can do to break or damage this comb, ladies and gentlemen. It is absolutely indestructible, one hundred percent guaranteed. You want one, lady? Thank you. How about you, sir? Shrewd move. You won't be sorry. Say, stick around for a minute, will you? I'm gonna show you something really amazing in a minute."

When he'd drawn a crowd and had sold a half dozen or so, he'd snap one of the combs in half, an easy twist in his fingers, a satisfying *crack*. "Hey, guess what – I was lying. You're all a bunch of suckers."

He'd wait a beat, watching their faces. He already had the pennies in his hand, ready to dispense before anyone's anger got out of hand. "But if you think *I* exploited you, that's nothing. How many times has your boss sold you a bill of goods? Or city hall? The school board? How about Mr. Bennett up in Ottawa – how many indestructible combs has he sold you?" And he'd be off.

"It really *was* a gift in the mouth," Zelda said.

"Maybe."

"And you don't look a gift in the mouth, isn't that what they say?"

"Maybe. Maybe."

Dave Margoshes

Oct. 11, 1988 – Went for a walk after seeing the shrink. Along Seventeenth Avenue, a lot of restaurants, craft stores, interesting stuff, nice-looking people on the street. Girls even. Even one who looked at *me*. I need to get my own place, this is the area I'll look. Abe would like me to stay, move in with him permanently, and it's tempting – the A to Zed Brothers riding off into the sunset together. Sure. If only the dear man didn't drive me crazy. Feel like I've been cooped up for a long time – funeral home claustrophobia following me around for weeks, my legs cramped on the plane, the hospital, Abe's place – I needed air. It's all an illusion, I know that. I got all the air I need, all the elbow room. Still, it was good to be out, just walking, getting the machinery going, as Abe says. That poor bastard, he really suffers. Me, some aches and pains and stiffness but nothing so bad. Two months since Myrna died. Still feel hollow, numb. All the experience I've had with this sort of thing, I know it'll pass, but that can't come soon enough. Stopped for coffee, thought maybe it's just Abe's that's tasteless, but no, this stuff too. Everything in the mouth tastes the same, cardboard and cotton. Eyeballed the waitress but if there's any blood moving below my neck it's news to me. Just numb.

Thought about Annie Buller today – she came up at the shrink's – a woman I haven't seen for seventy years, haven't thought about more than once or twice since, yet I remember her so clearly, remember her name like I just heard it. "You have my sister's name," I told her; "Can't we share it?" she replied.

I've written a few names on a piece of paper – Luna, Goldie, Rose, Myrna – taped it inside the cover of this journal. I don't want to lose them.

CHAPTER 4

October 18, 1988

"HOW ARE YOU TODAY, ZAN?"

"Fine, fine, feeling fine. And you, Miss Zelda?"

"I'm fine, too, Mr. Wiseman, thank you. Let's talk a little more about your childhood, shall we? You mentioned once falling out of a tree. That seems to have made an impression on you – more than just the bump on your head. Were there other things like that that stand out in your mind?"

"Other trees?"

"No, but other memorable moments?"

"Memorable? Sure. We used to play on Selkirk Street, just one block over. That was a big street, always people, commotion. I remember a trick we used to play, my brothers Abe and Adam and my friend Bootsy – Abe we called Benchy, me, I was Pantsy, where those nicknames came from I have no idea, and what we called Adam I don't remember. This was when we were eight, nine, ten. There were wooden boardwalks in those days, elevated off the ground a foot or more, so a skinny kid like we were could squeeze under them. We would nail an old tin can under the sidewalk and run a long string, waxed at the end, through a hole. When you pulled on the string just right, it made a squeak, like a mouse. Then we'd lie in wait in an alley till a woman walked by, or some girls. Sometimes nothing, sometimes the can would squeak just right and the girls would scream. You're smiling, Dr. Zelda – you think I'm making this up? This is how boys used to amuse themselves before television."

"Sounds like fun," Zelda said. "Boys being boys. I have a brother too."

Zan cocked his head, still transported back seventy years and more. He hadn't always run with the pack, he told her. "Sometimes, I liked to get off by myself, imagine that I was an only child, an orphan even."

Getting off by himself usually brought him to Lord Selkirk Park, almost at the end of Flora Avenue, across from the Hebrew school. It had a fence all around and caragana bushes, and gates at each corner, locked at night and Sundays, so he couldn't always get in. Most of it was grass, bisected by cobblestone walkways, and some sort of a statue in the middle, a metal tower, with the British flag, and sweet-smelling yellow marigolds growing around it. He loved to go there by himself in the years before his and Adam's illness, when he'd felt crowded by his brothers, and look for four-leaf clovers. "I almost always found some, but whether they brought me luck or no, I can't say."

Still, sometimes he'd find a penny, too, maybe even a nickel, in the grass, where some big shot must have been sitting, smooching with his best girl. Right away, off he'd go a block way to Selkirk Avenue, to Saidman's Five-Cent Store, to get some candy or sunflower seeds. He loved to lie in the grass in that park, and eat sunflower seeds and spit the shells out and imagine that they'd take root and someday the park would be filled with sunflowers, big bright yellow ones. Then they'd have to change the park's name to Lord Wiseman Park!

"One day, I must have been nine or ten, I found a five-leaf clover! And nearby, a nickel! And a streetcar ticket. So that clover *was* lucky. That ticket was worth a nickel itself and I knew I could trade it for five cents' worth of candy at Saidman's or somewhere else, but instead I got a great urge to have an adventure. I'd never been on the streetcar and now I thought, why not today?"

All by himself, he'd walked the whole way down Selkirk Avenue west, till the end of the streetcar line, a mile or two, probably two, and him just a little *nebbish*. And what a walk! Every block, there were grocers, butchers, barber shops, pool halls, churches, *shuls*, sign painters, watchmakers, everything he could imagine. So much to look at. Past Salter he went, past Powers, past Andrews, McGregor, McKenzie, past Parr! He was sure he'd never been past Parr before. Arlington, Sinclair, Artillery Street and Battery Street! And on and on.

After awhile, on the south side, the stores and house petered out and there were the CPR yards as far as the eye could see. And gradually there was less and less on the north side too, just some houses, empty lots, a church here and there, livery stables, junkyards, and then the tracks ended. There was a big metal barrier to stop the streetcar if its brakes didn't work or if the driver fell asleep. And beyond that, just open prairie.

"By the time I get there," he told Zelda, "it's late in the afternoon and I'm tired, pooped. But I'm excited at the thought of taking a streetcar ride. All during the walk, the cars kept passing me, both directions, and I'd think, 'okay, big shots, soon it'll be me, Zan Wiseman, with my feet up like the rest of the swells. Just you wait and see.'

"I sit down on the barrier and after awhile, a streetcar comes, clanging its bell, big as a house, wood and metal and glass, maroon and yellow. I wondered if it would crash into the barrier, so I scampered off, but no, it came to a stop right in front of it, and I thought what a grand job that must be, to be a motorman, and I decided right on the spot that was what I'd be. The motorman and the conductor got off and lit up cigarettes. There weren't any passengers on the car to get off and I was the only one waiting, so they were in no hurry and had no one to please. 'Got a ticket, young feller?' the conductor asked me, and he winked.

"I watched them unhook the cowcatcher from the front and take it around to the back and hook it on – presto, now the back is the front. If only it were that easy to turn your life around.

"Then the conductor switched the electric wire connection, swinging the cable around and rehooking it up with a lot of sparks and crackling, and then he's back in and clanging the bell. 'All aboard if yer comin', young feller,' he calls out, and I climb on and hand him my ticket, all crumpled up and sweaty from being in my hand so long. I remember the conductor squinted at it, 'This ticket's been around the block a few times on its own, I see,' he said, and I had a moment's scare, thinking he might not take it and I'd have to walk all the way back, all those long blocks. But then he just winked at me again and put the ticket in his little metal box, rang the bell one more time and off we went.

"I remember there were long benches on both sides of the car, and straps to hang onto if you were standing, and I was surprised by how old and drab everything looked, the upholstery on the seats worn, the floor dirty, and how musty it smelled inside, not at all elegant and grand, as I'd imagined. There was a stove by the motorman's seat and a charcoal box and a box of sand and a shovel – all unused because it was summer now – and there was lots more to look at but I was too tired and my eyes were drooping, so I didn't enjoy the ride as much as I'd been hoping."

Dave Margoshes

"The anticipation was better than the real thing," Zelda said.

Zan looked up, surprised by her presence. "Yes, so often. Still, it was a great adventure. I remember I got off at Powers and walked the rest of the way, tired as I was, because I didn't want anyone to see me, afraid Momma and Pop would give me hell, and they would have too. And I never told anyone, not even Adam or Abe."

"Quite a memory, Zan."

He smiled. "Memory! Some things I can't remember, some things I can't forget."

CHAPTER 5

October 25, 1988

"AND HOW ARE YOU TODAY?"

"Today? Today I'm tip-top. Tomorrow may be a different story, but today, tip-top."

"I wonder if you can remember anything where perhaps you got hurt in some way, like falling out of the tree you told me about a few weeks ago. For example, I can't help noticing that your nose has been broken. When and how did that happen?"

Zan laughed. "Ah, that. Not exactly Cyrano, but still, it gives me a certain..." – he waved the fingers of his right hand beside his head – "...distinctive look, don't you think? Like Brando in *Streetcar* or *Waterfront*. Women go for that, so I've been told."

Zelda smiled. "It's a distinctive feature, yes. Also a defining one."

"Defining!"

"I mean that it says something about who you are."

"Is that right? A nose is more than a nose? And what does it say, Lady Doctor?"

"It says that you're very adept at changing the subject, at manipulating the conversation."

"Ah, you're getting to know me so well, in so short a time, just three or four visits. I'm impressed, very impressed."

"So let's get back to the nose, shall we? When did that happen? Were you a boy?"

"A little older than that. Seventeen, eighteen."

"Ah, no longer a boy. You must have thought of yourself as a man when you were eighteen."

"If I didn't before the punch in the nose, I certainly did afterwards."

"And who was responsible?"

"Responsible? *I* was responsible. I knew what I was doing. Besides, I should have ducked."

"I meant – as you know very well – who was it who delivered

the punch?"

"Ah. That was Abe. My brother Abe. My nemesis and protector. Not so much a protector that day."

This time Zelda laughed. "Oh, yes, the famous A to Zed boys. The protective bigger brother. Was this sibling rivalry gone to extreme, or what?"

"No, nothing like that. It was in a boxing ring, at a gym, gloves and mouthpieces, the Marquess of Queensberry, all very proper. A demonstration that went awry."

"Awry."

"It was an accident. I left my chin unprotected, he aimed too high. *Always aim high*, that's what they taught us at school, but this was an accident."

"Your brother was a boxer?"

"Wise Crack. You're smiling, Zelda, but that's what they called him, a little play on words. Golden Gloves welterweight champion of Winnipeg three years running, 1923, '24, '25. You should have seen him, he was something to see then, a sight to behold, slim, dark, muscles, an Adonis. Not the tired old man he is today."

"And he was giving you a lesson?"

"That's it exactly. I was no boxer, no athlete at all. Scrawny, a caved-in chest. No Charles Atlas, for sure, but maybe not exactly his ninety-eight-pound weakling either. I'm eighteen, things are going on, and Abe says, 'Zannie, come down to the gym, I'll show you how to defend yourself.'"

"Excuse me," Zelda interrupts. "Things were going on?"

"Oh, nothing too serious. I was working at the railway yards – the CPR – and it was a tough bunch. There were card games, sometimes sore losers, sometimes fights. So Abe says 'Come down to the gym,' and I go. He dresses me up in shorts and special shoes, we work out on punching bags, skip rope. Then we're in the ring. 'Keep your gloves up,' he tells me, then he pokes me in the belly. I drop my gloves and bang! He makes his point. A little higher, a little harder than he meant. An accident. Well, I think it was. That's what he always claimed."

"You were knocked down?"

"Down but not out. Still, Abe throws in the towel for me. Blood everywhere. A TKO."

"And pain?"

"Not right away. Just blood, salty, thick. And seeing double, two of everything."

"And how did you feel?"

"Feel?"

"Were you angry at your brother?"

"Angry? No. I wanted to break *his* nose, break his head, his neck. I wanted to punch *him* in the nose, show him how it feels, how his blood tastes. But angry? No. This is my brother we're talking about. And just an accident, after all."

Zelda smiled. "There's a school of thought, you know, that there's no such thing as an accident."

Zan smiled too. "So I've heard, Dr. Zelda, so I've heard."

IT WAS THE BOXING that caused everything, Zan once explained to Jack, the trigger that, once pulled, could not prevent the hammer from striking the bullet. But no, that couldn't be right. The boxing had been supposed to replace the trigger.

Saul and Hersh had been the wild ones, tough guys; the eldest, twins, they were novelties in the neighbourhood, grew up thinking they could get away with anything, "that they were bulletproof," Zan told Jack. "They liked to scrap. God only knows where they got it, not from our mother or father, they weren't like that. Maybe throwbacks to some outlaw in the family."

There was a gap of seven years and more between them and the rest of the kids, so, growing up, none of the other boys was ever close to them. But Abe idolized them, Hersh in particular. Still, if Hersh hadn't been killed in the war, Zan said, things might have happened differently. "Saul came home alone, and Abe sort of slipped into the vacuum where Hersh had been."

It hadn't happened right away, but the magnetic field had shifted.

"Especially after Adam died, he should have been closer to me," Zan said, "but he kept being pulled toward Saul."

"And he got in trouble?" Jack asked. "The two of them?"

"Trouble, you could say that. Saul and Hersh, they were the original trouble twins. They were hanging around the Main Street saloons and pool halls even as kids, some petty crime." Zan paused to shake his head, remembering. "Where they got that itch, I don't know. Not from our parents, that's for sure – hard-working, religious – well, my mother, not so much my father, but always his nose clean, my father, always straight home to the family after work, if he took a drink it was at home, not in a barroom. Maybe from our uncle Leo the boys got that itch, he was a rabble-rouser, a brawler, but not a thief, not a gangster, like Saul almost became. He was a bouncer at one of the Annabella Street whorehouses, my big brother! But that's later. Saul comes home from the war tougher than ever, and sullen, gets into trouble during the 1919 strike – the General Strike, you know about that? – then drifts away from home, gets involved in a robbery in Vancouver, winds up in jail. Abe's getting into his own scrapes, schoolyard fights, that sort of thing, but nothing like Saul, nothing like Hersh. Then he's doing boxing, amateur stuff, Golden Gloves, that's supposed to – what's the term, Dr. Freud? – *channel the aggression.*"

"It didn't work out?"

"It did and it didn't."

EVEN NOW, SO MANY YEARS LATER, he could feel the cold square of the watch against his wrist, even – he imagined, as he imagined then – the spidery incision of the letters: "Abe 'Wise Crack' Wiseman, Golden Gloves, 1923, Winnipeg." What a thrill it had been when Abe gave it to him, the next year, when he won his second, to have it on his wrist, the feel of it, the constant reminder, when he glanced down to check the time, of what could be accomplished. Even the deception, the revelation that followed, the metal taste in his mouth, didn't take away that feeling, not entirely.

And where was the watch now, what had become of it?

On that day, the policeman had it in his hand, what appeared to be the watch anyway. They were crowded into a small room at the police station downtown, two all-but-identical cops in plainclothes, Zan, Joe Zuken, a law student he'd become friends with when they acted together in an amateur play, and Adrian Fox, a law professor at the university who was active in the Party and had represented members on occasion. Through Joe, Zan had become a little friendly with Fox, and at Joe's suggestion, he'd called him the previous week when his brothers had gotten in trouble. Fox didn't usually do criminal work, but he was glad to oblige as a favour, at last to give advice. Zan's brothers had been arrested after being implicated in the hijacking of a truck leaving a Point Douglas warehouse. Apparently, they'd been linked to other robberies, as well, though Zan had known nothing of them, but this was the first time they'd been arrested. Fox had been able to get them out on minimal bail, since, aside from the word of a man who'd been caught, there was no real evidence against them, and he was confident they'd be able to get the charges thrown out. Now, when Zan had been summoned down to the police station, he'd called Fox again.

Zan knew one of the detectives who'd shepherded them into the interview room – he'd been the one who'd interrogated Abe while his more senior partner was in with Saul the previous week. "What's this all about?" he asked him.

The bull glanced at Zuken and Fox and smirked. Then he turned his attention back to Zan, handing him the watch. "Ever seen this before?"

They'd all been standing and Zan sat down on a bench now. He glanced at the watch and then, without thinking, checked his own, cocking his elbow and sliding his wrist forward. It was, he noted, 3:15, and he'd have to be going soon or he'd be late to the class he taught two afternoons a week at the *Arbeiter Ring* school in the old neighbourhood. "It looks like mine."

"It isn't yours?"

"No, you can see, I'm wearing mine."

"Inscribed on the back, is it?" the cop asked. He was a big man with thin, sandy hair and a drooping mustache, Irish most likely. He wore a vest mismatched with the rest of his suit. In fact, it looked like he might have swapped vests with the other cop, who didn't speak a word. "Kin I see it?"

Zan glanced at Fox, who made a face and shrugged. "Sure." He started to unbuckle it.

"Let me guess what it says." The cop glanced at the back of the watch in his hand. "Abe 'Wise Crack' Wiseman, Golden Gloves, Winnipeg, something like that?"

"That's Abe's watch?" Zan asked.

"Why'd you think so?"

"He's got one just like mine. There's three of them. He won three titles. I've got the first one, our brother Saul's got the second, Abe wears the newest."

"All the same?"

"Except for the date, sure."

The bull checked the back of the watch in his hand. "Nineteen twenty-three. What's yours say?"

He didn't have to check, he knew the inscription by heart. "That can't be right. Mine's 1923."

The cop laughed and winked at his partner, who stood silently by the door. "Yours and half a dozen others we've found so far."

"I don't understand..." Zan began, but Fox cut him off.

"That looks like a Waterbury," the professor said. "Pretty common watch. I've got one not much different myself."

"Pretty common is right, counsellor," the cop said. "A jeweller on Portage Avenue lost a box of them in a burglary a while back. Forty watches. Two bucks each, wholesale." He tapped the face of the watch in his fist. "Worth more inscribed, of course. Keepsakes. Collector's items."

"You're lying," Zan said. He was on his feet now, blood pounding in his temples.

"Take it easy, Wiseman," Zuken said.

"Yeah, boy, take it easy," the cop said. He was grinning. "Sit down and tell me again about your watch. Where'd you say you got it?"

As it happened, Zan would tell Jack years later, there were serial numbers on the watches and the one on Zan's was way earlier than those on the cops' list; it really had been issued in 1923, so he was off the hook for possession of stolen property, which is what Fox told him later the two bulls probably had in mind for him. Nor, except for the circumstantial evidence of Abe's name on the back of the half-dozen watches that had turned up, was there ever any evidence to link his brother to the jewelry store burglary – Saul's watch, and Abe's own, dated '24 and '25, both appeared to be authentic, and the people who'd bought the bogus watches, all from a man at the bar of the St. Regis Hotel, all denied the man was Abe. The cops were just fishing around for other things to bolster their case against Abe in the hijacking, Fox said. As it happened, those charges were soon dropped against both brothers, as he had predicted.

"They did make a phone call to the dean, though, or someone did," Zan told Jack. "Let him know about the trouble my brothers were in, about the watch, that they had all they needed to prove possession of stolen property on me but were dropping it."

"Harassment."

Zan nodded his head. "Not that the dean needed anything new on me. I was already the celebrated Commie kid, always getting into trouble passing out leaflets, organizing students – we had a strike once almost, over what I don't remember. All they needed was an excuse to kick me out. The scholarship I had, it had a morals clause or something like that – I had to be of high moral calibre to keep it. They pulled it and that was it for me."

"When was this?" Jack asked.

"Ha ha, 1929. The crash – you remember that? I had one of my own."

But it hadn't been so bad. "The hell with them," Luna had said. "Write that novel you've been talking about."

FROM ZAN'S JOURNAL

Oct. 25, 1988 – That woman got me thinking about all that old stuff today, the robbery, the watches – and what the hell has become of mine? – the boys in jail, all of it. Haven't thought about this garbage in a long time. No, I think about it all the time – it never really goes away. I look at my mug in the mirror, see that flattened shnoz, and how can I not think of it? I see Abe – which I do every day now – and how can I not think of it? But really think about it, be there again, no, I haven't done that for awhile. "You are who you are today, not who you were yesterday," Myrna always said. Wise woman. Then she would kiss me, as if that would make everything better. Usually it did. That woman had healing power! Nothing ever goes away, not really, but you can make it still. Myrna could do that.

This woman, this Zelda, she likes to do the opposite, rile things up. She knows how to get under my skin. Just the way Luna did. And Rose. Just the memory of them prickles.

Just heard on the radio news: in Palestine, they're calling themselves a state now, a state! That too gets under my skin. Well, good luck to them. Israel called itself a state too, forty years ago, and still it's not quiet there.

If only things were that easy. I could drop the "failed," just call myself a novelist. And presto, I'd be one!

CHAPTER 6

November 1, 1988

"GOOD AFTERNOON, ZAN. HOW ARE you today?"

"As good as can be expected." He smiled. "Considering my low expectations."

"I asked you the first time we talked about wife and children," Zelda said, smiling over her notebook. She liked to take her time settling herself in her chair, Zan noticed, moving her hips, adjusting the collar of her white blouse. He was getting to like her. "You were a little vague. I'm getting used to that, but can we get back to that question. You were married?"

Zan looked at his hands, spreading the fingers. "A little vague. Only a little? I'm surprised. I must not have felt well that day."

"You'd been in the hospital a few days before."

"Is that right?"

"You don't remember being in the emergency ward? Being constipated?"

"You think I would discuss something so indelicate with you? But no, I don't remember. I was constipated yesterday, I'm constipated today, so that's nothing to talk about, nothing worth remembering. To tell you the truth, though, I don't remember anything about that week. I was in shock."

Zelda hesitated. "And what was the cause of that shock?"

"You think I'm avoiding the subject again, isn't that right, Lady Doctor? Deflecting? I'm not. You asked about marriages, so I'll tell you. But first I have to tell you that the woman I lived with for twenty years died three months ago. Well, four months now. We weren't married, but in every way but the technical, legal way, we were. Twenty years, we were together every day, almost, eating meals together, sleeping in the same bed. She was a professor, I was a notorious writer, so sometimes to conferences we would go, she to hers, me to mine, so not every day together. But almost. Living in each other's pockets. If that isn't married, what is? Then she died, I sold or gave away everything we owned, I left my home of all that time – in Las Vegas, of all places, did I tell you? I did some travelling, and I came here..." He laughs. "If I *hadn't* been in shock it would be of more interest to you. I was dazed, that's all, like I'd been punched in the nose, something I have some experience in, as you can see." He raised his chin and gestured toward his face. "But that I don't want to talk about. Not today. Ask me again some other time maybe."

"Actually, you told me about that."

"I did? Okay."

"You told me, too, I think, that you'd been married several times. Do you want to talk about the earlier marriages, or is that off limits today too?"

"No, they're not off limits. But let me tell you a story, Dr. Zelda. This is a story I've tried to write, a dozen times maybe, but it's never come out quite right. It's called '*Kaddish.*' You know what *Kaddish* is? The prayer Jews say for the dead. It's tough for a rich man to get into heaven, tougher than getting a camel through the eye of a needle, you read that in the Bible? The truth is, it's tough for anyone to get into heaven, rich or poor, and some Jews believe unless your son says *Kaddish* for you, it's even tougher. Not a good prospect, especially for someone about to die. And even more so for someone without a son.

"So anyway, I'll tell you this story. It's about my great-grandfather. He was a rabbi, a big man back home in the old country, a scholar, respected throughout the district for his piety, his wisdom, his charity. Great-grandfather, is that what I said? My grandfather's father. My father never knew him, he was an old man, died long before my father was born, but he heard stories, in the village he'd come from in Galicia – you know where this is, Galicia? Part Poland, part Ukraine, all the Austrian Empire back in those days. Anyway, everyone knew what a big man my father's grandfather was, what a wonderful man. Just as an example, here's a story they told of him: A traveller came to the village and stopped at the *shul*, asked if he might attend services. My great-grandfather said, 'Of course, you're welcome. Our door is always open to a Jew, any Jew. Excuse me, sir, but you are a Jew?'

"'Yes,' said the traveller, 'but maybe not such a good one. It's been years since I've been inside a *shul*. Perhaps you could tell me, show me what to do?'

"'There's a lot involved in being a Jew,' my great-grandfather told him, '613 *mitzvahs*. Few know them all, though we're supposed to. I will explain one to you. I will be satisfied to see you following even that one, rather than complaining that you lack the other 612.'"

Zelda smiled. "A wise man indeed."

"Yes, didn't I tell you he was? And here's the thing: by teaching the traveller one *mitzvah*, he was performing one himself, so doubly wise he was.

"Here's another example, just a brief one: after a pogrom, when a nearby *shtetl* was attacked by Cossacks, houses burnt, people injured and even killed, he was asked, this great rabbi, why is it that God allows such things to happen. 'Yes, God did this to us,' he admitted, 'or allowed it to be done. God is not answerable to anyone, nor are His ways understandable. We're not permitted to ask Him why he does this or doesn't do that, but we are permitted to ask, please, God, don't do it again. This is prayer, and that pleases God very much. So much so that, some-times, He answers. But you know, even when we don't get what we pray for, when we don't *seem* to, that doesn't mean God hasn't replied.'

"But I'm getting away from the story, sorry. Okay, I think I've shown this is a pretty wise man. But in his life, the life of this great man, there was a great tragedy...a loving wife, whom he dearly loved, but no sons, no one to say *Kaddish* over him.

"They went to the doctor, to other rabbis, to the village priest even, to the witch even – oh yes, in the *shtetl* there was always a witch. Under her direction, the direction of the witch, the wife of this great man lay naked in the light of the full moon, she drank potions, they said prayers, incantations the wife of a rabbi shouldn't say but she did, noth-ing worked. Daughters she produced by the carload, six of them, strong, healthy girls with arms like peasants, there was no problem get-ting the work done. But no sons, no son, and what to do? A big rabbi, a spiritual man, and no one to say *Kaddish* over him? This can't do. Can you guess what he did, my great-grandfather?"

"He divorced his wife?"

"You must have a rabbi in your family tree, Dr. Zelda, some of Solomon's blood. Of course, he divorced her. The watch doesn't work, you clean it, you oil it, you wind it, you shake it lightly..." Zan brought his cupped hand to his ear and shook his fingers gently, "...just so. It still doesn't work, you get a new watch. If you want to know what time it is, you do, anyway."

"And the woman, your...well, no, *not* your great-grandmother...the woman gave him a divorce?"

"The term in Hebrew is *get*. The husband gives a *get* – I know, it doesn't sound too grammatical – the wife receives it. She gets the *get*. Again, of course. There's not much choice involved. What else could she do?"

"It might have been your great-grandfather's fault, you know."

"It might have been, but the proof of the pudding, as they say...."

"He remarried, your great-grandfather?"

"He did. Even in his sixties, with a big belly and a white beard, he was still a good catch. He found a woman, a widow who already had two sons – the proof of *her* pudding, and a hedge against the bet maybe."

"And his new wife bore him sons?"

"Here I am, the proof in the other pudding." He gestured to indicate himself. "Two sons, one of them my grandfather. And two more daughters for good measure. But then, here's the joke – my father always laughed when he came to this part of the story, my father wasn't so religious, you can see, that was my mother's department – he died while they were all still children – too much exertion, maybe. The boys said *Kaddish*, yes, but their Hebrew wasn't all that good, and it probably didn't count anyway because they were not yet *bar mitzvah* – you know what that means? Thirteen years old and adults. Before that, they're not really Jews. The stepsons said *Kaddish* too, but they were only stepsons. Who knows how much trouble the old man may have had getting through the gate, him *and* his camel."

"And the woman? His first wife?"

"Ah, the first wife." Zan brought his right hand to his chin and rubbed it vigorously. "It would be nice to be able to say she and her six daughters lived comfortably and happily in the same household as her former husband and his new family, that she lived to a ripe old age in comfort at the hearth of her successor. It would be nice to be able to say that, and if I ever write this story maybe that's the way it will end.

As to what really happened, I'm afraid that isn't part of the story, not the way my father told it, anyway. So that's the story. Some story, eh?"

"Very nice," Zelda said. "Well, not so nice, maybe, but a good story. And you told it to me...why exactly?"

"You can't guess?"

"As a metaphor?"

"Metaphors, you'll pardon my bluntness, are my stock and trade."

"As a metaphor for why you've not been able to hold onto a relationship...."

"Twenty years is not so bad, and ended just by death."

"Prior to that. You said there were several."

"All right, a metaphor, okay. I'm good at them. But for what?"

Zelda put the eraser end of her pencil against her lips and studied him with a level gaze Zan turned his own eyes away from.

"Are you telling me you went from woman to woman to assure you had sons?"

"Ha. You can do better than that. What does one want sons for?"

"To say *Kaddish*...."

"And what do you care about a silly prayer said over your cold corpse for anyway? You can't hear it."

"To get into heaven..."

"There, that wasn't so hard, was it?"

"So you're telling me, Zan, that your inability to...excuse me, your *difficulty* in maintaining a relationship...or is it *disinterest?*" She raised the hand with the pencil. "Well, whatever it was, and the most recent one excepted, that the reason for that pattern was an attempt to get into heaven?"

"I see you're an atheist, Zelda. Just like me."

She smiled, just a hint of exasperation flickering on her lips. "An attempt to get into a heaven you don't even believe in?"

"You play poker, Lady Doctor?"

"Poker?"

"You know, cards. A big pot on the table. You know the cards you hold, but not what the other guy's got."

"Bluffing. I know the term."

"You never know what the other guy's got. Or if there even is another guy."

"So it's a good idea to keep your options open, to make sure you can get into heaven...just in case there really is a heaven?"

"Pascal – you heard of him? His famous wager? He put it this way, it's better *to* believe in a God that doesn't exist than *not* believe in One Who does, and Who might take it personally. Words to that effect."

"Hedging your bets...that the expression?"

"It's not a bad way to live," Zan said. "Wouldn't you agree?"

Nov. 1, 1988 – Zelda asked about marriages today. We never did get to talk about Goldie or Rose, not to mention Luna, and just as well. At the time I couldn't remember any one of their names for the life of me.

Speaking of names, I asked her finally about her own name – or maybe she already said and I forgot. Turns out she's named after Fitzgerald's Zelda. Her parents were romantics, obviously. Does that make her better able to understand me, or worse?

And since when do I care about being understood, anyway?

I broached the subject of race too, or tried to. "Your skin is a lovely shade, Miss Zelda," I said. "Is your father black and your mother white, or the other way around?"

She brushed that off. "It's *your* parents we should be talking about, Mr. Wiseman," she said, all formal all of a sudden, a little cold.

"My parents, white on both sides, all the way down from Adam, by way of Abraham, Moses and the Wiseman clan of Galicia," I said, making a little joke.

"Oh, what makes you think Adam was white?" she asks, a twinkle in her eye.

I *like* this woman. So like Luna – there, I remembered her name now.

DUET 2

"So, you're coming to *shul*, Zannie?"

"I don't think so."

"Why not? You want to meet people, *shul* is people."

"No offence, the people I've met so far have not exactly greeted me with open arms."

"So they're old."

"Old? *I'm* old, *you're* old. This is some sort of excuse?"

"Not an excuse, it's an explanation. *You* always feel so cheerful?"

"Cheerful I don't ask for. Just common decency, common courtesy. A simple 'hello' would be nice."

"They don't say hello?"

"So they say hello. That much I'll give them. Hello and goodbye."

"And you'd like an invitation to dinner?"

"An invitation to dinner would be nice. So would a cup of coffee. At *kiddush* or after."

"We don't do *kiddush*, I told you. Just the wine, no food."

"*Wine!* That thimbleful of grape juice – this by you is wine?"

"It's the tradition here, so sue me, sue them."

"Believe me, I'm thinking about it. At least in court, they'd talk to me."

"Zannie, give them time. They get to know you, they'll talk your ear off, believe *me*."

"Time! Excuse me, Mr. Plans-To-Live-Forever, time is something I don't got too much of."

"On that score, don't get too lonesome, baby brother. I'm ahead of you in line."

"So who's pushing? Just don't...."

"Don't what?"

"Never mind."

"What? Don't leave you alone?"

"Not with this crowd, thanks."

"You got a better crowd, go schmooze with them. Beggars

can't be choosers."

"For people to talk to, I'm no beggar."

"So what are you complaining about?"

"Is it too much to ask, a new Jew in town, to get a greeting at the synagogue?"

"Synagogue! How many times I gotta tell you, it's *temple* here, *temple* is what we say."

"Temple, synagogue, what difference does it make? It's *shul*."

"Temple is what we say here."

"Synagogue is what we said at home."

"So go home. This is here."

"Synagogue is what we called it in Winnipeg."

"So this looks to you like Winnipeg? This is here, not there. That's so hard?"

"Believe me, Benchy, I'm not too likely to make the mistake."

"And all of a sudden, anyway, you're an expert in Jewish terminology? How many times you even been in a temple – synagogue, whatever you want to call it – since your *bar mitzvah?*"

"*Bar mitzvah?* You must be thinking of a different baby brother, *Abela*."

"Ha, that's a good one. Aren't you Alexander Wiseman?"

"Guilty as charged, Your Honour."

"Then you were *bar mitzvah*."

"I was?"

"I was there."

"Really?"

"*Oy*, what a head you got. You don't remember the agony, every afternoon after school for, what? Two years at the Talmud Torah? Learning Hebrew, getting ready for *bar mitzvah*, you don't remember Rabbi Goldenberg with his pinched-up nose, 'what kind of a Jew is that?' we kids would say. 'With a nose like that, how did they let him into rabbi school?'"

"The rabbi with the skinny nose, yes. But the rest.... I was *bar mitzvah?*"

"Were you *bar mitzvah?* Why wouldn't you be? You didn't

think you'd be able to get through the Hebrew prayers, remember? But you did, and I was proud of you."

"You were proud of me?"

"Sure, and so was Momma. You made Momma happy."

"I did?"

"You did, Zannie, take my word for it. Don't you remember the old ladies upstairs in the balcony throwing down little candies on you, to sweeten your life. Little chewy candies wrapped in pink paper."

"Like saltwater taffy."

"That's it. Honestly, Pantsy, like swiss cheese your head is, that many holes. Thank God, I ain't got that problem. Bad hearing is bad enough."

"I don't believe you, *Abela*. Maybe your memory's as bad as your hearing and you ain't heard the news yet. I don't think I was *bar mitzvah*. Studied, yes, but something happened, I got sick, that must have been it. Anyway, even if I *was*, just for the sake of argument, I should go to *shul* now and sit with a bunch of old Jews, they got their thumbs up their asses, a cork in their mouth?"

"So who invited you?"

"Invited? By you I need an invitation? To go to *shul*? Maybe I need to join the club, get a key, learn the secret handshake."

"You did learn it, you *shmuck*, that's what *bar mitzvah* was all about. Anyway, an invitation, no. That you don't need. God invites you."

"God? He lives in your so-called temple? God, if He existed, would make me more welcome."

"So maybe He stepped out for a minute."

"An absentee landlord, some god!"

"So maybe He got something in His eye, maybe He looked away. That much I'll give you."

"Thank you very much. I'll take it."

"Maybe He blinked."

"You still believe in this God fellow, Abe?"

"Don't blaspheme, Pantsy."

"I shouldn't take His name in vain? Why not? That's how He takes mine – except there is no God."

"There is."

"He's just looking away."

"Maybe He is."

"He stepped out for a minute."

"Why not?"

"To take a call."

"Could be."

"He blinked?"

"You never got a speck of dust in *your* eye?"

"He was distracted by the Holocaust? Not to mention the Crusades, the Inquisition, the pogroms, Charles Manson and any other nickel-and-dime horror."

"He created the world, Zannie. He didn't say it would be easy."

"Not easy. That's for sure. Some god, this god of yours, Abe. You'd better get off to *shul* and say your prayers to him. Put in a good word for me."

"Don't mock, Zannie. Yes, God did bad things to us, let bad things happen. We can't ask Him why, but we can say, 'please don't do it again.'"

"You really believe that, Abe?"

"That's so hard to believe, Zan? That I believe?"

"That's the hardest thing to believe. It's the one thing I really don't believe at all. Not that there's a God – who knows? But that people believe in Him – *that* I can't believe."

CHAPTER 7

November 8, 1988

"YOU'RE LOOKING DAPPER TODAY, ZAN. A flower in your lapel!"

"It feels like spring today. With these chinooks I'm still a novice. One day it's the dead of winter, the next, it's spring. You don't know if you're coming or going. Yesterday it's the deep-freeze, today it might be March 21, the infernal equinox! An interesting word, equinox. It sounds like a cross between a horse and a steer. Almost two months I've been here – see, Lady Doctor, I change the subject, but then I get back to it. I'm not the prognosticator you think I am. How come I can't remember what happened yesterday some days, but I don't forget a word like 'prognosticator'?"

"A different part of the brain involved. But aren't you changing the subject again?"

"I don't know. What *is* the subject?"

"I don't think we've settled on one yet, for today. I did have something in mind. Tell me, how are you getting along with your brother?"

"My brother? Abe, you mean?"

"You have another brother?"

"Sure, three others. Saul...I...I can't think of the other two's names just now."

"They're alive?"

"Alive? No. They're dead. Hersh in the war, the first war, World War I, in France, there, that's his name, Hersh. And Saul, that was Hersh's twin, he died young too, a heart attack, in a prison hospital, he was born with a weak valve, that's what they said. Me, I had to get scarlet fever to get my weak valves, he was born with his. Adam.." He paused. "That's the third one, Adam. Hersh in the war, blown up by a bomb. Saul, his heart. Adam in the scarlet fever, same time as me but...him not so lucky. Dead at ten."

"Scarlet fever?" Zelda interrupted.

"First scarlet fever, then rheumatic fever, I meant. Adam rheumatic fever, Hersh in the war, Saul, heart, he was sick a long time. Nothing like Dolly, but weeks, months maybe. For his sins, he said."

"Dolly?"

"Abe's wife. A dozen years in a coma, every day he goes to visit her, every day. And before the coma, an invalid for, I don't know, another dozen years, more."

"Oh, yes, you mentioned that."

"Abe, he's the subject?"

"Why not? But first, let me get these brothers straight. Hersh, Saul, Adam...."

"Right, Hersh in the war, Saul in prison, Adam the scarlet fever. All dead. Oh, and there was another one, actually, born dead, but that didn't mean our mother didn't continue to mourn him. Anyway, all dead, and Annie too, our sister, also from a bad heart. All gone, just Abe and me left, and Abe's Dolly, hanging on by a thread. That's the Wiseman family in a nutshell. Some nieces and nephews too, but I've lost track of who's who."

"Sounds like an interesting family. Tell me more about your early life. What kind of upbringing did you have?"

"Upbringing? Perfectly normal. You know that line in *The Glass Menagerie*, maybe – you know, the Tennessee Williams play? The son describes his father as a telephone lineman who fell in love with long distances. I wish I had written that. *My* father was a milkman who was just a little short of the milk of human kindness, later a locksmith who couldn't find the key to success. Poor but honest. Died young as his reward. That's God's way of saying 'screw you' – pardon my French. My mother was a saint – would have been if we were Catholic. She'd have been a *mensch* if she'd been a man. A just man. She was a pillar. Yet that's the way God treated her, taking her husband from her, her sons. My sister was made of the same stuff, steel lace. She was a good girl whose heart was broken because of something other people did, something she had no control over. I did, but I didn't.... Well, she didn't deserve what she got, let's just say that, though what she wound up with wasn't so bad. A good husband, not the one she wanted first, but a good man just the same. Good children, a happy home. Even a fast death – her heart, poof, she's gone. A lot of bum tickers in my family. As frailties go, that's not a bad one. No suffering. We're lucky to get what we do, but we don't always see it that way, isn't that right?"

When Zelda didn't reply, he went on.

"My brothers – did I mention this? – were jailbirds, holdup men who couldn't shoot straight. There was another brother, killed in the war, I told you already. How he would have turned out it's hard to say except his twin brother was one of the holdup men. But then, so was mine."

"Two sets of twins," Zelda interjected.

"We were famous in the neighbourhood, I can tell you that."

"Sorry, I didn't mean to interrupt."

"What was I saying? Oh, my brothers. Hersh, killed in the war, the First World War, this is, I don't remember how or where or when – I don't know if I ever knew. Saul, his twin, was with him, so he knew, but he'd never speak of it.

"Saul and Abe wound up in jail and Saul died there, he had the family curse, a weak heart." Zan paused. "Well, he might have died in prison, but they released him just in time and he was able to die at home, that was the government of Canada's gift to my family. He was just as dead, but our mother was able to tend to him, there was some…dignity. The government saved the cost of his burial. It cost us…. It cost something. But it was worth it."

"Ah. I understood from what you said before that he died in prison," Zelda said.

"I didn't mean to deceive you. It was as I said, he was in prison, in the hospital, they knew he was dying so they let him go home. In my mind, it was as if he'd died there, but, no, he was at home. That was what we wanted, what we paid for and got."

"Paid for?"

"Just a figure of speech, Dr. Zelda."

"And there was a third brother who died? I understood that right?"

Zan paused again. "Adam. It was so long go, I forget about him sometimes. He and I, we were…we were close. We both had the scarlet fever. Ten years old, something like that. We both had it. I got better, he didn't."

He took a sip of water from the cup on the end table beside his chair. Zelda waited.

"Good Jewish boys, all of us. Saul and Hersh, how we younger kids idolized them, our big, dangerous brothers. Saul and Hersh, Hersh and Saul, they could do no wrong, but the truth is that all they did was wrong. They were always in trouble, or in danger of it, or just getting out of it, scraping by by the skin of their teeth, the Main Street bars and pool halls they hung out at and worked at, the whorehouses. Hersh especially, he was the master. It scares me even to think what might have happened if he'd been with Saul and Abe later on their robbery – attempted murder nothing!

"I never could tell those two apart by eye, but their senses of humour were different. Hersh was the practical joker, there was never any shaking hands with him without getting a shock or a squirt or a stink on your hand you couldn't wash away. Saul was slyer, a putdown artist. 'I've never met a man I didn't dislike,' he'd say, W.C. Fields was his idol, so deadpan who the hell could know if he was serious or not, unless you knew him, in which case you knew he was never serious.

"The last thing he ever said to me, Saul, lying on his deathbed, was 'Pantsy' – that's what he called me – 'Pantsy, give me a little drink water.' Saul, who never drank water, not since he was a kid and got pleurisy from bad water, or that's what the doctors said, not a drop since unless it was boiled for tea or in soup – milk he drank, whiskey, lots, boiled tea, that's it. No coffee, no juice, not even a bottle of Coke. So dying, he asks me for water, thinking he could trick me: if I'd brought it, what? He'd say 'Pantsy, this is some way to treat a dying man'? Always a joke with Saul.

"But the upshot is, I didn't bring him water, before I could decide what to do he fell asleep. I sat with him awhile, then I went to get a cup of coffee, a bite to eat – my own drink of water. When I came back, half an hour, no more, he was dead. So maybe he wasn't pulling a trick after all, maybe he was saying goodbye. And me too dumb to realize, to say goodbye back.

"Hersh, if he was around, if he was still alive, he'd have brought him a cup of hot soapy water from the sink, said, 'Here, drink your tea,' and watched him spit it out. Always a joker, Hersh."

Zan fell silent and, after a minute, Zelda remarked, "Quite an interesting family."

"Oh, you don't know the half of it. 'Good Jewish boys,' I said, but Abe and me both wound up marrying a *shiksa*, one time or another.

You understand *shiksa*, Miss Zelda? A *goyish* woman, a Christian. Abe, a jailbird, then a war hero, then a tailor, a trade he learned in prison camp in Germany. His own shop, over forty years in this city, very respectable. Me, you know.

"Upbringing, she asks. Perfectly normal. All screwed up, and completely happy."

Zelda smiled over her notepad. "Tell me more."

Zan shrugged. "Funny you should ask about family. I was just thinking about my mother this morning. I lit a candle for her."

"It's her birthday? Or the anniversary of her death?"

"Her *yahrzeit*, yes, the anniversary of her death. Except I don't know if it really is, I forget when exactly. I just woke up thinking of her, so I thought maybe it was."

"Your brother would know, wouldn't he? Abe? From what you've said, he sounds like a methodical man who keeps records."

"Records and records of the records, lists of lists. You got that right. You know that expression 'anal personality'?"

"So you could ask him."

"I could but his lectures I can do without. Better to remember my mother than have Abe play the mother. Better to light a candle on the wrong day than take a chance and miss it. Like Pascal – remember, I told you his bet?"

"Let's get back to your brother Abe now, if we can. You told me when we started that you moved here to be close to him. So, how are you getting along?"

"Getting along? Fine."

"So you'll be staying at his place?"

"That, probably not, no. Twins, we are; Siamese twins, we're not."

"So there's some friction between you?"

"Lady Doctor, we're human beings, and we're alive. Friction, sure."

"So just normal friction – nothing related to being brothers? Issues from your past? From childhood? From his breaking your nose, perhaps?"

"Ah, more with the Freud. I keep forgetting."

"Forgetting? Forgetting what?"

"That you're a head-shrinker."

Zelda smiled. "Three different sizes. Small, tiny and microscopic. How much shrinkage would you like today, sir?"

"Do your worst, but go easy on the starch, okay? I'm stiff enough as it is, except where it counts, if you'll excuse a little off-colour."

"I won't excuse it, but maybe we'll talk about that one of these days. For now, I'll let it pass. Tell me more about your brother. Tell me *something* about him."

"He's...I told you...we're twins?"

"Yes. He's the older?"

"Thirteen minutes, or maybe it's thirty, I forget, but it's like ten years. Always, he's the one in charge. A babe in arms, sucking at our mother's breast, *both* breasts he's got to have. Five years old, ten years old, fifteen years old, you can't tell him anything. Now, just the same."

"That sounds like a little bit of bitterness in your voice."

"Bitterness? Not at all. I'm trying not to laugh. You can imagine a baby suckling at *two* breasts at a time? Some mouth."

"But does it make you angry, that mouth? Always being in charge?"

"No, of course not. He's in charge because...he's the one to be. He's the eldest, he knows what's best. Just ask him. Besides, he's got a mean right cross. I'm the kid brother, I've got to listen. Do what he says."

"And do you?"

"Listen? Sure."

"Do what he says?"

"Sometimes. Not always. Once in awhile. Not for a long time."

"Hmmm. Tell me more about him."

"About Abe? What's to tell?"

"He's your age. He's retired, I imagine. What did he do?"

"Do? I told you, he's a tailor. His own shop, here in Calgary, Hill-hurst-Sunnyside, over forty years. Right after the war, he comes home, the Veterans Affairs helps him get established here with a loan and so on. Why Calgary, not Winnipeg, I don't remember. But he's not retired, he still goes there every day."

"A tailor. I would have expected something different, more active. A former boxer."

"A former boxer has to make a living."

"How's his health?"

"His aches have pains, his pains have aches. In this department, he's got me beat. His heart is like Big Ben, it keeps such good time – if he wasn't my twin brother, I'd swear he must have been adopted, the Wiseman curse he doesn't have. Strokes he doesn't have either, cancer, no, indigestion, yes, the way he eats, but no ulcers, no problems like me with the back door, no plumbing problem. He looks the same as he did when we were thirty, almost, strong as an ox – not an equinox, but a musk ox – built like a post stuck in concrete. Suckling two breasts at a time, he got all the calcium from our mother's milk, I just got the leftover whey. Still, hair I got, him not so much. Active.... He skates three days a week, swims the other three, when he goes over there, to the Y, he's got his pockets full of hard candies he gives to the kids, they call him Candyman, follow him around on the ice like he's the Pied Piper, something to see. Oh, and he rides one of those whatchamacallits...."

"An exercise bike?"

"That's it. In his bedroom, a bike. Every morning, fifteen minutes when he gets up, at night, fifteen minutes before bed. Without the morning ride, he can't move around so good, without at night, he can't sleep. Without the swimming and the skating, he seizes up. That's what he says. He's like an old machine you're afraid to turn off, not sure it'll start up again."

"So he's a real athlete."

"A boxer, Golden Gloves champ. A hockey player. Weights he used to lift. Even in prison, he boxed."

"He was in prison? I thought that was..." She glanced down at her pad. "Saul."

"Saul, yes, Abe, yes, both of them, for armed robbery. Saul, he was in a few times. Hersh probably would have been too, except the war got to him first, the first war. He was a scrapper before he went, always in trouble. If we littler kids got into a fight on the street – and on Flora Avenue, believe me, you could get into a fight easy, there were plenty of Jews on our street, but plenty of Poles too, and it wasn't always détente. If we got into a fight, and if Hersh was around, like the US Cavalry, here he would come charging to rescue us. But you were asking about Abe. In prison, yes; they let him out early to join the army when war came. And later, in Germany, prisoner of war camp."

"That's interesting. Why don't you tell me more about this? Come to think of it, you mentioned another brother, the one who died as a boy. Adam? You talk so fast, I never got a chance to ask you about him."

Zan rubbed his face, pursed his mouth, thinking. "It's Dolly who really suffered," he said. "A hard-luck woman like her, there aren't too many who stay so faithful, so loyal. If I was writing a novel about my brother – not that I am, but if I were – it's her I'd make it be about. An angel she was, believe me, but cursed by my mother when they got married. Then hardly married before he's arrested, and then five years in prison, all those years she waits. Then they let him out to go into the service, he's shipped overseas, I don't even think they got to see each other before he's gone, maybe once. A tail gunner in bombers, two years, shot down twice, almost killed, the first time in the ocean, picked up, not a scratch on him, the second time over Germany, again, not hurt at all but the rest of the war in a prison camp. More than ten years she stands by him, waits for him. That's something, eh? That's some woman. Then later, her son dies, from drugs. And she's sick for years herself, and, I told you already, in a coma now, what, a dozen years?"

"Yes. Maybe you *should* write a novel about her. Why don't you?"

"You got any patients with impotence, Dr. Zelda?"

"I've had some."

"Do you ask them why they don't make love with this girl or that?"

"Point taken. But tell me this – how come when I ask you about your brother, you tell me about his wife?"

"Oh, that's easy. It's a metaphor."

"It's evasion, I'd say," Zelda said, but she was laughing.

"Evasion...what the hell do you think metaphors are for?"

HE HAD BEEN ASLEEP when the phone call came from the lawyer. He'd always been asleep, he remembered. Luna answered, jabbed him awake with the receiver.

"Zan? This is Joe Zuken."

He'd immediately thought of Saul. Since his big brother had come back from his prison term on the coast, he always seemed to be getting in trouble again or on the verge of it. Zuken had helped him out a couple of times on minor things, got him off. He was a practicing lawyer now and already had a good record at the provincial court. But Zan and Joe were friends, so it could have been about anything.

"This about Saul?"

"I don't know if I can get him off this time. Your brothers have been arrested, both of them. They're down at the...."

"What? Both? Abe too?"

"Yes. Can you...."

"Both of them! What, this is the James gang?"

"Your mother is hysterical. Can you come down?"

He dressed in silence, aware of Luna's eyes on him from the bed. As he was tying his shoelaces, she got up and came to sit on the edge of the bed beside him, putting her arm around him. He stiffened, but she didn't budge, never did. "I've got to go..." he began but she put a finger to his lips, silencing him. Over the years they were together, she had developed a sure intuition for things relating to his family, a subject she had little or no interest in. She didn't ask, didn't want to know. So at that moment, was it she who turned away from him, or he from her?

Funny the way that had stuck in his mind, years after; it wasn't his mother's sobbing, the embarrassment in Abe's eyes, the downcast look on Saul's face, their hands in cuffs, the stare of the copper standing in the corner of the room, just out of earshot, the drone of the lawyer, none of those things stayed with him the way Luna's fingers to his lips had, the way he had shrugged away from her, the way she had seemed to shrug away from him. Everything between them had come to a head and begun to slide away months before, but they had fiercely ignored that, he as much as she, had put it out of their sight and minds; now, with that shrug, those shrugs, he would realize later, the falling apart began in earnest. That wasn't something he could tell Zelda, though – how tell her about the end when they haven't even gotten to the beginning?

Except, of course, it hadn't happened that way at all, the memory false. The boys' arrest had been in 1935, while Zan was in Toronto, and that moment of separation between him and Luna had come a good year earlier. There had been no phone call then, just his own decision to go. Eventually there had been a call, yes, that much was correct; though it wasn't from Joe Zuken, but a neighbour of his mother who somehow knew where to reach him; everything else happened much the way it comes back to him in the dream – except that the next day he was on a train back to Winnipeg, Zan to the rescue, as always. But, Luna, no, that part of his life was already over. "Somehow, in the swamp which is his memory, the two strands had conflated. Did he dream, this? Imagine it? Why not? Wasn't imagination his domain?"

Nov. 8, 1988 – Moved into the suite today – that's what they call an apartment here. Not bad, only one story up, one-bedroom, clean enough, plumbing that growls but doesn't leak, $350 plus utilities. Just a block off Seventeenth Avenue, just south of downtown, restaurants around, suits me fine. I can walk from here to see that Zelda easy. From my window, I can see the street, I like that, the passing parade. From the roof, maybe, I can see the mountains. The suite is in good shape, freshly painted, white. It has that almondy smell of new paint that lodges in the back of your throat. The moment I walked in, the landlady chattering away, it was so familiar, the suite itself, the white walls, that smell.

Abe and the fellow who does odd jobs for him, mows his lawn and shovels his walk and so on, helped me. Some odds and ends of furniture Abe had in his basement and a good desk I bought at the Goodwill. Some dishes and pots and pans from Abe's but I need a coffee pot, that'll be about it. You need a dresser, Abe says, but cardboard boxes work fine, for now anyway. That's the system I used in Toronto when I became a bachelor again. We went down to one of the cafés on Seventeenth after, coffee and pie all of us, my treat. Eventually, they went away, I walked back here on my own, through heavy, wet snow – it'll take some getting used to again, snow, cold. Can't shake the thought of how much this place is like the one I had in Toronto after Rose. That's twenty-four years ago, before Myrna, but it feels like just last year maybe, the year before, that close. Everything different, everything the same. Jack then, now this Zelda. Maybe I'll get one of these computers that are all the rage – imagine, a typewriter where you don't have to scratch mistakes out on the paper, just a few keystrokes and it's fixed. That would be different.

I miss my old portable. That typewriter should be in a museum somewhere, instead of in storage, along with most of everything else I still own, or a rest home, which is where I suppose I belong too, will certainly wind up. But until then, I'd rather it was with me.

●

The US vote today – somehow they managed to get it done without me being there, but look what a cock-up they made of it. Looks like it's Bush! Nixon, Reagan, Bush.... Is this a trend? The country's going downhill. And I'm the one they say is crazy?

ABE 2

Dolly, darling, hello, hello. Let me give you a kiss, sweetheart. Ah, your hands are so nice and warm.

Weather's taken a turn for the worse, Dolly, cold now, snowing like all hell. You're smart not to go out. Let me give you another kiss, if you don't mind my cold lips on your cheek.

There, that's better. It's comfortable in here, as always. You got it good, Dolly, never have to go out in the cold or the heat or the rain or snow, never have to get your feet wet, your ears cold. *And* they wait on you hand and foot. Yeah, you got it good, Dolly darling.

So, sweetheart, my big news, Zan's moved out, thank God. Got a place of his own and we moved him in this afternoon.

He was driving me nuts. Don't get me wrong, I love him – well, you know, Dolly, but how that woman in Las Vegas lived with him for twenty years I don't know, I couldn't live with him for twenty days, not another twenty minutes probably.

This is for the best, he's here, close by, but not in my pockets, I'm not in his.

Every day an argument about something. I say high, he says low, I say yes, he says no.

And he lives in the past – that's not my sort of thing, you know? I told you this already, Dolly, I think: we take a drive into the mountains. He'd been saying he wanted to see them. So we go to Banff, yeah, my old jalopy still works good enough to get us there and back. We walk around in the town with the tourists, go up to Lake Louise, some of the other places, and what does that *farshimmelt* brother of mine do? Does he look? No, he's too busy talking about Nevada, New Mexico, Colorado, other mountains he's been to. I look at something, I see what's there. Zannie looks at the same thing, he sees something else entirely that the real thing reminds him of. He's not of this world, that brother-in-law of yours, Dolly, not of the real world.

This morning on Gzowski, Dolly, this guy is talking, and he says, apropos of what I forget, that everybody is divided into

Dave Margoshes

two camps: those who say the glass is half full, and those who say it's half empty. I have to laugh. That's me and Zan in a nutshell. At our mother's breast, I said, hey, great, milk; Zannie, he yells, what, no chocolate? I always see the best, he the worst. I'm not saying I've always been right, or even smart, but it's an outlook on life, Dolly, that makes life a little easier. What am I telling you?

I'm thinking about this later when I'm at the gym taking my skate. The kids come around, yelling, "Hey, Candyman, Candyman," and I give out a few treats, like always. I never give out all I have, or to all the kids – I don't want them to think it's an automatic thing, that the world owes them a living. I want them to know that some days there's candy, some days there ain't, but there's always a chance of it. It's that chance that makes getting up in the morning worthwhile, especially when you hurt like me – but what do those kids know about that? For them it's just school and fun. I know, they don't have to work like Zannie and me did, still it's the principle.

Even bigger kids, they all have jobs these days, but it's to buy cars and records and hamburgers, not to help put food on the table and pay the rent. Me and Zannie were breadwinners already when we were ten, well, I was, he was sick then, but he was out on the street when he was twelve, thirteen, but I'm getting off the track a little. Well, maybe not so much. We were working – we both had paper routes, I was a pin boy, a hot walker at the track, all those other things, Zan had his jobs – you know all this, Dolly, all of this is ancient history to you. What I mean to say is that it's not that we were different, but here's the difference: with Zannie, it was always, not a chore, not even a responsibility, but a noble calling, this big selfless gift, a sacrifice. He let you know how much he was chipping in – even now, he lets me know. If I say, 'Zannie, I worked too,' he looks at me like this is news he's hearing for the first time. With me, it was just part of being in the family. See what I mean? Half full, half empty. Maybe that's not exactly right, but you know what I mean.

CHAPTER 8

November 15, 1988

"LET'S TALK ABOUT WOMEN TODAY, SHALL WE?" Zelda was wearing a beige suit, a red blouse. *Crisp* is the word her appearance suggested. "Last week, I tried to steer you in that direction, but you outwitted me."

"Me, outwit you? No, you're confusing me with another patient. But keep your lovely red shirt on, Zelda. Women. Sure. Great idea. I love them, admire them, can't live without them. Do you have some particular women in mind? Helen of Troy? Cleopatra?"

"I was thinking more of the women in your life."

"The waitress who poured my coffee this morning was nice."

"I'm thinking of women closer to you."

"She was as close as you are. Closer. She leaned over, I could smell her perfume, *eau d'bacon and eggs*."

Zelda smiled, recrossed her legs. "I'm thinking of the women in your life, who've been important to you."

"There's my mother. There's you. With some distance and time in between."

"There are two – or three? – wives. I've lost track. Could we start with them? Then, perhaps we can talk about your mother."

"And you?"

"Let's leave me out of it."

"Why should that be? Believe it or not, Doctor Zelda, but right now you are the number one woman in my life. Well, the *only* one. You and the waitress this morning. Edna. That's her name. Can you believe it? An eighteen-year-old girl called Edna? And you a Zelda. Where have I landed?"

She smiled again, nodded sympathetically. "Just the same, let's leave me out of our discussion this morning. Tell me about the wives – am I right, were there three?"

"It depends on how you count – but who's counting? It depends on what you mean by wife."

"What do *you* mean by it?"

"Ah, another trick question, Madame Freud. Twice there were actual, legal marriages, with licences, the whole *megillah*. Though only one was what anybody would really call a marriage, the licences and other niceties aside. Two other times, what they call these days *relationships*."

"Common-law marriages?"

"There wasn't anything common about them, but, yes, you could call them that."

"By common-law, I mean, they were for an extended period of time, with joint households...."

"Four years, twenty years, you could say they were extended."

"Twenty years is certainly a marriage, legal or not."

"I'd say that."

"Why didn't you make it legal?"

Zan shook his head. "You ask difficult questions, too difficult. I honestly don't remember. Did I ever get divorced? Maybe not, maybe that's why. I'm not being evasive, as you might think, I just don't know. These last twenty years, in some ways they're a blank. You ask me about my mother's cooking, I can describe whole meals, right down to the soup and nuts – not that we ever had nuts. You ask me about Myrna's cooking, I couldn't tell you a single thing she ever made. How do you figure that?"

"All right, we'll let it go. Maybe you'll remember as we talk."

"Maybe."

"So tell me about these women."

"Frankly, I'd rather talk about you, Lady Doctor."

"Please, Mr. Wiseman...."

"Okay, okay, I know all about ethics, professional and otherwise. Excuse me if I offended you."

"You didn't offend me."

"Good."

"So, can we...."

"Me, you mean."

"You, yes. Can you...."

"Tell you about my wives? These women? Yes and no. Luna, Rose, Myrna.... I'm sorry to say I forget the name of the other one. She's the one who doesn't really count anyway. So, in order...Luna, she was so long ago, it's hard to talk about her. She was a professor of literature who made me her project, her *thesis*. Whatever I am as a writer, I owe most of it to her. She made me. But then, well, maybe she got bored, maybe I did. Who can say? Next, the one whose name I can't remember, there's *nothing* memorable about her, except that she made my life miserable. No, that's not fair, not her – the *marriage* made my life miserable. And, I'm sorry to say, I made *her* life miserable. But, believe me, she doesn't bear talking about. It was a marriage but not really a marriage. It was...a convenience. An arrangement that was later unarranged. Finally, Myrna. Of Myrna, what can I say that I haven't already told you? She too was a professor of literature who made me her project. What's that they say? What goes around comes around? Or is it the other way? But Myrna wasn't interested in making me, I was already made. When we met, she said to me, "You're that overnight sensation thirty years in the making." I wasn't her thesis. Her project was to preserve me, take care of me. An old man can't ask for better than that. We lived together for twenty years, we were...happy. The word sounds odd to me – I don't think I would have used it then, but I realize now that that's what we were. We shouldn't have been, but we were. Of those four women, Myrna is the only one who doesn't haunt me. Well, maybe she will in time, if I live long enough. But I don't think so."

He paused, as much to catch his breath after the long discourse as to think.

"You know, you find someone in middle-age – you're too young to appreciate this, but you're a psychologist, you know people so you probably know this – it's different than when you're young. You love them, but the passion doesn't burn as hot. People don't die of love in their fifties and sixties and seventies. Also, you're a little smarter – you don't take some risks, you don't do some stupid things. Maybe you even think about the other person more. So Myrna, yes, happy, but no bad dreams. Beyond that, I remember little. She died. To me, those are the overriding facts: twenty years, happy, she died. No, that last one, *she died*, that's *the* overriding fact."

Zelda glanced at her notes. "And Rose? You skipped over her."

"Ah, Rose. She was...different."

"Different. How so?"

"That *was* a marriage."

"And can you tell me about it?"

Zan laughed, rubbed his face. "I have to laugh. Her father was a famous artist – Ernest Rosenberg, the painter. You know his name? I was at the museum here, the Glenbow? They have a couple of his pieces. I always used to say of Rose that she was not an artist but had an artist's temperament, that she inherited from her father, but me, I was an artist, or tried to be, but without the temperament, or so I liked to flatter myself. Was that the undoing of us? I don't know. It didn't help."

"I see. Tell me more about Rose."

Zan pursed his lips, looked down at his hands. When he looked up, his eyes went to the window, where a smear of snow from the previous night's storm had obscured the view of cityscape and sky.

"You know the story of Eurydice?"

"Yes, of course. A Greek goddess."

"Not exactly. A goddess, maybe, but not a Goddess, with the capital G. She was a wife, Orpheus's wife."

"That's right. She died."

"You could say that. A more celebrated death, a more dramatic death there never was. Anybody ever get mad and tell you to go to hell, Dr. Zelda?"

"Once or twice."

"That's what happened to Eurydice. Not that anybody got mad, but she went to hell, literally. Hades. A serpent bit her on her perfectly turned ankle and she died, and she went to Hades, the underworld, where the dead live – and if ever there was an oxymoron, that's it. Hades was the name of the big cheese down there, what we call the Devil these days, and he was such a big cheese that his name was also the name of the place where he lived and ruled. In those days, you didn't have to be damned to go there, just die. It was the place for the dead. Obviously, there isn't room up top for both the living and the dead, there are too many of them. And in those days, there was no heaven above – just Mount Olympus, reserved for gods only. So to Hades went the dead."

"And Orpheus pursued her. I remember."

"Pursued her is right. He pleaded with Hades and made a bargain. Orpheus, you remember, was the great poet and singer and musician.

He was a novelist, like me, except not a failed one – not yet."

"Didn't he lose his head?"

"He did, but that was later. Then, as a failure he makes me into a piker. He was a roaring success as a failure. But first he lost his head over Eurydice. He sang and played his lyre for Hades and his court, he recited poems and he softened Hades' heart. 'Okay, okay, take her,' Hades tells him. 'Just one thing: Don't look back.' You understand? *Don't look back.'*"

"Or she'll turn to salt."

Zan laughed out loud. "You got your myths all mixed up, Doctor Jung. That's Lot's wife, from the Bible. Another wife. Another devoted husband, another wayward wife, another warning about looking back, another disastrous glance. Makes you think, eh? It's probably the same story, though, you're right about that. You're not the only one to get these stories mixed up. There are only so many stories, but an infinite number of ways of telling them. But this is Eurydice. Hades tells Orpheus not to look back till they're back above ground or the deal is off, that's all, back to the underworld she comes. Sounds simple enough, and don't ask why Hades made that condition, he just did, and he was a god so he could do whatever he wanted. So, off they go through the dark, Orpheus leading the way. Across the river Styx they go, on the ferry – you know the story of the ferryman? Well, that's another story, never mind. Off they go, over the river, along the way, up the hills, and there's the end of the road, Orpheus can see the light, one more step, there's sunshine on his face, they're almost there, the sun so bright he has to turn away – and he looks back, to make sure his darling girl is there!"

"Just as he promised not to do."

"That's it! You got it. He looks back, and presto, Eurydice is gone and even Orpheus knows there's no point in trying to get her back this time."

"Why's that?"

"Why's that? A bargain's a bargain, even in ancient Greece. Maybe *especially* in ancient Greece."

"I see." Zelda glanced toward her lap, made a brief note. "And the connection of all of this to you is...?"

Zan's slow smile. "That isn't obvious?"

"You looked back?"

"I looked back. You put the nail on the hammer, Doctor Freud."

"And why wayward?"

"What?"

"You said Eurydice and Lot's wife were both 'wayward.' Why do you call them that?"

He laughed again. "Lot's wife looked back, not Lot. So she's salt. That's wayward, wouldn't you say?"

"Granted. And Eurydice?"

"You're right, this time I took the Freudian slip. It's the husband who's wayward, Orpheus, isn't it?"

"I'm not suggesting that. Just...."

"But you're right. I'm the wayward one in this story, not Rose."

"Yes, but maybe that's where you like to be." Zelda smiled. "Wayward."

"Maybe so, Lady Doctor, maybe so."

"We're almost out of time, but let me ask you one more question before you go: you said you were happy with..." She looked down to her notes. "Myrna. I don't imagine you've been happy since."

"Shock, mourning, grief. Sherlock Holmes you don't have to be to figure that out," Zan said.

"But it's only been a few months. You've moved, been through a period of transition. These things take time."

"Time heals all wounds, so I've heard. Time is also something I don't have a lot of. I once had all the time in the world. Not any more."

"No. But that doesn't mean you can't be happy again. What do you suppose it would take?"

"To make me happy again? Ah. That's too hard a question for this old head today. Ask me another time, maybe."

"I will."

LATER, WALKING BACK to his apartment, Zan chided himself for being so evasive. This woman would lose patience with him. And there wasn't any need for it. He'd never been so coy with Jack, he remembered that.

Luna, Rose.... He'd told Jack this story the very first time he'd asked about them.

"I was with this woman Luna then. I was young, pretty young still, she was older, a professor. We'd been together for awhile, a few years. She was.... Well, she made me, I was a figment of her imagination, she created me out of whole cloth."

"This is pretty interesting," Jack had said.

"But you asked me about Rose. One thing at a time. I'll tell you about Luna another time. Rose was the daughter of Ernest Rosenberg, the painter, you know? One of the Winnipeg Quartet, the only one to really endure. When I knew him, he was penniless, pretty much. He'd made some money, he'd squandered it. He was a drunk, a womanizer. Not much of a father or a husband. Whatever he made went right out the window. Now, his paintings sell for a pretty penny, if you can find one. We used to have a dozen of them in our house in Toronto. Can you imagine the ego on a fellow named Rosenberg, naming his daughter Rose, making her a little echo of himself. Rose Rosenberg, what a handle to inflict on a kid. Anyway, that was Rose.

"One night, Luna and I went to a New Year's Eve party at the Liberty Hall where I'd often been to political meetings or gone to hear a lecture. This is in Winnipeg. Luna would rather I'd gone to lectures on campus, she thought that's where my future was, but there it was, it was politics I was interested in then. Some fellows I knew were involved in a theatre group that was always putting on performances or skits, usually political, or staging fund-raising events, either for itself or for one group of strikers or another, left-wing stuff.

"On this night – New Year's Eve, 1932, that is to say, the night before New Year's Day, 1933 – it was just a party, but there were a lot of artists, writers and theatre people there and there were periodic skits along with music from a jazz band. The skit I remember best, even years later, even today as vivid as if it were yesterday, was this girl who came on the stage wrapped in a blanket, shivering. She had a mop of brown curls surrounding a baby face, enormous brown eyes set in a broad frame of clear, pale skin. Enchanting. Beautiful. The drummer played a roll and the lights dimmed as the crowd fell silent. A spotlight shone on the girl and there was a voice on a microphone, like those March of Time newsreels they used to have: 'And now, ladies and gentlemen, an important political pronouncement.'

"The girl threw open the blanket and stood there in her underwear –

panties and bra, and let me tell you, she filled them – one hip cocked, her head tilted, eyebrows raised, sexy as hell. She had a violin tucked under her chin and she played a sort of seesaw introduction to get our attention, as if all eyes weren't already on her. Then she announced: 'Workers of the world, tonight!'

"The drummer hit his cymbal and the light went out. Everybody laughed."

"I can imagine," Jack said.

"Wait, I'm not through. Luna leans over and whispers to me: 'I suppose you'd rather see the new year in with her, than a tired old last-year's model like me.'

"I said, 'That's ridiculous, don't be silly.'

"But she was right. That's just what I was thinking. The truth is, we were almost done, Luna and I. I asked about the girl later. That was my first sight of Rose."

FROM ZAN'S JOURNAL

Nov. 15, 1988 – That Zelda! Again she asks me about Luna, Rose, the others. She's a therapist, if that's what she is, but she's also a woman, and like all women, she wants to know about the other women in your life. A few hours over a few weeks and already I'm her darling, she's possessive, jealous. Luna wanted to know about girlfriends, didn't believe there hadn't really been any. Goldie wanted to know about Luna, Rose wanted to know about Goldie *and* Luna. Myrna wanted to know about Rose and Luna – I probably never told her about Goldie, never even mentioned her name.

There, I remembered Goldie's name finally.

But maybe I'm being unfair to my Zelda. Jack asked the same questions. In his case, just horny, I always thought. He liked the details.

One thing I never told him: that New Year's night, the first time I saw Rose. Later, Luna and I went back to our place. We made love to celebrate the new year. It wasn't long before I'd be on my way to Toronto, Luna and I would be through. My novel had crashed, I was on fire to write another and I thought I needed new scenery to do it, shake myself up. So this was one of the last times we made love. Afterwards, falling asleep, this new woman – Rose – came into my mind for a moment. She must have been in the mind of every other man who'd seen her that night. A vision!

Damn that woman, that Zelda. I'll dream of Rose tonight too, I'm sure of that. Maybe of Luna too. If I sleep at all.

Dave Margoshes

CHAPTER 9

HOW CRUEL IS MEMORY? This cruel: the things he needs to know, he forgets; but some things he can never forget, they go beyond mere memory, they're part of the rhythm of his breathing, of his blood, burned into the flesh of his brain like a brand.

"If you go, don't bother to come back."

He and Rose had argued, he knows that, but about what? Not a clue. No, that's not exactly right, he has clues, but that's all. They hadn't *argued*, that's not the right way to put it, rather they'd *been arguing*, and probably for some time. It had something to do with their house, he was certain of that, but they were no longer in their house, hadn't been for some time...months? Maybe over a year? He wasn't sure. Drinking had had something to do with it too. He was certain of that.

Talking about this with Jack had been different. It was all fresher in his mind then, and his mind itself was...fresher. That was over twenty years ago, before his life had taken a couple of right-angle turns, before his brain had started turning to sponge. And Jack, he wasn't like this woman – well, he wasn't a woman, for starters, but he wasn't like her in any way, he had been more like...like Zan himself. His friend Joe Zuken always used to say Zan should have been a lawyer, that he had a taste for the jugular, and Jack was definitely like that, he had that taste. "Don't give me this 'I don't remember' shit," Jack would say. That was no defence against him. He'd pry it out of you, *make* you remember.

Argued, argued, argued...yes, they'd argued, he and Rose, been arguing, but about what? Over the years they'd been together, there had been plenty of arguments, often over money, often over his – his what? Failure to get things done? Fair enough – many novels started, none finished. Failure to make decisions – fair enough there too. Inadequacies? She never used that word, but it wasn't hard to figure out what she meant. They'd argued over whether to have a baby; argued, after she became pregnant, over his desire to join the army – it was June 1941, and was it his fault the pregnancy was coincidental with Hitler's attack on the Soviet Union? They'd even argued, after the miscarriage, over whose fault it was, if fault there even was to assign. But what was it they'd been arguing over this time? This was twenty years later, the war, the miscarriages all long behind them. The house? Could it really have been that? They'd agreed, hadn't they, to sell the house, much as they liked it. They had bought it with one thing in mind, really, a place for a child; that hadn't worked out and now everything in the house, the house itself, was a rebuke. So what was the point of persisting, of sticking with it? Who had argued that, him or her? It didn't matter, because the other, whoever it was, immediately agreed. They were of one mind on the subject of the house, he was certain of that. But then why had she been in tears as he was packing, useless, why had she been pulling at his arm, his shirt, beating against his back? And was that even then, or some other time entirely? Jack would worm it out of him, could do, but Jack's long gone, his brain's long gone, that was all long ago.

Still, there was something about the house that was wrong, he was sure of that. She or he, or perhaps both of them, had had regrets. But it was "If *you* go," she had said, not "if *we* go," so it wasn't the house she was referring to, no, it was the apartment they were in, somewhere on Lake Shore Boulevard, he thought, or maybe nearby, a tall building with a view of the lake, Toronto Island, the little airport; a lovely, airy living room that she had fallen in love with right away, "oh yes," she said, "let's take this one," except maybe they *hadn't* taken it, maybe that was the one she'd wanted but he'd thought they couldn't afford, maybe it was another one they were living in, maybe that's why she was so unhappy, why they'd been arguing. He couldn't remember.

But "If you go, don't bother to come back," he *could* remember that, *did*, couldn't forget. Where? To the corner store, like in that old joke about the man who went out one evening for a newspaper and a quart of milk and never came back? When they found him, years later, he explained that while glancing at the headlines he saw one that said something about opportunities out west, so he'd taken the subway as far out of town as he could and stuck out his thumb, sharing the milk with the trucker who picked him up, drinking from the bottle, the old-fashioned kind of glass bottles, the glass hard against his teeth, the milk cold in his throat. What was unreasonable about that?

"There's the novelist in you," Jack had said. "You're turning this into a story."

What was unreasonable about *that?*

"Is that what you wanted to do?" Jack persisted. "Run away? Go west and seek out new opportunities?"

And what was unreasonable about that?

"Well, you do have a wife – did. A wife and a life. You had opportunities right here."

That was true: a wife, a life, opportunities, though he couldn't remember much about any of them now. The wife – he knows he loved her, deeply, fiercely, passionately, truly, did at one time, anyway; but he doesn't remember what it was about her he loved. For all the pain she caused him – and, undoubtedly, he caused her – it's remarkable how little he remembers about Rose, how little he knows of her, he's told Zelda that – hasn't he? She's no Jack, this Zelda. Jack could pry anything out of him, Zelda, she gets some things, but she doesn't push the way Jack did. And the life – again, he knows he had one, but it's mostly a blank, a grey wall like the curtain of fog pushing against your chest as you walked along the beach not far from that house at night. There's the whole of Lake Ontario on the other side of that fog, or inside it, you can hear it, it's getting your feet wet, you *know* it's there, but there's nothing to see, not a fucking thing. If Zelda asks him questions, specific questions – what did you do, what year was that, what did it look like, how did you feel – sometimes he could answer. But left to his own devices, no, just a curtain of fog, something beyond it, yes, but not a fucking thing to be seen.

And he had run away, later – gone west, anyway, looking for new opportunities, and found them, Myrna, and a life that was also greying out but in which form and even some detail could still be perceived: their life together in Las Vegas, the house on Brindlewood Drive near the university, the blanket of blossoming ice plants, the bee farm in the valley, the bees, the honey, visits from her children, and later the grandchildren, his mostly unused typewriter, her sudden transformation from a woman of flesh into a walking ghost, her death. Left alone again. But had he actually run away from.... Rose, that was her name – had he run away from her? No, he didn't think so. "If you go, don't bother to come back," that's what she'd said, and he'd gone – yes, he remembered that, he'd gone, all right – but running away, no. He was certain he hadn't been doing that.

"If you can't remember, reconstruct." That's what Jack had used to say, challenging him. Zelda didn't do that – too gentle – but that's what Jack would have done. Taken him by the short hairs and squeezed. "Come on Zan, you're a novelist. Spin me a yarn."

Well all right, he would. It wouldn't be the truth, but everyone knew that fiction is based on fact, flows out of it, and the yarn he'd spin would be close enough, close enough to give him a clue, at any rate, to give him a feel for what might have happened, what it might have been like that day.

It was that house, the damn house, he was sure of that.

It wasn't an extraordinary house, just a very ordinary three-bedroom bungalow in the Beaches, no view of the lake though just a few blocks from it, not even Cabbagetown, where they'd rented when they first came to Toronto and where he would have preferred to stay; where, he thought, he'd be more comfortable with working-class neighbours and, he liked to delude himself, his work would have gone better. A very ordinary house, although there was a beautiful stained glass window in the front room. That window was what had sold Rose on the house. "Look at how that simple addition transforms this room," she'd said, a bit of her father talking through her, although it had seemed to him that the window – an intricate blending of lead and coloured glass forming hexagons, triangles and circles within which were contained flowers and birds – and the way it had been installed were far from "simple."

Rose was no artist, but there was enough of her father in her to give her an eye and a definite idea of what she liked and didn't. She'd had ideas for the house immediately, another stained glass window in the room that would be turned into an office for him, removal of a false ceiling in the kitchen and construction of skylights above to let in light, air – light, air, so important to her, though he was largely indifferent to them, then. One of the upstairs bedrooms would be the nursery, of course, and there was plenty of room for two children, maybe even three. This was before the miscarriages, when so much of Rose's hopes had been directed toward the family she wanted them to become, so different from the one she'd come from, her tyrant father, vanishing mother. The basement could be finished, plenty of room down there, and maybe an addition later on, something with lots of glass extending into the fine backyard where she also had designs, a rock garden and fish pool replacing the vegetable patch. To all of those things, those plans, Zan had not only acceded but enthusiastically agreed, adding his own suggestions, touches. It would fall to him to do much of the renovation work, he alone or the two of them together, the way they went at the repainting that first summer, so he might as well be enthusiastic.

And over the years, through his failure to finish another novel, her stoic shouldering of much of the breadwinner role, going from substitute teaching, which she preferred, to full-time, her miscarriages, then her failure to conceive again, through Zan's failure to achieve what had once seemed so close, through his adherence to the Communist Party followed by his break with it, through his drinking, through all these things, some twenty-five years' worth, it was the house – that damned, damnable house – that more than anything else figured in their arguments, rasped at them, rubbed at their dreams as they slept at night, be they twined in each other's arms or cold and alone in separate beds, separate rooms. That house....

No, no, no. Don't you know anything about telling a story? Have you forgotten even the basics? Show, don't tell.

What about that image of them twined in each other's arms, or cold and alone in their separate beds? Flesh out those scenes, man! That's showing. Hint at the secret – foreshadow!

And can you hear yourself? The house this, the house that...too abstract. Give us something concrete – and I don't mean the basement.

Why not? What could be more concrete? For years, it had been a sore point, filled with the boxes their belongings had been in on the trip from Winnipeg to Toronto, stored in the Cabbagetown house they'd rented for two years, then used again to move them to the Beaches house. He had stacked them as neatly as possible, knifing off the tape that held many of them into box-shape, collapsed and stacked on their edges against one wall, but there were also boxes full of things that had never gotten unpacked, *tchachkas* from Rose's place in Winnipeg and many more later, inherited from her father, boxes of books, of manuscripts, letters – his papers, which a university or library might conceivably want someday – as relics of a failed writer's life to hold up as warnings to want-to-be-writers, if nothing else, "for God's sake, don't do this," that sort of thing – and other things he could never bear to let go of. All of it was covered with a sheer layer of dust and, along the walls, a voracious coat of mould thick as Zan's hand, which breathed its pollen into the air, aggravating Rose's allergies.

There wasn't any point in finishing the basement – they weren't able to finish the work they had begun upstairs, and, with no children in the house, the last thing they needed more of was usable rooms – so all she wanted was for him to *clean* it – throw out the damp, mouldy cardboard, give away some of the books and *tchatchkas*, the never-used tools Zan had somehow accumulated, mostly through his various machinist jobs. "Put those tools to use for once, for God's sake," she had berated him. What she had in mind was building shelves to get what was left off the floor, scraping and hosing down the walls, disinfecting.... If he wouldn't do it himself, she would gladly hire someone to do it, a gang of people so it would be over with quickly, but there was always some reason why not – he couldn't give away books, no matter what; sorting through the tools and other things would take time, he'd get to it, he really would; hiring people, no, he couldn't work with people tramping around in the house, no, that was out of the question.

The truth was that he couldn't bear to throw away the boxes, so sure was he that they'd be needed again, and soon, so sure was he that he couldn't possibly be a homeowner, stuck in one place. That would have meant there was little hope of whatever it was that was holding him in place changing.

This went on for years – four or five, at least, until, while he was away in Winnipeg for a week, she hired the "gang" she'd threatened. When he came home everything that was most likely garbage had been thrown out; the tools and other bric-a-brac were in boxes in the unused garage; the books and papers were on newly built shelves in front of freshly plastered walls. The cracked, chipped concrete floor had been sealed and carpeted. There was a new humidifier on the furnace. It was several days, though, before he discovered any of this – he rarely went into the basement, and she didn't say a word about it. Nor did he, after he stumbled on it.

Dave Margoshes

He was at his desk, wheels spinning as always, when he noticed the smallest of wobbles in his chair, checked and found a loosened screw. He went downstairs to look for a screwdriver – expecting to have to rummage through the pile of small tools heaped on the workbench as usual – and was greeted by an unexpected scene, discovering it in stages: first, the smell of fresh plaster, paint and ammonia in his nostrils when he opened the door, then, halfway down the steps, the opened expanse swimming into view, taking shape. He felt, what...surprise? Of course. Anger? Yes. Rage? Perhaps. Confusion? Definitely. All of this took only a moment or two, his body battered with emotions like a small boy in a hail and windstorm. Then it passed. He continued down the stairs, discovered with pleased surprise how easy it was to find a screwdriver – a row of them and other hand tools of various sizes were clipped to a board against one wall over a spotless workbench, newly lacquered. He went upstairs, tightened the screw, slipped the screwdriver into a drawer, went to the living room cabinet where the liquor was kept, poured himself a shot of the very cheap scotch he favoured, downed it and returned to work. He wouldn't give her the satisfaction of admitting what a fine job had been done, or even alluding to it by asking about it, nor would she give in and speak of it first. So frozen to each other were they already. They went about their lives, never mentioning it, while beneath them, the pristine basement vibrated like the string of a bow.

The struggle over the skylight was more protracted.

Within their first year in the house, the two of them, working together, had removed the false ceiling in the dining area adjacent to the kitchen, exposing the slanted beams. The idea was to cut open a space and construct a skylight that would flood the room with light – an evocation of her father's Winnipeg studio. But after her first miscarriage, Rose had shied away from such physical work, and Zan, who had no real interest in the project, promised to get to it but always found reasons not to. The summer after Rose's move on the basement, he'd finally roused himself to take some measurements and make drawings. He refused to hire a carpenter, and had begun the process of sawing through the roof, but was interrupted by an organizing trip out of town – in those years, the Party often made use of Zan's oratorical skills during strikes around southern Ontario. By the time he got back, he'd lost interest and energy. That winter, they'd endured the seeping of cold, wind and snow through the cuts, and in the spring, he boarded up the damaged area with plywood and plastic, leaving the room with the look of someone with a bandaged head wound. There he'd stopped, and there matters stood. He would return to the skylight in the summer. He had made a New Year's resolution that the work would get done this year, next year, the year after, but always either the novel or the Party work took precedence. Eventually, she stopped asking him about it. Nor did she take the opportunity to have the work done during one of his infrequent absences, as she had with the basement. His paralysis appeared to have been contagious, affecting her as well. They'd long since stopped using the dining room for meals, eating instead at a small table in the kitchen. They rarely went into the area.

When they put the house on the market, the agent had suggested they get the skylight done or the roof properly repaired and a new ceiling installed. "It doesn't look very good the way it is," she said.

"It wouldn't take a new owner very long to fix it," Zan protested. "Or you."

"I just can't be bothered," he said, nor was he. The house did sell, for less than they wanted, but the agent told them that could have been for any number of reasons. The skylight wasn't the only project they'd left undone.

His last view of the botched job, though, was through a ring of open cardboard boxes; the empty dining room had finally found a use, a holding area for boxes as they filled them. He was bending over one of them, stuffing something in, and Rose's fists were beating on his back.

"I don't want to go," she wailed, sounding like a cartoon child being pulled from the playground, *"Ahdonwannago, Ahdonwannago."*

"Dearest, we have no choice," he explained, turning, taking hold of her fists, first with both his hands, then joining them, grasping them with his left hand while his right encircled her waist. "It's a little late now. The moving van will be here any minute. And the new people's van will be along this afternoon. The house is sold, remember?"

Too late. I don't want to go. Those phrases echoed in his mind all that day, that night at the hotel, the next day as they began the search for an apartment – left till the last week, then the last day, then not done at all until after the fact – and all that week and the following one, as the hotel bill piled dangerously high. She had agreed they should sell, that the house had become a burden to them, that they didn't need anything nearly that large, that the house was...an anchor, but not one giving stability, an anchor pulling them down, drowning them, certainly drowning *him*. And the reissue of *The Wise Men of Chelm*, which had come, completely out of the blue, just two years earlier, was a sign, he'd told her, and half believed himself, that his career had taken a significant turn, that he might be able to get another novel done after all, but that he needed a change in order to accomplish that.

They'd both agreed: they'd put the house on the market, they'd start looking for an apartment. But she'd refused to look, hadn't cooperated with the agent, had said neither yes nor no when the offers came in, had refused to help in the packing, turning her back on the whole thing, burying her head in the sand, leaving it all to him, a peculiar switch that – the idea certainly wasn't lost on him – may have been deliberate, some sort of ironic revenge. Or may have been unconscious paralysis, that's what Jack would suggest, a few years later, when Zan pulled himself out of the rain into his office.

"All of a sudden, out of the blue, she was crying," he told Jack. "She didn't want to move. She pleaded with me like a child. She didn't threaten."

"And she'd given no hint?" Jack was a tall man with a neatly trimmed moustache and a high forehead, prone to wearing grey or brown tweed or camel hair jackets. He looked more like a university professor, perhaps of medieval history, than a clinical psychologist. Of course, he *was* a university professor, which maybe explained that, even if he didn't have a beard. That was psychiatrists Zan was thinking of, Jack had explained, and even that was a stereotype, there probably hadn't been a bearded psychiatrist since Freud and Jung themselves.

"Hint?" The cartoon image of an ostrich with its head in the sand came into his mind, tail feathers dominating. "Yes, she...."

"She what?"

"She was less than enthusiastic."

"She didn't want to go."

"I didn't say that. *She* didn't say that. How was I supposed to know? No, she was busy, grading papers, preparing lessons, I was free, between jobs then, it naturally fell to me to do the work."

"And she didn't say anything?"

"No."

"Not a word?"

"Not a word I could reasonably interpret to mean she didn't want to go. We had talked about it, we both agreed."

"Don't you mean *you* talked about it, *she* reluctantly agreed?"

"I didn't see it that way."

"So you admit it might have been something like that."

"Admit, admit.... You missed your calling, you should have been a lawyer, a prosecutor. Okay, maybe it was something like that. Am I supposed to be a mind reader?"

"How long were you married?"

"Twenty years, something like that."

"Then, yes. A mind reader, most definitely."

But he hadn't read her mind and finally, though she would have hesitated forever, they chose an apartment, the pre-selected furniture, books and so on were delivered – the rest to stay in storage and now, another twenty-five years later, Rose dead almost a decade, he had no idea in the world what had become of it – and they'd moved in. Was it to the airy apartment, the view of the lake? He wasn't sure, but why not say it was. It was what she would have wanted, and, yes, more than they could afford, he was sure of that, but why not? She was hurting, he could tell that even if he didn't know why, so why not placate her this way. And – miracle of miracles – he was actually starting to make some money himself, the new paperback *Wise Men* a surprising hit and royalties beginning to roll in. Everything those next few months, though, was a blur, resisting even reconstruction, even wholesale fabrication, let alone memory. A blur. But there'd been an argument, he could be sure of that. Somewhere he wanted to go, somewhere she didn't want to go *with* him, didn't want him to go.

"If you go, don't bother to come back."

The timbre of her voice, the pitch, the tone. When he wrote the words down, he was amazed at all the vowels, six "o"s, one in every word but the first and last; a nicely constructed sentence.

But that was only later, much later. At the moment he first heard them, the words had curiously little effect on him. True, he was in the heat of anger, when people neither hear nor think clearly, but neither do they speak rationally or necessarily mean what they say and so, since she too was in the heat of anger, and he knew that, he hesitated only for a moment. "Maybe I won't," he said, and he slammed out the door.

Where had he gone? What was he doing? Did it have something to do with writing? With *The Wise Men of Chelm*? He thinks maybe so. Since the novel had been republished, he was often being asked to talk to an editor or an interviewer, academics, so much so that the belated success of that old book had eventually become his favourite excuse for why he could not produce another. "I'm hounded," he told Jack. "When it came out, no one cared, the world shrugged its shoulders. For thirty years I didn't make a dime from that novel, not a penny, nobody knew my name, nobody gave a shit about me. Can you wonder why I couldn't write during that period of stifling indifference? Now it's out again, I'm discovered, the world beats a pathway to my door...and how can I work with all that clamour?"

"You're good, Mr. Wiseman" – this was an early interview, before he and Jack were on a first-name basis, before Jack was writing articles about him for academic journals, bringing him in to his class to visit with his students – "very good. You can turn everything to your advantage."

"Not being able to write when all you want to do in the world, this is your idea of an *advantage*?"

"Having an excuse to *not* write, no matter what happens, failure or success, yes, that's an advantage. Some people have to hunt for excuses. You stumble over them, you have so many." Jack grinned at him – a grin that Zan found most attractive, most conducive to frank talking. "But maybe I should say instead, you can turn everything to your *dis*advantage."

How well Jack had known him, and how quickly. And they agreed, though Zan couldn't remember where he'd gone that weekend, that it probably had something to do with the book – a conference at a university in the United States, he's pretty sure that's what it was, and that's certainly what he'd like it to have been, perhaps even the conference where he'd first met Myrna, that would have been a lovely irony – but that, ultimately, it didn't really matter. "Unless, of course, you're looking for one more thing to blame on that poor novel," Jack said. "You've blamed everything else on it."

"*That poor novel....* What about that poor novelist? That poor novel turned me into a cripple."

"You're pretty agile today, Mr. Wiseman."

All right. Enough of that. Jack was right, it didn't matter where he went – what mattered was that he *went*, period.

"If you go, don't bother to come back," that's what she'd said. He hesitated, just for a moment, and then he went. And by the end of the weekend, the threat – if that's what it was – had long since been forgotten. As the plane floated in for its landing, as Zan gathered his bags, as the taxi approached the apartment block, as he paid, as he stood in the lobby awaiting the elevator, as he hurtled upward on the strength of cables and pneumatic pressure, as he strolled down the corridor, searching in his pants pocket for his key – through all of these actions, the thought that he might not be welcome was the farthest thing from his mind, no, it didn't exist in his mind at all. "Why should it?" he asked Jack. "Do you remember every offhanded comment *your* wife makes?"

"'Don't bother to come home,' that's hardly an offhand comment."

"All right, a threat. Do you remember every threat *your* wife makes?"

"Actually," Jack said, grinning again, "actually, I tend to."

"All right, all right, I didn't. What can I tell you? All I *can* tell you is that I found my key, I put it in the lock – and the damn thing wouldn't turn. And even *then* I didn't remember what she'd said."

In fact, he'd stood there for a moment, suitcase at his feet, his mind completely blank. He tried the key again, and again no result. Now he was confused. Was he at the wrong door? He glanced at the number, 7C, which was correct, and to his left and right for further reassurance. Again he tried the key. Nothing. He withdrew the key and held it up to his face, squinting at it. There were actually three keys on the ring: one for the door, which would also work on the storage locker in the basement; one for the outer door; a much smaller one for the mailbox. He was certain he had the right key, but nonetheless he tried the other large key, the one he was sure was for the outside door; sure enough, it didn't fit at all; and, he recalled, it had opened the outside door. He tried the door key again, sliding it in and out of the lock – smooth, no problem there – then attempting to turn it. He stood dumbfounded, leaning against the door, the key still in the lock, his hand still on the key. Gradually, a sound began to echo in his head, growing louder; the sound took the shape and form of words, the voice familiar: "If you go, don't bother to come back."

He knocked, a short, sharp rap with the knuckle of the pointer finger of his right hand, quickly repeated several times. Nothing. After a few seconds, the knock again, this time with two knuckles, producing a slightly louder effect. At the same time, he stage-whispered: "Rose." Nothing.

He took a deep breath, turned and walked down the corridor as far as the elevator, turned and walked back to the door. Didn't bother with the key. Knocked. "Rose," he called, no whisper this time, "it's me, Zan, open the door." This time, he used the ornamental brass knocker, but it seemed to produce a sound less loud than his knuckles. He rapped on the door again. "Rose. Open the door. I know you're in there."

"How did you know that?" Jack interjected.

"Because she never went out, that was part of the problem. She didn't like the neighbourhood, was afraid of it. A perfectly safe, upper-middle-class neighbourhood like we had never before lived in, not ever in our lives, *afraid of it*, that's what she said. She wanted to be back in the house, that's all, she wanted the hands of the clock to turn back."

"And you were less than sympathetic."

"Less, more, I wasn't sympathetic, you got that right, Dr. Know-it-all. She agreed to sell the house, agreed to move, agreed on this apartment. Picked it. Well, agreed. And life was moving on, with or without her."

"But mightn't she have been at work? At school?"

"No, it was evening."

"Ah," Jack said.

"It was Sunday!"

"Ah."

"At any rate, I know she was there because eventually she spoke."

First, though, he'd gone downstairs, rang the bell, long and hard, just in case she was in the bathroom and couldn't hear his knocking, then took the elevator up again, pounded on the door with his fists, worried at first about what the neighbours might think, then finally oblivious. Stood leaning against the door. Heard footsteps. "Rose, I hear you in there, I know you're there. Open the door, please, sweetheart."

Nothing. "Open the goddamned door, Rose."

Nothing. Pounding, his fists, again. Nothing.

Then, a whisper; not cold, certainly not frigid; not hot, certainly not searing; not a shout, a whisper, not like a child but more like a child than like a woman: "Go away" – did she say "Go away, Zan," did she use his name? Later, he couldn't be sure. "Go away, you don't live here any more. Remember?"

DUET 3

"I like that bell, Abe."

"I've been listening to it for forty years."

"So this is it?"

"This is it."

"It's..."

"What? It's what?"

"Not what I expected."

"And what was that? A palace?"

"No, but...?"

"Something from Saville Row, maybe? The posh shop of a bespoke tailor to the gentry?"

"That's it exactly, Abe. And a lineup of swells at the door."

"Lineups, you won't find here. Swelled heads, maybe, swelled bellies...that's as close as we come to swells in this neighbourhood."

"The neighbourhood is nice."

"It's colourful. Character."

"Like the old neighbourhood. Flora Avenue, Selkirk Avenue. The whole North End."

"That's it exactly, it's what I like about it. The smells are different, but the street around the corner, not so different from our old block."

"And this street, not so different from Selkirk. I was there before I came here – I told you. Not so different."

"Some things are the same all over, Zannie."

"I didn't know Calgary had neighbourhoods like this."

"Sure."

"Where I am, it's all coffee houses and florists."

"This is more hardware and Chinese grocers."

"And business...is good?"

"Business is what you see. A few *shmatas* in for mending, on that table waiting for the fix, on that rack hanging, waiting to be picked up."

"The sign, I saw on the door...you're just open a few hours."

"Every day but Saturday. Even Sunday I'm here, for the customers who can't come other times. It's enough for the business I have."

"They know when to come."

"Sure. Walk-ins, I don't have too many. But old customers, still plenty. Loyal. They wouldn't take their mending anyplace else."

"And there's enough...."

"To send me to Acapulco every winter? No, to pay the light bill, the heating, maybe part of the taxes. But I listen to Gzowski every morning anyway, so why not here? After lunch, to the gym. Then to visit Dolly."

"It's a place to be."

"Pop used to say, 'you have to be somewhere, so why not here?' Remember?"

"A philosopher, he was, our father."

"'Why count dollars when you can count your thoughts?' He used to say that too."

"A *real* philosopher. But thoughts...not blessings?"

"Blessings you don't always have enough of. Thoughts, too many sometimes."

"You're a philosopher too, *Abela*."

"That's me, a regular Spinoza."

"This cash register, Benchy, you don't see them like this any more."

"It's a relic, like me. Like you, Pantsy."

"Still works, though, eh?"

"Still works."

"You said something about tea."

"I'll put on the kettle. Turn on that radio, will you?"

"It's about time you had me over here."

"It's about time you expressed an interest."

"It's about time you suggested it."

"If I'd known you needed an engraved invitation, I would have sent one."

CHAPTER 10

November 22, 1988

Nov. 19, 1988 – I'm starting to think about starting a novel.

Why not? I'm a novelist. And what a delicious word that is! I stood in the shower this morning saying it aloud: novelist, *novel*-ist, novel-*ist*, *no*-vel-ist, no-*vel*-ist, no-vel-*ist!*

What could be so difficult? I did it once. Like riding a bicycle, once you know how, you don't forget, that's what they say.

What I'm thinking is this: a writer comes home, an old man, back to where he was born, where his people are, whatever is left of them. He's not fully a success, but neither fully a failure, like George Weber in Wolfe's *You Can't Go Home Again*. He's old, but not dead yet, not a dead writer like me. There's enough time left for one more try. Try at what?

And no, this is not autobiographical!

Still, maybe this old writer has a brother. Why not? Lots of old men, writers or not, have brothers. What could be more true to life? And maybe these brothers argue – not all the time, but once in awhile. And maybe out of these arguments...what? Arises truth? Epiphany? Self-awareness?

And maybe this writer, this old writer, this *ancient* writer, this relic of a bygone age and style and school of writing, this not-quite-dead-yet writer, maybe in his long, dark, distant past had a muse, a woman, an older woman, an older, wise woman (though perhaps not so wise in the ways of the heart, her own heart), an older, wise woman who saw things in him he couldn't see himself, who urged him to become the man she thought he was capable of becoming. Maybe her name was even Luna, or something like that. Muna, Fawna, Dawna, Lacuna. Luna.

Why the hell not? This is a novel I'm talking, not history.

ZELDA TOOK HIM BY SURPRISE this afternoon. "You really seem to enjoy our sessions."

"I do, but I've been wondering – no offence intended, Lady Doctor – why I'm here."

"You were referred from the hospital, remember? You were admitted after you came to Emergency, confused and in pain."

"This I vaguely remember. I had a bellyache, right?"

"It was a little more than that. Severe constipation. And you were, frankly, in shock. And, though you say no, maybe suicidal. Depressed, at the very least."

"Still, that was weeks ago...wasn't it? Months. I'm not in shock now. And depressed..." He smiled. "No more than usual. I'm not exactly a happy-go-lucky fellow. Never have been."

"No, you're doing very well. But it doesn't hurt for us to continue to talk. You don't object, do you?"

"No, certainly not. But I'm eighty-two years old, and of relatively sound mind. I was just wondering what I'm doing here. There are people more in need of you than me, that I'm sure of."

The therapist laughed.

"Don't worry. The province of Alberta can afford to let you see me for a few more sessions. Let's make sure everything's okay with you, okay? We don't want you getting plugged up again, or worse."

"Plugged up! I can assure you, Dr. Zelda, I'm no more full of shit than the next guy, excuse the language, please. And *worse?* What could be worse? But, okay, okay, I'm glad to accept your hospitality, yours and the government of Alberta's, thank you very much to you both. But *sessions*, such a clinical word. Chats, they're chats, my dear Zelda."

"You like to chat?"

"With you, yes."

"Good, I'm glad to oblige. Perhaps today we could chat about what you were doing before you moved to Calgary. You talk easily about the Winnipeg years, and not quite so easily about how you feel now, but what about in between? I believe you said you were living in Las Vegas? That must be an exciting place to live. And I know the woman you were living with for many years died. Myrna? Would you like to talk about that today? About her?"

Dave Margoshes

Zan blinked, stared at her, the question buzzing around his head like a fly. She was right, of course. His life, he had thought more than once, was like a bagel – substance in a circle, a hole in the centre, notwithstanding a wisecrack Abe liked to make, that with a bagel, the best part is the hole, so save it for last. In truth, the hole was just the hole, the best parts of his life were the beginning and the now, the beginning because it really had been the best, the now because, well, for no other reason than its proximity, its freshness in his mind, the immediacy of coffee this morning, the promise of cherry pie this afternoon, his reward to himself for enduring this session. All the rest was a blur, a hole from which little could be retrieved. What was it Jack had said? "Our youth makes us, old age defines us. A person's teenage years and middle-age years – who remembers them, really? What happened of consequence? It's just rhythm and noise."

Jack was full of those slightly distorted insights. Another time he said: "There are four Zans, you know?"

"Four?" Zan had laughed. "I have trouble enough with one."

"No, four."

"Only four? I'm so simple? Someone like you probably has half a dozen."

"Four's plenty, believe me." He began to tick them off on his fingers: "Zan the writer, Zan the lover and husband, Zan the brother, and also son, Zan the family man, you might say."

"That's four?"

"That's three. Fourth is Zan the *mensch*, the social Zan, the political Zan, Zan connecting with the world. The trick is getting all those Zans into some sort of balance, packing them all into one phone booth."

"That's some Zan," he'd said then. Now, shaking away the memory, he said: "Before here? Before, there was there. What happened there? What happened happened. Life happened. I did this and that, went here and there."

"Now there's an evasive answer if ever I heard one," Zelda said. "And none of it meant anything? Nothing that happened to you in the last twenty years, thirty years, had value? Nothing memorable at all?"

"Did it mean anything? Of course it did. It meant plenty while it was happening. I had a life with a woman again, something I didn't think could happen. I was, without the benefit of marriage, a real husband.

She had children, Myrna – grown, yes, with children of their own, but they came to visit. In some half-assed way, I was a father, a grandfather even. My novel, I'm talking about *Wise Men*, I told you about that, it had a new life – that's something I never dreamed would happen. This was how Myrna and I got together – did I tell you? She was a professor, at the university there, in Las Vegas, she wrote a paper about my book, about me. I was, at long last, a *Writer*, capital W. I visited her classes, I went with her to faculty club parties and people wanted to talk to me, I was a man of substance. Did all this have value? Sure – it had value then, it meant something then. Memorable? No. She wasn't the love of my life, the children weren't mine, it wasn't a *new* novel.

"She used to introduce me to colleagues, 'My husband Zan, the famous novelist,' the idea of my fame obviously giving her pleasure, and I would invariably add, 'Infamous, she means,' more to undercut myself than her." He shook his head. "Damn fussy, ain't I?"

"Yes and no," Zelda said, smiling. "Yes, it is fussy, very fussy, some people might say, especially people to whom what you had might seem like a lot, a lot more than *they* have. But no because, well, it's your life, you have a right to be fussy about it."

Zan gave her an appraising look. He kept finding new things about this woman to appreciate. "Very enlightened of you, Lady Doctor. Very enlightened. Anyway, fussy or not, no, no more memorable than today will be memorable next week."

"But you *do* remember some of it, obviously. You with your notoriously bad memory, or so you say."

"The bad memory is no fiction, I assure you. And not, I'm reasonably sure, the result of encroaching Alzheimer's disease or any other form of dementia, just too many late nights, too much cheap scotch, too many years under the bridge and, oh, yes, that bump on the head when I fell out of the tree. Age ten. Now that I remember clear as a bell. But I take your point, yes, I *do* remember some of the last twenty years, even the last thirty, blank spots, whole years, notwithstanding. So I concede some of it *was* memorable.

"For example, for a few years, in Nevada, I was a beekeeper. Don't look so surprised, over the years I had plenty of jobs – teacher, machinist – I was a good machinist, I apprenticed with the CPR, and believe me, they know something about machines. Other things. That's what this was, just a job, something I did to earn money and occupy my time. Often Myrna was at home, marking papers, preparing lectures, so it was better for her for me not to be there during the day. Every day I drove from our place in Las Vegas out into the country to a farm where there were hundreds of hives. There were people I worked with, tasks to do, and the bees, of course, thousands of bees. This occupied me for – I don't remember, two, three years. I don't remember the name or face of a single one of those people, don't remember the name or location of the farm, somewhere near a lake, Lake Mead maybe – was that an attempt at a pun? Another thing I don't remember. I don't remember any of the tasks I did, except in the most general of ways – the feel of the bulky costume we wore, the mask, and the sensation of the bees swarming around you. All I really remember is the music of the bees – they call it a drone, but it's more than that, filled with highs and lows and even melody, a very subtle music. And I remember the remarkable taste of honey. But that may not even be from Nevada, the bee farm – maybe I'm thinking of honey I had as a kid."

"And were you stung? Surely you'd remember that."

"You'd think so, wouldn't you. But no, I can't say, I really don't remember."

Zelda made a long note on her pad. In the silence, defined by the almost inaudible scratching of her pen, Zan could almost hear the singing of bees.

And from there, he was transported into the sunroom of Myrna's Las Vegas house, Myrna in her favourite chair, head bent over a book, the sun in her face and hair, him bending over her to kiss her temple, the smell of honey in the air. When was this, early on? No, her auburn hair, cut in an old-fashioned pageboy, is streaked with grey. Her silent period?

"And today, today's a good day?" Zelda's voice brought him back.

"As good as I can expect, as good as I can hope for. I'm alive. There's no pain – no more than I can bear, I should say." He flexed his hands, rolled his shoulders to demonstrate. "It's cold but the sun is shining. There's pleasant company – what, you think I come here to get cured? I come because it's nice talking to you, and who else is there to talk to? As you said, I enjoy our chats. God, if there is such a thing, has a sense of humour, that you've probably already noticed. I'm a man who likes to talk, cursed to have very few people to listen."

"I find that hard to believe. What about your brother? He's why you moved here, right?"

"Ha ha. You don't talk *with* Abe, or even talk *to* him, you talk *at* him."

"He doesn't listen?"

"No in two ways. He doesn't listen and he doesn't hear. First, he's deaf, almost stone deaf. He hears a little – that is to say, when it suits his purposes. Secondly, he is constitutionally deaf to me, always has been. Comes with being older by thirteen minutes."

"And friends...."

"All dead. Or turned to enemies." He grinned. "Not really, but you take my point. No, Zelda, it's been years since I've had anyone to chat with, as you put it."

"I think 'chat' was your word, Zan."

"Was it? All right, but you know what I mean."

"I do. But what about Myrna?"

Zan stiffened imperceptibly. "Myrna. She's dead."

"I know that, I'm sorry, I didn't mean to.... What I meant was, you must have been able to talk to her."

"Ah, well, yes and no." Zan was uncharacteristically silent, and Zelda waited. "Not just a sense of humour, this God of yours has, but sick humour. A regular Lenny Bruce, God is. Myrna was the perfect listener – that's what drew me to her, I suppose. I am a man who loves to talk, she was a woman who loved to listen to me. Or so she said, so it appeared, so I believed.... You know, maybe I was *meshugener* all along, maybe...." He waved away the thought. "No, then what would have been the point?"

"The point of what?"

"Of the accident. Oh, I didn't mention it, maybe? An automobile accident, a few years ago. Guess who was driving. Guess who was driving but not hurt a bit, not a scratch. You guess me? You are sharp, Dr. Zelda. Guess whose fault it was. Mine? No, wrong there. It actually wasn't – someone ran into us. But guess who felt it was his fault just the same.

"Now guess who was hurt, and how. Myrna? Yes, of course, who else? No, she wasn't killed, well, you know that...but there was an injury to her head. It wasn't life-threatening – that's the term they use, so matter of fact – but she was in a coma for awhile, nothing like Abe's Dolly, just a few days, her brain is resting, they said. Gradually, she came back, soon as good as new...except for...one thing."

Zan paused and let his eyes roam around the now familiar office, as if searching for something to assist him, prompt his memory. Zelda sat patiently in silence.

"Except for one thing, her hearing she left behind. Deaf, stone deaf for real. Not off-and-on like Abe, I mean deaf, completely, and beyond repair. Not the most conducive situation for conversation."

"No," Zelda said, but nothing more, and they sat in comfortable silence for several minutes. Eventually Zan laughed.

"What you just heard was the sound we made together the last three or four years or more that we were together, this silence. There was nothing wrong with her speech, but it seemed to be connected to her deafness, in her mind, anyway, and she pretty much stopped speaking as well. So we really were silent. Oh, we learned to deal with it. We both learned sign language and Myrna got to be pretty good reading lips, mine anyway. I can't tell you what a spectacle we made, the two of us, walking down the street in Las Vegas, two old people, their hands flying about them like a pair of lunatics, chattering away in complete silence like a couple of mimes. A sense of humour this God has like a razor blade, giving a man who likes to hear the sound of his own voice a woman who can't..." His voice tapered off.

"I don't suppose your brother has learned sign language," Zelda said.

"Abe? Learn something? Something that might make his life easier? Or someone else's? You got the wrong older brother, Lady Doctor. No, me and Abe trying to talk with our hands really would be a pair of lunatics."

"So, to get back to my question... This has been a good day?" She smiled. "It must have been, since you've had someone to talk to – someone who actually listens."

"Sure it's a good day. Let there be plenty more of them. But you were also asking about memorable – see, I do remember that. Has today been memorable? No. That much, I don't kid myself."

The therapist glanced up at the wall clock above Zan's shoulder. "We out of time?"

"No, sorry. Just reflex. You were about to say something?"

"You were asking me about before...remember? Before I came here, to this place, I mean...what's it called?"

"The clinic?"

"No, this city, what's..."

"Calgary."

"Calgary, yes. How can I forget that? You were asking me about what I was doing before I moved here. You said I was in shock, I told you Myrna died. But I forgot to tell you I'd been on a 'world tour.' Well, *my* world, the world according to Wiseman.

"Myrna died. Twenty years together and she dies. Fifteen years younger than me, and she dies. Smart girl. She knew my history. All the other women in my life, I left them. She beat me to the punch.

"So there I was, not the end of *my* life, not the end of the century or the millennium or anything so dramatic, but the end of *something*, wouldn't you say? And I always had a sense for the big gestures – you'll have to take my word for that."

"I'm getting to know you, Zan."

"Okay, so you know. Anyway, I'm not so young myself..."

"Are you waiting for me to contradict you?"

"Certainly not. I was just trying to remember.... Well, it doesn't matter. No longer young, let's just say that. How many more chances would I have? I thought I'd travel around, visit relatives, old friends, take another look at the old places.

"I bought one of those Greyhound passes. Buses are the only way to really travel. You see the country, talk to the people, *smell* them. You get in touch with your tailbone and every other bone too. And time – people who ride buses have all the time in the world. You could write a novel between one end of the country and the other, easy, if you had one of those little computers that sits on your lap. I went to all the old places, well, all the ones the Greyhound goes to, Winnipeg, Toronto, I guess that's really all but that was plenty. But you know what? All the relatives are dead, or they're nieces and nephews I never really knew, and who even knows where to find them these days or if they'd even know who I am, *Uncle Zan, aren't you the one who moved away, a long time ago?* And all the old friends, they're all gone too. Dead or in nursing homes or moved to Florida. Suddenly, you realize you're old.

Dave Margoshes

"'*Damn you, Myrna,*' I said, '*this is a fine time to die and leave me, when I'm all-of-a-sudden old.*'"

"Most of the old places are gone too, or changed in some way. Winnipeg, Toronto, it had been years since I was there but I didn't need a map. My eyes closed, I could find the old neighbourhood, Flora Street, the house where I grew up, except the house is gone, another house there, I'm pretty sure it's different, but still pretty much the same, the same narrow, clapboard shotgun house. A dump. The door falling off, windows broken, a yard full of kids. How can anyone live like that? I wondered; then I remembered, *we* lived like that. And were happy, most of the time. Until we started to grow up and the world intruded.

"In my day, it was mostly Jewish, but plenty of Ukrainians and Poles too, even the odd person named Smith or Jones or Brown. Or Mac-Something, no offence. Now, the Jews are pretty much gone but the Polish church is still there, a Ukrainian centre, and the people on Flora Street are mostly Indians, from one of the lost tribes of Israel most likely. So everything changes, everything stays the same. One thing that doesn't change at all is how poor everyone there seems to be.

"Some of the restaurants are still there, the Top Hat Café, still there, Oscar's Deli, still there, everything the same except a corned beef sandwich costs ten, maybe twenty, times more than it used to.

"Went around to the old places. Aberdeen School, gone, but Strathcona and St. John's still here – completely different buildings, but still there. The Jewish school, gone. The Walker Theatre downtown, where I saw Harry Houdini once, still there, spiffed up, even. But not one familiar face. Suddenly, you realize you're old."

He grew silent, looking down at his hands. The therapist waited.

"You know," Zan began again, "back when I was a kid, I used to dream about running away to sea. That's the Canadian joke – kids from the prairies long for the sea, kids from the Maritimes want to climb mountains.

"The biggest body of water I saw in those days was the Red River, which was pretty big in spring when it flooded, but still a long way from a sea, just a river. The year after I was sick, we went up to Lake Winnipeg on the train one weekend – how my parents afforded that, I don't know. That was pretty big, though, as big as an ocean as far as I was concerned. But long before that I was dreaming of the sea. I read

Kipling, *Treasure Island, Robinson Crusoe*, that sort of stuff. When I was twelve or thirteen, something like that, and all the way till when I was sixteen, I had what you might call a mentor, a man who liked to be called the Commodore, dressed like a sailor, said he had a sailboat on the lake. I never saw it. He used to fill my head with tales of the sea, though. He always said he went to sea young, it made a man of him – he was a businessman, did pretty well, though he made boxes, nothing connected to sailing or water.

"I always thought I'd get to sea, but the closest I ever got was flying over it a few years ago, went to a conference in Italy. I tried to get overseas during the war – first to Spain for the civil war, but that didn't work out. Something...something came up. Then with the army in the war itself – I'm not talking Vietnam or even Korea, I mean the real war, Second World War – but no dice there either. I wanted to go, Rose – that was my wife then – didn't want me to, she was pregnant – we argued – then as it turned out they turned me down because of my heart anyway. And Rose miscarried." He paused, rubbed his eyes. "Well, that's another story. The point is, both times, I thought I'd be on a ship, a troopship, something, but no.

"Why am I telling you all this? Because the closest I get to adventures these days is a ride on the Greyhound, that's about the closest I've ever gotten. Suddenly, you realize you're old. And you realize, when you die, maybe it won't be a crossing over, like they say, a pathway of light, maybe it won't be a ferry on the River Styx, maybe it'll just be another stop on the Greyhound, another bad cup of coffee."

"Tell me more about this mentor of yours," Zelda said. She had made a brief note in the file on her lap.

"The Commodore. I've got to laugh. I had my first real job when I was eleven or twelve, the year after I was sick. I told you I had scarlet fever? That's what kept me out of the war, by the way – they listened to my heart and sent me home. The year after I was sick, I was a paperboy, standing on a corner at Main and Selkirk selling the *Free Press* for an hour every morning before school. The paper was a nickel then. For every one I sold, I got to keep three cents. Maybe it was two. An Extra was eight cents, and you kept a nickel. You tried to sell as many papers as you could, but in those days everybody bought a paper, maybe more than one, so you could make some pocket change. I was selling papers there the day the war ended, when they signed the armistice, 1918, what they call Remembrance Day now. I didn't go to school that day, stayed on my corner and sold papers all day that day, made close to sixty dollars, I remember that, though maybe that was before paying the paper its share. Either way, sixty dollars was a fortune. I remember they kept bringing out extras, every hour or so, and people kept buying papers, some people bought three, four, five different editions from me, and across the street there was another kid, selling the *Tribune* and doing just as good. Our pockets were bulging with nickels and pennies, I remember. Every hour or so, a truck would come with more papers and the driver would give us bills for our change. I was a press baron that day, a millionaire, Lord Wiseman of Selkirk Street! And it felt good handing that money over to my mother – we ate like kings that week!

"Oh, and I should tell you this: This morning, on Gzowski, they're talking about the death penalty – it's been twenty years since the government said no more, and Gwowski's asking should it come back. It made me think about this fellow called Lombardi, used to buy a paper from me every morning at my corner. He was the hangman for Winnipeg – I don't know, maybe for all of Manitoba. Before him, there was a fellow named Haberman, a Jew, he'd done the same job in Russia and had lots of experience. But some Polish murderer complained, no, if he was going to hell, he'd be damned if he'd have a Jew send him there, so they got rid of Haberman, and Lombardi got the job. He was a barber and he was good at making men feel comfortable.

"This Lombardi had a shop on Main Street in the lobby of the Occidental Hotel, near downtown. He lived further north and in good weather he would walk down Main to his shop in the morning like he was lord of the manor, swinging a cane. His suit would always be dark, dignified, like he was on his way to a hanging. He wore white gloves, summer and winter, and spats on his shoes. He was a big man, but graceful you might say, with dark hair and long lashes a stylish woman like you would kill for. He always bought a paper from me, always gave me an extra penny for myself. If he had a hanging that day, he'd say to me, 'save some space on the front page tomorrow for a big story,' and he'd wink. This happened two, maybe three times. Then the next day, he'd say, 'Better read my notices. Not that we care what the critics say, eh, Zan?' Yeah, he knew my name, always called me Zan.

"But I was telling you about the Commodore. One morning there were people on the street and a car had to stop. A man in a fancy suit was in the car and I ran up to it waving the paper and yelling, and he bought one. He offered me a job just like that. Before I knew it, I was his darling."

In fact, there had been a little more to it than that, but not all that much. He'd inherited the paper job, even the specific corner, from Abe, who was always one step ahead of him, had gone on to other things. The two boys had convinced their mother it wasn't too much for Zan. "He stands on the corner, he lifts a paper, that's all there is to it, Ma," Abe said. She reluctantly agreed. As always, even then with their father healthy and working, every penny mattered.

The day after selling a paper to the man in the car, without incident, he noticed the same car go by, a big black Packard with isinglass windows: it was early, before school, and the car was going south on Main, into the city. The day after that, he watched for the car, and when he saw it coming, stepped into the street waving the paper, almost in front of it. It wasn't going that fast, but he had an inexplicable, absolute conviction that it would stop.

The same man was in the car, a big man with a reddish face wearing a blue blazer with brass buttons and a captain's hat with a shiny black beak – Zan had seen pictures of such hats in magazines but never seen a real one, on a real head – and first he frowned, then he smiled. "You should be careful, kid," he said. "You could get hurt playing in the street." But he bought the paper.

"I'm careful," Zan said. "I got you to stop, didn't I?"

After that, the man bought a paper from him every morning on his way to his factory, which was a mile or so further south in Point Douglas. Over a period of weeks, Zan gradually learned about the factory, that its red-faced owner was called the Commodore, and that he lived in Sandy Hook, one of the little towns miles north on Lake Winnipeg, where he sailed his boat, the finely dressed man behind the wheel of the Packard dropping crumbs of information from its rolled-down window the way ashes drifted from the end of his cigar, crumbs the boy scooped up with hunger. Summer came and school ended, and the job offer did come, as much as out of the blue because the Commodore gave no hint that it was coming. Just one morning, when he stopped for his paper, saying: "Why don't you come work for me? Nothing too strenuous now, boy, just running errands and making yourself useful. A dollar a week. Just till school starts in the fall. Ask your mother for permission." He winked. "Tell her you're going up in the paper industry."

He didn't *ask*, he *told* his mother, breathlessly, "I got a job, I'm goin' to work for a *goy*," and the very next day was on the job, at a low-slung building on a dead-end street just off Sutherland Avenue where cardboard boxes were produced by cranky, noisy machines, folded and stacked and loaded by hand into railcars parked on the siding that came up alongside the factory. He'd stand on his corner selling as many papers as he could until the Commodore came along, then give what he had left to another boy and scramble through the open passenger door into the back seat, sinking into cool leather upholstery more luxuriant than anything he'd ever seen or felt. The Commodore, whose name was McLean but who was called by all his employees Commodore McLean, not Mr., or just "Commodore," and referred to as "The Commodore," always wore the blue blazer and captain's hat, though Zan had no idea where the title or outfit came from. In the summer's heat he loosened his necktie and removed the blazer, handing it to Zan to hang up, along with the hat, as soon as they reached the confines of his office, which was cooled by the languid rotations of an electric-powered fan.

In the large building behind them, and on the loading dock outside, Ukrainian and Polish men wearing undershirts and heavy boots, and murmuring in their own languages, went about their mysterious business, but the world that Zan inhabited was in the office, heavy oak desks and a large bottle of water that gurgled when you drew a glassful, large polished oak blades of the fan circling overhead, a man in a stiff collar and patent leather shoes who kept the books, and two women in flowered dresses – one elderly, the other young – with shoulder-length brown hair that seemed to whisper as she walked. Zan sorted papers, fetched and took out the mail, went down the street at noon to get a sandwich and jug of iced tea for the Commodore from a lunch wagon, generally made himself useful. He was paid two dollars – two, not one – each week, which he delivered to his mother in exchange for two nickels.

That and a few of the pennies from selling the morning papers were enough for a day-old five-cent pie once a week from the pie factory on Selkirk that he and his pal Boots, who had no regular source of income, shared, and anything else he wanted. He could still remember the sweet, sticky taste of cherries as he buried his nose in pie, syrup and crust crumbs lodging in his nostrils and eyebrows. That summer, and the summers after – except for the year away in Toronto – for as long as he continued to work at the box factory, he always remembered, he lived high on the hog, his pay rising from two dollars eventually to five.

YEARS LATER, TELLING JACK about the Commodore, he had wondered if the man hadn't been too good to be true, the ascot and jaunty captain's cap, his hearty way of speaking. He wondered about that again now.

He'd had his own suspicions, confusing the red-faced, white-haired memory with that of a British film actor he particularly liked – Trevor Howard, was it? – but it was Jack who really planted the seed – seed! more like planting a bomb. "He sounds like somebody you might have made up," he'd said.

"Made up? What do you mean?" He was mildly affronted. "He was somebody I knew."

"I didn't mean to suggest otherwise. I'm sure he was. But you describe him in such detail – I'm just wondering if you haven't embellished."

"Embellished."

Jack smiled, that slow, almost sly smile Zan had come to relish. "It's what you do, isn't it? Make things up? Isn't that what a writer does?"

"It's what we do on the page."

"And isn't the mind a page? Memory?"

"Are you a psychologist or a philosopher?" Zan had snapped, inexplicably irritated.

"There's a difference?" Jack looked innocent as a schoolboy, butter wouldn't melt, but Zan had. He commanded his mind to focus on the Commodore, and the sharp-detailed picture he'd always been able to summon came up fuzzy, the large man looming over the small boy more an indistinct shape, a blur, than a distinctive collaboration of limbs, clothing, eyes and flashing teeth.

Dave Margoshes

"All I'm saying," Jack was continuing, "is that the man sounds too good to be true. Maybe, in your imagination, over the years, he's become larger than life. Maybe some things you remember – things that seem so certain to have happened, that he said – were merely imagined, and over the course of time have taken on their own truth."

"The same could be said for anybody, everybody."

"Of course."

"Even a mother, a father, a lover."

"Of course."

"Anything you remember is suspect."

"Yes."

"And some things forgotten."

"That goes without saying."

"Goes without saying..." Zan had smiled then, strangely pleased. "So what you're telling me, doctor, is that basically you don't believe a goddamned word I'm saying."

"Oh, I believe what you're saying," Jack had shot back, laughing. "I certainly don't think you're lying. I just don't necessarily believe that everything you say is true."

"I WORKED THERE, FOR THE COMMODORE, for the next few summers," Zan told Zelda now. "When I was sixteen, something like that, then my father had his first heart attack and couldn't work for months. I dropped out of school and asked him for a regular job in the factory, where the money would be much better."

"Not on your life," the Commodore had said, and Zan remembered he put emphasis on "life" as if it were something of real value. "Not in my factory. Those Polacks and Ukes would eat you alive."

"But I work here already," Zan had protested. "The men don't bother me, they like me."

"In the office they like you, sure, you're another girl, no slight intended. On the factory floor, you're another kike, believe me, I know. If it's not a strike, it's an accident. Either way, it won't be good for you, it certainly won't be good for me."

What the Commodore had been willing to do, though, was call a friend, get him a job at the CPR yards, just south of where he lived, loading cars a few hours a day, "the skinny Jewboy working side by side with the *schvartzes* and thriving on it," he said, "going from boxes to boxcars." The Commodore was sure, he'd always believed, that Zan wouldn't last long on that job, the work would be too hard, that he'd come running back to the box factory office begging for his old job back. Instead, Zan had put on twenty pounds, much of it muscle, found himself, perhaps for the first time since his childhood illness, exulting in the workings of his body. After a few months, he was transferred to the repair shops, the boiler room, where he helped to fix locomotives, learning the machinist skills that would earn him a living for years afterwards. For months, he was a helper, then, because he was a quick learner, moved to an operator's job, making better money. It pleased him to be working with metal, like his father.

"*Schvartze*...." Zelda interrupted.

"Black men." Zan paused, watching her intently. "But said with contempt, like 'niggers,' pardon my language." She registered no discomfort, so he carried on. "The same word as the name of my father's horse, Blackie, *Schvartze*, except that word was said with affection. They weren't really black, these men, that's just the word my brother Saul picked up in jail and we used for them all, Poles, Ukrainians, Hungarians...like honky today."

"Not to their faces, though...."

"No, Lady Doctor, not to their faces. Not if we wanted to live."

"And this was all right? I mean, those men accepted you? There was no trouble?"

"No trouble, just crap games every Friday night. I had to lose a couple of paycheques before I figured out why God told Moses no gambling on the Sabbath. And accidents, of course – dangerous work, a machine shop. I cut my arm once, so deep I could see the bone. Still have the scar. While I was at the infirmary I remember, another guy came in, he'd chopped off a couple fingers."

"So you had a real education."

"You might say that. A better one than I got in school. I had lots of teachers. Abe – he taught me to duck." Zan grinned and touched his nose. "That was after he gave me this keepsake. My uncle Leo, another mentor. He was something."

"You father's brother?"

"My mother's. A veteran of the first revolution in Russia, 1905. Another family jailbird, but he escaped, got out of Russia somehow. Later, when the real revolution came along, he tried to go back but couldn't, I don't remember why. He finally made it after the war, became an officer in the Red Army. He never came back, so we never saw him again, but my mother would get a letter from him from time to time. 'Greetings from the workers' paradise,' that sort of thing. We used to eat it up. Only much later, after we stopped hearing from him, did it occur to me that maybe he was bullshitting us all along. But in Winnipeg he was a *makher* in the garment union, a big deal. He used to hang around our place when we were kids, he and some others, and talk about the old days in Russia. This is where I first heard about Lenin and Marx – you heard about them?"

Zelda smiled. So did Zan.

"He never lost the faith," Zan said. "Politics *or* religion. He'd been raised Orthodox, like my mother, but naturally Marxism had knocked most of the religion out of him. He never went to *shul*, and used to kid my mother about going so often, about keeping kosher, that sort of thing. But he continued to believe in God, continued to read the Bible. He used to say, 'I've got Marx in one hand, the Bible in the other. I think I'll be pretty safe when I get to eternity.'"

They'd been walking on Selkirk Avenue one day, he remembered, he, about twelve or thirteen, and Leo, on the way to the bakery. Was this before Toronto or after? He couldn't remember, but there were still wooden sidewalks, he could almost hear the click his uncle's boots made on the boards. They'd passed a nicely dressed woman walking a dog, a big dog, a Lab maybe or something bigger, with a rhinestone collar and a leather leash. A pretty woman, with a bag of pastry under her arm. "See that dog?" Uncle Leo said. He was a whip-lean man with a grizzled look that made him seem older than he was, and always wore an ancient leather jacket with frayed sleeves. "You think he wants to be patted by that woman? Hell, no – he wants to fuck that woman, right in the tush like she were another dog. But you think he ever does that? Don't be stupid. If he did, he'd be out on the street, eating from garbage cans, sleeping in the rain, his balls in the garbage can at the vet's. No, he lets that woman walk him on his leash, lets her pat him anytime she wants, lets her scratch his ears. At night, he dreams of her tush, but is he stupid? Is he suicidal? No." Uncle Leo took a deep breath and was silent for a moment. His jaw clamped shut, his fierce moustache bobbed above his lip. "Is the working man stupid, Zannie? Is the working man suicidal? No."

They walked on. "Uncle Leo..." he'd started to say.

"Don't say anything, Zannie," Leo said. "Don't say anything. Just think about what I told you. Just think about it."

"And did you?" Zelda asked.

"Think about it? How do you suppose I became a Communist? I thought about it all the time. I thought about it a lot at the box factory, and I thought about it even more when I worked at the rail yards, I can you tell you that. I thought about how the Commodore would scratch me behind the ears and call me his darling. Pay me two dollars a week and go home to his big house on the lake in his big Packard. How could I not think about it?

"I thought of it so hard, so long, that dog reappeared in my novel. Don't worry, it's not a dog story, *Lassie Come Home* it ain't. But there's a dog. And there's an uncle too, I almost forgot. And a boy. Where did all these characters come from, I wonder. And there's a wise man, a rabbi, so wise he's almost a fool, or maybe it's the other way around.

"The uncle says to the boy, 'My dog can see well – look at him at the window, riveted on the activity of that fellow in the courtyard below. They say dogs have poor vision, but not mine – his eyes are good. His hearing is good. His nose is good. All his senses are good. Yet he has no sense. There's a riddle for you. What would the wise rabbi of Chelm say to that, I wonder.'"

"And what does he say?" Zelda asked.

"Ah, for that, you'll have to read the book."

AS HE TRAMPS HOME OVER FRESHLY FALLEN SNOW, it's not the Commodore, or Uncle Leo, who accompanies him, but Myrna, the first time, he realizes, that he's allowed himself to really think of her since the funeral, more than three months ago. Were they happy, Zelda asked awhile ago. Yes, they had been, *he* had been, and never happier than during the silent period, her deafness a curse, yes, but also, in some perverse way, a blessing. There were times when, their hands and arms

Dave Margoshes

tired from signing, they would sink into their respective chairs, into books, into reveries. The house would be truly silent then, only the ticking of the grandfather clock in the hallway, the occasional purr of a car creeping slowly by on their cul-de-sac. He would revel in that silence, gazing fondly at Myrna, her face lined with age but her Bette Davis eyes and bangs as youthful as the day he'd met her. She would sometimes sense the heat of his eyes and raise her own to gaze fondly at him, as thoroughly comfortable as he'd ever been in his life. Other times, the silence would feel oppressive, and he would begin to talk, oblivious to Myrna's deafness, chattering away like a boy home from school telling his mother about the day, an imitation of the one-way conversation he knew Abe conducted regularly with *his* wife. Once, he remembered, in the middle of one of these soliloquies, Myrna had, without looking up from her book, spoken, "What would you say to a cup of tea?" He hadn't heard and continued talking. She looked up, about to repeat herself, and caught him with his mouth open, a smile slowly spreading across her face. "You don't need me at all, do you?" she said, but warmly, not offended or hurt but amused. "Oh yes I do," he'd replied. "You don't know how much."

FROM ZAN'S JOURNAL

Nov. 22, 1988 – The twenty-fifth anniversary of the Kennedy assassination today, the paper is filled with it. To me it was never such a big deal, but Rose thought a lot of him, I remember, she was shaken. And Myrna – of course, she was American – she remembered exactly where she was, what she was doing that day when she heard. Years later, tears would come into her eyes on the anniversary, telling me. He was not a hero to her, but an icon. Is there anyone like that in my life? Lenin once, Trotsky maybe, I used to know their birthdays, the days they died. Not any more.

That woman, that Zelda, has me dizzy. Today we were talking about the end of my life and its beginning, like a yoyo. The Commodore! Haven't thought of him in years, of those times. All just a hazy dream. Me working at the box factory, the rail yards! Did all that really happen? To me? It seems like a dream, like a story I wrote or imagined but never got around to writing. About some other Zan. I could ask Abe, but why would he remember such a thing? Or have even known? The Commodore – did he really even exist? I wonder if I didn't just make all that up, the Commodore and everything else, like Jack suggested once, like I've made up so many other things.

Myrna was real enough, so was Rose. What about Luna? Was she real? Or did I conjure her up too? Dream her, fabricate her, hallucinate her out of some bottle? Was she just some character I tried to write?

CHAPTER 11

November 29, 1988

"I'D LIKE TO TALK ABOUT YOUR MOTHER TODAY, if that's all right," Zelda said. "We were moving in her direction last time, I think, but didn't quite get there. You loved her, I'm presuming."

"I loved her, you presume right." Zan hesitated.

"And?"

"And she's dead. My father died, my mother remarried, twice, once didn't take, then again, the new guy died, she died." He smiled, just a bit ruefully. "They all die, you notice that, Dr. Zelda? There's a pattern here."

"I have. It's not unique to your family, though. Have *you* just noticed?"

"No, it was called to my attention some time ago. Charles Darwin pointed it out. Before him, there was some mention in the Bible. Shakespeare had a thought or two on the subject. So did the Greeks. It's a popular topic."

"Death? Yes, though these days most people don't like to talk about it."

"No. It's everybody's favourite for not talking about."

"And you?"

"Me? It seems like I talk about nothing else. Isn't that what we're talking about now?"

"Yes, it is." Zelda smiled, consulted her notes for a moment. "I was asking about your mother."

"And I'm telling you, she died," Zan said, perhaps a bit more sharply than he meant.

To soften what he'd just said, he added this: "The other day, Abe, my brother Abe, and I argued about our mother – a stupid argument. She had beautiful brown eyes, I said; no, no, Abe protested, blue. Then I realized, I really had no idea."

He remembered everything about her – almost everything. He

remembered her voice as clearly as if he'd heard it that very day, remembered the touch of her hands rubbing mustard plaster onto his skinny chest when he was sick, the smell of her, sweat and talc and flour – and always a slightly sour smell for a minute or two, lingering on her skin, after she went to the toilet, a warning perhaps of the cancer inside her that her children never even dreamed about, though she lived a long life, outliving three of her sons. He remembered his repeated surprise, once he had grown, over how small she was, no more than five feet tall. He remembered the force of the palm of her hand on his face! Who could forget that? The curve of her arm below the elbow as it came out of the basin of water or a tub of bread dough, like the neck of a swan or a goose about to take flight. He remembered all those things, everything about her, everything but one small thing, one thing, that's all: her face. He saw her standing by the kitchen stove, stoking the fire or stirring a black cast iron pot, saw her approach the table, saw her hand go up to brush away a curl that had come loose from the net around her hair, to smudge a smear of flour on her chin. He saw all these things, clear as if he had seen them last just that morning, but between the flour smudge and the loose curl there was a blank, nothing.

The last time he'd seen his mother, she had recently become a widow again, a woman twice widowed, once divorced, four times bereaved over her children, counting the son who was born dead, and only a few months away from her own death, though he didn't know that. She was eighty-eight – just five years and a bit older than he himself now was – an old woman but with none of what he thought of as the failings of an old woman, seeing poorly, hard of hearing, forgetful, arthritic, complaining. "At eighty-eight, she was in better shape than I am at, what am I, eighty-two?" he said. She was, or appeared to be, strong, healthy and still sharp as ever, still stranded somewhere between the Old World and the new, as he'd been thinking of her for years, a woman who still had difficulty with the language of the country she'd lived in for almost seventy years, though she loved it with a fierce passion.

"She had not the softest life," Zan said. "She lost her beloved husband early, took a fool as a second husband and came to a happy third marriage only late in life. That was to a man I barely knew, I only met him two or three times, I don't even remember his name or what

Dave Margoshes

became of him – well, he died, I know that, but nothing of the cause or circumstance – and my knowledge of the happy marriage is merely hearsay, to tell the truth. She visited three of her sons in prison and sent packages to one son in a prisoner-of-war camp in Germany, packages he never received. One of her sons died in an earlier war, another of a weak heart just days after being released from prison, a third.... I told you about Adam. Rheumatic fever. Just a boy. Oh, and there was another son, born dead.... I mentioned him, I think. She'd seen her daughter jilted and heartbroken."

And one son – the one she was with the last time he saw her – would soon be committed to the mental health facility on Queen Street in Toronto, would be behind a locked door on the day of her funeral. Zan said nothing of that. Nor did he mention that she'd cursed the *shiksas* two of her sons had married or taken up with, though she came eventually to like her daughter-in-law Dolly well enough, even love her – nothing remotely like that with Luna – and had, at one time or another, disowned three of her sons, himself included. He doesn't say, can't *bring himself* to say, the things his mother called Luna and Dolly, the invectives she poured out at her sons for their involvement with these gentile women. It had taken a long time for his parents to find out about Luna, and when they did, though the reaction was severe, somehow the fact that she was a professor, that she was helping Zan – in other words, that there was a bargain, even if with a devil, and their son was benefiting from it – somehow all this mediated the harm, and his banishment from the household was short-lived, though their dislike for Luna herself was not extinguished and his mother had continued to rail against her for years, even after Zan was, by all appearances, happily married to Rose, a "good Jewish girl" in his mother's eyes, at least by virtue of birth if not practice. "That viper," she always called Luna, refusing to dignify her through the use of her name; "that viper almost ruined you," deaf to Zan's objections that, on the contrary, she had *made* him.

With Abe, the reaction was stronger, the banishment more determined, going on for months – his parents had told him he was dead to them, not to come to the house, not to attempt to see them or talk to them. When reconciliation came, it was, ironically, Zan who brought it about.

It was uncanny how similar to Luna Dolly was, "but more so," Zan had once told Jack, as if Abe had been determined to outdo his brother. Like Luna, she was tall and slender, but even taller than Luna, towering a good four inches higher than Abe, and when she was in high heels, they were almost comical together; and like Luna, she was fair-skinned and light-haired, the auburn running almost to bright red in the sunlight. And where Luna was Scottish and Presbyterian, Dolores was Irish and Catholic, the daughter of the man who ran the gym where Abe continued to go to spar and work out, years after he'd stopped boxing in the Golden Gloves. She too had been disowned by her parent when they married, and Abe barred from the gym. How they'd gotten together was never explained, although the common ground of the gym was the obvious part of the answer, and the basis of her attraction to his brother was as mysterious to Zan as that of Luna to him.

He remembered so clearly a funeral for a neighbour he attended months after Abe married Dolly. They were living in a small apartment in the West End, and, though Abe was banned from his parents' house, he continued to see Zan often, and Saul almost daily, as they were partners in the trucking business at this point. "I don't know why I suggested he come to this funeral," Zan had told Jack, "I just had a feeling that maybe something could happen."

"Emotions are close to the surface in situations like that," Jack observed. "Were your instincts good?"

"Better than expected."

In all of this drama, at least as far as Zan remembers it, his mother was the central player – his father, not as religious, more practical, would not have initiated anything so severe as banishment for his children, would have been more willing to accept, but went along with his wife's decisions. In Zan's memory, his father is absent from this drama, as he is, he realizes with a sudden slap of certainty, from so many family scenes. But there, etched in his mind as if by acid on glass, is his mother, dressed in black as always, her arm on his, and there, not more than ten yards away, is Abe, looking miserable in a tight black suit.

"Look, there's Abe, *Momela*," Zan said, but his mother refused to acknowledge him. "Momma," he persisted, "there's Abe, your son Abe."

"I have no son Abe," his mother replied.

They crowded in closer to the grave. The body had been lowered, the rabbi's words finished. As earth was being thrown on the coffin, Zan took his mother's hand roughly. "Would you rather be throwing earth on your son's coffin? Would you really rather *he* were dead?"

She'd burst into tears, "and that was all it took," he'd told Jack. Zan could see her softening, as if the tears were melting the glue that held her resolve together. He gestured to Abe and, when he appeared beside them, she took him into her arms, right there at the graveside, though it would take some time before she was willing even to meet Dolly, let alone embrace her. But it wasn't too long afterwards that Abe and Saul were arrested and the two women thrown together in a common cause. Soon, Dolly had even moved in with her mother-in-law, the better to pool their resources through what would turn into a long wait.

"When my mother saw how faithful Dolly was when Abe went to jail, that melted the last of the ice around her heart," Zan told Jack.

But he can't tell Zelda that, any of that. Or won't. "No, she had not the softest life," he repeated. "'A life full of woe, for all its pleasures'— is that Shakespeare? And yet" – he shook his head in genuine bewilderment, "she believed all her life in a good, well-meaning, all-knowing God. Believed as firmly, as fiercely, in God at the end of her life as she ever had."

The last time they were together, they were in the lounge of the nursing home Abe had arranged for her. The eldest son now, he was living in Calgary, a thirteen-hour drive to Winnipeg, but the responsibility for her had fallen on him anyway, a responsibility he was happy enough to take on. He figured, he told Zan and Annie, he owed her more than he could ever repay. Not that a nursing home was a proper way to repay a debt or honour a mother, in Zan's view, but that was easy enough for him to say, more than a thousand miles away in Toronto and with no financial resources to back up any alternative wishes he may have had. He might have taken his mother in to live with him, since the others wouldn't or couldn't, made the offer, at least, except that his own living situation was so precarious, having so recently left Rose and staying in a cramped basement apartment, the first thing he'd found, and he knew she'd be reluctant to leave Winnipeg at any rate. But it hadn't gone that far. "Money talks. I got it, you don't," Abe had said when Zan questioned the choice, not that he was wealthy but his tailor shop was doing well in those days. "So shut up."

Now he was here to visit her, the first and, as it would turn out, the only time he'd see her there. She seemed happy enough – said she was – with several old friends in the same home, and some new ones, and the place was clean and well run, as far as Zan could tell, the staff obliging and friendly. It was likely that it was only he who was unhappy about her move there, one more failure of his own he'd been powerless to prevent.

Still, it grated on him, and her persistent faith in the face of what seemed to him as so many mounting injustices – he'd found her in her room, praying, but with gratitude – grated all the more.

"Momma, do you really still believe in God?" he asked, in Yiddish. His had grown rusty, but her English, never very good, had worsened.

She looked at him, surprised, her eyes still clear. "What kind of a question is this? You might as well ask me if the sun and the moon are in the sky, if day is light and night dark. What a question! *Zanela*, where do you learn such questions? From that viper? Or is it those lousy Reds?"

The sound of that phrase, "those lousy Reds," in his mother's mouth triggered a memory so painful Zan shook his head violently to fend it off. He laughed, again as a way of driving out the hobgoblin of memory, and also because he wasn't in the Party any more, hadn't been for some time. Mostly he laughed, though, because he'd stopped believing in God long before he'd become a Communist. If anything, it was the Party's staunch disbelief that had, at least in part, attracted him to it. In North End Winnipeg, in the '20s and '30s, it was one of the few organizations where such an idea was considered palatable. But *stopped believing* was going too far – he never really had believed in a god, one or another, he was certain of that, any more than he'd believed in Santa Claus or the Easter Bunny, Christian concoctions his parents themselves had told him were fictions not worthy of a child's belief, or the tooth fairy, or fairies of any sort. Even as a small child, he recalled, when Abe and Adam were still frightened of the dark, of imagined monsters under the bed, Zan had been fearless. How had a child, let alone a child of an Orthodox Jewish family on Flora Avenue in the Winnipeg of the early part of the century, been so clear-eyed? He didn't know, just that he had, that he had been that child.

"Momma, don't be angry at me," he said, first in English, then in Yiddish, getting up and kneeling in front of her. He put his arms on the arms of her chair, his hands on her shoulders. She was so small, the bones, beneath the faded flower print of her purplish dress, so brittle, so close to the skin.

"Angry? Who said I was angry, *Zanela?*" She put her hands on his head, the hair still thick, still black then, and he let it drop until his face was in her lap, the way he had loved to sit with her when he was a child, supplicant at the feet of a saint. The stale smell of her, a bathroom smell, washed over him, and he could hear gurgling from her stomach. He knelt there with her for a long time, would have stayed all day, despite the ache creeping into his knees, but after a while she touched him gently on the arms. "Get up, *Zanela,*" she said. "Be a *mensch.*"

He spent the afternoon with her, but he remembered nothing of the visit other than that first brief exchange about God, and that posture of prayer he'd affected, the last time they'd ever held each other in their arms. When he left, he gave her arm a squeeze, her cheek a peck.

His breakdown had come about six months later, a year or so after the breakup with Rose, and was precipitated by a combination of sleeping pills and whiskey, more likely an accident than deliberate, the doctors and psychologist agreed – Zan himself had no memory of the incident. *Breakdown, breakup* – those two words were inextricably linked in his mind. The point was that he was in hospital when his mother died, and no one knew how to reach him. Abe phoned the Toronto apartment he and Rose had been in for the year since they'd sold their house, the last number he had, but Rose had no idea where he was staying, didn't give a damn, she told Abe, though she was very sorry to hear of *Buba's* death. That part would have been true. The two women had always been allies and friends. If she and Zan had been together, and he able, there's no question that she would have accompanied him to the funeral. As it happened, neither went, and it was only weeks later, after Abe made some more calls, that Zan learned his mother had died. Yet another stone on the pile weighing him down.

The following year, when he was seeing Jack, Zan had described that last meeting with his mother, so vivid still in his memory he could feel the rough carpet under his knees, the fragility of her shoulders on his fingers. Looking over Jack's shoulder to the square of blue sky framed in his window – the therapist's office was on the tenth or eleventh or twelfth floor – the stabbing memory that had threatened to engulf him that last time with his mother, a memory of being high above the city, in their own elevated world, again buffeted him, like waves batting against a swimmer. He shook his head and the memory retreated.

"And death," Zan had said. "Religion, death, my mother. They all seem to go together. When I think of my brother Saul, or my father, I think of their deaths, and then I think of my mother, her tears. Not *my* tears, *hers*. But when I think of her, I don't think of *her* death. I see her alive. Maybe because I missed her death and funeral, didn't hear about them until they were long past. It makes them not real for me somehow. For me, she's not dead, I just haven't seen her for awhile."

"That's all understandable enough," Jack said. "Your mother brought you life, it's understandable that she represents life to you." He jotted something down in his notes, puffed thoughtfully on his pipe. "And sex," he said.

"What's that?"

"Sex. You said you link your mother with religion and death. I'm tossing sex into the mix."

"Don't get Freudian on me now, Doc."

Jack grinned. "Why not? I'm a Freudian. Besides, you got something against sex?"

"Now there's a loaded question if I ever heard one. No, I'm all in favour of it. I'd rather be having some right now than be here talking about it. But I have to say my mother doesn't make me think about it."

"Are you sure?"

"Sure is something I'm not," Zan said. "About anything."

Again, his eyes were pulled, as if by a magnet, to the blue square of sky in Jack's window, again that sickening feeling of vertigo, as if the window had fallen away and he was outside, on the ledge, the precipice. Again, he successfully fended it off, though that night, as he lay in his bed, he allowed himself to succumb to it, and it washed over him, with all the finality of grief. And for the first time, he wept for his mother's death.

"AND YOUR BROTHERS?" Zelda asked gently after Zan had been silent for several minutes. "Maybe you'd rather talk about them. I've been meaning to ask, how are you getting along with Abe now that you have your own place?"

"Better, thanks."

"It stands to reason – you're not stepping on each other's toes all the time. Do you see a lot of each other?"

"Friday night, at his house, every week like clockwork. We light candles, he makes dinner, chicken. A few times, the movies, dinner out – I like Szechwan, he likes Vietnamese, it's a harmless enough argument. Sometimes something else. Temple, Saturday morning a few times."

"You never invite him to your place for dinner?"

"I would, believe me, Lady Doctor. He won't come. He says I can't cook."

"Can you?"

"I think so. You don't see me wasting away."

"And your brother? He can cook?"

"He too isn't wasting away, but he's no gourmet chef."

"So you're both probably not wonderful cooks, but you eat his food, he won't eat yours. Does that bother you?"

"Again with the sibling rivalry stuff. Believe me, with Abe and me, it's way past rivalry, way past '*bother*.'"

"All right then, let's talk about your other brothers. You've told me a bit about them already."

"Ah, my brothers," Zan said. "I am a man with brothers. Well, I *was*. Haven't we *been* talking about them?" He remembered having had a similar conversation with Jack, perhaps he'd used that phrase then. Jack would have sucked on his pipe and considered the answer. "Does that mean that you're your brothers' keeper?"

"Oh ho. That's too religious for me, Doc. It means just what I said. I have brothers. Had brothers, now just one. They're important to me, always were."

"And sisters?"

"One, but she has a husband to look after her."

"A father and mother?"

"Both dead. Well, my father for sure, my mother, so I've been told. It's only my brothers I got to worry about. Some of them are dead, just one alive. I worry about them all, regardless."

"And why is that?"

"You're asking me? Now you're getting theological. I thought you were supposed to come up with answers."

"That's not the way it works." Jack would have smiled, showing big, slightly crooked teeth, stained yellow in the front. He was a slender, almost bony, man with an exaggeratedly large head that seemed mismatched to the sharp shoulders pressing against the cloth of his wrinkled tweed jacket. "We talk, we poke into things together, but you come up with the answers yourself."

"So poke," Zan had said.

And Jack had, sometimes gently, sometimes with a sharp stick that felt like it was lodging itself in Zan's ribs.

Even before Saul and Hersh there had been another brother, still-born. That boy, if he'd been born, was to have been called Isaiah, though what he would have actually been called, Zan had no idea. All of the kids had three names, he'd told Jack, or even four, some of them: their real name, in Hebrew, and its English phonetic version, and their "English" names, the ones their mother used when she registered them at school. And then a pet name or a nickname that seemed to evolve on its own. Zan's own name, Isaac, was one neither he nor his family had ever used, except his mother and the teachers at the Talmud Torah Hebrew school where he and Abe had studied for their *bar mitzvah*. His brothers called him either Zan or Zannie or Pantsy, a childhood name that had something to do with his first pair of long pants. The teachers at Aberdeen School had used Alexander, the full name he was registered under, and Luna, in their first years together, would sometimes teasingly call him Alexander the Great. But that was just in bed. It had been years since he'd been called Isaac or Alexander by anyone, and years since he'd heard any of his brothers called or referred to by anything but their regular English names, Abe and Saul, Hersh and Adam, though the latter three were long dead. Their Hebrew names were inscribed on the headstones on their graves in Winnipeg, but the last time Zan had been there was for Annie's funeral, four years earlier, same cemetery, the Shaarey Zedek, different section, she beside her husband and members of his family. On his most recent visit to Winnipeg, just a few months ago, he was fresh from Myrna's funeral and had avoided the cemetery and graveside visits. But that earlier time, for Annie, he and Abe – the A to Zed boys together again, and now it was just them – had made the rounds of the other graves, their brothers' and parents', all close together, but he had no clear memory of them. Abe might remember the names, maybe yes, maybe no.

In the house at 424 Flora Avenue, all the boys had been crammed into one room. Oh, how they used to squawk about that, the injustice of Annie, just a little girl, having a room practically of her own, sharing just with the succession of young women boarders who always were living with them, while the five boys were sardines sleeping foot to head in two sets of double bunk beds their father had built, Saul and Hersh in one set until they went off to the war, Zan and Adam in the other, Abe by himself on a cot wedged in between. Sometimes, when they were small, on cold winter nights, Zan would climb into the upper bunk with Adam, he remembered. But for all the complaining, they loved that downstairs room, with its one small window looking out on the backyard garden and the barn where in the morning they could hear the jingle of harness and *Schvartze* stamping his feet and whinnying for food or attention. At night, they'd be draped over each other on the beds or the one small desk the bigger boys took turns at as they laboured with their English or their sums, safe and secure in the total warmth of complete acceptance. No matter what might happen on the outside, in school, the playground, the street, where the taunts of boys with English names sometime grew hostile – even in the kitchen, where their mother might scold and their father's occasional flashes of anger might erupt – in their room they were equals and anything would be forgiven. "That's the way I remember it anyway," Zan had told Jack. Now he told Zelda.

"So it was a happy childhood?" she asked.

"I think so." Zan laughed. "It shouldn't have been – how could it have? Five boys crammed in one room, eight of us in the family in a house the size of a postage stamp, until Hersh and Saul were old enough to work, all dependent on the one lousy pay envelope my dad brought home from the dairy, anti-Semites all around us.... How could it have been happy? But I think it was."

And as childhood does, it had seemed like it would last forever, but then the war came, and Saul and Hersh were gone suddenly and the three remaining brothers rattled around in that room, he remembered, the two empty beds, still with the same sheets his mother had been too superstitious to wash, somehow seeming larger than they'd been before. "Oh, they seemed so empty," he said.

By the time Saul came home alone, Zan had been through his lost year of sickness, leaving him stunted and still weak, Adam had died and the room was even emptier. Saul filled it up again, though he was quieter than he'd been before, and would often not come home at night, staying out who knows where. Even when he was there, there were only three now where there had been five, and their father took out one set of bunks, creating more room, Saul and Zan, the oldest and youngest, in one set, when Saul was around, Abe still on his own in the cot. But the bedroom was no longer the fun place it had been and the boys avoided it as much as possible. Going to bed seemed solemn now when Saul was there; Zan remembered Saul and Hersh as racehorses, all gangly limbs and nonchalance, but now Saul would often thrash in his sheets through the night, waking with a gasp in a sweat, rattling the homemade bunk's slats, and Hersh's absence was all but palpable. Saul never referred to Hersh – the rest of the family could only speculate on whether he knew any of the details of his twin's death at Vimy Ridge – and never spoke of his own wounding in the same battle. The closest he ever came to a war story – what Abe and Zan longed to hear – was a veiled reference to the nurses at the hospital in France where he'd recuperated, that they were "clap traps," a pun that Abe had to explain to Zan.

Zan was twelve then, in 1918, and already it felt as if childhood was over because it would never go back to the way it was. No, not the way it had been, the five of them in that room, all elbows and ankles and smelly armpits and feet.

"With that spread in age, you'd think the eldest wouldn't have much to do with the youngest," he said, "but that isn't the way it happened. Thick as thieves, all for one, one for all, that was us." Saul and Hersh had been eight when Abe was born and naturally took his well-being upon themselves. And Abe, who was big for his age, just as naturally had became protector for Zan and Adam, who were small, the physical gulf between Abe and Zan widened, while the emotional narrowed, all the more after Zan's sickness, Adam's death. And they had all looked after Annie, the baby girl, treating her more like a pet than a sister, like the monkey their father called her, until she started school.

Saul and Hersh had been the only twins in the neighbourhood at first, and their mother used to say, he remembered, that they'd been immediate celebrities, a distinction that followed them through their childhood and teens, all the way until Saul had come limping home alone from France in 1918. Was it that celebrity that had made them tough guys, tougher than most of the other boys on the block and the surrounding neighbourhood, the need to live up to their celebrity, defend it, grow into the space it forced on them? Or was it simply the mathematical fact that there were always two of them, always one to watch the other's back, a second for any duel? (With Zan and Adam and Abe – the original A to Zed boys – that same mathematics was intensified, the boys more like triplets than twins and one slightly older brother.) Zan didn't know, but his earliest memories of his big twin brothers were of them being in trouble, in detention at school, kept after class, extra homework, or kicked out of school entirely, doing penance. There had been, he remembered, an endless stream of broken windows, fruit stolen from pushcarts, fights and chases – and one memorable incident when the two of them had hidden giggling and muffled in the hay above the horse's stall in the backyard barn while their mother, with Zan and Abe and Adam still in short pants by her side, bluffed a cop in the kitchen, convincing him her eldest boys were up at Winnipeg Beach, visiting an uncle. Then, gradually, as Zan had been six and seven and eight, the nights when the boys hadn't come home from their saloon jobs downtown to sleep became more frequent, the nights sometimes turning into weeks. When they were home, he remembered, things were as always, his older brothers always finding time for him, always the gentle cuff to the shoulder, the tousle of his hair, the questions and answers – but less and less frequently were they there. Then the war, and they were gone entirely.

"I don't even think they came home to say goodbye, we're going," he'd complained to Jack. "They were afraid of what Momma would say when she heard they'd enlisted. They just sent word. So I never did get to say goodbye to Hersh. He just disappeared and never came back. At least Saul did."

"Did that make you angry?" Jack had wanted to know.

"Don't play the doctor with me," Zan snapped back.

"No? What should I play then?" Jack had stirred in his chair and the two men gazed at each other, the heat of the sudden eruption already dissipated. Flare-ups like that were exactly what he no longer had the energy for, he thought as Zelda dug into similar territory, but more gently.

"Things changed when your brother came home from the war?" she asked. "How so?"

"Ah, you ask the hard questions," Zan said, as he liked to do. The hard questions were, in fact, what he both longed for and shrank from.

The Saul of his memory would always be fifteen, the age he was when Zan was six, when he would come by the schoolyard afternoons to pick him and Adam and Abe up and chase away the circle of bigger boys habitually gathered around them, a tall, skinny boy in overalls and a tweed cap from which tufts of unruly black hair curled. And Hersh would always be with him, same coveralls, same cap, same curls, but a blue shirt to Saul's green. Even without the shirts, Zan could always tell them apart. Saul's smile was the bigger, showing his broken front tooth – how had that happened? – and he was always in the lead, Hersh lagging slightly behind. For some reason, it was Saul who was more real to him. "I'm Eenie," he would announce himself, Hersh echoing "I'm Meenie."

And Abe, whose belligerence would have been the cause of the circle of bigger boys in the first place, would shout: "Oh, yeah, then I'm Miney." And Zan would follow: "And I'm Moe." Where was Adam's voice in that chorus? He couldn't remember. Curiously, even then, four years before his death, Adam was beginning his slow fade from Zan's memory.

And the five of them would singsong: "Catch a Polack by the toe."

Now Adam was gone and Zan and Abe teenagers and seemingly headed in the same direction their older brothers had followed, Hersh was gone forever and Saul was a grown man who walked with a slight limp and rarely smiled or laughed. His hand, when it came to rest on Zan's head, seemed heavier than it had.

"Just be careful," he liked to advise his younger brothers, as if care were all it took to navigate the dangerous world.

Saul was involved in the big strike in 1919, but in what capacity Zan was never sure. He and Abe had been messengers themselves, carrying intelligence back and forth from the strike leaders to the picket lines and back again on their bikes, as had many boys from their neighbourhood, and they had a good view from the roof of one of the Market Square buildings of the Mounties' charge into the assembled strikers on Bloody Saturday. Later, Abe had come up with what he swore was the truth that Saul was one of the men who had set the streetcar on its side and afire on Main Street later that afternoon, but Saul himself would only scowl and gesture aimlessly with one hand when they asked him about it.

A few months after the strike, with their father out of work and money tight in the house, shortly before the family moved to Toronto, Saul took off suddenly, leaving the family dependent on no more than the little income Abe and Zan brought in from selling papers and the rent paid by the single-women boarders, now two of them, crammed into Annie's room. It was weeks before they heard from him, a picture postcard showing the Rockies but postmarked in Vancouver. "I'm okay" was all he'd scribbled on the card's back, no signature but Saul's oversize scrawl immediately recognizable. Zan thought he could see the old broken-toothed smile flash across Saul's face as he mailed the card.

"I didn't see my big brother again for almost three years," he told Zelda. He explained how the family returned to Winnipeg after the year in Toronto, their parents disappointed with their fortunes there, and were able to move right back into their old house.

"We hadn't sold it, just rented it out, and I don't know what happened to the tenants but they were gone, we moved right back in. My father's horse *Schvartze* was still in the barn in the back, the tenant had been using him to pull a peddler's wagon or something. It was like we'd never been gone."

"And you went back to school?"

"For a while. I did good – I actually won an essay contest, a scholarship to university. That was the beginning of me as a writer. My father had learned the locksmith's trade in Toronto and he did okay for awhile, I didn't have to work, but then he had his first heart attack and was laid up for awhile. I had to quit school."

It was around then, too, that word had filtered back that a bank robbery had gone wrong and Saul was in prison in British Columbia. "I had to see him," he said, "just had to. I didn't think about it, didn't think about the danger, about the worry my mother might feel, nothing. I didn't tell anyone, not even Abe. Just packed a few pieces of clothing, a notebook and a pen and went down to the rail yards to catch a freight heading west."

Some things Zan remembers, plenty he doesn't, but one thing he remembers with perfect clarity is the look of surprise on Saul's face when he walked into the visitor's room at the prison, and what Saul said: "What's that on your face, Pantsy? Dirt?"

"No," Zan had protested, "it's beard."

"That's beard?" Saul said, incredulous. "Wash your face."

Zan was sixteen, his brother twenty-five, and childhood, if it hadn't been already, was certainly over.

"I'm sorry, Pantsy," Saul said after the bluster had subsided. "I did it for the family, to get money for the family."

"With a gun, Saul?" Zan asked.

"With a gun, yeah, Zannie. Sometimes...." His voice trailed off and Zan had no idea, really, what was implied. The shape of a gun, the imagined feel of it in his hand, lodged in Zan's mind and stayed there for a long time. Now, more than sixty-five years later, he can still feel that weight.

Nov. 29, 1988 – I think I'm through with that woman. Who needs this pain?

Dave Margoshes

DUET 4

"Look at us now, Zannie, it's hard to believe we're identical twins. Isn't that what you used to say?"

"Identical? I thought we were similar."

"We're not even that any more. You've got hair, I've got this head of skin and fuzz."

"No, not so close any more."

"You still walk straight, not like a question mark, like me. Nobody confuses us for twins these days."

"Confuses? Wait a minute, *Abela*, you mean we're not?"

"Brothers, yes, we still look close enough for that."

"But not twins."

"Definitely not identical."

"Well, we were. Before I got my nose broken...."

"By me."

"It was a lucky punch."

"The hell it was lucky, I was aiming."

"And you lost your hair...."

"And three inches. Life pounded me down like a fence post in mud."

"But made up for it with a few pounds."

"And I was always the better-looking one, identical or not."

"Identical? Really? Were Adam and I really identical, Abe?"

"Like peas in a pod, Pantsy. Momma used to say she tied different coloured ribbons around your necks when she brought you home, to tell you apart, don't you remember?"

"Blue and red. I remember she said that. I think I was blue."

"Red, more likely."

"Maybe. Maybe it was Zan that died, maybe I'm Adam."

"Maybe."

"Then you became the twin, Benchy, remember?"

"That's what we used to say. Before Adam died, we used to pretend we were triplets, remember that?"

"No. Did we get away with it?"

"Sure, sometimes. We were all about the same size, and I

looked close enough like that we could maybe convince someone it was true, if they didn't look too hard. Triplets! And it *was* true – for that three weeks in February, every year, we were all the same age."

"We were always so close, the three of us, isn't that right, *Abela?*"

"Sure, we were the three musketeers, the Three *Pischers.*"

"All for one, one for all, everybody together."

"After Adam died, even more so, Zannie. Sometimes, I swear, there'd be a push on my shoulder and I'd spin around and there was no one there. You swore you felt it too, remember? 'Adam's ghost,' we'd say, 'pushing us together.'"

"I remember, we used to play a game with an empty mirror frame we found somewhere, out in the alley, I think. We'd take turns, me holding it up and you looking in it, posing, then we'd switch places, making faces at each other, pretending we were looking at our own reflection – like we really were twins."

"And sometimes we'd switch shirts, and I'd call you 'Abe,' and you'd call me 'Zannie.' We'd even get Momma and Pop *farmisht.* That close we were."

"Yes, close."

"But not identical."

"Identical, you gotta have same mother, same father, same egg, same sperm. We had that? Twins, we were for sure. Born minutes apart. First you, then me. I'm the kid brother."

"Well, same egg, maybe not same sperm."

"Then that wouldn't be.... *Abela!* Such disrespect for Pop, I'm surprised at you."

"Maybe not even the same egg, but same mother, that's for sure."

"Well, maybe not even same mother, but same hospital, same day, that part is guaranteed."

"Maybe not same hospital, exactly, but same city. Same city, same week, that's for sure."

"Same province, same year, that's as far as I'll go. Manitoba, 1906. You can put money on that."

"Well, maybe not the same year. Same decade, that's for

certain. Same decade, same country, absolutely."

"Absolutely. Identical. Or close enough."

"Any closer, no one would want to be. Any closer, it would be supernatural."

CHAPTER 12

December 6, 1988

"YOU LOOK TIRED TODAY," ZELDA SAID. "A little...ragged. How've you been sleeping?"

"Sleeping? Who sleeps?"

"You can't fall asleep, or you wake up in the middle of the night, what?"

"I can't fall asleep, I wake up in the middle of the night, yes, all those things. What's that old saying, 'Early to bed, early to rise'? With me, it's 'late to bed, early to rise and not much action in between.'"

"And dreams? When you're asleep, do you dream?"

"Freudian Lady Doctor, you know I dream. Do I remember them, that's what you mean to ask."

"Of course. And?"

"And what?"

"And do you remember your dreams, Mr. Wiseman?"

"Sometimes."

"Do you write them down ever?"

"If I could get this right hand of mine to work better, maybe I would. I could use them in a novel. You got a cure maybe for arthritis and mini-strokes?"

"There is medicine...."

"Medicine I take. I mean beyond that."

"Afraid not."

"Oh, well."

"Can you tell me about a dream? One you had last night, perhaps? Do you remember? Try."

"Sure. I can tell you a dream. This is easy. Freud I've read, Jung too. It's the dream I had last night, so it's fresh. It's also the dream I had the night before and the night before. You asked me last time about brothers, remember?"

"Yes. You dream about your brothers?"

"Listen, you'll find out. I'm in a prison, it's easy to tell what that means – but I'm just visiting, don't jump to conclusions. Still, the heavy door clangs shut behind me, the men in uniform are tall, stiff, no expression on their faces, our footsteps echo as I'm led down the hallway, it's hard to breathe, as if all the oxygen's been used up, sucked up by the men in cages. I can't see them as we walk, but I can hear the sound of their breathing, short, sharp breaths, murmurs. How'm I doing so far?"

"Fine, fine. Pay less attention to me and more to the dream."

"Okay. Wait.... Ah, yes. I'm wearing a long overcoat, long, almost to my shoes, scarf, a bowler hat, all dark. My steps echo, and I look down at my feet.... My shoes are dark but scuffed, unpolished. I hope the guard won't notice, but his eyes are straight on the door we're approaching, he's not looking at me at all. At the door, another guard is sitting, he has a clipboard, a baton, a gun on his hip. He stands up and approaches. I hold my breath. He pats me down, the palms of his hands hard against my ribs, my chest, my hips and thighs. But he doesn't open my coat and we pass safely through his door, Erebus at the gate.... Are you getting all this, Dr. Zelda?"

"I'm listening, Zan. Go on."

"I'm in a big room, tables and chairs, men in striped uniforms, women and children. There's noise, laughter, chairs being scraped back, the crack of a baton on a table when one man hugs his wife too long. I'm at a table with a prisoner, striped pants and shirt and cap, short, like me, heavy shoulders, powerful arms. My bowler hat is on the table. He takes off his cap, places it on the table next to my hat."

"This is your brother? Saul?"

"No, not Saul. Close but no cigar. He takes off his cap and we sit facing each other, looking into a distorted mirror."

"Abe, then."

"Very good, a point for you. You've been paying attention. Abe it is. We sit, talk, our arms on the table. He takes a cigarette from behind his ear. I lean over the table to light it for him. The sulfur of the match is sharp in my nostrils, the smoke burns my eyes, Abe nods his head, sucks on the cigarette.

"I sit back in the chair and begin to unbutton my coat, first at the collar, then down the chest, all the way down the legs to my feet. I hold my arms close in, so the coat doesn't fall open. I slide the scarf off, put it on the table next to the bowler hat. This is all in slow motion, like at a striptease show, something you'd see at Minsky's Burlesque. Abe is saying something, talking to me, but his eyes are across the room, his head is nodding.... Suddenly, there's a commotion. Across the room, a prisoner and his wife are arguing, they're on their feet yelling insults at each other, raising their arms. Everybody looks, the guards go running. Abe and I are on our feet, my coat is thrown off, Abe is pulling it on, we're moving around the table, Abe is buttoning, buttoning, so many buttons, sliding into my seat, his hands nimble over the buttons up his chest, the cigarette still glowing in his mouth. He slips the scarf around his neck, tucks the ends in, fastens the final buttons. I'm sitting calmly where he had been before, striped pants, striped shirt. I put the striped cap on my head. Across the room, the tumult is over, guards are dragging the prisoner away through a door, another guard is escorting the woman through another door, everyone else is sitting down, their conversations resuming. Abe and I stand, we shake hands. He places the bowler on his head, tilting it slightly. He turns to go, stops, puts his hand in the right pocket of the overcoat, takes out a package of cigarettes, hands them to me. Then he goes; the guard opens the door for him, I can hear his footsteps and those of another guard retreating down the long hallway. I pick up the cigarettes, hold them tight in my hand as a guard leads me through a door, down an iron hall ringed with bars, back to the cell I've never before seen."

Zan stopped and closed his eyes. He was silent for a long time, his breath lengthening.

"Are you all right, Zan?"

"Sure I'm all right. Why shouldn't I be?"

"I thought maybe you'd fallen asleep."

"So, why didn't you let me? You said I needed more."

"You're right, I'm sorry."

"Apology accepted."

"That's quite a dream. Very vivid. Are you sure that it's not a memory?"

"Memories that vivid I don't have. I can barely remember what I had for breakfast."

"So this didn't actually happen."

"I didn't say that."

"So it did?"

"That I didn't say either."

"And?"

"And what?"

"And did it happen?"

"Ah...that's the question. You're the one who's supposed to be able to interpret dreams, Zelda. There are enough archetypes in there to keep you busy for awhile."

"Yes, but answer the question."

"Question?"

"Did it happen?"

"Ah...how could it have, Lady Doctor. How could it have? Don't be silly."

THEY SAT IN SILENCE for a minute. Zan coughed, then another minute passed.

"You asked, when we began, if I'd been sleeping. In all honesty, not so good sometimes."

"Ah. *In all honesty*, that's a good turn of phrase. I don't know if I've heard you use it before."

"Maybe not, Dr. Zelda, maybe not."

"So, in all honesty, tell me why you didn't sleep well last night. As an example."

"That's easy. Some nights, I couldn't tell you. Last night, easy. Today's the anniversary of my sister Annie's death. I've mentioned her?"

"Yes."

"Last night, we were in *shul*, Abe and I, for the lighting of her *yahrzeit* candle, the saying of *Kaddish* for her. You remember, I told you about *Kaddish*."

"You did, but you also told me you're an atheist."

"So?"

"So isn't there a contraction in an atheist saying a prayer? A prayer to a god you don't believe in, in aid of getting into a heaven you don't believe in? Or is this you hedging your bets?"

"Ah, very good, Dr. Zelda, you remembered about Pascal. You're smiling, but these are serious questions you're asking. To which I'll put just one simple reply: Life is a contradiction. You live so you can die. Compared to that, all other contradictions are *bupkis*."

"Not much I can say in response to that, Mr. Wiseman. So tell me about your sister."

"Ah, Annie. You ask about contradictions! She had a good life, or so Abe reminds me – we were talking about her last night. A happy childhood, a good husband, lovely children, a pleasant old age and a quick death, another of the famous Wiseman heart attacks. But when I think about her it's always two sorrows that come to mind first."

"Two sorrows – without meaning to denigrate them – in a long, happy life, two sorrows seem not too bad."

"Another contradiction. But you're right. We all have sorrows, but some are worse than others. They cast shadows. She married a good man, but not the man she'd wanted. Who's to say how different her life might have been."

"Yes, but not necessarily for the better."

"You keep trumping me today, Dr. Zelda."

"I know. It's usually the other way around, isn't it? I don't know what's gotten into me. And the other?"

"The other?"

"You said there were two sorrows."

Zan laughed. "Yes, two. Last night, Abe and I argued about which was worse. He said the broken engagement was, but I say if that son of a bitch she was engaged to – excuse my language – would abandon her over something her brothers did, then good riddance to him. What kind of a husband would he have made anyway? No, I say the other was worse.... But now it seems – almost trivial. Just a slight."

"Tell me anyway."

He looked down. "Poor Annie, she was so bright, so smart, she did so good at school, and she had friends, all kinds, she liked everybody, everybody liked her, but one in particular, a Polish girl, Anna. Anne and Anna, one dark, the other, the Polish girl, blonde, with braids, I remember. Two Annies, except Anna was always called that, not Annie, and our Annie was never called Anne, even Mom didn't call her that. Always Annie. The other kids, all the kids but especially the Poles, would tease them: "Annie, Annie, bend over and show your fanny," and sometimes the girls would, a sort of quick half-bend, and then run away, all giggles.

"This girl Anna had polio when she was little, and she died in the influenza in 1919, when she and Annie were eleven or twelve. In between, she was all right, but frail, and if she got a cold, she'd be out of school two weeks. Chicken pox, measles, she didn't do so good with them. Blonde and pretty, but thin, she looked like a waif, and Annie always looked out for her. When she was sick, Annie would go to her house every day after school, on Stella Avenue, just three blocks away but a Polish block, a different world from ours. She'd tell her what they'd learned that day, the gossip, cheer her up. She was there in Anna's house all the time, sick or well, she knew the mother and the brothers, but not the father, he was a blacksmith for the fire department, he was never there in the daytime and Annie didn't go there at night. He was home Saturday, but Annie didn't go there Saturday, because of *shabbos*. Sunday, she would go in the afternoon, if Anna was sick, but the father worked on Sunday, so they never crossed.

"On this day, though, Annie went over there after school and was met by a man in the doorway, a big man, Annie said, with curly yellow hair just like Anna's, a big man in an undershirt with reddish skin and big, thick hands. The boys were around too, Anna's brothers, three or four of them, some older, some younger, Annie knew them all, including one who was in the same grade as she and Anna were because he'd been left back one year. 'Who's this?' the big man asked, not to Annie herself but to the boys.

"'It's just the Jew girl, Anna's friend,' one of the brothers said. That was the first sting, Annie said, this boy referring to her that way, not calling her by name, or just 'Anna's friend,' but 'the Jew girl,' like she was an insect or some piece of dirt."

He looked up. "We boys got that plenty of times, 'Jew boy' and plenty worse, but I think maybe Annie hadn't, she was so sweet and nice and everybody liked her, who would dream of hurting a girl like that?

"'We don't want any Jew girls here,' the father said. Just like that, again, not talking to Annie really, or even looking at her.

"She came home her eyes all puddles, wouldn't say what it was until I wormed it out of her. Abe wanted to go beat the crap out of those Polish boys, and I would have come too. But Saul said no. What, and start a war? So then they and their friends will come and kill us? Not that Saul was afraid of them, their brothers, their father and all the

Polish firemen in Winnipeg – not the Polish army – but he was too smart to be stupid, always was, even if it was him that always got caught, that spent more time in prison than the rest of us put together."

"So you did nothing?"

Zan's laugh was harsh, bitter. "Nothing. That's what sticks in my craw, even after all these years. Annie cried and her brothers didn't do anything about it, not right away, anyway. Again, I didn't do anything."

He'd said the same to Abe the night before.

"Not doing something stupid isn't not doing anything," Abe told him. "And besides, do you think Saul and his gang didn't catch up with them some day when they weren't expecting it? Do you really think there wasn't a time when those brothers of hers went to bed hurting and not knowing why?"

"But that's just it," Zan said. "They didn't know why. So what value was it? What goddamn value?"

"So do you think, even for a minute, it would have made a difference to Annie if somebody got a bloody nose that day?" Abe asked. "If you got a bruised knuckle?"

"Not to her, maybe," he admited, "but it would have made a difference, yes."

"To you, maybe."

"Not to me. Not just to me. God was watching."

"God! You don't believe in God. Remember? It wouldn't have made a difference, believe me."

"You didn't do anything," Zelda echoed him. "It sounds to me like that bothered you more than what happened to your sister."

FROM ZAN'S JOURNAL

Dec. 6, 1988 – There's a man with brothers. How many? How many do you want? Three? Four? Five? Pick a number. The number doesn't count. What counts is there are brothers. A sister or two, too, for good measure. Obligations. Am I my brother's keeper? My sister's? If not me, who? God? Don't make me laugh.... God has problems enough with His own family, *ach*, that son of His....

Dave Margoshes

I'm just doodling. Thinking about this new novel. It's going round and round in my head like the load of laundry I had in the dryer at the laundromat the other day. It's about.... What the hell *is* it about? It's a family history, family arithmetic, yes, a family arithmetic problem, it's about a man with brothers....

And a woman, of course. Always a woman.

CHAPTER 13

December 13, 1988

"WE'VE TALKED ABOUT YOUR MOTHER and your brothers a number of times," Zelda said, "and last week your sister, but I've noticed you only rarely mention your father, usually in passing. Why do you suppose that is?"

She looked a little tired today, Zan thought, endearing dark smudges under her eyes.

"So you *are* a Freudian, Lady Doctor. As I expected. You think I'm a momma's boy."

"That's not what I meant at all."

"Maybe not, maybe yes. It's how it comes out. Even Freudians can have Freudian slips. A nice young woman like you, with so much sex on your mind, it's not healthy."

"Thank you for your analysis, Mr. Wiseman. Should we switch chairs?"

"I'm comfortable here."

"Would you like the notebook and pencil?"

"Notes I never took." He tapped his temple. "In here, I keep notes. Novelists are very observant. That's our nature. Like I observe today that you're wearing dark clothing, your suit is, what, navy blue? Even your stockings – forgive me for looking at your legs – are dark. So what do I deduce from this? Not that you're in mourning, no, nothing as solemn as that, but that you're feeling serious today, you're in a serious mood. I hope nothing is amiss on the home front."

The therapist was smiling, her small, wry smile that Zan found particularly appealing. "No, nothing like that. Nothing amiss at all."

"And yet, your mood is serious. You can't deny that."

"No, I can't."

"And we never forget a detail, we novelists. So when, just to conjecture, next week you're wearing a red dress, a comparison will be inescapable."

"But you complain about your memory...."

"True, true, but I'm a failed novelist, like I already told you. Not the writer I once was, at any rate. Isn't that the problem?"

"I don't know what the problem is. That's what we're trying to find out."

"Very good, Zelda."

"Or if there even *is* a problem."

"Better yet."

"Usually it's a collaborative process."

"Ah, and I'm not collaborating."

"You could be more helpful. Truthfulness is the key to understanding." She smiled.

"Ah, truthfulness. In my line of work, we get to the truth by fabricating."

"I've noticed that's your approach."

"It's not lying, understand that. Just a different way of getting at the truth."

"I understand."

"And who's to say that one way – your way or my way – is better than another?"

"Understood."

"So ask."

"I did. I asked about your father. You novelists are very observant. Without getting sidetracked, what's your observation about him? Why you speak of him so rarely, that is."

"I'll be serious. I don't know. I don't remember him so well, maybe."

"Did you love him?"

"Yes!"

"All right, no ambivalence in that answer."

"No, no ambivalence."

"You mentioned that he died young. Of a heart attack? When was that?"

"Of a heart attack, yes – that's the Wiseman curse. When, I don't remember exactly – during the Depression, for sure. Nothing to do with the Crash – he wasn't one of those stockbrokers who jumped from windows on Wall Street, that I can assure you."

"What sort of a man was he? A professional?"

Zan reared his head back with laughter. "He was a locksmith. I already told you that, I'm sure, so you clearly have no memory for detail. He had his own business, a wagon pulled by a horse, everything he needed in the wagon. So he was a businessman, you could say – a pillar of the business community. Before that, a milkman, he drove a milk wagon for Crescent Creamery for a dozen years or more, different wagon but same horse, same lousy weather, more steady wage. That ended with the strike, 1919. The Winnipeg General Strike, you've heard of it, maybe? After the strike, he lost his job, couldn't find work and we moved to Toronto for a while. That's where he learned about locks, working with a cousin who had his own shop. When we came back to Winnipeg, somehow Pop managed to buy back his same old horse, *Schvarzte*, we called him, Pop loved that horse. This was in the '20s, most businesses that delivered used automobiles by then, but Pop liked the old way. 'What's the hurry?' he'd say. No point calling up if you were locked out – Pop wouldn't get there till the next day. No, he did most of his work for builders putting up new houses or renovating old ones, he'd go to a job and stay there all day. But sometimes there'd be calls – not phone calls, we didn't have a phone till later, but someone would send a boy with a message – and he'd stop by a house in the morning to fix a lock. He used to say he met some very nice women that way, and he'd wink and my mother would get mad.

"He had a few heart attacks before the one that killed him. I forget how many. He was supposed to take it easy for a few months, that's what the doctors said, but he couldn't sit still, so he started doing metalworking from the barn or out in the summer kitchen. He knew how to weld and already had the equipment for that, and he scrounged up a second-hand power grinder and power drill, and started doing small jobs, anything metal someone needed fixing, my dad could probably do it, for a fraction of what it would cost you to buy a new one, like the grate on a coal stove – he fixed I don't know how many of those, for a quarter or fifty cents each. A metal cobbler, he called himself. Then, when he'd start feeling better after a few months, it was back on the wagon he went. He probably made more money from the metal business at home, but he didn't like not being behind a horse part of the day. *A professional!* Abe will get a good laugh on that one."

"Sounds to me like you remember him fairly well."

"Yes and no. The broad strokes, I remember. The fine ones, not so well."

"Well, let's see. Sometimes we remember more than we realize. Was he a gentle man or a hard one?"

"Hard. He was – stern. No nonsense, and took no nonsense from us. One time, I remember, he jumped on a junkman's wagon when he saw him beating his horse, gave him a thump with his fist. 'Your horse is like your wife,' he used to say. 'Take care of her, she'll take care of you.' So did he take good care of his wife? That I don't remember. He didn't run away, the way some husbands do these days, that I can tell you. I can't remember him smiling. He must have, but I don't remember that."

"He was the disciplinarian in the family?"

"He must have been.... I don't remember. Mom – my mother – disciplined us, she was always there. But she would tolerate our nonsense more. Beyond a certain line, then a *frosk* on the *tuchas*, a *frosk* in the *fresser* maybe. Or a swat with the broom in the *tuchas*. Pop – I only remember him hitting me once. A slap in the face, so hard my ears rang for hours after, my teeth ached. You could see the red marks, the shape of his fingers, on my cheek in the bathroom mirror."

"That must have been some slap. What did you do?"

"Before or after?"

"Before. To provoke the slap. Did you deserve it?"

"I don't remember. Something I said, maybe. I think we were at the table. There was no talking back at the table. This was like the round table, Pop was King Arthur. He was supreme. I must have said...something."

"You don't remember?"

"No."

"And afterwards? After the slap? Were you angry? Did you run away from home?"

"I don't remember that either. Run away from home, I did plenty. Later. This time...I don't know. The slap, I remember. Like it was this morning. I can still feel it, on my cheek, right here, in my teeth. Before and after, no."

"What else? What's your one clearest, sharpest memory of your father? The two of you doing something together, maybe?"

Zan rubbed his face, looking down. "I don't...ah. Ha." He paused, eyes still closed. "I'm eight, nine, ten, maybe. Maybe eleven. Twelve maybe even. I can't see myself clearly, just him. He's...I want to say a tall man, but I know he isn't. My own height, five eight or nine. But powerful, his shoulders like a bull, his arms and legs like tree stumps, heavy hands, blunt fingers, broken nails, black and blue – this must be later, when he's a locksmith, when he was a milkman his hands wouldn't be like that. But I've got things mixed up because I was fourteen, fifteen when he went to the locks, and in this memory I'm younger. Anyway, I see him tall, towering over me. Then I see him next to the horse, putting on the harness, and he's not that tall, really, he's small. Powerful. Not a bull, a bulldog.

"I'm eight, nine, ten.... Was it before I was sick or after? I don't remember. Playing hooky from school. I'm under a tarp in the back of the wagon. I hear the jingle of the harness, then the motion of the wagon as we set out. To the dairy first, to load up, then off on his rounds. I hear him singing to the horse. After we're off, I creep out. He yells, sure he yells a lot, but he doesn't hit me, he doesn't send me home. We're only a few blocks away, he could. He lets me sit up front, beside him on the seat like a man, lets me hold the reins. This I remember."

HE WAS ELEVEN, ACTUALLY, not as young as he remembers, the year after his year lost to sickness, the year after Adam's death. For a long time, everyone had treated him as if he were made of glass, but he was better now, and gradually things had returned to normal. There was a hole where Adam had been, everyone seemed to tiptoe around it, like a hole in the ice you had to be careful not to fall through yourself. There had been a hole even larger where Saul and Hersh had been, but that was different somehow – the older brothers were away, fighting the Huns, but there was no thought that either or both of them might not come back. In fact, on this particular day, Hersh was already dead, Saul wounded, in the fierce battles around Vimy Ridge, but the family had not yet been informed.

He hadn't meant to stay away from school that day, though he did do that often enough. Sometimes, he and Abe would run off together, spontaneously – they'd leave for school with good intentions, their lunches and books under their arms, walk a block west on Flora Avenue toward Aberdeen School, then whoever had the idea would nudge the other, they'd look at each other and burst into gales of laughter, double back through the lane to drop their books off in the barn, under a loose board. Then they'd be off, and, depending on the season and weather, fishing in the Red River off a pier at Point Douglas they liked or playing ball or pitching pennies in front of the pool hall on Main where Saul and Hersh had sometimes worked before the war, or sledding on the riverbank at St. John's Park. This day was different.

He was awoken by a something, not likely a sound what with Abe snoring in the bunk above him – just the two of them now rattling around in a bedroom that once held five – and he lay in a fuzzy world between sleep and waking for a moment, staring up into the darkness, words starting to come to him out of the nebula, taking shape, "He lay in the darkness...." He smiled with pleasure at his agility and rolled over, grasping at the edges of sleep, but now a new sound attracted him, a creaking beyond the door, from the kitchen. Opening his eyes again, and craning his neck, he saw the slice of light under the door and knew his father was up. Though he had never shared his father's morning, he knew its movements: stoking the stove, the rattle of the coal shovel, heating water for tea and shaving, the latter effected over a basin next to the sink, the water gradually turning black and white from the swished-around razor. He thought now he heard the steady *thwop* of the razor on the leather strap, and in the story he was beginning to write in his head the man lathered his face, lifted the razor, its edge glinting in the light thrown haphazardly from the flickering kerosene lantern. The story raced ahead, faster than a real man could accomplish these simple feats: towelling off of the face, pouring the tea, breaking off a heel of bread from the dark loaf on the counter, slicing an onion in half – this, he knew, was what his father liked to breakfast on – and before his father could have sipped half his glass the man in the story was outside in the foot-stamping cold, slipping the harness on the horse, lifting himself into the wagon, unaware of the muffled shape behind him, snapping the reins against the horse's flanks, setting off....

Zan scrambled out of bed and fumbled into his clothes as quietly as he could. In the darkness, he could barely make out the shape of his brother sprawled across his narrow mattress, one arm hanging through the railing, his feet protruding slightly beyond the reach of mattress and blankets of his bunk. Zan's heart battered against his chest as Abe half rose in his bunk, a string of unintelligible words spilling from his mouth, but his eyes remained closed and he lay down again immediately. Zan pressed his ear against the door, listening, breath half held, until the crack of yellow glow at his feet suddenly extinguished and he heard the creaking of the outer door.

He opened the bedroom door and slinked through, holding his breath as he closed it behind him. Then he threw off caution and raced to the entrance hall, threw on his jacket and boots, not bothering with the laces, and was out in the bracing night air, blood pounding in his temples. The sky was completely dark except for a sprinkling of stars and a heel of moon hanging low to the west, and Zan knew it would be another hour or more before there was even a faint glow diffusing the darkness to the east, toward Main Street and the river. He stood by the side of the house for a minute until his eyes adjusted to the darkness, enough to allow him to see the vague, looming shape of the barn. It was late April, more than two months past his eleventh birthday, the air cool but heavy with the sharp scent of pollen and damp earth. He raced toward the barn, where he could hear Schvartze stamping in his stall, and, as he drew closer, his father's voice, cooing to the horse. The wagon stood beside the barn, so solid a mass of horizontal planes and circular shapes it was hard to imagine that it could move, no matter how many horses were attached.

The horse was his father's own, but the wagon was provided, for a monthly fee deducted from wages, by the dairy. It was heavy-duty, built to carry weight, with spoked wheels almost as tall as Zan was, and covered over with a wooden superstructure, the shape and size of a small house, and white tarpaulin emblazed with the large slogan "Crescent Creamery" and, in only slightly smaller type, "Pure Milk Supply." His father would first drive it to the dairy, in Point Douglas, and load it with cases of glass milk bottles, then start in on his rounds. Zan leapt over the wheel into the rear wagon bed, this playground as familiar to him as the floor of the kitchen or the boys' room, and slid himself under the tarp at the very back, his shoulders up against a crate of empty bottles, careful not to set off a riff of tinkling. The wagon was redolent with the rich odour of sour milk. Then he waited.

He heard the jingling of the harness and the heavy clomp of the horse's hooves, his father's muffled voice. Then the wagon lurched forward and back, stilled, and he felt his father's weight climbing up and settling in the seat. His father called to the horse and they lurched forward again, the wheels pulling free from the mud's grasp with a kissing sound that made Zan smile in his suffocating tent. He squeezed his nose to keep himself from sneezing. "Across the moors, they rode," he dictated, the brooding, rolling landscapes of *Wuthering Heights* and *The Hound of the Baskervilles,* both of which he'd read during his long period of confinement the previous year, vying for his attention. He lifted a flap of canvas, exposing the wagon's rear gate, and watched the trail of hoofprints and wheel ruts freshly cut in the mud of the lane roll out behind them like slow motion film as his father sang to the horse like he'd never heard him sing to his mother, telling her in Yiddish what a good girl she was, how soft her coat, how beautiful. Zan grinned into the ghostly light of the shopworn moon.

The swaying motion of the wagon, the steady *clip-clop* of the horse's hooves first on mud, then pavement, gave added weight to the tarp, and to his eyelids, and he was almost instantly asleep, but for less than a minute. He was awoken by a jarring, the rim of a crate prodding his ribs as the wagon wheels rattled over a pothole. He lifted up the tarp and peered out. They were on King Street, plodding along south, toward the market at Dufferin Avenue. He took a deep breath and scrambled out of his secure cave and through the interior of the wagon, and stuck his head out through the tarp directly behind where his father sat. "Hi, Pop."

His father – he remembered this now as if it had been filmed in slow motion – turned his bullet head, the hair still damply slick along the contours of his skull beneath his cap, and the expression of surprise etched across his eyes and mouth flickered between amusement and anger, then turned to amusement again. He wore the dairy's regulation white shirt over a grey wool sweater, and a black leather apron over it all.

"Abraham?" he said, pronouncing the Hebrew name, "what are you doing here?"

"It's Zan, Pop. Not Abe, Zan. I wanted to come help you today," he said in Yiddish. "I hope you don't mind."

"Zan." The expression continued to flicker, as if the mind behind it was uncertain of how to respond, how it felt. "Where's your brother?"

"He's...he's still in bed, Pop. Or just getting up. I'm on my own. I did this on my own."

His father continued to gaze at him, confident in the horse's ability to find its own way. "To show me what a man you are?"

"That was Abe, Pop. I just.... I just wanted...."

"You think I need help, is that it? You think I can't lift crates of milk bottles any more?"

"No, that's not it, Pop, I...."

"You think, maybe, I need help making change? That I can't do my sums any more?"

"No, Pop, that's..."

"You think maybe I need help with the reins? That *Schvartze* won't listen to me any more?"

"Pop, I just wanted to be with you, that's all."

There was a long silence and when he looked up, he saw his father's lips turned up, the eyes so black they sucked in moonlight rather than reflecting it, and his hand was raised. It hovered in the air and the slap his father had given him only three weeks before tingled on his face again.

"I'm a man," Abe had said, pushing away his father's rough face.

"A man? Not even *bar mitvzah*, and he's a man? Chaika, you heard that? Already this one's too big for his father's birthday kiss. Thirteen, that's when you'll be a man. One more year."

"Today," Abe had insisted, switching to English. "Zannie, ain't that right? Ain't I a man today?" But Zan had been silent, turning away, and when the slap came, it was with complete surprise; Abe had disappeared, and it was Zan's face their father's hand landed on, not his brother's, it was his alone, not for them to share.

"Pop," he'd protested, "it wasn't me. I never...." but his father was already walking away, his shoulders hunched and rolled, his mother was in the kitchen, Abe gone, Saul and Hersh not there to defend him, Annie disappeared, he was alone with the ringing in his ear, the burning, the sudden, absolute sense of despair and rage – and confusion: had his father really mistaken him for Abe? Or was his choice deliberate, some secret message from father to son it now fell upon Zan to decipher?

Now, the hand raised in the glinting moonlight again was for him alone, but it landed on his face with the softness of comfort, stroking his cheek for a moment, then sliding off, up his brow, where it tousled his hair, and on, landing on his shoulder, where it perched and stayed. The silence continued but, after a moment, his right hand still on Zan's shoulder, his father passed the reins from his left hand into the boy's smaller ones. The thin leather felt cool and dry in his warm, damp hands, comfortable. His skin, wherever his father's hand had passed – cheek, forehead, scalp, shoulder – tingled, but it was his heart that battered against his ribs in protest, calling out in pain.

"That's all you remember?" Zelda asked again, her voice rising slightly.

"What? Oh, yes. That's all I remember. The wagon, the tarp, the rear end of the horse swaying in front of me, the reins." He looked up, grinning. "That's all, Lady Doctor. It's not enough?"

Dolly, darling, Ana sends you hugs, kisses, all her love. I talked to her yesterday.

I've told Ana all about Zan, several times, "your uncle's here, actually moved here, he asked about you," but she has little interest. Who can blame her, she hardly knows him.

Of course, Dolly, she always asks about you, how are you doing, sends her love, but when I ask her when she might be coming for a visit, she changes the subject. The last time we talked, she said maybe for *Chanukah* – well, a Christmas break she gets from work, but no, not this year. Maybe in the summer she'll come, she says. I know, I shouldn't nag, she has a life of her own, and...it's hard. That I know, believe me.

What worries me more than anything, Dolly, is that I'll die before you, that Ana won't move back here, that you'll have no one to visit with.

I asked Zannie if he'd come by and he promised he would. He surprised me – swore he'd be as faithful as I am, that's the word he used, "faithful," that he'd come every day.

"You can die in peace knowing that, Benchy," he says, "not that I'm saying you should die."

"I know that," I tell him. "What, and miss out on your company now that you're here?"

It's good that Zannie's here – I'm glad he is, pain in the *tuchas* that he is. He's my brother, my only brother left, and what good is family if you're not there for each other? And it's a comfort to know that he would come to visit you, even if he *doesn't* come every day – I *could* die in peace, like he says. Zannie is not the most reliable man in the world, this you know, Dolly, but I think he'll be true to his word on this. Faithful.

I'm ashamed to say I haven't always been faithful, Dolly. No, not in the way you might think, although that too, but a man has needs, you know that, you wouldn't begrudge me, I'm sure of that.

But sometimes – is anyone listening? No. Sometimes, Dolly, I can't help thinking that you would be better off dying –

not me, I don't think that. Coming to visit, to see you, that is not something I begrudge, believe me. But you. Lying here all these years and who knows what goes on in your head. The doctor tells me you might hear, that I should talk to you, and if you hear, then who's to say that you don't understand, that you don't remember. God forbid that you should have to lie here day after day with nothing but your memories. No, even the God who let six million of His own people die, who lets innocent people die every day, who lets children suffer – even that God couldn't be that cruel, of that I'm certain.

But what if He is?

What if you do remember, that terrible, cruel burden? The terrible things Momma said to you, though she came to love you. Those years with me in prison, those years when I was in the war, those years when I was in the POW camp, all those years alone, waiting. Then your sickness, losing the use of your legs, tied to a wheelchair, now a bed. Losing Benjy. Ana – I might as well say it, it's no secret – her indifference. It's not even anger – if she was angry at us, okay, I wouldn't know why, but maybe I could do something different so she wouldn't be, maybe even I could beg her forgiveness.

But no, she's not angry at me, at you – she just...doesn't care. She doesn't care. And who knows why? She probably doesn't know herself. If you asked her, she'd deny it, say "Oh, Dad," the way she does.

But that's the way it is.

It's hard, hard to accept, Dolly, but so much more for you it must be than for me. If you know, and I think you must. A mother knows when her daughter doesn't come, no matter how deep the coma.

So yes, I admit it, Dolly, sometimes I think of your death, even wish for it. In that way, I'm faithless, because doesn't God tell us that life is everything?

And it is, I believe it is.

Still, some things are too much to bear. Even God knows that. Memory, that's one of them, for sure.

CHAPTER 14

December 20, 1988

FROM ZAN'S JOURNAL

Dec. 20, 1988 – Thinking more about this novel. I keep typing pages, crumpling them up and tossing them away. Another fresh page, another ball of crumpled-up paper. Soon I'll need my own tree.

But some pages get saved. Gradually, something is starting to take shape.

Brothers, a woman, a robbery, a gun.

Something. That's something.

LATE IN DECEMBER, the streets he passed along all decked out in inexplicably cheering Christmas finery, and having woken with an idea and scribbled a few words before breakfast, Zan was looking pleased with himself when he arrived at Zelda's office, and she remarked on it.

"I've started work on a new novel, if you can believe it," he told her. "Well, not work, exactly. Work toward work. A new year coming, why not a new novel?"

"That's an excellent attitude, Zan. Anything is possible...although I didn't mean that the way it might sound, like the idea is so far-fetched. Anything *is* possible, for you and anyone else. It's a matter of making up your mind."

"So *you* say. Easier said than done, I say. Still, I guess I made up my mind. Oh, and my typewriter arrived finally. I wrote to the storage place weeks ago asking them to send it."

"Maybe you should think about getting a computer. It makes it easier, doesn't it?"

"That's what I've heard. But I'll stick with my old Underwood. I've used it for sixty years." Unpacking it the other day, he couldn't help thinking the typewriter should be in a museum somewhere. The University of Nevada had offered to buy his papers, and the typewriter could go with them, but he'd declined. The universities of Manitoba or Winnipeg would be a more suitable home, but he hadn't heard from them.

"Well, good for you," Zelda said. "And this novel – you're happy about it? Will it make you happy?"

"Happy, *shmappy*. Who knows from happy? I'm a writer, I write. Is a fish happy because it swims? No, it doesn't know anything else."

"Yes, but if you take the fish out of the water, it gets pretty unhappy."

"You're right about that, Lady Doctor. Touché for you."

"I asked you another time, I believe, what could happen that would make you happy, remember?"

"The question I remember, not my answer."

"You didn't answer. So how would you answer today?"

Zan laughed. "Another woman asked me a question like that once: 'What would make you happy?' Or maybe it was, 'If you had one wish, what would it be?' Or maybe something as simple as, 'What would you like for a graduation present?' Well, however it was put, it wasn't just a rhetorical question, I knew that. This was a very generous woman – not that there wasn't always an ulterior motive behind every gift. I said – and I didn't have to think about it, I knew – 'the time to write a novel. No pressure, no other things to do, just sweet time.'"

"'Okay,' she said, 'move in.' It was that simple. They have nowadays, the Canada Council, you know about this?"

"I think so."

"It gives grants to writers, not just writers, artists, all kinds, to give them time. I had my own personal Canada Council."

It really had been that simple, or nearly. He had just been kicked out of the University of Manitoba, a guilt-by-association thing in which he actually was innocent that time. He'd been a thorn in the university's side almost from the beginning, leafleting and helping to organize rallies for the Communists, on campus, but he had a scholarship and Luna's support, which carried a surprising amount of weight – Luna McGowan, professor of English, someone any university administrator would think twice about before offending. Still, the fact that he was Jewish didn't help either, and a couple of times someone from the Jewish students' group had begged him to tone down his activities. "It makes us all look bad," one fellow had told him, to which Zan had made a rude reply. Now the trouble Abe and his other brothers were in with the law was enough to tip the balance. He wasn't actually expelled, as he liked to boast – that brazen the university wasn't – but an excuse was found to withdraw his scholarship, and even Luna was unable to intervene. But she came to his rescue in a different way.

Although he spent most of his nights during the school year at Luna's apartment near the campus, he'd returned to his parents' home for the summers, and as his third year began, he remained there, unsure, as he usually felt, where he stood with Luna. Now, he moved permanently into her apartment on Balmoral Street. She'd been his mentor and constant supporter for more than three years and they'd been occasional lovers throughout that time. There were no other women in Zan's life, he was immune to the pretty girls on the campus, and if there were other men in Luna's life, and he suspected there were, he didn't want to know about them. But this was something different: he packed a suitcase she'd bought him, put the typewriter she'd given him three years earlier into its case and put a few books and other things into some boxes, and Abe drove him over from Flora Avenue in the battered old truck he and Saul used in their cartage business, the logo "Wiseman Brothers" emblazoned on its side following a giant, stylized W. Both boys were living at home then, Annie too, still unmarried and going to teacher's college, so it was a relief to get rid of him, Abe said, providing a little more room. All of them, as well, with the exception of Zan, were working and helping out financially since their father's most recent heart attack, even Annie, who had a part-time job downtown at Eaton's, so Zan could leave with a clear mind. "Go, go," Abe exhorted him, "*gay avek*. Who needs you around here? Go write your novel, wear a beret, be an *artiste*."

That didn't stop him from cautioning Zan on the drive over, though. "You sure you know what you're doing, Pantsy? A *shiksa*, older, an *Englisher*...."

"You're a fine one to talk, the women you take up with ain't exactly rabbis' daughters."

"No, but I keep my eyes open, Zannie, I'm no dreamer like you," Abe said, and his scepticism deepened as they turned onto Balmoral, with its tall canopied buildings.

Luna had made space in the closets and dressers. "This is your home now," she said, "I mean your real home, not just a dormitory," and led him into a room she'd had renovated into an office, with a large oak desk. Together they placed the typewriter on it and took it out of its case, as if it were a sacred chalice, placing it squarely on a large green blotter. Zan took a deep breath. When he'd first enrolled at the university, it was housed downtown, mostly in the Wesley College and Manitoba College buildings on Portage Avenue, just a five-minute walk from Luna's apartment. They'd often run home for lunch, or to make love. But now, with the university having moved most of its operations to its new campus in Fort Garry, a drive of half an hour or more, Luna was spending more time in her office there, almost all day most days, so Zan really would have the apartment to himself. He looked around him. Although the surroundings were extremely familiar, he felt as if a new phase of his life was beginning.

"This may take a while," he said.

"Take as long as you want," Luna said, and it occurred to him that she'd have been happy if he'd never finished, taken forever.

"This is what you've wanted all along, isn't it?"

She laughed that effervescent, tinkling laugh he loved, music over ice. "I couldn't very well have one of my students living with me, now could I?"

"I don't think I've stopped being your student," Zan said.

"Well, let me teach you something right now."

They came together, Zan's hip sharp up against the edge of the desk, one arm around her, the other by his side, his fingers caressing the smooth oak.

That moment, and the weeks and months that followed, while he was writing *Wise Men*, were, he thought now, the one time of his life when he really had been happy, day after day.

"OKAY, LET ME ASK YOU SOMETHING SIMILAR," Zelda intruded. "Do you recall what your ambitions were when you were young, what your goals were?"

"You ask too easy questions. A child can answer them." Zan took a sip of water from the cup she always offered. "Sure, I wanted this, I wanted that, anything I put my eyes on, just like a child. Breakfast in the morning, supper at night. No bedtime, and if there is a bedtime, a goodnight kiss."

"How about when you were a bit older?"

"Older? How old? One of my ambitions was to live to be a hundred. Now I'm almost there, I'm not so sure it's a good idea."

"Why did you want to live to be a hundred?"

"I had a lot I wanted to do. I figured it would take me that long, at least."

"Have you done them? Most of them? Some?"

Zan laughed. "I got a start on some of them. Just a start."

"You wrote the novel, the one you finished, published. You did that."

"When you're a writer, you don't ever want to write just one novel."

"You had love affairs."

"Those I had plenty. But what did I do with them?"

"What *did* you do with them?"

"Ha. Now you ask the tough questions. What did I do with them, indeed?"

"And?"

Zan took a good look at Zelda. What the hell, why not?

"All my life I've had good women wanting to take care of me. First my mother, may her soul rest in peace, and my sister Annie – may *her* soul rest in peace – good women both of them. Then I go directly from the bosom of my family to the somewhat bony bosom of a university professor. That was Luna. If I am anything today, whatever it is I am, it's that woman's doing. I end my life – well, my life up till now, there might still be a bit more worthy of note – with another professor, a somewhat more ample bosom, again taking care of me, trying to make me into somebody. This is Myrna. Along the way, another good woman, Rose, my wife.

"You know, it's funny, in the grass-is-greener department maybe, when I was with Rose, I was happy enough, but sometimes I thought back to my time with Luna and I thought, 'ah, I was happier then.' Then, years later, with Myrna, and I was certainly happy with her, as I told you, I think, I thought back to my time with Rose, maybe not thinking I'd been happier, but wistfully, at least. With regrets, certainly.

You're the psychologist, Miss Zelda, is this human nature, to think back like this?"

"To wish you were with someone else? It's certainly a common thing, Mr. Wiseman. And who are you thinking back wistfully about now?"

"Ah, now, now I'm thinking of them all, missing Myrna, that would be natural, wouldn't it? Dead just a few months. Have I mentioned how my Myrna loked like Bette Davis, in her prime? And how she always smelled of lilacs?"

Zelda merely smiled as an answer.

"And Rose, still wistful, and with regret. Ten years dead her, I think, something like that. No chance of making amends there."

"Not amends, no. There's always a chance of coming to terms, though. Making peace with yourself. And Luna?"

"Luna? I think of her, sure. I think of her all the time, I don't mind admitting it. I have to laugh. It's over fifty years, I don't even know if she's alive or dead, where she might be if she is alive. She was older than me, I forget how much, so probably she isn't."

He shook his head, laughed. "All these women. All looking after me. And now, Lady Doctor, you, another good woman, wanting to take care of me. Some charm I got, eh?"

"And you don't deserve all this good fortune, is that what you're implying, Mr. Wiseman?"

"We all deserve what we get, Dr. Zelda."

"The good and the bad?"

"The good we earn. The bad we earn too, in reverse. Then there's luck. We deserve the luck we get too. But some things it's best to leave to God, even if you don't believe in Him."

Zelda made a note. When she looked up, she was smiling again.

"Tell me about the new novel. What's it about?"

"About?"

"Is it a love story, about growing old? About two brothers, maybe? What?"

"I'm an authority on all those topics. It's about – I'll tell you the title, you can surmise what it's about. This morning, I wrote out *God Blinked*."

"That's the title?"

"You don't like it?"

"It's fine. And what can I surmise from it?"

"Well, you know God has his eye even on the sparrow. The Bible says that, no?"

"Yes. So?"

"Well..."

"Ah, I see. But even God has to blink. And then what?"

"Then what? If I'd known there was going to be an exam today, I wouldn't have come. Then what? You ask the tough questions. Okay, you know this joke? God creates the world. Eve screws up, so He kicks her and the boyfriend out of Eden. Cain screws up, God marks him. Abraham is tempted, so God tests him. Job has troubles, he complains, so God sends him even worse troubles. Then there's Sodom and Gomorrah. God says enough's enough, He brings on the rain, and lets Noah save just enough that life can go on. But then, God says 'never again.' He won't meddle any more, He'll let nature take its *own* course, notwithstanding that He created nature. Just the same, He'll back away and see what happens. So, man goes his own way, there's sickness, war, famine, ignorance, pogroms, the Holocaust, AIDS, you name it. Eventually, *nuclear* holocaust, everything's *kaput*, burnt to a cinder. God turns to St. Peter and says, 'Tch, you look away for a second....'"

Zelda laughed and jotted something on her pad. He could never be sure whether her laughter was genuine or mere politeness, a practiced clinical gesture. "So your novel is about – can I put it this way? – the willfulness of mankind."

"Bingo. Mrs. Dr. Freud you are today. I couldn't put it better myself."

"And how do you fit into this scenario?"

"How do I fit? I'm supposed to know the answer to that? This is what I'm writing the novel for, Dr. Zelda: to find out. Ask me in a few months, a year better. Maybe I'll have a glimpse."

"And what brought on this outburst of creativity?"

"Oh, now you're making fun? That's ethical behaviour? Should I be reporting you to someone? A man comes to your office, pours out his heart, unburdens himself, reveals his weaknesses, then you stick it to him – this is therapy?"

"I'm sorry if you think that, Mr. Wiseman."

"Well, you know I don't. But I could, so watch yourself. This outburst

Dave Margoshes

of creativity, it's not that much of a deal, actually. I've started lots of novels over the years, as I think I may have mentioned. It's the sticking with them that's tough, the finishing them – that's the $64,000 question. Still, this one may be different."

"And why is that?"

"Why? A new year approaching, as I said. Isn't that a good enough reason?"

"Maybe it is."

"And I'm in a new place. Maybe that's another. Talking to you is part of it too – it churns up all sorts of old stuff, stuff I thought I'd forgotten but, it turns out, I merely mislaid. Beyond that, I don't know. Well, maybe I do. Today I was thinking about dying. I've been thinking about it."

Zelda gave him a look. "Oh? Are you not feeling well?"

"I'm feeling fine. But who's kidding who? I'm eighty-two years old, I'll be eighty-three soon. I'm not the man I was, and I never was all that much of a man – but I was what I was, I'm not arguing that. Everybody I ever loved and most of the people I've known are dead, with the sole exception of my brother Abe, which is the sole reason why I'm here in this cowboy town, no offence, your lovely little city. So soon it'll be my turn. I woke up thinking that. Not that it's any secret."

"And how did you feel about it? How *do* you feel?"

"Feel, *shmeel*. What's to do? You can't cheat the Ragman."

"Pardon?"

"Oh, it's something my father used to say. Look, I lie awake watching the light come through my window. My head's either filled with thoughts bouncing off each other like pinballs, or empty, a complete blank. It doesn't make a difference. Either way, sooner or later, I get around to one solid thought: Why me? Even the way I am now, with half my brain in mothballs, I still have more going on up there than most people. So I haven't written a novel in over fifty years. Who's to say I won't? And Hitler I'm not, not even Mussolini. My point is, why should I die when there are so many others less worthy – or more worthy, depending on your point of view. But my father always said, you can't get someone to stand in for you when the Street Cleaner comes, the Ragman. You understand?"

"Death."

"Death, of course – except not *Death* Death, this disembodied... thing, this abstract idea, no, I mean Death the Angel of Death, the Street Cleaner, the Ragman, this fellow with a wisecrack and cold hands who invites you out for a stroll and a cup of coffee. Emily Dickinson – you know that poet? She called him the Gentleman Caller. When he comes, you can't say no, you can't even say maybe. No 'not tonight dear, I have a headache.' He throws a pebble at your window, you go."

"And this led you to start a new novel how?"

"Ah, again with the tough questions, Madame Zelda. I'll tell you, this is how. So the Ragman comes to your window, he tosses a pebble. You poke your head out, see who it is. You know you've got to go, but still...it's worth a chance. 'I'm in the middle of a good book,' you tell him. 'Just let me finish this chapter.' Or maybe you're more modern, you're watching TV. 'Wait till the commercials,' you say."

"Are you thinking about death a lot?" Zelda asked after a pause.

"I'm thinking about death not at all. If anything, it's Death thinking about me, that's the worry. Like I said."

He turned his head and glanced at the clock on the wall over his shoulder. "I won't see you for a few weeks, that right?"

"Yes, we're closed over the holidays."

"So, just so you won't forget me, I'd like to tell you a story. That okay?"

Zelda was smiling. "I don't think there's much chance of my forgetting you. But certainly, go ahead. What sort of story?"

"Listen, Lady Doctor, you'll hear. It's something from my novel. My old novel, I mean, *Wise Men of Chelm*. You haven't read it, have you?"

"No, I mean to, but not yet."

"But you expressed interest, I think, so...may I?"

"Yes, please, go ahead."

YEARS AGO – I MEAN HUNDREDS OF YEARS – in Spain, there was agitation against the Jews. You may have heard something about it. There were too many of them, they were too good at what they did, their scholars too smart, their businessmen too rich. People were jealous. People complained to their priests, priests to the bishops, the bishops

Dave Margoshes

to the archbishop and eventually the complaints went all the way to Rome, to the cardinals and the Pope. People also complained to the representatives of the royal court and news of this upset reached the ear of the King, who consulted his advisers. While they were dithering about this matter of state, the cardinals and archbishops in Rome were putting their heads together and they came up with the idea of an inquisition: they'd give the Jews the chance to convert, to turn over their wealth – most of it to the church but some to the King – and promise to lead good Christian lives of humility and piety – and those that refused, well, they'd just kill those few ingrates, and who could object to that?

They took this plan to the Pope and he agreed it seemed like a good solution, a Christian solution: the choice would be theirs. "It's important," the Pope said, "that there be no pressure. Let them make up their own minds. We're not barbarians, after all. We're Christians and must do the Christian thing."

The cardinals and archbishops nodded their heads in agreement. The king of Spain was notified, and he and his court also agreed that this was a reasonable solution. Very reasonable – who could object? Everyone agreed that's the way it should be.

But the Pope was a cautious man. Before he gave his approval, the Pope prayed for guidance and God spoke to him, speaking just two words: "Remember Moses."

Remember Moses? What could that mean? The Pope couldn't very well ask God for clarification. He pondered this peculiar message from God and discussed it with his most trusted prelates, and they decided the Pontiff should travel to Barcelona and Seville and examine the situation for himself. The king was merely the king, after all, but the Pope was God's man and he couldn't afford to make a mistake.

So he did. He travelled by carriage, in a convoy of carriages, north through Italy, across France and down the Mediterranean coast of Spain, and he arrived in due course, after many wearying days, in Barcelona, where he conferred with the archbishop and the bishops, and he went out into the countryside and conferred with the priests, and wherever he went, he put on the robes of a simple priest himself and said Mass and heard confessions, and always he heard from the lips of the parishioners this complaint about the Jews. They were pushy. They were greedy. They were too clever. Their women were seductresses.

And there was ample evidence of their terrible blood rituals, involving Christian children, virgins and other innocents. It would be good riddance to be rid of them, that was certain. But still the echo of God's simple message to him rang in the Pope's ear: "Remember Moses." And because he was a pious man, and anxious that there be no mistakes, no mistake at all, the idea came into the Pope's head that he should confer as well with a Jew. Moses, after all, had been a Jew, and this reminded the Pope that Jesus too was a Jew, as had been all of His original disciples. The Pope didn't want to make a mistake, and perhaps a Jew could shed some light on God's enigmatic message. Who better to ask about Moses than one of Moses's people? Not just any Jew, though, but a Jew who could speak with authority for all of his brethren, just as the Pope himself spoke for all of Christendom.

So an invitation was sent out to the Chief Rabbi of Barcelona to come to the cathedral and meet with the Pope. The Chief Rabbi was no fool – the Jews well knew the complaints about them and already word had filtered back from Rome as to what was being contemplated – and he realized that the fate of Iberian Jewry was on his head, that the conversation he would have with the Pope would be the most significant exchange in the history of the Jews perhaps since Moses consulted with God – ah, there's Moses again. One wrong word on his part, and the darkness would descend – but, should he acquit himself skillfully and cleverly, perhaps disaster could be averted.

The Chief Rabbi knew all this, and he also knew he wasn't up to the task. He was an old man and he was no longer completely in possession of all his faculties. He would have liked very much to send the First Assistant Chief Rabbi, the Chief Rabbi's trusted confidant, to go in his stead, but the First Assistant had contracted malaria and was too ill. The Second Assistant Chief Rabbi, a cunning man who had gone far on his abilities with language, would have been the next logical choice, but he too was indisposed – he had fallen from the roof of the synagogue and broken his leg in several places; he lay in bed now, in excruciating pain should he move even an inch. The Third Assistant was a brilliant young man but had a speech impediment, making him all but impossible to understand; the Fourth Assistant had a similar problem: he was brilliant, and fluent in both Hebrew and Spanish, but could speak not a word of Latin or Italian. And so it went down the line, exhausting first the remainder of the assistant chief rabbis and then the ordinary rabbis of Barcelona and the surrounding towns: all were indisposed, unavailable, afflicted or, quite frankly, insufficient. Not all of the rabbis of Spain were as brilliant as they should have been, alas. There were a few possible choices in Seville, but it would take too long to send word there and for the candidates to come to Barcelona. What to do? The Pope was awaiting a reply.

Word came to the Chief Rabbi that there was visiting, in an out-lying village, a certain rabbi from the town of Chelm, in Poland, who was known for his wit and his willingness. Even in Barcelona, the fame of Chelm as a community of fools was well known, and a rabbi who could preside over such a flock was clearly a man of some talents. And, as if to underscore the appropriateness of this man for this particular assignment – almost as if God Himself were guiding the hand of the Chief Rabbi – the rabbi of Chelm was reputed to be well versed in Latin, a skill he had apparently learned at the knee of his predecessor and mentor, who had learned it from his predecessor and so on, down through the centuries dating back to the first refugees from the Holy Roman Empire to reach Chelm. In fact, in Chelm, where knowledge of Hebrew was weak, the reading of the weekly portion of the Talmud was done in Latin.

The Chief Rabbi sent a messenger to fetch this man.

The rabbi of Chelm, whose name was Yonkle Schmegegge, was honoured to receive such an invitation – the Chief Rabbi of Barcelona! – and quickly presented himself. "What can I do for you, *rebbe?* Ask anything."

The Chief Rabbi briefly explained the mission: to break bread with the Pope of Rome who had asked, the Chief Rabbi said, being perhaps just a bit duplicitous, to confer with a typical Spanish Jew.

"I'll be happy to comply," the rabbi of Chelm said, "but I feel I must point out – though surely the Chief Rabbi already knows this – that I am hardly a typical Spanish Jew."

The Chief Rabbi recognized in his Polish colleague a man of humility who could be trusted with this mission. "Oh?" he inquired. "And are the Jews of Chelm so different from the Jews of Barcelona? Any better?"

The rabbi of Chelm was indeed sharp-witted and he saw at once that he was cornered; moreover, his sense of duty and his willingness were strong. And so, with that, the matter was settled. Word was sent to the cathedral that a delegate from the synagogue would arrive promptly at noon the following day to lunch with the Pope.

And sure enough, on the next day, just before noon, Rabbi Schmegegge arrived at the cathedral, alone, and riding a jackass, which he had borrowed from his host in the small outlying village. The rabbi's host, I should mention, was a distant relative of his wife's, and the host's own wife, a pious woman who knew it was unlikely that kosher food would be available at the cathedral, had prepared a lunch for the rabbi, a leather sack containing a simple meal of black bread, celery and radishes, salt herring and a hard-boiled egg, with hot – now warm – tea with lemon in a glass jar, wrapped in a rag.

The rabbi was ushered through the halls of the cathedral, into the basement – it was felt it would be inappropriate to host a Jew on the cathedral's main floor – and into a large, lushly furnished room lit by both torches and candles. A long, narrow table covered with a lace-trimmed linen cloth was set for twenty at least, with fine china, linen napkins, silver cutlery, cut glass. The rabbi was greeted by the Pope himself, who was surrounded by several cardinals and all the archbishops and bishops of Spain as well as a number of functionaries of the Vatican and the king's own Special Adviser for Religious Matters and the Spanish ambassador to the Vatican. Other than the ambassador and the special adviser, there were no other representatives of the king present, as this was considered, as of now, to be a religious matter, for the Church to settle, not the State. Whatever was decided here by the Pope would be accepted by the King.

The Pope, who had already been apprised that his guest would not be the Chief Rabbi of Barcelona, but his special emissary, took a moment to size up the simple man who appeared before him in a shabby dark suit, its lapels and elbows shiny, its cuffs frayed, wearing shoes bound with rags and twine and a hat one size too large. This emissary was indeed special, he could see, and the Pope's guard was raised to its highest, all his senses at razor pitch so as to miss nothing. This rabbi was clearly a formidable man, but the Pope was confident he could best him.

"Welcome," the Pope said. "I am honoured to have your company." He spoke in a Hebrew that was grammatically correct but heavily accented.

"It is I who am honoured," Rabbi Schmegegge responded in flawless Latin, tainted by just an echo of a Polish accent. "I am your servant, as I am God's, to the best of my abilities."

The Pope was momentarily taken aback by the rabbi's command of Latin and his mention of his relationship with God – was this a subtle reference to Moses? – but he extended his ringed hand for the rabbi to kiss. The rabbi, whose father-in-law was a jeweller, took the other man's hand for a moment and examined the large silver and ruby ring on the middle finger. "Excellent workmanship," he observed.

This too rattled the Pope, for the comment seemed a jibe against the materialism of the Church, a criticism he was particularly sensitive to.

"Let us talk," the Pope said, and he led the rabbi to the head of the table. He – the Pope – sat himself at the very head, and gestured to the rabbi that he take the seat at his right. With another gesture, he indicated to the cardinals, archbishops and others that they were to wait at the other end of the room. Servants immediately appeared to pour wine and to unfurl napkins for the two seated men. "What can I offer you?" the Pope asked.

"Perhaps a little hot tea," the rabbi said. "Mine appears to have grown cool."

He put the sack containing his lunch on the table beside him. "I hope you won't be offended, Your Excellency, but I have brought my own lunch. A special diet, you understand? Perhaps your holiness would be pleased to share some of it with me?"

The Pope glanced at the rabbi's lunch with surprise, disdain – and suspicion. He demurred.

A waiter with a ruffled shirtfront and white gloves ladled out soup for the Pope, a rich, pungent broth into which cream and eggs had been blended, but the guest waved him away. While the Pope consumed his soup with an exquisitely carved silver spoon, the rabbi peeled and ate his egg, scattering bits of shell and bright yellow yolk crumbs onto the tablecloth and the richly brocaded rug. The hot tea hadn't arrived so he took a few sips of wine, but it was too sour for his taste and he made a wry face.

A large bowl was brought to the table containing a variety of fresh greens, wedges of vibrantly red tomatoes, intricately carved slices of cucumber, asparagus tips, hearts of artichoke and baby shrimp, in a sprinkling of the most virgin of olive oils and vinegar from fine red wine. While the Pope enjoyed the salad, the rabbi ate his celery and radish, crunching them between his molars.

The next course was fish – freshly caught sole from the deep blue waters of the Mediterranean, served steaming and swimming in butter sauce – accompanied by baby potatoes and fresh corn. "Are you sure...?" the Pope asked, gesturing with his fork.

"No, thank you," Rabbi Schmegegge said. He waited until the Pope had deboned his fish, then ate his salt herring, washing it down with a few sips of his now lukewarm tea.

When the Pope was finished with the main course, the waiters cleared away the dishes, poured more wine and served a magnificent chocolate cake layered with cream and studded with cherries. "Certainly I can tempt you with this cake," the Pope said. "It is truly memorable."

"No, thank you once again, it's too rich for me," the rabbi of Chelm responded. He ate his crust of black bread, which he first brushed roughly against the paper in which his lunch had been wrapped, to sop up any crumbs.

Finally, the two men arose from the table. The cardinals and arch-bishops and bishops and the others, who had been watching intently from the other end of the room, pressed forward, but the Pope gestured to indicate that they were to maintain a distance.

"This was a great pleasure," the Pope told his guest.

"Ah, the pleasure was all mine, I assure you," the rabbi of Chelm said.

Once again, the Pope extended his hand, but the rabbi was bending over the table, gathering up the jar that had held his tea and the leather sack, into which he swept with the back of his hand the few crumbs left from his simple meal. He was escorted out of the dining hall and through the cathedral to the front steps, where a man in a scarlet uni-form was holding his jackass.

The Pope, meanwhile, summoned his retainers and they gathered around him, the cardinals, the archbishops, the bishops and the func-tionaries. They could see that the Pope was white-faced, shaken. "This is a formidable man, this rabbi," he said. "I fear we have underestimated our opponents."

"What did he say?" the cardinals and archbishops and bishops all clamoured at once.

"It's not what he said," the Pope replied, "but what he did." He allowed two of the younger bishops to help him to his chair. He took a sip of wine and stared at his glass.

"What did he do?" the chief cardinal finally inquired.

"I offered him wine, and first he drank it, to show that he was my equal," the Pope said. "Then," he added, with a dejected tone, "he disdained it, to display his superiority.

"I offered him soup, and in response he produced an egg, to show me that he was familiar with the teachings of the church on the trinity, the Father, the Son and the Holy Ghost. The egg was hard-boiled, to indicate he knew well the blessed state of virginity of Our Lord's mother, but that he was unimpressed. You should have seen how he cracked it, how he peeled it with seeming disinterest."

The bishops and the functionaries gasped.

"I offered him salad and he countered with a simple stalk of celery, a radish still bearing soil from the garden. With these he signalled that the Cross was powerless in a struggle against the Star of David."

"I see," said one of the bolder cardinals.

"I offered him fish and he produced his own fish – salt herring! – a symbol of the fish our Saviour used to feed the multitudes and a clear indication that the Jews consider themselves capable of outlasting any threat."

The archbishops paled and nodded their heads.

"Finally, I offered him cake and he countered with bread, a symbol of life, its vicissitudes and the everlasting mercy of God, and a clear signal that he has access to the wrath of God, just as the Hebrew people did in biblical times."

The Pope looked around at his trusted lieutenants, looking each man in the eye for a moment. "Remember Moses," he finally added. "Remember indeed."

One of the cardinals fainted and had to be revived with smelling salts.

"I offered him my ring to kiss – twice – and he refused, showing his disdain for the power of Rome. And yet" – the Pope rose, shaking his head in wonder and holding up a hand – "always he spoke gently, humbly and with a smile. He gave every impression that he means us no harm. This is indeed a learned and wise man, a man to be reckoned with. We must pray and seek heavenly guidance."

That very evening, the Pope and his party left on the return journey to Rome. He would pray, he would take counsel, he would consider, but already it appeared clear which way he would rule.

The rabbi of Chelm, for his part, after leaving the cathedral, rode his jackass to the main synagogue of Barcelona, where the Chief Rabbi and those of his assistants who were available were anxiously awaiting him in the street.

"What happened?" the Chief Rabbi asked before Rabbi Schmegegge had barely dismounted.

"What happened? Nothing happened. There was a fine lunch and we talked, though I must say the Pope is not much of a conversationalist. His Hebrew is marred by a thick Italian accent – although, of course, I didn't mention this. And his manners, I'm sorry to say, are somewhat lacking. I asked for hot tea, but I never got it."

And so, the Inquisition was avoided. The people of Spain continued to grumble against the Jews, but there were no forced conversions, no mass executions. It was, you might say, a happy ending.

ZAN LEANED BACK IN HIS CHAIR.

"A very nice story," Zelda said. "But there *was* an Inquisition. Have you forgotten?"

"Ah, that was a few years later. You thought maybe anti-Semitism would go away? No, the rabbi of Chelm may have been clever, but that clever he wasn't. The Pope died, there was a new one. And also, in real life, there really is a Polish town called Chelm, and in the Holocaust, most of its Jews were killed, thousands of them. That was no story, no joke. But in my story, for a few years, a generation, all was well."

"Ah, I see. And tell me, the chocolate cake...."

"Chocolate cake?"

"The cake served to the Pope. Wasn't chocolate something Columbus brought back from the Americas? And corn? Wouldn't that have been later?"

"You may be right."

"I mean, there couldn't have been chocolate cake then, I mean, could there have been?"

Zan looked at her, smiling. "Zelda, who's the crazy one here, you or me? This is a story."

DUET 5

"Abe, do you remember when I went out to Vancouver to visit Saul?"

"Saul? Our brother Saul?"

"Of course, our brother Saul, what other Saul would I be asking about?"

"Saul is dead. Maybe you forgot."

"I know Saul is dead, Benchy! I'm not asking about yesterday. I'm talking about years ago – remember, the year we went to Toronto..."

"That's where I learned to box."

"Sure, and other things, too, I'm sure. But while we were there, Saul went to Vancouver, remember?"

"Sure, after he came back from the war. Went out west on his own, he said, just to see the country, *meshugener*, meant to get off the train here in Calgary, he said, but overslept, woke up in mountains and was scared to jump, just hung on."

"Is that what happened?"

"I should know? I wasn't with him. That's what he always said. Overslept, and so became the first of the Wisemans to see the Pacific. He'd already been across the Atlantic, just like Pop had, when he and Hersh shipped out to France. He inherited that wanderbug from Pop, I guess."

"And he got in trouble, remember?"

"*Tsuris?* He robbed a bank. Got caught with a gun in his hand."

"A gun? I didn't know that."

"Wound up at the BC Pen for three years and lucky, he always said, lucky he had a clean record and was a veteran. The judge went easy on him. Lucky he didn't shoot the copper who barged in on him, he'd come *that* close, he always said."

"A gun? I never knew that."

"You just forgot. Fell in with a bad bunch, as they say. Robbery, gun...sound familiar?"

"Too familiar."

"He used to say jewelry stores were easy, pieces of cake, compared to banks. What made him think that, where he got that idea, I don't know."

"It was his idea, Saul's idea, the robbery, later?"

"I wouldn't say it was his idea. But it was him put the idea of *robbing* in my mind, not me putting it in his, like Pop and Momma always thought. They never knew about the trouble Saul was in out west, thank God. But he fell into bad habits out there on the coast, our Saul, brought them back with him."

"Mom and Pop never knew?"

"They thought he was working on the docks, he wrote them a postcard. But somehow we kids knew what was what. You don't remember that? When we came back from Toronto, Saul was still gone, we were worried. I remember I asked around."

"And then I went out there to see him, remember? That's what I was asking you about. What year was that?"

"*You* went? What are you talking about?"

"That's what I'm telling you, I went out there, hopped a freight, just like Saul did."

"*Oy Vay!* Zannie, the head on you. Hopped a freight, sure, but it wasn't just you, me *and* you, little brother. What, you don't remember *that?*"

"Me *and* you? You went too, *Abela?*"

"*Meshuge!* Like you had the *chutzpah* to do that on your own?"

"You went with me? I didn't remember that."

"Still, it was your idea, I give you that. Just a kid and already you're trying to play the peacemaker, like you're the person responsible for holding the family together, Mr. United Nations, a regular *makher*, a big shot."

"So when was that, *Abela?*"

"When? After Toronto, the next summer, maybe. Now you got me as *farshimmelt* as you. We were sixteen, seventeen, something like that, the same age Pop was when he and Uncle Moishe came to Canada."

"We took the train, though, a freight, I'm not imagining that, am I?"

"A freight, sure. We set out as soon as school was over – I'd quit already, but you were still in school then, where you should have stayed, would have if you'd listened to me, but when did you ever? Hopped a freight down in the CPR yards just like Saul did, wound up on a siding for hours in the first one we jumped, then switched to another. You almost lost your footing and fell, thank God I grabbed you. 'You stick close to me, Pantsy,' I told you."

"We were in a boxcar, right? I didn't imagine that?"

"In a boxcar, sure, like real hoboes, free as birds, rattling across the prairies like peas in a dried-up pod, you lying on your belly scribbling away like you always did, making up stories, me looking out the open door at the country flying by."

"That's right, I wrote stories."

"In my mind, I was Pop, you were Moishie, I was in charge, taking care of the kid brother, we were on our way to a new world. 'Make up a story about us, Pantsy,' I said, remember?"

"I do now, *Abela*. It's coming back."

"This was before I broke your nose, flattened it across your face, poor *schmuck*. When you lifted your head, it was a good-looking kid with clear brown eyes and a straight honker, not a bump in sight, I was looking at. 'Make up a story about us,' I said, and damned if you didn't, right there, something you wouldn't believe."

PART 2

AND NOW A NEW YEAR

ZAN HAS THE NEW JOURNAL TO PROVE IT, the numerals 1-9-8-9 pulsing like the heart on a plaster statue of Jesus in front of an evangelical church in Las Vegas.

Better yet, he's four chapters into the new novel, *God Blinked.* "He hasn't yet," Zan writes in the journal this morning. "Not yet."

He writes this on the first page of the journal:

Jan. 1, 1989: No session with Dr. Zelda last week, the holidays. Looking forward to this Tuesday. I miss her.

CHAPTER 15

January 3, 1989

"HAPPY NEW YEAR," the therapist says.

"Same to you, Dr. Zelda. Same to you. And you know what? I think maybe it will be a happy new year for me. But better I shouldn't say so, maybe, for fear of the jinx."

"I thought you believed you make your own fortune. Isn't that what you've told me?"

"Ah, maybe I did, maybe I do. What I say, though, what I say I believe, and what I actually believe, that may be two different things, that well you should know me by now."

Zelda's smile is appealing, her lipstick a subtle pink. "I guess I do. And, frankly, I can't help wondering why. Let's talk about that, shall we? But first, tell me how you're feeling today."

Zan shifts his shoulders, his hips, settles himself, considers both the comment and the question. How long has he been seeing this woman? Three months, so far. And already she's seeing through him. Or has she all along?

"How I'm feeling today?" he begins slowly, some of his exuberance from just a few minutes earlier drained. "I'm alive."

"And that's good?" Zelda's mannish jacket is on a hanger on a hook behind her and her white blouse looks crisp, businesslike. He likes that.

"That I'm alive, yes, that's good. The things that come with, maybe not so good."

"Shall we begin to talk about those things today? Tell me something – not all of them – tell me one thing in your life that isn't so good, that you could see a way for it to be better."

Zan laughs. "That's easy. Health, wealth, my love life, a diet with more cherry pie and ice cream, these are all small things. It's easy to pick out one thing, it towers above everything else."

"And what is that?"

"I told you several times already, I'm a failed novelist."

"Ah. Your novel. I read your novel over the holidays. Thank you for suggesting it. Not what I expected, but it's wonderful."

"Really!" Zan opens his eyes wider so as to see more of her, take her deeper in. "Not what you expected – which was?"

"Oh, I don't know. More like the story you told at our last session, the rabbi and the Pope."

"Ah, no. There is some of that, but it's the boy's story...growing up in Winnipeg, the family... You would have liked more of the fable?"

"No, I liked the mix, the way you move back and forth between the real world and the imagined. Really wonderful."

"The real world and the imagined. Well, it's all real, *and* it's all imagined. Figuring out which is which, where you are and when...this is the trick. The novelist is a magician, you know, but the magic doesn't always work. Sometimes Houdini doesn't get out of the box and he drowns. It's a miracle there aren't more failed novelists. How anyone ever finishes one, that's the real miracle.

"But thank you very much, Lady Doctor. My opinion of you has just gone up, for your literary critical perception for sure. Your psychological perception, the jury is still out. No offence intended."

"None taken."

"And impressed too with your efficiency. I mention a novel, mention that it might – just *might* – play a small role in my – how would you put it? Tangled web of neuroses? And off you go and read it. That's dedication."

Zelda is smiling. "It would have been dedication, perhaps, if I had to force myself through it. But this was a pleasure."

"And you learned something, maybe?"

"About you? I already knew I can't necessarily take everything you say at face value. 'Failed novelist' is hardly the term I'd apply to you. According to the back cover, your book was quite a hit."

"Yes, agreed. A million copies in paperback, that's just in English, who knows how many in French and Italian and Japanese and so on, and still going strong. Can you believe, over thirty languages it's been translated into? Korean! Serbian! Russian! Polish. Swahili I'm not so sure about. Arabic, probably not. They love me in Italy, God only knows why – there's that God fellow again. In Italy, they teach it in university, maybe some other places too. I told you, I think, it made me a few dollars and brought me plenty of free meals. But only thirty years after the fact. Have I mentioned anything about luck? I was languishing in well-deserved obscurity – well, just how deserved it was is open to debate maybe – when some professor in Winnipeg I didn't know, a professor who'd heard about the book but had never actually seen it – it wasn't even in libraries then! – came on a copy in a used book store, where, I forget. Chicago, maybe. I have been the lucky recipient of the attention of professors all my life – I told you, I think, about Luna and Myrna – and this time I hit the jackpot."

Luck! That's all it really had been, nothing he'd done. Obscurity, and then, almost overnight, celebrity, first small, then large. And along with that, almost as if one had triggered the other, the years with Rose were careering to an end. He wasn't so much sorry over that as bewildered, as bewildered by the impending and then actual end of his marriage as the rebirth of his writing life, not so much lonely or heartbroken by one or excited by the other as adrift. And somewhere in there, at an academic conference in Los Angeles where he was an honoured guest, he met Myrna, who was an English professor at the University of Nevada. He wasn't writing – book reviews, yes, a paper for a conference, yes, but his own writing, the new novel he'd been thinking about for several years already, not a word. "Let me help you," Myrna said, those enormous brown eyes of hers full of him, and Zan, pleased and flattered, shivered nonetheless, hearing the echo of Luna's voice, then the unmistakable ironic chant of all his brothers, those alive and those dead in harmony, "What's the matter? Someone walking on your grave? Someone pissing in you ear?"

All of a sudden, he'd found himself telling this woman – a stranger until only an hour earlier – all about the new life breathed into *Wise Men*, talking as freely and excitedly as once he had talked with Luna, as once, but not for some time, he had talked with Rose.

"I'm minding my own business, the phone rings," he told her. "It's this voice I've never heard, a name I never heard, Olafson, an Icelander from Gimli. A big voice over the phone that matched the size and shape of the man when I got to meet him a few months later. I imagined a beard and blue eyes behind that voice and I was right."

"I know, I've met him," Myrna said. "At a conference in Chicago. Yes, a big man. He claims he discovered you."

Zan laughed. "*Re*-discovered, I give him credit for that. Someone else gets the credit for discovering me. Another English professor, but you wouldn't know her. This was long ago.

"But rediscovered, yes. 'People talk about your novel in Winnipeg like it's the holy grail,' he tells me.

"'Is that right?' I say. 'That's very nice to hear.'" He paused, took a closer look at the woman who'd sat down beside him in the lounge. Fiftyish, trim and well decked out, vivacious, girlish haircut, enormous brown eyes. A bit of Rose in those eyes, a bit of Luna in her mouth, the slightly lopsided smile.

"I was at home in Toronto," he told her. "Hadn't thought about *Wise Men*, except in the most passing of ways, for years." He'd been marking papers when the phone rang – since his break with the Party, Zan had stopped doing the machinist work that had occupied him for so many years and had found a part-time job teaching first-year composition at one of the suburban colleges. It wasn't exactly "if the workers don't want me, then fuck 'em," but something not far beyond. The way Rose put it, he was finally growing up, learning to accept who he was. Zan noticed with wry amusement that she expressed this in the present active tense, not the past. Now here was something from the past reaching out and tapping him on the shoulder.

"All sorts of people swore by it, but no one had a copy," Olafson was saying. "There's not a single copy in the Winnipeg Public Library, if you can believe that. There were some, apparently, but they took a walk, some time ago. Neither university has it. Same thing, apparently. Collectors, most likely."

"I think the book burners got their hands on it back in the Fifties," Zan said. "Whatever copies there were left would have made a pretty small fire, just enough for a marshmallow or two."

"I think you're right about that," the professor said. "I finally found a copy, though. Dog-eared, coffee-stained, well-thumbed. But readable." Here he paused, as if for dramatic effect. "It's everything I was told it was. Well, maybe not the holy grail, but a damn fine novel. Damn fine novel."

"Thank you," was all the response Zan could muster. Was he really having this conversation? He looked around his familiar workroom, cluttered with books, magazines and piles of student papers, as if for confirmation that he was awake, not submerged in some dream, either his own or someone else's. The phone was on the desk across the room from the armchair he'd been sitting in when it rang and he stood now staring down at his typewriter, untouched for months.

"I'm not being polite, Mr. Wiseman. May I call you Zan?"

"Of course."

"When you get to know me, and I hope you will, you'll find I'm not that sort. When I say it's a damn fine novel it's because I really think so."

"Thank you again," Zan said. He could think of nothing else to say.

"But I'm not calling just to heap praise on you. I'd like to republish the novel."

"You say what?" Zan said, stunned.

Olafson explained he'd photocopied the novel – "I hope you'll excuse the copyright infringement," he said with a nervous laugh – and he'd written a paper on it, would be delivering it at the Learneds conference in Toronto that spring – perhaps they could meet? Then he'd started thinking about teaching it as part of a CanLit course he was putting together, but where to get copies?

"I've got a few," Zan interjected. "You can have them cheap." He laughed.

"I'd like to go further than that," Olafson said. He was involved with some other people in a small press in Toronto. So far, they'd only published poetry and a handful of first novels, but he'd been talking to his partners about *Wise Men* and they'd agreed the time might be right for a revival. "It never really got a chance. I consider it a lost masterpiece – I hope I'm not embarrassing you."

"Embarrass away," Zan said. He'd slumped down into the desk chair and was holding onto the desk with his free hand.

"The question is whether you're agreeable," Olafson said.

"Agreeable? I'm ecstatic."

He used the same word, "ecstatic," retelling this conversation to Myrna.

It was the sort of thing writers dream about all the time, the bolt from the blue. But nothing like it had ever happened to him, and he'd stopped dreaming long before.

"You probably don't know this history," Zan told her, "no reason why you should, but *Wise Men* came out in the depths of the Depression,

1932, from a New York publisher. A few weeks later, the publisher goes belly up and the book simply vanishes. There were a handful of reviews, but after the first copies in the bookstores sold out, there were no more to be had, no place where they could be ordered. I had no idea what became of the others – shredded probably, the plates melted down. It was like the book never happened."

"I know," Myrna said, "Olafson told this story at the conference," but nothing in her face suggested she didn't want to hear it again, from Zan.

"That right? You know, for years I held onto the thought that someone might want to do another edition. Even that small hope extinguished in the early Fifties, when I heard about some of the few copies left disappearing from libraries. McCarthyism was running rampant in the US, well, I don't have to tell you, and I'm ashamed to admit I burned most of the manuscripts and journals I'd been carrying around for years. I wasn't worried about something in them incriminating me, but other people maybe." He smiled ruefully. "If I wasn't depressed enough about writing, that was the icing on the cake."

"All that time, you never published anything?" Myrna asked.

"A few stories, some articles and book reviews in little magazines. But I never came anywhere near to finishing a novel. After the burning, though, my output dried up entirely. And I certainly forgot about the idea of a new life for *Wise Men*.

"So rediscovered, yes, Olafson did that, and if he wants to take more credit than he's maybe due, wants to boast, he's welcome to it, he won't get an argument from me. He breathed new life into me."

"But no new novel," Myrna said gently, "at least not yet?"

"No, things don't work out as you expect." Zan laughed, tried to keep the usual bitter tone out of it. He was liking this woman, didn't want to scare her off.

"Olafson's paper was published, and I made a sort of footnote appearance at the conference. The novel was republished the following year, and you know the rest yourself, good reviews...."

"Glowing reviews," Myrna interrupted.

"Some, yes."

And the novel had sold reasonably well, mostly on campuses, where other professors, like Myrna, followed Olafson's lead and put it on the curriculum. There was talk of a new US edition. For the first time in his life, Zan was invited to do a reading, first one, then another, then a whole tour was arranged. He had to decline a course at the college to keep up with the demand.

"But I had no time to write."

"That damn novel is a millstone around your neck," Rose had told him, her eyes slanting in a way he once found irresistible but he had come to find annoying. She had always, correctly, associated its writing with Luna, and viewed it with skepticism. And, though she was always supportive of him, in a wifely fashion, she had little patience for his blocks and excuses.

"What a couple of damn critics said meant more to you than all the people who read it and loved it. You fretted for years that you'd done the wrong thing, ran from it, hid from it – now it's overwhelming you." She was right, too, but there wasn't any way he could see that or, even if he could, any way he could have admitted it. Ultimately, it was another wedge in the growing distance between them. But it was also, in a way he couldn't have predicted, giving him a new life. Four years after the call from Olafson, *Wise Men* was published in New York again, in a trade paperback edition, with a vivid cover, something from a Chagall painting, and a brooding photo of Zan on the back. To his astonishment, there was a full-page review on the cover of the Sunday *Times'* book review section and the book began to sell, not enormously but slowly and steadily, nudging its way onto university reading lists all across North America. It was published in England, then translated into French, Italian, Chinese. Zan had an agent. There was a problem getting royalties from China, she reported, but just knowing thousands of people were reading it there made that not matter to him. He was already making enough from the novel that he'd never have to work again.

There were even more invitations, readings, conferences, a request that he be writer-in-residence at McGill for a year, which, terrified, he declined.

"But no new writing," he told Myrna.

"Let me help you," she said.

Zan was taken aback. "What do you mean?"

That was the weekend the marriage to Rose ended.

"so you were a success," Zelda says.

Zan clears his throat, looks up. "A success, sure. All of a sudden, my novel is alive again, and I'm a celebrity, invited to speak, to read, to attend.... But all of this, as I say, is thirty years and more after I wrote it, after it came out, after it disappeared as if it had never existed. And all that time, and all the time since, not another word. Well, no, that's not right – other words, I wrote plenty, but not another word in print.

"So, wonderful, much as I might agree with you, Madame Zelda – and thank you very much – is beside the point. The point is that it was written over fifty years ago and since then...*bupkis*, as my brother Abe would say. Nothing. Dry as...no, dry as the kiss of an Arab princess."

"That's a nice metaphor."

"You complimented me on my metaphors once before, remember? But to return to the point, I haven't exactly been putting them to good use."

"And this is something that you see as not being good in your life? Something you're unhappy about?"

Zan laughs again. "You could say that. Yes."

"And...." She consulted a note. "Nineteen thirty-two. That's fifty-six years. You've really written nothing since then?"

"Written, plenty, published, *bupkis*. No, that's not completely true. Odds and ends. During the dark days years ago, occasionally a short story, even a poem or two, somehow, miraculously finished – there's method in setting your sights low – and published in some little journal no one reads. And since *Wise Men*'s revival, a few book reviews, an article or two, in academic journals. And interviews – well, I didn't write them, it's me being interviewed. Another short story or two, not new ones really but old ones revived, published in *The New Yorker*, no less. A lecture, even. Through no fault of my own, as I said, I became a celebrity, people wanted to hear me talk about not being able to write. I was in demand. But novels, no, not a one. Not even close. Lots of words written, not a word in print. When you're a novelist and you don't write novels...you might as well be dead."

He raised his hands. "Would you believe these are hands that braved the hives of honeybees? Oh, yes, for years I was a beekeeper."

"Yes, you said."

"I mention it only because I wrote articles for the beekeepers' journal, if you can believe there is such a thing. I was not exactly an authority, but enough of one for them."

"But no novels."

"Not for not trying."

"You attempted another novel?"

"I attempted plenty of novels."

"And...?"

"And nothing. You're familiar, maybe, with the sound of wheels spinning in the snow?"

"I believe the term is writer's block, is that right?"

"That's the hammer on the nail, Zelda. Writer's block. Most writers, it lasts a day or two every other week, or a week or two once or twice a year. Some writers, it's worse. For me, it's the *Guinness Book of World Records*. It's the Goddess of Writer's Blocks."

"And this...you say this is the biggest thing in your life that isn't good, that you're unhappy about?"

"Lady Doctor, suppose you hung out your shingle and no one came. Or put it another way, suppose all your suicidal patients killed themselves, all your depressives went into comas, all your..."

"I take your point, Zan. Tell me how you became a writer."

Zan laughs.

"What's so funny?"

"I've got to laugh. This is a one-hour appointment, not all day."

Zelda smiles, jots something down. Taking notes with pencil, he had thought before, was a sign that she quickly transferred them to tape or computer disk. Pencil was comfortable to write with, but too impermanent. No one knew that better than he: a dozen stories or scraps of stories, written in pencil on wide sheets of newsprint from the box factory, pressed together between the covers of a scribbler, hidden in the basement, in a shoebox, over the summer he'd ridden the rails to Vancouver and back, the summer he was sixteen, and then forgotten until five years later, all the pages blurred and illegible when finally he returned to them, the lines he'd laboured over so lovingly smudged. He'd cried on Luna's bosom that day, and the very next week she'd presented him with the typewriter, a portable Underwood, used but certainly serviceable, the same one he wrote *The Wise Men of Chelm* on, the same one he continued to use – or *not* use – for over sixty years.

"Give me the nickel version," Zelda says.

"The nickel version, sure. But you know that in my day, a nickel could buy a whole lunch. There really was a free lunch then, in the taverns, sliced meat, bread, pickles, you helped yourself, but you had to buy a beer, and a schooner of beer was only a nickel. So I can still fill up the hour, don't think I can't, but okay. It was school, of course, not the Jewish school I went to later, public school, Strathcona, in the North End...."

"This is Winnipeg?" Zelda interrupts.

"Yes, of course, Winnipeg, who's giving this nickel tour, me or you? Strathcona School, the one good thing I got out of that place, a German teacher, of all things, Mr. Goodman. Grade Five, I'm, what, ten years old. Wait – was it before I got sick? I don't remember, maybe it was the next year – I lost most of a year of school – maybe I was eleven. No, after I was sick I was in Aberdeen School, and this was Strathcona. So ten, let's say ten. Mr. Goodman sets us this assignment: write a descriptive paragraph. Ohhh, the class groans. What can we describe? Use your imaginations, Mr. Goodman says. Describe your mother, your father, your kid sister, the tree in your backyard, the magic pumpkin Cinderella's fairy godmother turns into a coach, whatever you like. Just one paragraph, three sentences. How hard can it be? Ohhhh, *three* sentences! That's hard. So okay, describe me, Mr. Goodman says. Here I am. He strikes a fancy pose and we all giggle. And that's what everybody does: Mr. Goodman, his bald head gleaming under the ceiling lights, the moustache bristling under his nose, the soup stain on his necktie. His name is Goodman but probably originally it's Schultz, he makes like he's a German Jew but everyone knows he's German as the Kaiser, the war on but somehow nobody holds it against him. German as a dachshund, believe me, but for some reason he looks like an Italian singing waiter. Easy to describe. Thirty pupils in the class, twenty-nine Mr. Schultzes."

"And your paragraph something else."

"Of course, Zelda. You're getting to know me. I'm going to do what everyone else is doing?"

"Or take the easy way."

"That too. Though this is easy. A horse! A horse, I write about. My father's own horse, that pulls his wagon. I don't have him standing in front of me like Mr. Goodman-Schultz, to copy, but all I have to do is close my eyes and there he is, *Schvartze*, Blackie, his mangy tail, nostrils drooping, big yellow teeth, slobbering lip. This is no noble stallion, no Trigger or Silver, no Man of War. This is a workhorse worked half to death, but I love him, and I know every inch of him. All I have to do is close my eyes and there he is. And the words leap onto the paper. Like magic."

"Mr. Schultz was impressed, I'll bet."

"You'd win that bet. Flattered as he was by the twenty-nine portraits of himself, whatever instinct he had as a teacher was stimulated by my paragraph. Words of praise fell from his lips, dripped from his lips like honey, and I basked in them, *bathed* in them. Intoxicated, I was. It was the first time that had ever happened, I can tell you that. All of a sudden, I was writing descriptive paragraphs about people, my brothers, sisters, my friend Boots, the butcher, the man at the pie factory where in those days you could buy a whole pie, day old, for a penny or two, maybe a nickel, the Commodore – did I tell you about him, this fellow I worked for? Well, that came later. Just close my eyes, there they are! And even people I don't know: I close my eyes, and like magic, the faces appear. Then, not just descriptive paragraphs, but stories, adventures, first about the horse, a magic apple he eats that turns him into a noble stallion; then about a boy, not *me*, mind you, but a boy *like* me, a runaway team of horses like in the movies, the boy riding up on a noble stallion, hurling himself onto the backs of the runaways, the boy bowing before the girl in the coach he's saved.... All of a sudden, I'm a writer!"

"A ten-year-old writer," Zelda said. "I'm impressed. And wasn't that the same year you started to work at the box factory? A lot going on for a ten-year-old."

"Maybe I was eleven. Maybe twelve. Definitely eleven at the box factory – *after* I was sick."

"Even so."

"And I fell out of the tree, don't forget. Maybe that was the year before."

"And both – I mean the writing and the working at the factory, if I understand right – involved a mentor of sorts, an older man taking an interest."

"If you mean diddling, Lady Doctor...."

"No, that's not what I meant at all, Mr. Wiseman. I think you know that."

"Mentor. In the *Odyssey*, if I remember right, Odysseus asks Mentor to look after Telemachus while he's away at the wars. It's from him, I suppose, the boy learns the skills he'll use to help his father kill his mother's boyfriends.... You're writing furiously, Zelda. Taking notes on Greek myth?"

"Taking notes on your adeptness at changing the subject. The idea of having a mentor makes you uncomfortable?"

Zan laughs. "No. Not at all. But we were talking about my becoming a writer."

"All right, let's return to that. You were ten or eleven, and starting to write stories. Then what?"

"Then what? Then nothing. I wrote. I wrote and wrote and wrote. Sometimes just in my head – you don't have to actually have a pencil in your hand to write, you don't have to actually put the words down on paper. But sometimes on paper too. From the factory later, I got paper, all sorts, and filled up pages and pages. I wrote. When I was sick... Oh, there's this. I was sick, my brother Adam was sick, both with the rheumatic fever, I told you. All the time I was in bed, I filled my head with stories – I didn't actually write them down, but I made them up, I told them to myself, I took them apart and looked at them from all angles. *That's* what made me a writer, if anything did – those months in bed, sometimes with a fever that made me imagine all sorts of unworldly things, filling my head with stories. I had that, Adam didn't. Adam died, I didn't. Writing saved my life!"

The furious scratching of Zelda's pencil on her pad fills the silence that follows. "I've turned you into a writer too, I see," he says softly.

"Yes." She looks up, smiling. "Do you really believe that? It saved your life?"

"I don't know. Maybe better to say it cursed my life, poisoned it. But that's what I believed then. I looked at Adam's empty bed, and that's what I believed. I had...you know the word *mojo?* Like in the blues song?"

"Yes."

"That's what writing was for me then, my mojo. And it was for a long time."

Zelda writes another sentence or two of notes, then looks up. "Okay, you're ten, eleven, you're writing, you have your mojo, as you say." She smiles. "Then what?"

"Then...I won a contest. For an essay. One of those things service clubs sponsor, 'What Canada Means to Me.'" Zan rolls his head back on the stuffed imitation leather chair and considers the ceiling for a moment. "That's how I met Luna. She was one of the judges. Schultz, the Commodore, you think *those* guys were mentors. Compared to Luna, they were pikers."

THEY'D MET UNDER ONE OF THE GLITTERING CHANDELIERS in the ornate lobby of the Fort Garry Hotel on the evening the award was presented, he a gangly seventeen-year-old in a way-too-large suit borrowed from his eldest brother, far away in a Vancouver prison and not in the need of it, she the cool, distant university professor, her flat chest camouflaged by the ruffles on the bodice of her dark blue dress, who surprised and embarrassed him by offering her hand to shake. "You do know how to shake hands, don't you, Mr. Wiseman?" she said when he hesitated, reddening his face all the more. A half smile flickered on her lips, which were thin and vividly painted, both mocking and encouraging him. The people around them, all men, other judges and officials of the contest, laughed politely but then, miraculously, melted away, leaving the two of them alone in the lobby. A wide, carpeted stairway beckoned them upwards to the ballroom where the Lieutenant Governor of Manitoba, Sir James Aikins, in a uniform with a brocaded front, would personally present Zan with a framed plaque and an envelope representing the scholarship he had won.

"Sure, Miss, I just..." The hand was no larger than his, soft and cool, and she surprised him further by allowing it to linger in his grip longer than he expected, all the while her curious grey eyes locked fast with his own gaze, the touch and look thrilling him in a way that was not only totally unexpected but unlike anything he'd ever before experienced. "Thank you for picking me," he finally managed to get out.

"No thanks necessary," she replied with a cool laugh. "Your essay was the best, simple as that. It deserved to win." Her voice had a not-unpleasant nasal drawl to it that required him to listen hard. "You won't find literary success as simple as that ever again, I wouldn't be surprised. The best story doesn't always get published, nor the best book. Nor does the best book always win the prizes or sell the most." Her mouth pursed, as if she were trying to swallow the involuntary smile, revealing slightly protruding teeth, but her eyes softened, making the smile clear. "Are you a poet, Mr. Wiseman? Zan, is it? What kind of a name is Zan, anyway?"

"It's Alexander, but...."

"Ah, well, I like the sound of Zan. *Xanadu!*" She said the word with feeling, thrilling him, for he loved "Kubla Khan."

"Are you a poet, Zan?"

The professor's little speech, and her question, thrilled him even further, and so disarmed him he didn't hesitate to answer yes, even though, until that very moment, he had never thought of himself as a *poet*. He *had* written some poems, but most of his writing efforts had been directed at stories, narratives in which the hustle and bustle of plot and the vivid descriptions he was so good at had shouldered out any specific considerations of language. His mouth was still open and he was about to say something else – though later, he couldn't remember or imagine what it might have been – when one of the men who had made the introductions minutes earlier was back at their side, taking each of them by the elbow and directing them toward the stairs and the ballroom above. Everything that had followed that afternoon – the meal which, as his mother had instructed, he left untouched except for the salad; the speeches, his own clumsy words of thanks as he accepted the certificate and envelope – was a blur and remained so as, that night, he lay in his bed trying to reclaim his moment of glory, Abe snoring noisily above him. The only moment of clarity was that in which his hand and that of the woman had touched, their eyes met, and she had spoken to him, first sarcastically and then in so offhanded and frank a manner as if to imply that, despite all evidence to the contrary, they were somehow equals.

He didn't see her again for four years, though she often invaded his dreams – a slim, white figure in a flowing gown and hat with long fingers trailing toward him from a veiled distance – so when he did meet her, just by chance on Portage Avenue not far from Main, there was no awkward hesitation. It was February, just two weeks past his twenty-first birthday, and they were both bundled up in heavy coats and boots, Zan in a black cap with earflaps that he immediately pulled off, feeling awkward, she in a dark blue woolen cloche that allowed some russet curls to frame her face, but he recognized her immediately, as if it had only been a week or less since they'd last spoken. She too, apparently.

"Oh, I know you," she said, her distinctive voice immediately familiar. She took a step back, better to appraise him. "You're the poet. Zan, isn't it? Your name makes me think of Zanzibar."

"Yes, miss, Zan Wiseman. You were the judge." He was amazed that she should recognize him, even remember his name.

"Luna McGowan," she said, extending her hand, gloved in soft kid. Zan struggled to get his mitt off to take it, acutely aware that this was the second time their hands had touched. "Please don't call me *miss*. It makes me feel like an ancient spinster, and I'm not. Not ancient, not a spinster." A flash of colour sprang to her cheeks, already red from the cold. "And I wasn't *the* judge, just one...." Her voice trailed off, and her eyes, so grey they seemed to contain an inconsolable sadness, darted away from his face for a moment to the street, people in heavy coats and exhaling steam passing by, cars moving slowly on ice, the clanging streetcar, then back to him.

"And I'm not a poet," he said, amazed at his own boldness.

"No? Too busy with your courses? I haven't seen you on campus. You haven't taken my class. Why not?"

Why not? So many reasons. During the years since their first meeting, he'd ridden the rails west to Vancouver with Abe to see Saul, who was in prison there, dropped out of school, worked full-time in the box factory, then at the CPR yards, immersed himself in the union and the Communist Party, had his first experiences with sex – not love, no *that* was something he was saving – and scribbled, as always, his breathless stories, poems too, poems of heat and desire, as often as not directed at her. But he still wouldn't think of himself as a poet.

"I'm not in school, miss.... I'm sorry."

"Oh, for goodness sake, *Luna*, my name is *Luna*. Like the moon. I'm the woman in the moon. What do you mean you're not in school? You won a scholarship."

"I haven't even finished high school...." He couldn't bring himself to say her name aloud, not in front of her, though he'd pronounced it silently to himself a thousand times, and shouted it from the open doors of boxcars. "I mean, I was. St. John's. But I quit. Got to work, help the family. My father's sick. My brother Abe, he's the smart one. He wants to go to law school." The lie rolled so effortlessly off his lips it didn't even seem to be a lie.

"This doesn't make any sense at all. You win a scholarship and you quit school to help your brother go to university? The scholarship goes to waste so you can work so he can.... I can't make any sense of that at all...." Again, her eyes darted away from him. It had begun to snow, large, airy flakes that fell lightly on them like kisses. "I'm sorry, I was expecting to meet someone.... Listen, let's go in that restaurant and have a cup of coffee. It's not seemly, standing on the street. And much too cold. Or are you in a rush to get somewhere, Mr. Wiseman?"

He was amazed again at the sound of his name in her mouth, amazed at the invitation, amazed to find himself moving beside her across the wide, slushy street, holding up his hand to slow an approaching car, her hand on his arm as they manoeuvred over the streetcar tracks and patches of ice, holding the restaurant door open for her as she stamped snow from her boots, amazed to find himself in a restaurant seated across from her, the smell of coffee sharp in his nostrils. Later, he was amazed even more that she had persuaded him to apply to the university.

"It's intolerable that a mind like yours should wither," she'd said, her voice so fierce Zan had to blink.

"I'm not withering. My mind isn't."

"Not yet. You still have poetry. A box factory! Loading rail cars! A machinist! Riding freight trains! That box factory will produce its biggest and best box yet, the one that encloses you."

Not finishing school was no problem, she told him. He was over eighteen and could go directly into university, take whatever classes he needed to catch up there. Money was not a problem either – she would inquire about the scholarship, make certain it was still waiting for him. If more money was needed, well....

"I can't do that," he protested. "I can't take money from...."

"An ancient spinster? I told you already, I'm not either of those things." Her bucktoothed smile was an arrow that pierced him, holding

Dave Margoshes

him fast to the café's hard wooden chair.

"...from a lady, I meant. From a stranger."

"And now I'm a stranger? Aren't we having coffee together? Are you hungry? Do you want something to eat? How can you say I'm a stranger?"

"My parents wouldn't like.... My father would never...."

"Does your father object to the rail yards? Where you could slip and lose an arm or a leg in the blink of an eye? Or be killed? I imagine the machine you operate could take a finger or a hand off in a second, or an arm, isn't that so?"

He admitted it was.

"Does your father object to that?"

"No."

"No, I didn't think so. So it's not your working your parents don't like, and your wasting your mind obviously doesn't bother them. I'm a professor, I hire students occasionally to do research for me. You'll be my assistant! The hours are flexible. I can afford to pay you, I assure you. I have a stipend from the university to spend as I see fit on research. It won't be charity, and it won't be a loan. You'll earn your pay."

All of this, she'd said, because he was a writer, a poet, whether he admitted it or not, whether he wrote poems or not, all because of something he'd written in his essay. "I read a hundred essays and it wasn't just that yours was better than the others, it was, but that it had in it something entirely different, poetry. I read student papers all the time – you'll see, piles of papers to mark, you'll help me – but I don't find poetry in them. The right answers, regurgitated, maybe even processed, often. Graceful writing, sometimes. Insight, occasionally. Poetry? Never."

The ironic thing – *irony*, that was a word he learned that day – was that she couldn't remember what he'd written that moved her so much – just that it had – and he hadn't kept a copy of the essay, so whatever it was, was gone forever. "It doesn't matter," Luna had told him. "The mind it came from is still here, still with us, and about to be unboxed. I don't remember what it was you wrote exactly, but I do remember how it made me feel when I read it. I want to feel that again. There'll be lots more poetry from you, Zan. I guarantee it."

THEY BEGAN TO MEET WEEKLY, Thursday evenings. Zan would rush home after work, his ears still ringing from the noise of the machine shop, have a wash in the sink to get off the stink of the hot oil spray, bolt his supper, then hurry back across the Salter Street overpass to meet her in a coffee shop on McDermot she liked, the Top Hat Café. Outside, at Speaker's Corner in the Market Square, where Zan was often drawn on his own on Sunday afternoons, the number of orators jostling for attention increased as spring progressed, and Zan was amazed to find Luna was as familiar with the Socialist and Communist arguments as he was. He had been active in the radical movements in the city and around the fringes of the Party for several years, not always clear on which particular organization he was involved with at any given time – the Arbeiter Ring, for example, was run by a rainbow of differing leftist groups, he knew, and some of them occasionally bitter enemies – helping with leafleting and selling newspapers, including the Party's paper, *The Worker,* even occasionally talking at meetings, but was surprised to learn she was a member. "Do you believe in a better world, Zan?" she asked him at one of their first meetings at the Top Hat. It was March now, the winter starting to crack, though the streets were still deep with snow.

"Sure. It's a matter of breaking the chains that...."

"And do you believe you can make a difference?"

Interruptions like that coming from Abe would have the brothers wrestling on the kitchen floor, from his mother or father would have him burning with resentment, but from Luna they seemed only to whet his appetite.

"I don't know. I think so. Every man is of value, just like each link on a chain..."

"Yes, yes, I know all about the chain. Forget about what you heard Joe Penner talking about in the square. I'm asking *you,* I want *you* to answer, use your *own* head. Can *you* make a difference?"

Zan bowed his head, watched discs of light shimmering in his coffee. "I don't know."

"How *could* you? Make a difference. What could *you* do to help make a better world?"

"I don't know. I mean, I could...."

"Join with your fellow workers? Knock on doors? Hand out

leaflets? You do all that already, I know. And has the world gotten better?" She smiled wickedly. "No need to answer, I know – no, of course not. What next, then? Give speeches? Take up arms? Storm the barricades? Line the capitalists against the wall and shoot them? What?"

"Yeah...all those things...but also...." The "gift of the mouth" some of his friends in the Party had remarked on seemed to fail him in Luna's presence.

"Also? Also what?"

"...I don't know. I guess...."

"All those things? Anyone could do, can do, some will do. See that man there?" She pointed to a balding man with a mustache and a red scarf around his neck, reading a newspaper at the counter. "He could do those things. I could do those things – well, some of them. What about *you?*"

"I could...I can...write...." His voice sank to a whisper but he was rewarded with the purse-lipped smile he'd come to love so much.

"There! That wasn't so hard, was it? Saying that word? You can *write!* And I'm not talking about leaflets, pamphlets, tracts. I'm talking about poetry, Zan Wiseman, do you hear me? Now, what did you bring me to read?"

And then, as if to give weight to her argument, an argument he no more fully believed than he did those of the speakers across the street, Zan reached into the canvas bag at his feet and brought out a handful of scribblers for her to examine.

Some of them were recently done, stories with a clear proletariat bent, often set at the rail yards, crude morality tales of worker justice. Others were writings inspired by or actually composed during his trip to visit Saul four years earlier, wild, vivid stories rendered barely legible, even to him, by the jerking of the train as he sat, back up against the shimmying wall of a boxcar, in what a hobo he'd met called "the cheap seats." But one of the older scribblers contained the loose pages that had been ruined by dampness and mould, found just that morning when, having remembered them the night before, he went into the basement to retrieve them, his heart sinking. He had thought perhaps a copy of the prize-winning essay was in the folder.

"I don't know why I brought this..." he began.

Luna was leafing through the others, pursing her lips, and when she came to the ruined pages she made an exasperated sound. "For goodness sakes. Where do you keep this, in a grave?"

Zan laughed, but tears came suddenly to his eyes. He shook his head, holding up a hand as if to ward her off, but she artfully negotiated her way around it, enfolding him in her arms. A few people at surrounding tables glanced at them with mild interest, and Zan, conscious of their gazes, pulled away. What must they think, he wondered; Luna was not old enough to be mistaken for his mother – a young man and his sister, or his lover?

"Do you know how to type, Alexander?" Luna asked, surprising him by her use of that name, but what was more surprising was her unfamiliar tone, something like a parody of a schoolmarm.

"Type?" There were several typewriters in the office at the box factory where he'd worked, and more than once, when the office was empty over the lunch hour, he'd crept in to sit before one of the machines and peck out a few words. "No, not really."

"Well, no matter. There's nothing to it, really. You'll pick it up. A university student needs a typewriter. No professor other than me – and I'm not so sure about me – is going to suffer through this atrocious handwriting." She smiled, to indicate she was only half serious. "I know where I can put my hands on an old machine. No protestations, please. It's not a gift, just a loan. But I'll really expect you to put it to use. And I don't just mean compositions and term papers." She smiled again, as endearing a smile as Zan had ever seen. "I mean poetry, with a capital P."

"AND DID YOU?" Zelda asks.

"What?"

"Write poetry."

"Poems, no. Poetry, well, I hope so."

Dave Margoshes

Jan. 3, 1989 – Luna Luna Luna. A Luna-tic I am, talking about her so much, thinking about her so much. This Zelda is sharper than I realize – she gets under my skin, gets me thinking about things I don't want to think about, shouldn't be thinking about. They call it the past because it's passed.

She should be the novelist!

I might as well work tonight – I know I won't sleep.

CHAPTER 16

ONE SPRING SATURDAY AFTERNOON, warm enough that Luna wore only a light cotton coat and Zan his one good sweater, a light grey wool his mother had knitted, the two of them went to see a show at the city art gallery at Main and Water, an exhibit of paintings by some-one Luna knew, a bewildering blur of shape and colour that mystified Zan and left him with a headache and a feeling that he had somehow displeased her. Afterwards, walking idly along St. Mary Avenue, she was silent and Zan felt conspicuous and awkward in his heavy work pants and boots, as if he should be a step or two behind her, carrying her parcels, as he had observed other boys doing. He was twenty-one, hardly a boy any more, but he felt like one at this moment, hesitant and clumsy. The story he had been dictating in his mind all afternoon, though, was about "the two lovers," with no reference to age – or, for that matter, class, religion or any other difference.

"University is going to do a world of good for you, Zan," Luna said abruptly. They had come to the corner of Hargrave Street, and she steered them north. She took his arm and fell into cadenced step with him, slightly taller than him in her heels. And then, equally abruptly, "You do have a suit to wear to the interview next week, don't you?"

"A suit? I don't have a suit." He laughed nervously.

"You wore one to the ceremony. Well, that was five years ago. You've outgrown it certainly."

"That was my brother's."

"Your brother who's in prison? I doubt he wears the suit there." She took his hand and squeezed it and smiled to show she wasn't mocking him.

They turned west on Portage, where several shops were still open.

"He's not there any more. But I don't know what's become of it."

"And?"

"My father has a suit he wears to *shul*. I don't know, maybe...."

"Let's go in here." She took him by the arm, and suddenly they were walking through the door of O'Brien's men's wear shop. Zan's nostrils filled with the smell of linen and wool, and his eyes fell with a longing he had never before been aware of on the racks of dark suits, the piles of neatly folded, gleaming white shirts. It took him a moment before he realized, with fright, what she intended.

A clerk in a stiff collar and a black elastic band around his sleeve approached them. "My young friend would like to see what you have in a light-weight wool suit," Luna said. "Something in good taste, but well made. To last through three years of university." She smiled at Zan. "Maybe even longer."

"I don't think this is a very good idea," Zan protested, but the clerk was already ushering them into a different section of the shop, commenting on styles and material, fingering the soft yellow tape measure around his neck.

"Why not?"

"My parents will never allow this. My mother...."

"You'll tell her it's a birthday present. Didn't you say your birthday is in February? It *is* a birthday present, belated."

"You've already given me the typewriter," he protested.

"I told you, that's only a loan."

"But a gift like this.... No, my mother...."

"For goodness sake, you're going to be my assistant. Can't I give my assistant a birthday present? I'll call your mother myself and explain. I'm sure she'll understand if I tell...Zan, where are you going?"

But he was already on his way to the door, his heart in his mouth, tears stinging beneath the lids of his eyes, and he realized he was as disappointed that he wouldn't get a suit as he was certain that he couldn't, shouldn't; as amazed at himself for defying her as he was frightened of its consequence. He went through the door without a word and found himself on the sidewalk, halfway down the block, punch-drunk, his ears ringing, certain that he would never see her again, before he realized that the ringing he was hearing was her voice, calling his name.

"Zan, Zan, stop, wait for me."

It was a voice different in tone and pitch than he had heard before, and when he stopped and turned around, she was hurrying to catch up with him, brushing past several people on the street who looked back at her askance, her coat open, one curl flying loose from the neat arrangement of hair, a totally unexpected look – could it have been of fright? – in her flashing grey eyes. The feeling of being a boy in her company he had felt so strongly only minutes before was gone, he realized, but he wasn't sure what had replaced it. She came abreast of him and took his arm again. She appraised him, and the look in her eyes shifted, the grey darkening almost imperceptibly. Her hand on his arm tightened in accord. "Well, I take it you don't want a new suit."

"I'd love to have a suit, Luna," he said. It was the first time he'd managed to pronounce her name in her presence.

"I understand."

They began to walk, her head down, her eyes on the toes of her glossy, black high heel shoes, his eyes straight ahead. The story unfolding in his mind, broken off earlier, was beginning to unroll again: "Out on the street again, the lovers began to walk, her head down, her eyes on the toes of her glossy, black high heels, his eyes straight ahead, but filled with images of the suit he would now never have...."

They crossed Carlton Street, taking care in the traffic, and continued west. "If there was a destination in mind, the man was not aware of it," Zan wrote. The feel of her soft grip, of her weight on his arm was a solace, like Abe's head might be on his shoulder as they lay together on the floor, side by side, reading the funnies.

They came to a restaurant and Luna stopped. "It's gotten late. We're both hungry and tired and out of sorts. Let's go in here and have some dinner."

He felt the panic again as he glanced at the lettering on the restaurant's window: Hanigan's. Good, not only not kosher, but Irish to boot. Were the Irish persecuting him today?

"I don't think so, Luna. Let's go to the Top Hat. It's just a few blocks back."

"Oh, I don't want to go there. It's too far. My feet are killing me. I've got to sit down. This is a very nice place, you'll like it."

"Well...." He glanced around, the panic not subsiding. "How about Simon's deli. That's just two blocks, back on Hargrave. Or the Venice, up on Smith."

"Oh, honey, I don't want a sandwich. I want a hot meal, something nice. Come on." She tugged at his arm, like a child. "It's the money again, isn't it? You really are impossible today. Come on, it's my treat, to pay you back for making you drag after me all afternoon at the gallery."

Reluctantly, he allowed himself to be drawn into the restaurant. A hostess, an elderly woman with red hair in a black dress with a white apron, barred the way. "Good evening," she said, smiling at Luna, frowning as her gaze took in Zan, then smiling again. "I'm afraid I can't let the gentleman in without a coat and tie."

"Oh, that's so disappointing," Luna said. "Isn't there anything...?"

"We have a coat and tie the gentleman can borrow, if he wishes," the hostess said, arching her brows. "Come this way."

"Luna," Zan said. "Let's go."

"Oh, come on, don't be a spoilsport," she whispered, tickling him in the ribs as she shooed him along after the hostess. "This'll be a good chance to see how you look in a tie. You *said* you'd love to have a suit – think of this as a trial run."

A few minutes later, they were seated, Zan feeling restrained within the narrow shoulders of the borrowed jacket, choked by the sombre striped tie. It was a bit early for dinner and, to Zan's relief, the place was almost empty, with just one other couple at a table some distance from theirs. Luna ordered a cocktail and he a beer from a waiter who might have been a brother to the clerk in the men's wear store, his reddish hair slicked back with pomade, and they sat in silence for a few minutes, Zan fidgeting, as Luna studied the menu. "The duck is very good today," the waiter said, carefully placing the martini in front of her. He poured Zan's beer from the bottle into a tall, chilled glass, the foam rising just to the glass's rim and no further. It was, he realized, the first time he'd been in a non-kosher restaurant other than the Top Hat, the coffee shop on McDermot they liked, or the lunch wagon where he used to go to get the Commodore's sandwiches; the first time he'd been in any restaurant, with those two exceptions, outside the North End; and the first time he'd been in any restaurant in the evening. In the story in his mind, the waiter was suggesting the duck, but the lovers were preoccupied with champagne.

"I'm really not very hungry," he said. "I'm just going to have a cup of tea."

"Nonsense. You haven't eaten all day, you must be just as starved as

I am. I've had the duck here, it's marvelous. With a cherry sauce. Mmmmm." She looked up. "We'll both have the duck. Does salad come with that?"

After the waiter withdrew, they sat in silence again, and Zan was aware of a motion within Luna, as if she were re-marshalling her forces, moving troops from this flank to another.

"If you're going to be a university student," she began firmly, "if you're going to be my assistant, then you have to look the part, act the part, speak the part."

"You make it sound like I'm an actor trying out for a play," he said with bitterness that surprised him.

"But that's it exactly, don't you see? The interview you'll be going to is exactly like an audition. You're lucky, the scholarship is secure, so money won't be a problem. That's half the battle. But you still have to get in. Lots of other young men want to go to the university, and there isn't room for all of them. There certainly isn't enough money to give them all scholarships, to provide jobs for them all as professors' assistants. It is an audition, and it's not enough that you merely dazzle them with your brilliance, Zan. If that's all there were, there'd be no problem."

"And a good thing my name's Wiseman, not Wiseberg or Wisestein," he said, "and I don't look *too* Jewish."

"Oh, Zan, don't be silly. That will not be an issue, believe me." She placed her hand on his arm and squeezed. "But they will be watching you, taking a look at the cut of your jib, watching to see if you spill any water when they hand you a glass. All of these things are important. That's why we really have to get you a suit. Not just for the interview, but for afterwards. I mean to be seen with you, and I want you to look nice."

Zan looked down at his shirt front. The restaurant jacket, one button loose, the lapel fuzzy with loose thread, was shabby, nothing like the crisp suits at O'Brien's, and the tie was wrinkled, stained. Still, wearing them was all that was required for him to enter this restaurant that he never would have dreamed of coming to on his own.

"Do you know how much one of those suits costs?"

"No, I really don't know. I know I can afford it, that's what I know. And I know that I don't want to have to feel embarrassed when I'm with you. Do you understand what I'm saying?"

"Yes, you're saying you're embarrassed to be with me. Thank you very much." He started to rise, shoving the jacket back on his shoulders. "I'll spare your feelings and go now."

"Oh, Zan, please don't be melodramatic. That's not what I meant at all. What I'm saying is I want to be with you. Do you understand that?"

He sat again, straightened the jacket, took a long drink from his glass of beer to steady himself. "I...think so."

"And do you want to be with me?"

"Yes, of course."

"Then is it asking so much for you to do a few small things to please me?" She smiled coquettishly, not the sort of smile she'd shown him before. "That's what men are supposed to do for women, or hadn't you heard?"

"No. But...."

"I understand. It's not easy for you to accept a gift. Your parents will feel...diminished in some way." She raised a hand. "There's no reason for it, but I understand. I have parents too." She smiled. "Parents named McGowan can be just as impossible as parents named Wiseman, believe me. Perhaps we can find some compromise. Maybe you can do some work for me now, or I can pay you in advance, and you can buy the suit yourself."

"Maybe," Zan mumbled.

"There. See? That wasn't so hard, now was it?"

It wasn't, but Zan realized with a sudden twist of discomfort, that he was disappointed. He did want a suit from O'Brien's, a suit that Luna would pick out for him, and he knew that no suit he bought with his own money, no matter how much it was or how he'd earned it, no suit chosen by his mother from the tailor shops along Selkirk Avenue or Main Street, could ever be as nice. In his mind, the story began to unravel, its texture and colour changing. "The man didn't –" he began, then backed up and began again: "The man knew he wouldn't...."

The waiter brought the wine, smirking as he waited for Zan to taste it and nod his approval, all of which he managed to accomplish only by following a series of almost imperceptible gestures and head movements by Luna. The salads were served, delicious in a bath of delicate oil and vinegar and spices, along with a crusty bread, both of which Zan felt free to eat, lathering his bread with butter and resisting the urge to blot up the loose crumbs with a licked forefinger. He was famished, he realized. But when the duck came, sizzling and golden brown beneath a thick, purplish sauce, each serving in its own oval bowl with an accompanying dish, his heart sank. He knew he couldn't eat it, even if he knew how, and it occurred to him that Luna had ordered duck to make him squirm as he attempted to negotiate his way through it with knife and fork. He ate two of the quartered roast potatoes and a forkful of green beans, then folded his linen napkin and placed it beside his dish, which he used his thumb to nudge a half inch further away from him.

Luna raised her chin, eying him and the dishes from a slightly elevated distance, but said nothing. She sipped her wine, ignoring her own serving of duck. "That painting with all the dark angles," she began, "the one you said you couldn't understand and didn't think anyone could. You remember? What do you suppose would be the reaction of an immigrant, fresh off the train, who came upon one of your scribblers you'd dropped in the street?"

"I don't think it's quite the same," Zan said tentatively. "In the first place, I'd be more careful and not drop one of my...scribblers" – how he'd come to hate that word.

"And in the second place?" A small smile was playing around the corners of Luna's mouth, as if she already sensed a victory.

"If I *did* drop a notebook, it would be an accident. Putting a painting on display at the Winnipeg Art Gallery is no accident."

"Accident or not – let's say this immigrant knocked on your door and asked to see your latest story, or let's say you sent it off to the *Saturday Evening Post* and they published it – don't laugh, it could happen. But if the immigrant can't read English, he won't be able to understand your story. He *won't* have the tools to understand it, the *skills*."

The conversation looped around, with Luna leading, Zan losing his reserve – the beer and wine rushing to his head – and arguing his side with a zeal he hadn't allowed himself with her before, and the minutes sped by, the portions of duck cooling in their chafing dishes, the vegetables on their separate plate growing limp. Something he said brought a flush of colour to her cheeks and Zan's heart thumped in his chest, making him intensely aware of the connection between them: his words, her cheeks, his heart, like the ricocheting pins at the ten-pin alley where Abe worked Sunday afternoons, coming home with sore shins from crouching in the space above the lanes.

"My goodness, you haven't even touched your duck, Zan."

"I told you I wasn't hungry."

"That's nonsense, you haven't eaten all day and I dragged you through that show. You seemed to have an appetite with the salad and bread. Now go ahead, eat. What are you smiling about?"

"You sound like my mother – 'eat, eat.' Except she would say '*ess, ess.*' That's something I wouldn't ever have accused you of before."

Luna shook her head in exasperation, the auburn curls on either side of her face bouncing against her cheeks and temples. "Oh, for goodness sake, here, let me show you." She reached over, flicking aside the garnish of orange with the serving fork and expertly separating and lifting a portion of duck to her plate. She gave Zan a stern look and busied herself with her own fork and knife, her mouth forming itself into a thin-lipped line as she contemplated the congealed sauce. She ventured a taste before putting her fork down and folding her hands in her lap. "Oh, for goodness sake," she repeated. "This is ice cold." Her eyes were bright with a lustre Zan thought might be tears but he was struck dumb, incapable of either word or action as he watched her gesture for the waiter and brusquely ask for the bill. Removing the tie and jacket, Zan felt like a prisoner freeing himself from ropes, like the great Houdini, whom he'd seen at the Walker Theatre, tearing off handcuffs and chains.

"Walk me home," she said when they were out on the street. It had grown dark and chilly, and there were few pedestrians, and traffic on Portage had slowed. Through the tangle of electric wires and streetcar cables, Zan could glimpse a sliver of moon, like a Cheshire cat grin. Luna took his arm, adjusting her gait to match his, leaning her weight with the slightest of pressure against his shoulder. She lived, he knew, not many blocks away, in one of the apartment buildings along Balmoral Street where it curved and ran alongside the river for a block, and they headed in that direction in cool silence, down Kennedy Street past Broadway and the legislative grounds to its foot at Assiniboine Avenue, then turned right along the broad avenue, almost completely deserted of pedestrians. He had walked this route on his own several times in recent weeks, past the legislature and onto Mostyn Place, past the imposing Granite Curling Club, onto Balmoral itself and past her building, the Balmoral

Apartments, south on Young Street to Westminster Avenue, then back along the river itself, as if on an innocent idyll, daydreaming of running into her, but that had never happened. They approached the Balmoral Apartments now, the front of the building somehow garish in the light from the gas lamp on the corner. The story again began to unfold, the lovers strolling hand in hand on a gaslit street, fog rising around them like breath on a cold day.

"I suppose you'll never speak to me again," Luna said. "I've been a silly woman. I've embarrassed you, humiliated you, humbled you, patronized you, condescended to you, degraded you. I've forced you to my will...."

"You're patronizing me *now*, Luna," he said, amazed again, as he had been earlier, at his boldness.

"Yes, and isn't it fun? Don't you love it?" A smile was fluttering around the edges of her mouth like a moth against a screen door. "But don't interrupt. I've forced you to my will, forced you to bend your knee to my command, and now you'll never speak to me again, just as you haven't for the last fifteen minutes, this is your way...."

"I would," Zan began.

"...of punishing me, of showing me..."

"...if I could..."

"...that you're your own person, that you..."

"...get a word..."

"...won't be pushed around by a domineering..."

"...in edgewise."

"...woman. There is a way of shutting me up, you know."

The sweetness of that first kiss, the voluptuous explosion in his mouth, in his ears, reverberating throughout his skull, the electric current zigzagging down and up his spine, would inscribe itself on the fresh page of his memory with more clarity and force than anything that followed it, the lovemaking that night, the kisses and lovemaking over the next six years, the slow cooling that would eventually set in, as if the love that came pouring out of their mouths that moment were a cup of coffee, set on a windowsill in the sultry air until it became undrinkable. She led him by the hand through the door into an electric-lit entry hall, then up one flight of stairs and another, down a long corridor to a door that she opened with a key. Later, he wasn't sure whether it was embarrassment or pride that he felt for what he said when she enwrapped him in her arms: "I'm not sure we should be doing this."

"Oh?" she said, tilting back her head to regard him in the light that flickered in the living room window, its drapes pulled back. "Are we doing something?"

"Luna...."

"Well, at least you're not calling me Miss any more. I should be thankful for that."

"Made fun of me."

"Pardon?"

"Humiliated, embarrassed, patronized.... That long list of indignities you've visited on me. You left out 'made fun of.'"

"Then I'm glad you're here to correct me. I told you you'd make a good professorial assistant." She ended this sentence with a kiss, even more passionate than the first one, if that was possible. Her hands, remarkably, were on the back of his pants, on his buttocks, pressing his body tightly against hers.

"Luna," he began again when they broke apart for breath.

"If you're going to tell me your *mother* won't approve, I don't want to hear that, Zan."

"Luna, I...."

"Or that I'm not kosher."

"Luna...."

"Oh, do shut up, won't you. Just shut up."

What he remembers, if he dares to think of that night, which is rarely – rather, what he *would* remember, if he thought of that night, which he hasn't in years – what he would remember if he *could*, is this: that this wasn't his first time but it might as well have been, so exquisite, so piercing, so *memorable* – despite the loss of the details now – it was. It was, he thought later, when he allowed himself to think of it, the moment in which he became not just a man, but a *person*, that defining a moment was it, the moment that, for the first time in as long as he could remember then, he was freed of himself, went beyond himself. He remembers – *would* remember – that they made love through the night, three, four, five times, both of them insatiable, inexhaustible, insensible to anything but themselves, each other, drenched with the perfume of each other's bodies. What he would remember with a stirring, even now, was how his penis filled all of her openings, how it probed the warm, satiny caves under her arms, the crooks of her elbows and knees, the rich valley between her pushed-together breasts; and how her vagina and breasts were pressed against all his hardnesses, his hips, shoulders, elbows, knees, as if the simple act of lovemaking had been fractured into a web of myriad different functionings of a complex organism too blind to recognize the simplicity of its hunger.

What he *doesn't* remember, hasn't remembered for years, began to forget almost immediately, so dazed was he: that it was *she* who took him by the hand, finally, and led him to the bedroom, that it was she who undressed him, who led his hands to the buttons of her blouse, that it was she who pulled him over her as she backed herself onto the bed, that it was she who reached down and, taking him gently in hand, fitted him to her, that it was she who rolled over, cocking her hips, she who bent over him, she who lifted him to her, that it was she who pressed herself against him, she whose imagination knew no bounds, whose passion was bottomless, will without surcease. *Her* apartment, *her* bedroom, *her* bed, *her* hunger, *his* willing concert. What he doesn't remember is that, from the instant of that first violent kiss and for the remainder of the night, the dictating voice in his mind was silent, that there was no "man," no "lover," there was only him.

Dave Margoshes

CHAPTER 17

January 10, 1989

Jan. 7, 1989 – *Shabbos* dinner at Abe's last night, as usual. The same chicken, the same roast potatoes, the same *challah*, the same apple pie. Everything the same as it was when Momma made *shabbat* dinner. As if Abe could wipe away the years.

The same talk even.

I asked, very gently, about his Ana. I've done the same a few times before, always he brushes it aside. I thought maybe she'd come for a visit over the holidays, but no. "Too busy," he says. What she's so busy with, who knows. She has a job, a big job in a company – an accountant – but no husband, no kids. So how "too busy" is she to visit her lonely father, her poor mother, not to mention an uncle she barely knows?

"Maybe for Passover," Abe says. Okay, Passover, whenever she wants. It would be nice to see her. Nieces and nephews I don't have many more chances with.

Chances? At what?

"I HAVE SOMETHING FOR YOU," Zan says.

"A gift?" The therapist looks skeptical.

"Better than a gift, a memory."

"That's a gift for both of us then."

Zan pauses to give her a good look. "You surprise me sometimes, Lady Doctor – and I hope you know by now when I call you that, I do it with respect. Very good."

She smiles. "And what is this memory, then?"

"It's about my father. You asked me about him one week, I couldn't remember much."

"And you've remembered something?"

"A story he used to tell, how he and my uncle Moishe came to Canada. He liked telling this story, I must have heard it or pieces of it a hundred times growing up, but I haven't thought of it in years. The other day, I was having coffee in a café and it comes into my mind, I don't know what I was thinking. One minute, nothing, daydreaming, the next minute, there it is, all in one piece."

"And you remember it today?"

"Today, sure, like I heard it at breakfast."

"And you're going to tell me?"

"Tell you, sure. You have to earn your money somehow."

MY FATHER WAS IN THE RUSSIAN ARMY, the Czar's army. Jews were drafted but they were treated maybe like black men were treated in the US army during the world war, sure, join us, but don't get too close. He was a healthy young fellow, eighteen or nineteen, small but strong, so in the army he went. He didn't have a choice. But after a while, he saw it wasn't for him, so he ran away.

"I have to be in the army to kill Jews?" That's what he'd say when he told this story to us kids. "If I want to kill Jews I can stay home in my own village. But I *don't* want to kill Jews, I don't want to kill anyone."

The village my father grew up in was Gorodnize in Galicia, and there were plenty of Jews there to kill, if that's what he'd wanted to do, and plenty for the *army* to kill, which they did when they felt like it.

"Don't ever think your father was a deserter," he used to tell us kids. "That means you turn your back on something you believe. From the Czar's army, what's there to believe? Nothing!" And here, if we were outside, and if Momma wasn't looking, he would spit.

From where he was stationed, less than a day's ride by horseback to our home, it took him four days, he used to say, walking through fields at night, an officer's service revolver he'd stolen tight in his fist the whole time. His mother, the grandmother I never knew, was at the door waiting for him, a candle burning, breakfast on the stove.

"How did you know I was coming?" he asked.

"How I knew? I'm your mother. I *knew*."

The next day, the secret police, the *Cheka*, bang at the door. Pop – my father – used to stand up and shove his hand in the waistband of his pants to show where he had the pistol. "Give me the gun and be quiet," his mother says. "Sit right by the fire." She was kneading dough for the day's bread and she buried the gun deep in the bowl, right in the dough.

"Have you seen your son Paisy?" a policeman asks.

"I should see him?" Pop's mother says. "He's in the army, far away. You'll see him sooner than I will."

"And these two?" He nods to my father and Moishe, who were braiding rope in front of the open fire, their faces bright with heat. Moishe was fourteen or fifteen then. My grandmother says, "My youngest sons, Ike and Moishe, home from the fields with a fever. Not one sick, but two. Don't you be thinking they're ready for the army, no sir."

The policeman looks my father up and down but he had a baby face in those days, and had shaved close that morning, he said, and they believed his mother that he was only sixteen. He was a small man, and sitting, he said, he seemed smaller than he was, not much bigger than Moishe. "You'll have him soon enough," his mother complained. "Give me another year with him at least. You'll have all my sons soon enough."

The *Cheka* goes away and my grandmother winks, pulling the pistol from the dough. "Don't worry," she says, "the bread will taste all the better for it. And the gun, a little vinegar and it'll be good as new. Now get it out of my sight."

But my father didn't take the gun with him. He sold it, so Moishe could go with him. It was too dangerous to travel with it anyway, he used to say. "A gun like that, it's a magnet for trouble," Pop said.

How they came? They didn't swim, don't worry, they took a boat, nothing remarkable there. But getting *to* the boat, that was the story my father told. They walked, singing for their supper as they went. Singing! Begging is what I mean, working when they had a chance. From Galicia to Holland, all that way, I don't know how many hundreds of miles. Still, only three weeks it took – could that be right? It seems too quick. I don't know – that's what my father always said. Three weeks, sleeping in barns, chopping wood or helping with the cows in the evening for their supper and breakfast, but he didn't mind that, it was the walking he said he hated. That was why in Canada he always looked for jobs where he could ride on a wagon behind a horse. He didn't want to walk further than to the barn and back ever again, he would say, his feet were sore enough in those three weeks to last a lifetime.

My father's parents were poor, but he had a rich uncle. His own father – my grandfather, that is, though I never knew him – was a rabbi, his nose in a book and his head in the clouds, Pop used to say, his mother, my grandmother, a simple farm woman, she ran the household. But her brother had been footloose as a boy and wound up all the way in Vienna, and had married a woman with some money or some land, and then bought some more land, I forget how the story went, but he'd become rich. His wife died and he came home to the village in Galicia where he was born like the lord of the manor, so rich he was. He might have given them money but my grandmother was proud, she wouldn't ask him. Later, my father said, this uncle's own children, my father's cousins, also came to Canada, and for them, of course, everything was paid. Believe me, they didn't walk to the ocean, they didn't come across in steerage.

"Why didn't you ask our father," these cousins asked Pop when they met him years later and they talked about coming to Canada. This was the year we lived in Toronto, I told you? That's where these cousins wound up, and we met them there. "Why didn't you ask our father," these cousins asked.

"Why didn't he offer?" my father said back.

Well, whatever the reason, for my father and Moishe there was nothing. Somehow, though, selling eggs, selling chickens, his mother had raised enough money to pay for his passage. Another brother, poor like herself, had gone to Canada two years before, so she knew something of how it was done. It took her a year, Pop said – she began saving when he went in the army, he said, sure that he'd be home soon enough and would need the money – but she raised enough, just enough for his ticket, and a handful of coins for bribes, nothing else. The pistol gave them enough so that Moishe could go too.

"Bless you for that," Pop's mother told him, but there was no blessing in it, my father used to say, it was a *mitzvah*, an obligation. "What, you think you can leave a brother behind?" he would say, giving us boys a look.

When they set out, their mother gave them bread, cheese, onion, wrapped in a handkerchief, enough for two, maybe three days. "You'll have to find your next meal on your own," she told them, that's what he used to say. "And someday soon, in Canada, we'll all eat a meal together again."

The two boys set off by foot, overland through Galicia, south to Austria and then on to Germany, the long way to skirt around Poland where it wasn't supposed to be safe. Safe! It wasn't safe anywhere, my father said, but some places were less safe. In Poland, their mother had told them, they had enough Jews of their own and didn't want any others, even just passing through. And you think this was a nice walk in the sunshine? No, it was spring, not yet Passover, and the ground was muddy and it was still cold at night. There were anti-Semites, and highwaymen who didn't care who you were, everywhere, and even in those days there were border guards, police, army patrols because of the smuggling. The Poles didn't like Ukrainians and vice versa, and no one liked Austrians, not even other Austrians, Pop used to say.

Approaching a town near the border with Austria – what would be Czechoslovakia now – they fell in with two young men, peasants, one of them tall and skinny, with a scar the shape of a triangle on his jaw, the other short, a little shrimp, my father said. He and Moishe looked at each other and just with their eyes they agreed, if there was trouble, Pop would take the tall one, Moishe would take the shrimp. He was just a kid, my uncle, but he was strong.

The tall fellow had a cask secured by a leather thong around his neck, and a pack on his back, laden down. The cask bounced along against his side, and my father could tell it was empty. The beansprout explained in Ukrainian that he and his friend made the trip across the border all the time, several times a week, carrying cheap Russian tobacco into Austria, then brandy, which had no tax in Austria, back home.

"Maybe," my father says to him, "since you fellows know the way so well, my brother and I could tag along."

That was fine, the tall one says, but they'd have to pay.

That was okay too, my father says, he had a few coins, he'd pay when they got to the border.

No, their new friend says, better to pay now, just so we'll all know what's what.

They had to stop so my father could go into the bushes and dig out a couple of coins, half of what he had, from his underwear – the real money, for the boat fare, was in his sock. He said he had to shit – excuse my language – that he had to go right away, he'd pay when he got back, but he didn't think anyone was fooled. Moishe stayed with the Ukrainians – he said later they sat on the side of the road and took turns spitting across it, seeing who could spit the furthest. Pop comes back and hands over the money and the shrimp whispers to his friend, "I hope the Yid didn't wipe his ass with that," and the two of them laugh like idiots.

They leave the road and my father and Moishe follow them to an empty hut; he said it had been freshly plastered and the smell was so strong it stayed in his nostrils all the following day, when they were miles and miles away. They eat some supper there, the last of the bread and cheese their mother gave them and some apples and sausage and cider the other fellows had. My father had been in the army, so this was nothing new to him, but he knew it was the first time Moishe had eaten anything that wasn't kosher, but they'd known this was coming, he said, and they'd talked about it. There wasn't any other way. He thought maybe Moishe would be sick, but no, he was okay.

It gets dark but still they wait. The tall one digs some tobacco out of his pack and they smoke some from a clay pipe and my father and Moishe get dizzy. My father just took a couple of puffs and wouldn't let Moishe smoke more either because he thought maybe the other two were planning on taking advantage of them, but that didn't happen. It got later, and soon the moon would be up, which wasn't good. Nobody actually said anything, but it became clear that they wouldn't be leaving unless more money was paid. My father excuses himself, digs out the last of his bribe money, and hands it over. Then they set out.

They cross a field, then another, in single file, the two peasants first, then my father and Moishe. Pop saw some rocks and he reached down and put one under his shirt, a good-sized rock but not so big it was noticeable or weighed him down, and Moishe did the same. They walked and walked, through fields and meadows, passing no light or sign of any human habitation. The beansprout would call a halt every few minutes, holding up his hand, wetting a finger and tasting the wind, listening, for God only knows what.

"How much further to the border?" my father finally asks, whispering.

"Shhh," the tall one whispers back, sharply.

"How much further...." Pop begins, in the smallest whisper he could muster.

"Oh, we're well into Austria," the Ukrainian says, grinning, "have been for hours. Just over that hill is Nizke Tatry."

My father was so mad he hit the fellow with the rock he had in his hand. Moishe and the shrimp fell on each other, thrashing around, Moishe losing his rock, and Pop had to go help. He hadn't meant to do that, he always said, he'd picked up the rock just in case he needed to defend himself, but he was so mad. He went through the tall fellow's pockets and found the coins he'd given him, taking back just the second payment. "I didn't begrudge paying for their help," Pop used to say, "but I didn't like being held up. And I didn't like being made a fool of."

They left them there – my father didn't think either was hurt badly – and made for the town, then through it and were far away by first light. He said he kept that rock with him all the way across Germany, all the way to Holland, to Rotterdam, where they took passage. They wouldn't let him take it with him on ship so he dropped it over the side, plop, into the water.

In Berlin, they had no money for food and there was no work to be had, so they went to a *shul* but the German Jews took one look at them, took one listen to their Yiddish and turned them away. Finally, a woman gave them bread, a woman who had been leaving the *shul* and stopped to watch these bedraggled boys, my father with wisps of beard on his chin, Moishe just a boy not long out of short pants, both of them with mud and cow shit on their shoes. She took them home, told them to wait outside and brought them bread, a half a loaf. That bread tasted better than anything they ate on the three-week walk, my father used to say, Berlin bread.

My father and my uncle, somehow they made it all the way to Rotterdam, at the docks, on the boat, at sea, which stretched all around them, Pop used to say, like an endless field of wheat, blue wheat, swaying in the wind. On the boat – the *Umbria* it was called, and my father always called his wagons that, lock and key wagon, milk wagon, vegetable and fruit wagon before that, the *Umbria* – on that boat, he said, at least they had enough to eat, gruel and stale bread, mouldy cabbage, all part of the fare, not the best but plenty of it – but dirt? He said they didn't wash for ten days, twelve, however long it took to get there, and the steerage stunk of vomit and piss and shit – excuse my language again – all that, and disinfectant. When we were kids, my father used to like to take long baths Saturday afternoons, and he would say he was still washing off the dirt and stink from that boat, all those years later.

That first night on the boat, he said, that was when Moishe cried for the first time, because he knew he'd never be home again, that he'd never see his own Momma and Pop again, which he was right about. They never did eat that meal together again like their mother promised, and whenever Moishe came to our house for supper later on, or my mother and father to his house, there'd always be two empty places set, not for Elijah like you do at Passover but for their own mother and father. That was the way it was, Pop said, and there wasn't any point in crying about it.

ZAN SITS SILENTLY AFTER HE FINISHES THE STORY, looking at his hands, thinking of his own mother. After a minute or two, Zelda clears her throat.

"That's a pretty vivid memory. An awful lot of detail to remember over fifty or sixty years."

"Detail is my stock and trade."

"You sure that isn't a story you just made up, like the rabbi and the pope?"

"Made up? What a thought! No, embellished, maybe, that's what I do. But the story, no, that's the story my father used to tell. It's the family – what would you call it? Legend, the family legend. Who would make up something like that? Who could forget a story like that?"

"And yet you did."

"You got me there. My memory, as you know, is not the best. It has holes in it like a rusted bucket. But still, things come back. They never seem to be gone forever."

Zelda smiles. "And when they do, you embellish."

"Of course. Like I said, that's what I do."

But what he doesn't tell Zelda, won't, was that he hadn't remembered the story at all, it had vanished entirely from his mind. It was Abe who'd brought it back to him, at Friday night dinner four days earlier.

"There's so much about you that reminds me of Poppa," Abe said, surprising him. "Not looks, you don't look alike, any more than I looked like him – but the same pig-headedness, the same bull in a china shop."

The brothers laughed at this shared image. "Me, a bull?" Zan protested. "Pig-headed?"

"You know, it's funny, all these ghosts I carry around with me – Momma and Poppa, Adam, Hersh, Saul, Annie, all the guys I knew in prison, in the war, in the prison camp – of dead people I got plenty of minions, believe me. All those ghosts, they're with me all the time, but usually they stay in the back room, they're so polite. Since you've been here, *boychic*, the ghosts keep coming out, I bump into them in the morning going to the bathroom, trip over their legs while I'm tidying up.

"But it's Poppa's ghost I bump into most, he's hanging around, craning his neck to see what those *meshuge* sons of his are up to now."

Zan observed his brother, cleared his throat. "Abe, what do you remember about Poppa?"

"About Poppa? What do you mean?"

"Just what I said. What do you remember? Was he a good man? A good father? What was he like?"

"A good father! You're asking me? What, you don't remember yourself?"

"No, I don't."

"Your own father you don't remember?"

"My own name, some days I don't remember," he said. "My memory is like a sieve."

"He died, you remember that?"

"That he died, yes. When, no. What of, no."

"What of? The Wiseman curse, the bad heart, just like we all have. Just like Saul died of, just like Annie. Just like you got, like I got."

"You have a bad heart too, *Abela?*"

"Yes and no. Not bad lately, knock on wood. Same as you. Double bypass three years ago."

"You had bypass? I didn't know – or maybe I forgot. Double? I had six. *Abela*, you told me about this?"

"I did. *You* told *me*. We talked on the phone, remember? We used to talk on the phone once in awhile, remember that?"

Zan just nodded.

"Not even fifty-five years old, Poppa was – well, we're way past that, you and me, Zannie. We're old men, almost as old as Momma lived to be. If the Wiseman curse gets us, it won't be such a curse. It'll be a blessing. You really don't remember?"

"No."

"And nothing else about Poppa, really?"

"Some things. I remember his forearms, big, like a blacksmith's, covered with black hair. I remember one time he hit me. You, you bastard! It was you he wanted to hit, but somehow he wound up hitting me! You sassed him, I got the blame."

Abe laughed. "I remember that like it was yesterday. You were so mad."

They spent the whole evening, till late, talking about their father, chipping away at the bottle of cheap red wine Abe favours. And Abe told the story of how their father and uncle walked across Europe.

"It's funny," Abe said when he'd finished. "I don't remember all that much about Poppa, really, but that story I remember like I heard it this morning on Gzowski. It's Pop's memory, really, not mine, but it's what I remember about him best, clearest.

"In Germany, those years at the prison camp, the *stalag*, every night I told myself that story. Told it so I wouldn't forget home, wouldn't forget Poppa or Momma or any of them. Told it mostly to remind myself to be strong, to be tough, like Poppa was. All these years later, I still remember it as if Poppa was just telling it yesterday – all those times in the dark in that camp, the words of the story – not just thinking about it, thinking it, but telling it, almost out loud, just under my breath until I'd fall asleep. No, you do that, you don't forget."

The brothers sat in silence for awhile, a companionable silence.

Finally, Abe asked, "Zannie, you really didn't remember any of this? About Poppa? About your own father?"

"Not a damned thing," he said. "Not a Goddamned thing."

And yet to Zelda, he told the story as if it were his own memory, brazenly appropriating it. And why? Walking home afterwards, he ponders that. He stops to look in a store window on Seventeenth Avenue, finds himself starting at his own reflection, a stoop-shouldered old man with a frown on his mug, no, now it's a ridiculous grin. Vanity, that's all it was, he decides. Anyway, it wasn't the memory itself that he valued – memories, as he knows so well, come and go. No, it was the story he liked, the story and the telling.

ABE 4

I've been thinking a lot about Pop since Zannie came, Dolly.

Not about Momma? You would ask that if you could, I know. A bad start the two of you had, yes, but that was soon forgotten and you and she became bosom friends. I know she learned to love you like a daughter, you to love her like a mother, although I always wondered if you ever forgave her. The things she called you! *Shiksa*, witch and much worse. Still, she wasn't all wrong – an unhappy marriage she saw for us – though she was right for all the wrong reasons. Me in prison, in the war, the camp, you sick, our poor darling boy Benjy dead, Ana always sore at us, some honeymoon, eh? Not that any of that had anything to do with why Momma was against you, Dolly darling. And no, it's not an unhappy *marriage* I meant to say anyway – that was never anything but happy, sweetheart – but an unhappy life, filled with *tsuris*. And that's not right, either – a happy life we had, but with our share of unhappiness. Okay, okay, more than our share.

But no, it's not Momma I've been thinking of – what I mean is, I think of Momma all the time, so nothing new. But Pop, no, sometimes I don't think of him for the longest time, Pop's dead, buried, gone, not forgotten, no, but out of mind; Momma I think about. Zan says he wasn't there for Mom's funeral so for him, she's not dead at all. Me, I know the difference, I know she's dead, but it's *like* she was still alive. A fool or a *meshugener* I'm not. Still, often she comes into my mind. Pop, not so much. But lately, there he is a lot. It's Zannie who makes me think of him, so much like Pop he is. So different too, true, but so much like. So sure of himself!

All the bad things that happened – and not just to me, but Saul too, even his death – all come down to Pop, not that I blame him. He didn't lift a finger, let alone a hand, didn't will anything to happen, didn't push over a domino. So sure of himself, but such a dreamer, no, Pop never had any idea what was

Dave Margoshes

happening, let alone wanting it to happen. Zannie, too. A bull in a flower shop, he races around, breaks all the flowerpots, goes outside. Then he notices the sign: "Look, *Abela*," he'll say. "A flower shop. Let's go in and look around, smell the flowers." That was Pop too.

One time, I'm sure I told you before, lots of times maybe, but I'll tell you again – if you don't like it, just say so, Dolly – one time, we were going on a picnic. A Saturday, in the spring-time, the first nice weather after the long winter, Zannie and Adam and I were seven and eight, I think. We had been beg-ging him all week, a picnic on Saturday, and he said yes, sure, if Momma agreed, and she did. After *shul*, Momma is making the lunch, sandwiches and sweet pickles, hard-boiled eggs. Pop goes to the barn to harness the horse, *Schvartze*, and he notices the barn door is crooked. He takes off his jacket, rolls up his sleeves and begins to fix it. The frame is warped, from the win-ter, all the cold and snow. He has a jack, a hammer, a saw, he hammers, he cuts, I don't know what all he does. He *fusses*. Zannie and Adam beg, whine, cry, Saul and Hersh, they hang around watching, hoping he'll ask them to help, but would he do that, like a normal father? No. Momma, she goes to see. "Paisy, the children are waiting," she tells him. "I'll just be a minute more, Chaika," he says. Eventually, half the day goes by. When he's done, it's too late to go, Saul and Hersh already wandered off by now anyway. Pop can't see what the fuss is about – "The door was crooked," he says, "it needed to be fixed."

A dreamer he was, and so damn sure of himself.

But what I was thinking, that was something else.

I remember this like it happened yesterday. At the supper table, Pop with a heel of bread, wiping up the juice of the *shmaltz* herring he had on Friday, so it must have been a Friday, a Sherlock Holmes I must be, Zannie would say. "At the fish market," Pop says, with contempt, "Shatz is complaining, the protection he must pay to keep away the fires. I tell him, Shatz, the muscle boys, the leeches, you didn't invent, we all have the leeches sucking on us. 'Even you, Mr. Wiseman? A milkman?' This is how he says it, 'A milkman?' Like a milkman would maybe be beneath the dignity of the leeches. They shouldn't have to stoop so low. True, I have no shop to set on fire, but 'Shatz,' I tell him, 'you never heard of poisoning a horse? Of breaking glass? Not enough the leeches, but the police too,' I tell him. 'The police too?' This is a revelation. 'Certainly, the police too. Tribute to the leeches to protect you from the police, bribes to the police to make sure the leeches don't bite too deep. This is what makes the world go around.' Maybe with fish the world swims a little different."

Pop laughs at his own joke and Saul and I exchange glances. Zannie, he's listening too, his chin in his hands, elbows on the table in that way he had, his eyes far away. It's the words Zannie listened to, not the meaning, already he would be spinning those words into something else all his own. Saul and me, we were realists, after Mom we took. Saul gives me a glance and even though I'm only thirteen or fourteen, I know what that means, or think I do: we all know who the kids are, these leeches, they hang out on Selkirk, older than me, Saul's age or a little younger, some of them back from the war like him, he knows them, went to St. John's or *cheder* with some of them, he knows what they're up to, but what he didn't know, not till right now, is that Pop is one of their targets.

That's why I say it all comes down to him, to Pop, because the very next day Saul goes to talk to those *gonifs*. He couldn't threaten them, couldn't force anything – Saul was tough, but he was just one. So a bargain, that's the best he could hope for – this gang of leeches, these grafters and firebugs and *shtarkes*, they'll leave Pop alone, but Saul has to join them, that's the price he paid. And then, as they say, one thing leads to another, and there goes Saul, not exactly down the toilet but whatever it was he could have been, might have been – I'm not saying he was going to be a rabbi, no, not Saul, he was no doctor or lawyer, but more than the jailbird he became – whatever it was, it's pinched out that day, like the breath from Pop's mouth at the supper table was blowing out the candle in Saul's hand.

And everything else that happened – to me, to Annie, even what happened to Zannie, though most of that he brought down on his own head, *meshuge*, who *asked* him to do the things he did? Marrying that girl, as if the money that earned him could pay our way out of prison, just like that, where did he get such a *cockamayme* idea? But that's Zannie, bull in a flower shop, barging in without thinking, Zan to save the day – all of that, I lay that all on Pop too, one thing leading after another like one domino tipping over another and another till the whole wall of the castle or whatever it is you've built falls down. Bull in a flower shop.

But I know, Dolly, if you could, here's where you'd be butting in, if you hadn't already, "Wait a second, Abe, honey, why stop with your father, why not blame his father for having him? Why not blame the man who built the ship that brought your father and your uncle Moishe from the old country? Why not blame the Czar? Why not blame God? And going the other way, how about putting humility aside and taking credit where credit's due? How about blaming yourself for whatever bad may have happened to you? Isn't that what a *mensch* does?"

Ah, this is why I love you, Dolly darling. Always the pinch of salt on the tail of the peacock, even when you just lie there and gaze at me with those eyes blue as the sky and the Pacific Ocean all rolled into one, if only they were open. Why I don't blame God? I'll tell you that – you never heard of free will? God created Adam – not our darling Adam, may his memory be blessed, but the Adam in the Bible, you know that – and Adam himself and his darling Eve defied God, Adam himself chose to leave the garden. You think God put the apple in Eve's hand, in Adam's hand? No, they put it there themselves. "So why not blame yourself then?" I can hear you asking that, Dolly darling. "God didn't put the gun in your hand, and neither did your father." No, I don't say he did. No more than I've ever said Zannie should have hidden it, taken it away, thrown it in the river – that's his own *cockamayme* idea. No, the gun I put in my own hand. Pop, I say – I don't use the word blame – Pop, he pointed me in the gun's direction. That's all. Because he knew there was a gun? No. Because he knew the baby boy he liked to bounce on his right knee, Adam or Zannie always on the left, would be a grafter, a thief, a holdup man? A boxer who'd break his brother's nose? A lover who'd break his mother's heart – not that it didn't heal, Dolly darling, that you know. But no, no to all those things. But because he was a dreamer, that's why! Because he was a man who talked at the supper table of things no man should talk about in front of his children, because he shamed us, and didn't even know it, didn't pay one damn bit of attention. Thought he was making a little joke, some joke! That's why. Bull in the flower shop, yeah, just like Zannie. "Oh, look, a flower shop. Let's go in and smell the flowers."

Because he didn't take care, that's why.

CHAPTER 18

January 17, 1989

A COLD MORNING, THE SKY A SHINY METALLIC GREY that suggests the sun is there, trying to break through, the snow underfoot hard and crunching, the smell of fresh snow in the air, biting at his nostrils. A beautiful morning, Zan thinks as he walks along Seventeenth Avenue, then across Eighth Street toward Twelfth Avenue and the clinic, picking his way carefully around the icy spots. Then: Why do I call this beautiful?

He thinks of Las Vegas, the ease of the Nevada winter. Myrna loved it there, her flowers and perpetual tan, the mountains in the distance. She'd had offers at other universities but wouldn't dream of leaving. Zan hadn't liked it at first, the seemingly unchanging seasons, the dryness and the ridiculous, ostentatious opulence of the city, the overbearing arrogance and rudeness of the tourists, but gradually he'd been won over. Now he's relearning how to breathe.

"So, how are you today, Zan?"

"Tops. Thank you for asking."

"It's cold today. Have you gotten used to our weather here?"

"I grew up in Winnipeg, Zelda. To me, this is sissy weather."

"You've used that word before. Anything there, do you suppose?"

"What, Winnipeg?"

"Sissy."

"It doesn't mean anything, believe me. It just means I'm older than you. When we were kids, the worst thing you could call someone, the worst thing you could be *called*, was a sissy. But it didn't mean what it means today. Stop looking for things that aren't there, Dr. Holmes."

"Holmes? Don't you mean.... Oh, I see. All right. Let's look for things that *are* there, then. What do *you* think might be bothering you?"

"Bothering me? What I think? Nothing, nothing's bothering me."

"Okay, what *isn't* bothering you?"

"*Isn't* bothering me? That's a long list."

"No longer bothers you that used to." Zelda is wearing white today, white blouse, white scarf, cream skirt, even her shoes are white. Only her stockings are dark, calling extra attention to her legs, which she crosses now, as if to emphasize the point. "I'm trying to get a handle on your process."

"Ah." Jack, he thinks, would never have asked a question like that. He was both more open and more devious – could that be? "You think like a Jesuit, Lady Doctor."

"I'll take that as a compliment. What do you know of the Jesuits, though?"

"What do I know? Nothing really. I once thought about becoming a priest, though."

"Is that right?"

Zan laughed. "I'm exaggerating a little. I thought about it for about a minute."

"Okay, you seem to have picked something already. Let's talk about religion today, shall we? It's something I've been wanting to ask you about."

"Religion? What on earth for?"

"We don't have to – we don't ever have to talk about anything you don't want to talk about."

"I've heard that before."

She smiles. "I'm looking for ways of getting...*at* you. Glimpses into your head, you might say. Religion is often a good route. I know you're Jewish, you refer to God often, though usually in a mocking way. And you've even mentioned going to synagogue with your brother. Saying *Kaddish* for your sister, lighting a candle for her. But you don't strike me as being particularly religious."

"Jewish?" Zan interrupts, "what makes you think I'm Jewish?"

"Oh, I see, those Jewish characters in your novel, they were all from your imagination?"

"Ah, touché. Hoist on my own petard. I always loved that expression, don't you? Makes me think of a big, tall petard, whatever the hell that is, and block and tackle, thick rope. Sorry, I know, I'm evading again. All right, let's say I might be Jewish. And the relevance of that is...what?"

"Well, you grew up in Winnipeg, lived in Toronto, both cities where there are large Jewish populations. Las Vegas I don't know about.

Now Calgary. I believe there's only a small Jewish population here. Is that a problem for you?"

"There's a small everything population here. It's harder for me that I can't find a good Szechwan restaurant than that I can't take my pick of *shuls*, believe me."

"So, being Jewish isn't important to you?"

"Yes and no. I'm Jewish but I'm not Jewish."

"I don't understand."

"What's to understand? I'm a Jew but I'm not Jewish. You want to curse God, be my guest. You call me a kike, I'll punch you in the head. Or let me put it another way, I like a corned beef sandwich but I don't *davvin*."

She looks at him questioningly.

"Pray."

"So religion *isn't* important to you."

"I wouldn't say that. Better to say it isn't anything to me."

"You didn't have any sort of religious upbringing?"

"Upbringing, I had plenty of. Jewish school, Hebrew school, Talmud Torah school, the Peretz school, that's for Yiddish, *bar mitzvah*, I did the whole ball of wool. Well, no, wait a minute. I studied for *bar mitzvah*, but didn't finish – I don't remember what happened, I gave the rabbi a hard time and he kicked me out, I think. Anyway, no, no *bar mitzvah*. But everything else. Later, I even *taught* at the Peretz school, and the *Arbeiter Ring* school too, classes in Yiddish literature. These were leftist Jewish schools for Jews who weren't necessarily Jewish, if you know what I mean. Like me. But upbringing, sure. My father, the high holidays were enough to keep him going. He wasn't that religious. He used to say he'd made a bargain with God: you leave me alone, I'll leave you alone. But my mother, she was very devout. Friday candles, *shul* Friday night and Saturday morning, every week, the burial society. I can remember her coming home late from the funeral home in winter. She and the others had been washing a body, ritual washing, and gotten wet and there was ice in her hair. Around her, there was always plenty of religion."

"But with you, it didn't stick? Or something happened that made you see things differently?"

"Life happened."

Zelda smiles, makes a note, recrosses her legs. "That's it? Life?"

"Life's not enough? Life's plenty, you ask me."

THE TRUTH IS, HE COULDN'T HAVE SAID WHAT, if anything, had happened. Jack had asked him the same question, of course – they'd had almost the exact same conversation. But he didn't have any clearer idea then than he did now. He didn't know, he told Jack, if he'd ever believed a word of it, or, if he had, if it stayed with him any longer than Santa Claus and the tooth fairy might stay with another child.

"I remember being in *shul* with my family," he told him, "my father, my mother and the seven of us kids in a row, our faces and ears scrubbed and shining like that would make some difference to God, and mouthing these prayers in Hebrew, and thinking 'these hypocrites' – not meaning my mother and father specifically, but not excluding them, either – 'these hypocrites, they don't even know what they're saying. There's not a one of them except the last *bar mitzvah* boy who has the faintest idea what the Hebrew means.'"

"You were how old?" Jack wanted to know. "Twelve, thirteen?"

"No, ten or eleven. Younger maybe."

"And feeling that way, you continued on with Jewish school anyway?"

"Certainly. That's what was expected."

"So you were a hypocrite too."

"Sure I was. I was hypocrite number one. I don't deny that."

But eventually, he tells Zelda, "I rebelled. I couldn't do it any more."

Talking to Jack, he described the extra burden he felt, still so soon after Adam's death, over his twin brother's absence, as if that absence were a yoke around his neck, Adam's absence a rebuke to Zan's presence. "It was as if I was studying *bar mitzvah* for two," he told Jack. "Even if I'd been willing to give it up for myself, I couldn't. I had this...obligation."

He tells Zelda much the same.

"But then?"

"But then it got to be too much. I don't remember what happened exactly – just that I didn't go through with it. Or maybe the rabbi didn't *let* me go through with it. This was a long time ago, Dr. Zelda. I remember it hurt my mother, that I remember."

He remembers, too, denying then as he does now, that any of it would matter a damn once it was all over, that God, if there was one, would hold it against anyone for not praying, or even not believing. "I don't believe in God," he told Jack, "can't believe in God. But what I really can't believe is that if there is a God he gives a damn about you doing anything but living a good life."

"But what's a good life?" Jack had asked.

"Ah, well, that's religion," Zan said. "Trying to figure that out."

HE REMEMBERS THE EFFORT BY HIS MOTHER and the community at large to *make* him believe. The endless rituals of the home, the candle lighting, the blessings and prayers, the continual invoking of the name of the supposed creator and benefactor, that was just the background, the field of white noise upon which the more active drama of indoctrination had been played, always working against itself, in Zan's view. But the more they pushed, the more he'd pulled away, emboldened by the models of his skeptical uncle Leo and his even more avidly atheistic left-wing friends, "those lousy Reds," as his mother called them.

As if having to go to regular school – five days a week, seven hours a day, not counting the interminable homework – as if that weren't bad enough when any boy would rather be out exploring and conquering the world, then there were Yiddish classes, just bearable, and Hebrew school, at which the learning of that dead, tongue-numbing language by rote was forced upon them, by a teacher – the cantor of the *shul* – who either couldn't or wouldn't ever answer any of Zan's questions, any more than could or would the rabbi, who occasionally would deign to take part. Preparing for *bar mitzvah*, he remembered with irritation, the prayers and incantations were incomprehensible to him and the other boys.

"But why did God do it that way, teacher?" he would ask, and the cantor, a choleric old *melamed* thoroughly infused with the smell of tobacco and tea, would pull his eyes back in feigned terror, as if he had stumbled on the devil.

"You don't question God, Mr. Wiseman," he would growl, his loosely fitting false teeth grinding against each other.

"But why...?" Zan would persist and the thin wooden ruler the cantor kept behind his back would snake out and crack across Zan's knuckles like a fly swatter, ending the argument.

"This was God," he told Jack. "A revealed truth, and if you question it, a whack on the knuckles. What sane person believes in such a god?"

The private lessons were even worse than the classes, he tells Zelda, though the shape of his complaint has blurred. When he was seeing Jack, he still retained enough to describe it to him, including a vivid memory of sitting across a table from the malamed, chain-smoking and scowling menacingly as he listened to Zan go over and over the unintelligible Hebrew prayers and invocations, slapping him on the hand with the ruler whenever he stammered along with the repeated oaths: "Idiot. Golem." Or, if his gaffe was particularly bad, the old man would roll his eyes heavenward and exclaim: "Merciful God, what have I done to offend you?"

He'd had to learn many passages by heart, never understanding them, nor – and this was the part that rankled the most – was he expected to. "God understands," the cantor would say should Zan protest. "That's what matters."

ALWAYS, THERE WERE THE EXPECTATIONS of his mother to be reckoned with. Her older sons, both Saul and Hersh, had obediently done their religious duty, as their parents had required of them, despite their troublesome natures, and Abe had followed suit. Zan and Abe had what he remembered as innumerable arguments – in reality, there may have been only one or two – about the value of the *bar mitzvah*. For every point that Zan could argue against the practice, Abe, who had gone through the ritual the previous year, had one in its favour. He believed in God, he said, believed in the history and traditions of their people, was more than willing to bend to the greater will, to play his part. He didn't care that he didn't understand the prayers, accepting the rabbi's assertion that he would grow into an understanding – "Someday I *will*," he said simply – or that Zan's questions – he had none of his own – went unanswered. "But why..." Zan would begin, and Abe would make that characteristic, irritating gesture with his hand, like a symphony conductor lazily encouraging the violins. "Why, why, why," he'd mimic. "When you get the hang of that one, give zed a try."

Maybe, he tells Zelda, that was it, his reluctance to be bested by Abe, for surely if he'd gone through with the *bar mitzvah* ceremony, his stumbling would have been compared, and unfavourably so, with Abe's flawless performance the year before – perhaps the only time, he'd ever be bested by his brother in a contest involving the intellect. He was used to Abe beating him at wrestling, boxing, hockey and any other sport they might try their hand at, but he was supposed to be the one who was the brain, who could twist teachers around his little finger, though not the *melamed*. One way or another, he says, he'd blundered through right up to the point where he would have been welcomed into the community as an adult, a man, then abruptly backed, or was pushed, away.

"No, I'm pretty certain it was my choice. I decided not to go through with it."

"And there was a feeling of relief?" Zelda asks. "Or guilt for disappointing your mother?"

"Neither. It was...confusing." Before the decision, rather than elation that he soon would achieve something of value or relief that the ordeal was almost over, he'd felt hypocritical, since he knew he'd done nothing really to earn the honour he was about to be given, he says. "I felt a cheat, unworthy," and the congratulations his family and the members of the *shul* would heap on him illogical, even sacrilegious. "Instead, I turned away. I felt...not relief, no, not that, but like I was stepping at last into myself."

And from that point on, he had turned away from religion in general, following only observances that were unavoidable so as not to offend his family. At the same time, reading Goethe, he had come across this maxim: "Man should be noble, helpful and good." He took this as his secular religion. Whatever Marx and Lenin had to say on the subject would only come much later.

BUT HE DID HAVE A FLING WITH CATHOLICISM, he tells Zelda. "No, not really a fling, just a flirtation, if even that." One evening during the off-and-on years he was with Luna, he had come home excited from a class and said to her, only half joking, "I think I want to be a priest."

She was making a salad, and looked up from her work with her lopsided grin. He no longer remembers this conversation, but that grin is etched permanently in his mind, he sees it still on the faces of women he passes in the street.

"Fine," she said. "I'll be a nun. We'll go to a monastery or an abbey – hell, we'll get us to a nunnery – and fuck our heads off. But with piety."

"I'm serious," Zan said. He had been reading Thomas Aquinas and was swept away. He'd never encountered anything with the same sort of passion in Judaism, certainly not anything in his studies for *bar mitzvah*.

"Oh, that happens to everybody." Luna came around the counter to kiss him. "I'm surprised at you. Everyone falls in love with Aquinas second year. I didn't think *you'd* succumb."

"I'm not in love with him. I'm in love with you. When I look at another girl, that doesn't mean I don't still love you."

"You look at other girls!"

"Only when it's unavoidable."

"St. Thomas is some girl."

"So're you."

"So you say."

They fell into their other world then, coming out the other end an hour later, by which time the leaves of lettuce had grown limp and seeds of the tomatoes she'd been slicing stuck in a gelatine to the paring knife. The idea stuck with the same glue.

"That would be the end of us, you realize," Luna said. Now she wasn't teasing.

"What do you mean?"

"Priests are celibate, don't you know that? You do know what celibate is, don't you?"

"I know I wouldn't like it. What about brothers, monks, do they swear off too?"

"I don't know. I think so." She sat up in bed, her loosened hair tumbling over her small breasts. "You know, you would love that life, come to think of it."

"What do you mean?"

"Oh, it's a very ordered life the clergy lead. Everything set down in Bible and church law." She was trying to keep a straight face but when Zan laughed, she did too.

"Yes, maybe you'd fare even better as a monk than a priest, the abbot or father superior or whatever they're called making all your decisions for you."

She got up quickly, and Zan couldn't see her face, wasn't really sure if she was kidding or serious.

"I'll worry about celibacy later on," he said. "Don't worry, priest or monk, it'll take years."

"And I'll be too old to care then, right?"

"Hey, a boy has to look to his future," he cracked, though what he meant was there was no certainty how long their love would last. It amazed him in later years to realize that he had known that then.

"WE STARTED OFF TALKING ABOUT RELIGION," Zelda says into the silence, "but you seem to be avoiding the subject."

"This socialized medicine," Zan says. "You've got to be guardian of the almighty taxpayer's almighty dollar."

"Pardon?"

"Getting our money's worth out of the hour."

"Don't start in on that," she says, smiling. "But you're doing it again, avoiding the subject, that is. I really would like to talk about your Jewishness, if you don't mind."

"I *do* mind. Religion is my least favourite subject. In fact, talking about religion is *against* my religion."

"I have a feeling that isn't exactly true."

"Exactly...whatever is *exactly* true?"

"That's too philosophical a question for us, I think. Shall we stick to the concrete?"

"Nothing can be *too* philosophical. Not for me, anyway."

"Oh, yes, I forgot. You were almost a priest. But we were talking about you *almost* being a Jew."

"I *was* almost a Jew, you're right. It's not enough to be born one, you know. There's a covenant, a contract, and it has to be renewed each generation. That's what the *bar mitzvah's* all about."

"And you didn't do that."

"I came close, but it didn't take. I reneged, you might say." He laughs. "Good thing they didn't have small claims court in those days. The rabbi might have sued me. Or God. God Himself might have sued me."

"You say it didn't take. Why not?"

Zan shrugs. "I told you. I never had any real interest. And I couldn't abide the rabbi's insistence that this was the way to do things, this way and only this way. That wasn't for me. 'When I was a child I spake as a child, when I was a man I put away childish things.' That's Shakespeare. Do you remember which play, Dr. Zelda?"

"No, I'm sorry, I don't."

"Or maybe it's the Bible. It doesn't matter. You know what I mean, though, right? When you're a child, you do what your mother tells you. I tried to. After *bar mitzvah*, you're a man, so she doesn't tell you any more. And you only have one chance – you get to be thirteen, you either do it or you don't. You miss, you can't try again. So *bar mitzvah* or not, you're a man, you don't have to study any more, don't *have* to go to *shul*, unless you want to. You're a man and you can act like a man. That's what I did."

"But don't most Jewish men continue...the covenant, as you say? Don't they embrace it?"

"There's no sense in having a covenant with a god you don't believe in. I acted like the man I was, not like the man I was supposed to be. After awhile, communism became my religion, the Party my church."

"Ah," Zelda says. She makes a note. "We're almost out of time for today, but I'd like to come back to that."

"Of course."

"And what about your brother? How did he act?"

"Abe? I told you, he was a good son."

"You mean he stayed true to the covenant?"

"Well, it was complicated, but he tried. He was better than I was."

"A better son or a better Jew?"

"Both." He frowns, picturing the pain lines on his mother's forehead when she came to him – but he can't remember which time it was, which was which. "But it was complicated."

"What do you mean?"

He shrugs again. "He married a *shiksa*, a gentile. I told you already, I think. God punished him for that, if there is a god. He was in prison.... I told you that?"

"Yes."

"Regular prison, hard time, and war prison, even harder time. Later, a son who died, drugs, and a daughter who's angry at him, he doesn't really know why. And his wife, sick, in a coma, as good as dead. God punished him plenty, that god he believes in. *Still* believes in. He had a hard life, Abe, so it wasn't always easy being a good son *or* a good Jew. But he always tried. What he always was was a good man, a *mensch*, a just man."

"And you? You didn't try?"

"To be a good man, a good son, or a good Jew?"

"Any of the above."

"For the latter, I didn't see anything to try *for*. I still don't. A country is one thing, a god is another."

"Now that's an intriguing distinction. What do you mean, exactly?"

"I mean Israel is something a man can believe in. I don't, but I can understand how a man could."

When he'd told Jack something on this order, he *had* believed in Israel, or thought he did. The Six Day War was still fresh then, and he himself had been aflame with all sorts of pulls and pushes, not all that long removed from the Communist Party, still confused. Any lingering connection he felt to either the Party or the Soviet Union was severed then, when the Soviets backed the Arabs. "I never thought I'd be on the wrong side of an issue like this," he told Jack with genuine surprise. "But to me it seemed clear the Israelis were the ones to support."

"Why 'the wrong side'?" Jack asked. "Why must one side always be right, one always wrong? Can't they both be right in their own way?"

"Or both wrong."

"Can't they both be right *and* wrong?"

"I don't know, Dr. Freud, can any of us?"

Now, he says to Zelda, "As for being a good son, I was pretty much of a bust. As for being a good man – what Jews call a *mensch*, you know that term? Well, I tried, I always tried. I *keep* trying. I told you, Lady Doctor, I don't *davvin*, I don't pray. If I did, this is a prayer I might make: let me be a better man today than I was yesterday, let me be better still tomorrow."

CHAPTER 19

January 24, 1989

Jan. 24, 1989 – Salvador Dali died. Heard it on the news this morning. Born 1904, they said, so just two years older than me. A great artist, a great man.

If I had gone to Spain, as I wanted, maybe I would have met him, but no, he supported Franco, so not likely. I'd forgotten that. Like so much else. I don't remember any more who was on which side, who the enemies were, who the friends.

The *Persistence of Memory* – that's his famous painting, the melting clocks against that bleak background – I love that. *Persistence of Memory* – he got that right. Memories fade, memory persists.

ZAN IS RESTLESS THIS MORNING, and the therapist picks up on it immediately.

"Not sleeping well?"

"Well enough. I dreamed about Luna again." It's not so much a complaint as an explanation.

"Is that right? Well, we've been talking about her. It's not unusual."

The therapist is in blue today, navy blue skirt, sky blue blouse. Even her earrings, little ceramic studs, are blue. Zan realizes he doesn't know the colour of her eyes – brown or black to match her coffee-and-cream skin, he's guessing. He leans closer but can't make them out behind her black-framed glasses.

"Who would have thought, after all these years, she'd be haunting me again," he says, sounding more peeved. "It's like all the others didn't count – Rose, Myrna, even the other one, Whatshername – all the women in my life, it's Luna I'm dreaming about now."

"Are they pleasant dreams, at least?" Zelda is smiling, and he's not sure if she's mocking him or genuinely interested.

"It's always pleasant dreaming of a beautiful woman. At my age, especially. Maybe some night, I'll dream about you, Lady Doctor."

"Tell me more about Luna, why don't you. You've told me about how you met and so on, but not much of your life together."

"Ah. Our life together." Zan smiles ruefully. "Luna was not a woman you could live with easily," he says carefully. "It took me a while to figure that out. She was.... It was like the big bang, no dirty double entendre intended. You know the big bang theory of the universe?"

"Yes." Zelda was smiling more broadly now.

"That was us. We came together – boom, a big bang. Then we started cooling off."

AFTER TWO YEARS, IN FACT, Luna's breath had become heavy on his neck.

His first year at the university, he'd continued living at home at first but was at her apartment on Balmoral Street so often, spending the night so frequently, that eventually he'd be all-but living there during the week, returning home on Friday night for the weekend. His parents remained ignorant of Luna for months, Zan explaining that he had made friends at university, which was not exactly a lie. When they did find out about her, his mother especially was horrified, referring to Luna as *dybbuk*, a demon, though she actually knew very little about the woman who was, she was sure, perverting her precious son. He was twenty-one, after all, and could do as he pleased. From time to time, he'd go back home for awhile, and the summer between his first and second years at university, when he was working long days again at the rail yards, he was in permanent residence in his old bedroom, empty of everyone else – both Saul and Abe living elsewhere. He would be there the second summer as well, but doing something entirely different to make money.

His being back home suited Luna well, actually, as she liked to spend her summers travelling, or visiting her parents' cottage at Victoria Beach, where Zan was sure he wouldn't be comfortable – Jews were expressly forbidden to own property in the village, he'd heard. Her father, a lawyer, barely tolerated him when, on rare occasions, she dragged him along to family functions, though her mother was unfailingly polite. Her family lived on Roslyn Road, just across the river – though on the south side of the street, not the river side; "My folks aren't *that* rich," she told Zan – and, standing at her living room window, Luna could see, through the trees that shaded it, pieces of the house in which she had grown up. Was it Zan's Jewishness her father detested? His poverty? His youth? Or was it merely his daughter's passion for the embodiment of those faults that made him squirm?

In the fall of 1928, back in school for his second year, he fell into the same pattern – continuing to live at home, spending time at Luna's apartment, the occasional night, then the whole week. Evenings, they were the happy married couple at home, he in his easy chair, she in hers, he with pipe and slippers and the newspaper, she with a lapful of mending and a letter from the grandchildren – that's the way it felt. The difference was that he was reading for his classes or writing a paper, she was marking papers or preparing a lecture. Selkirk Avenue and its rough, insular world, its sidewalks alive with Yiddish and Polish and Ukrainian, the barking of dogs and clucking of live chickens from the butcher shops punctuating the clatter of the electric streetcars – that all seemed a million miles away when he was with her, but he continued to make the ride on the maroon and yellow trolley north to visit his parents every Friday evening, spending the weekend and, to save the nickel fare, walking back to classes and Luna Monday over the Salter Street Bridge spanning the railway yards, shoulders hunched and the earflaps of his cap turned down against the wind.

Some evenings, Luna would entertain, having a few of her colleagues at the university over for drinks or dinner – or they would go out to someone else's home. Either way would send Zan into a funk, as much over Luna's seeming disinterest in his discomfort as over the discomfort itself. He had gotten over his mortal fear of non-kosher food – had come to like it quite a bit, in fact, bacon and tomato sandwiches in particular – but couldn't shake his self-consciousness.

"Those people think I'm a freak," he complained. "Worse – they think I'm your pet."

"Oh, Zan, don't be such a silly goose," she would chide him. "They like you. Besides" – her grin turned impish – "what's wrong with being a pet? Especially *my* pet?" That rankled because, though she invariably would deliver such a line with a light tone implying she was joking, he was pretty sure she was serious.

Other times, they would go out to see a movie at the Metropolitan Theatre on Portage or the new Capitol, with its sweeping staircase entrance, just down the street, and afterwards go to the Princess Tea Room to share a banana split. This suited Zan fine. But most weekday evenings, they were home, leading what was, for all intents and purposes, a very conventional life – conventional for someone of Luna's age and station in life, at any rate, not Zan's.

Occasionally, what struck him as the absurdity of their life together erupted. Luna got up, crossed the room in a caricature of silence, skirt swishing, her hip brushing almost against his face, and padded into the kitchen. "Do you want a glass of wine?"

"Milk," he shot back. "A glass of milk, please, Mommy."

When she came into the doorway, the wine bottle in her hand, an empty glass in the other, a perplexed smile on her face, he shouted at her: "This is ridiculous. I should be at home, or in my own place. We can't live like this. For God's sake, Luna – we're in two different worlds, can't you see that?"

She was silent for a moment, then punctured his balloon: "My, my, we are being dramatic tonight. Are you reading Aeschylus?"

He'd laugh – how could he not? – and that would be the end of studying. He wondered sometimes if picking a fight with her wasn't his way of getting out of studies, of procrastinating, wondered too if provoking him wasn't her way out as well. They'd wind up in bed, where all the differences in the world – age, class, accents, money, education, everything you could think of – disappeared and they were equals. Almost. No matter how much he caught up, he was conscious that she was always ahead, always would be.

"What do you see in me?" he would ask her. "I mean, really?" His belly was flat and hard, his chest and arms muscular from his time at the rail yards, but he knew well enough that he was no beauty, his hair too unruly, beard too dense and dark, nose too big, too bent, teeth too crooked. Lying next to her, his fingers moving along the smooth arc of her spine as she curved to nest her head in the concave in the middle of his chest, he was conscious of how much shorter than her he was, the hairiness of his stick legs, the occasional rumbling in his belly, a lump of clay in the arms of a sleek, supple swan. He was almost fifteen years her junior, absorbed in second-year university classes, the Big Questions that arise then – the disinterest of the supposed God, the mean-spiritedness of capital, the meaning of it all – and just as aware that these were questions that no longer particularly engaged her, if they ever had. It wasn't that she knew the answers, but she had forgotten – or dismissed – the questions.

"What do *you* see in *me?*" she'd check him. "An old woman like me, worn out and dried up, skin like sandpaper, a head filled with dry old names and dates and theories."

"You're making fun of me," Zan protested.

"Well, of course, my dear. What else would you expect."

And again they'd laugh, again his bubble punctured. She was impossible, certainly impossible to argue with, *it* was impossible, their life together, but so, she'd convinced him, was any alternative. In the morning, he'd gather up his still-unread books, the unfinished papers, and head for the library and his classes. She'd already be in her office at Wesley College, crisp in a blouse and stockings and skirt, patent leather heels, sipping coffee, chatting with colleagues, preparing to deliver a lecture.

Money was another opportunity to express it.

His tuition and fees were taken care of – the scholarship he'd won covered some of them, and the rest, Luna insisted, were waived because of his connection to a faculty member, even if they weren't married or related in any way. Zan had suspicions she paid them herself, and, of course, she paid the rent, bought the groceries and took care of all other expenses connected to the household, insisting again that, except for the little bit extra for food, her weekly expenses were no more with him in her apartment than when she lived alone. Still, he couldn't escape the uncomfortable feeling that he was a "kept man," as his friend John Archer, whom he had met in Luna's first-year literature class, mockingly called him – "teacher's darling" was the phrase Abe used, laughing – and he felt the censure in the eyes of his classmates and Luna's colleagues, though, remarkably, none of them ever said a word to him about it, with the exception of Archer.

"If our sexes were reversed, you supporting me, no one would think a thing of it," Luna would say, exasperated.

"Yes, but that's the way of the world."

"Me Tarzan, you Jane, welcome to my cave? That what you mean?"

Against the blunt force of her sarcasm, Zan was usually reduced to silence.

"Besides," Luna would add, "I thought you hated that sort of conventional thinking. And what do you care what people think, anyway?"

It chafed, but he allowed himself to be convinced. Still, he'd drawn the line at his own expenses – books and pocket money – and would accept no allowance from her. "I may be a kept man," he said, "but I won't be kept."

"What?"

"Maybe it's the other way round – I'm kept, but I won't be a kept man." He grinned at her. "Either way, keep your money."

He didn't need a lot, and the little bit of money he'd saved before starting school lasted him through most of his first year, a loan from Abe filling the gap. Saul had been paroled and returned from British Columbia that winter, and he and Abe had bought a used truck and were operating what seemed to be a thriving cartage business. It wasn't lost on Zan that, if not for Luna, he'd most likely be in business with his brothers, his life going a different direction.

The money he made working the summer between his first and second year at university, back at the rail yards, was enough to repay Abe and keep him going all through the following school year, but just barely. Toward the end of the spring term, not knowing that his time at the university would be abruptly cancelled the next fall, when his scholarship would be pulled away, and feeling dissatisfied with the prospect of repeating the cycle, opportunity came to him in the form of Archer, with whom he'd become tight.

Archer was day to Zan's night, tall and graceful, fair-haired and blue-eyed, well-dressed and well-mannered. He came from an affluent family, growing up in a house on Wellington Crescent, just south of the Assiniboine River, easily four times the size of the Wisemans' Flora Avenue house. Archer's father, cut from the same cloth as Luna's, Zan was sure, was a physician and an occasional lecturer at the medical school, where the Jewish quota was infamous.

"If I'd wanted to go there, your dad would have voted to keep me out," Zan complained to Archer one night when a group of students were assembled in the tavern of the Clarendon Hotel, near the campus.

"First of all, he doesn't have a vote," Archer said. "Second, he wouldn't vote against you because you're a Jew. He'd vote against you because you're a *schmuck*." He delivered himself of this pronouncement with a wide grin on his smooth-featured face to make clear he meant no offence.

Archer had been a champion swimmer in high school and he should have been on the swim team at the university, or playing tennis, but he'd fallen in love with the Romantic poets and now, though he had no talent or desire to write himself, he was applying himself to an academic life with the same concentration and energy of an athlete preparing for a meet. He'd already plotted out the arc of graduate school, dissertation, publication, teaching career. His friend also had another passion, Zan had learned. When, years later, he described his former friend's fascination with all things Jewish to Jack, the therapist, without missing a beat, had come up with the term "Hebrophile." He raised his eyebrows. "Believe it or not, it's a fairly well-documented phenomenon."

Zan uses the term now with Zelda and she nods her head knowingly. Whatever it was called, the man was fascinated with Jewish food and customs, Yiddish expressions, even certain aspects of the Judaic liturgy, although his family was staunchly Episcopalian and John was a long way from considering conversion. "He wanted to be a Jew without being Jewish," Zan says. "When I was living in the States, I saw people who wanted to be Negroes – blacks – in the same sort of way."

"A Jew without being Jewish," Zelda says. "Isn't that the way you described yourself, just last week?"

"Touché, Lady Doctor. I guess I did. But with a bit of difference."

Where this fascination came from, Zan had no idea, and it predated their friendship, but it soon came to be of more than passing interest to him, in conjunction with his friend's own need for money.

John's father was displeased that he wasn't following his path into medicine and had curtailed his allowance as punishment. The prospect of it being restored was held out as inducement to return to the expected fold, but it had the opposite effect on Archer. He was eager to move out of the Wellington Crescent house and get a place of his own, to be, he said, "my own man and tell my dad to go to hell."

"Daddy wouldn't like it there," Zan observed dryly. "Too many Jews."

"Let's go into business together," Archer suggested one day as they sipped coffee in the student lounge between classes.

"Business? You want to go into business with me? Why me?"

"It doesn't have to be you – it has to be a Jew. You qualify. It would also be nice if the candidate were a charming fellow who made good company. You qualify there too. We'll be spending a lot of time together." Archer said all this with a good-natured but somewhat non-committal expression on his face that made it hard for Zan to tell if he was serious or not.

"I see. And why a Jew?"

"Because I want to make money, that's why. Everyone knows Jews are good at business." Now he was broadly grinning, and Zan relaxed.

"I've heard that myth too," Zan said. "Have you ever taken a walk through the North End? Maybe you'd like me to introduce you to my father, laid up and dependent on his sons. Even when he's in the pink of health, he goes from job to job gazing fondly at the rear end of a broken-down horse. One of the shrewd Jewish businessmen you're thinking of, I'm sure. If that's the rule, then most of the Jews I know are the exceptions that prove it."

"But Wiseman, what about Shylock?" Archer protested. "Surely you're not suggesting Shakespeare would make up such a character."

"Heaven forbid."

"And what of the Rothschilds, and Disraeli?"

"What about them?"

"They're proof of what I say."

"And I and the members of my family and all our neighbours on Flora Avenue are proof that you're wrong."

"More than likely, your family and your neighbours are in the employ of the Rothschilds, set up as a smokescreen to confuse the rest of us."

"Ah, and why would we allow ourselves to be so used?"

"For the greater good of world Jewry, of course. Plus, you'll be well paid, receiving your reward in heaven. Come on, Wiseman, you can trust me. Isn't that it?"

"Yes, I can see how trustworthy you are, Archer. And with the best interests of me and my brethren at heart."

"Well, maybe we should agree to disagree on this point. I still need a Jew to join me in this business venture."

"Oh? If not for my business acumen, then what?"

"For authenticity," Archer said. He was still grinning.

"Ah. So tell me, Doctor's Son. What kind of business is this you're thinking of, this authentic Jewish business?"

"Bread delivery. Nobody makes better bread than the Jewish rye from Gunn's, don't you agree?"

"Yes. So?"

"So they deliver in the North End, but it's impossible to get a good rye bread in my part of town."

Zan laughed. "The *goyim* aren't interested in rye bread from Gunn's. That's why they don't deliver."

"But you're wrong," Archer insisted.

"You're telling Gunn's how to run a bakery?"

"I'm telling them how to sell Jewish bread to gentiles, yes. But I'm *not* telling them. It's going to be our little secret."

And it was.

John hadn't known that Zan had a horse and wagon at his disposal, but that was exactly the equipment he had in mind. Both *Schvartze* and the locksmithy wagon had sat idle since his father's heart attack a few months earlier, and it had fallen to Annie, the only one of the kids still living at home, to take the horse out once every other day for a brisk trot through the neighbourhood for exercise, good weather or bad. She was delighted to get out of that chore. And their father, uncomfortable and irritable in his chair, was just as delighted at the thought that his horse and gear were being put to good use, bringing in some money, although Zan was deliberately vague about what use exactly.

FORCING HIMSELF INTO A SUMMER ROUTINE was no more difficult than if he were doing shift work at the rail yards. As he had the previous summer, he moved back home, with mixed feelings of regret and relief, leaving Luna to her own devices. He wondered if she didn't feel the same. Early to bed, his alarm set for four a.m., a quick wash at the sink and a bolted-down cup of coffee, then off in the darkness to the barn to harness *Schvartze*, conscious of how he was repeating the patterns of his father. Just at dawn, he would arrive with the rig at the bakery on Selkirk, only a few blocks away. Archer, who had given up his McLaughlin roadster for a bicycle when he left his parents' home, would already be there. The financial transactions were his responsibility, they'd agreed, and he would have bought as many loaves of day-old rye as the bakers had available, usually a couple hundred, at two cents a loaf, and several dozen assorted Danish pastries, at a penny, and as soon as Zan arrived the two of them would heap the loaves in their long, white paper bags into bushel baskets in the back of the wagon and set off.

They clattered past the produce market at Dufferin and Derby, where the horse would prick up its ears and whinny a greeting to its cousins, stamping their feet and snorting in the still-cool air as their owners unloaded heaping baskets of lettuce, potatoes, cucumbers, tomatoes. The smell of the horses, mingled with that of herring and pickles in great black barrels, assailed their nostrils, and they would grin at each other as the market women called after them, "Where you going in such a hurry? Don't be so stuck-up, come on over, sweet boys. *Vayher! Vayher! Sheyne gute vayher!* Oh, you darlings, you lovely boys, see what we have, so cheap and good! Don't be shy, come over and taste. How can you resist?"

"That's how we've got to sound," Archer would say, winking.

"Maybe just a bit deeper voice." Zan's feelings about the venture were never less than ambivalent but he would be most torn at this moment, as they passed the market, when he felt most like his father, felt most like he was an heir to some ancient inheritance, but at the same time felt most repulsed. This was what he had wanted to escape from, what he *had* escaped from, so why this pull? And later, years later, he would realize that the seeds of *The Wise Men of Chelm* were first planted here, in the smells and bickering outside the bakery and at the market. Indeed, a man selling bread from a wagon – a man not like either Zan or Archer but somewhat like Zan's father – and his young son – a boy not entirely unlike the boy Zan had been – would become characters in the novel.

They turned onto Main, the iron wheels of the old wagon grinding sparks as they crossed the streetcar tracks, then south on the wide street, over the CPR tracks and past Portage, across the Main Street Bridge over the Assiniboine River, then west on River Avenue and past Fort Rouge Park, where, finally, after a trip of almost an hour, they'd begin to sell their wares along the quiet, tree-lined streets just as the housewives of the Osborne and Roslyn districts were setting about getting breakfast for their husbands and children. At Zan's insistence, they avoided Roslyn Road itself, the wealthiest of streets, running parallel with the river, because that's where Luna's parents lived. John had no similar compunction about Wellington Crescent, happily selling bread to curious neighbours who had known him all his life.

Dressed in long, black frock coats with shiny sleeves they'd picked up at a second-hand store on Main Street and battered tweed caps, they looked authentic enough, Zan pronounced, as much like his father as his father did himself, no, even more. They'd put away their razors for the summer and grew dark beards – Zan's naturally dark, of course, Archer's as pale as his hair, most of which he concealed beneath his cap, but darkened with shoe polish, which reeked as Zan sat beside him on the wagon seat. Housewives bending close to John with their pennies or nickels would often catch a whiff of the polish and jerk their heads back, sending Zan into fits of uncontrolled laughter. "Don't mind my partner," Archer would say. "He's just come out of the hospital but he's harmless. A fine baker's assistant."

They sold the bread for ten cents a loaf, the Danish for a nickel, the same price Gunn's charged for them fresh, and always had most of their supply sold before nine a.m., when sales would slow noticeably. They could count on the rest being gone by noon. At Zan's insistence, they avoided the use of the word "fresh" – "I'm not going to lie about that," he said – instead crying out "good rye bread, real Jewish rye" as they clattered down the streets in their wagon. Occasionally, they would mimic the women of the market, calling out *"Vayher! Vayher! Sheyne gute vayher!* See how cheap and good! Just come over! Just taste!"

If a suspicious-eyed housewife would ask if the bread was fresh, Archer, who loved the transactions, would answer: "Just give a loaf a squeeze, Missus, take a whiff, decide for yourself. But, please, don't squeeze too hard." That was usually all it took, and only if a woman remained skeptical, demanding to know when the bread had been baked, did Zan, speaking up, confess that it was from the day before.

Dave Margoshes

"But listen, Missus, you think at your grocer's, the bread is any fresher?" John would throw in. "You know it isn't any better." A few sales would be lost with the admission, but only a few, and the loss of a sale here or there was hardly a setback for them. "Customers we got plenty," John would say, good-naturedly mimicking a Yiddish accent, "it's merchandise we need more of," and after only a few days they began to stock day-old pumpernickel, as well. Adventurous house-wives gave it a try and many liked it. There was never enough rye to meet demand. They tried bagels one day, Gunn's good chewy bagels flecked with poppy seeds or onion flakes, but the day-olds had a stale smell and a rubbery feel that was unappealing. In the second week, John made a deal with the bakery to increase its Danish output, so there'd be more left over. They had to pay an extra penny for the sweet rolls now, but it was still worth it.

Usually, their wagon would be bare by two o'clock at the latest, and the two of them would be splitting something in the vicinity of thirty dollars. It was a huge sum, and that was after the three dollars Zan set aside for his father – three dollars, he realized with a shock, being more than his father would sometimes bring in with his horse and wagon, loaded down with locksmith equipment, after a full day of work.

By summer's end, Zan had over seven hundred dollars socked away, more than enough to let him live just the way he wanted through the following year, buying a round of drinks when it was his turn or any book or magazine he wanted at People's Books on Arthur Street, where he loved to browse on Saturday mornings, despite his mother's dire warnings about transgressions of the Sabbath. And he put his foot down with Luna, insisting he pay his own tuition past the amount the scholar-ship covered. "Honestly, the tuition is free," she said with irritation. "The university won't even take it from you – it would be dishonest. Or if they do, by mistake, it'll be like throwing it in the garbage."

"All right, you take the money then, put it in the grocery fund. That's not throwing anything away."

There wasn't anything she could say to that, and she retreated with a smile that perplexed him. Damn that woman – even beating her was losing!

But he didn't mind. He soon was out of school anyway, making tuition a moot issue, and he'd started work on his novel. By the time his savings ran out, he was deeply immersed in the novel and barely aware that Luna was once again supporting him in every way, making him once again a "kept man," that label Archer had good-naturedly taunted him with. He was too absorbed in the novel, its evolving story and cast of characters – Jewish peddlers, women in a market, a boy and his father and an uncle – to care. His thoughts were most often there.

DUET 6

"Pass the bread, *Abela*."

"Pass? It's right there. You got a sprained arm, maybe?"

"Okay, okay. Bread like this, the least you could do is pass. It ain't Gunn's, you know."

"Gunn's? Gunn's Bakery?"

"What else?"

"On Selkirk?"

"Where else?"

"In Winnipeg?"

"*Abela*, take a look at me. It's Zannie, your brother, remember? What else would I be talking about? Gunn's Bakery, Selkirk Avenue, Winnipeg, Manitoba, Canada."

"So how could it be Gunn's? It *ain't* Gunn's. It's Superstore."

"Superstore! That ain't Raber's Grocery."

"Again with what it ain't. It *ain't* Raber's. Why should it be? It is what it is, not what it ain't."

"Gunn's was better, believe me. So was Raber's. Remember when that *cockamayme goyisher* Archer and I sold Gunn's bread from Pop's wagon? We were the original Superstore, on wheels no less."

"Gunn's was good, sure. This is too. Raber's was good, but it was small. And Raber always marked up too high. Superstore is big. Raber's in the winter had oranges. Superstore in the winter has oranges, melons, apples, grapes…"

"Just like in Las Vegas."

"But this ain't Las Vegas. You don't live there any more, remember? Again with what this ain't. This is here, now. Why not tell what *this* is?"

"What this is? This ain't the old neighbourhood. You remember Civkin's barber shop?"

"Remember it? I got my hair cut there ten thousand times. How could I forget?"

"And the conversation? Always, the old men in the morning

talking about yesterday's *Tag* like it was today's. Philosophy, art, politics. Playing chess."

"But would they buy the *Free Press* from you?"

"Not on your life."

"'War coming,' it says in *Der Tag*, that's yesterday. 'War breaks out,' in the *Free Press*, that's today. But will they buy the Free Press from you?"

"No, they sit and talk about the war that's coming."

"That's you."

"That's me?"

"Like those *alter kockers* at Civkin's."

"I got news for you, we're both old men, at Civkin's or anywhere else."

"You know what I mean."

"What, I'm reading *Der Tag?*"

"Not exactly."

"What exactly?"

"Yesterday's news."

"What about it?"

"You're reading it. No, you *are* it."

"What, because I'd like a piece of decent rye bread?"

"Because this is here and you're still walking down Selkirk Avenue like forty years haven't passed by."

"Fifty."

"Fifty? Sixty, you mean."

"Why stop at sixty? Seventy."

"Exactly, seventy years and you're still there, Zannie."

"So? It's not such a bad place to be. This is better?"

"Not better. This is this. That was that. This is where we are."

"And that's such a big deal?"

"A big deal? What, to be alive? Yeah, that's a big deal, Mr. *Makher* Las Vegas. Maybe to you it isn't. To me, it is. Aches and pains and all."

"That's not what I meant."

"So what you meant?"

"Never mind."

Dave Margoshes

"Now it's never mind. First you're on Selkirk Avenue by Civkin's barber shop, now you're on Nevermind Boulevard in Las Vegas, Nevada."

"Another place that's not so bad to be."

"I'll take this place."

"This place! Is there a Gunn's? Is Civkin's down the street? Or do I mean Misha's?"

"Now you're really talking *meshuge*. Misha's was two blocks east, closer to us."

"I'm crazy? It was just down the street, past the deli."

"The deli? Kirk's, you mean?"

"What else? Sure, Kirk's."

"Wake up and drink your coffee, Zannie. That's Civkin's on the Gunn's block."

"Civkin's?"

"Sure. With the picture of the fireman's dog in the window. What that fireman's dog was doing there, I never knew. To ward off fire, maybe. East from Gunn's, the Queen's Theatre, a hardware man every year a different name, the *Jewish Post*. The other way, Saidman's Seeds, Kneller the carpenter, Rabkin the dentist, Kirk's delicatessen, Civkin the barber, Manitoba Upholstery, Raber's on the corner. Across the street..."

"Okay, okay."

"Misha's, two blocks over."

"So why'd we go so far, if Misha's is right there?"

"You're asking me? Pop liked Civkin's."

"So how come you remember all this so good? I'm the one who's there, you say, you're the one who's here."

"How come? I don't have a head full of *drek*, that's how come. I don't think about it, that's how come I can."

"Can what?"

"Think about it, Mr. Big Shot. When I have to."

CHAPTER 20

January 31, 1989

Jan. 31, 1989 – Been working more on the new novel. *God Blinked.* I like that title more and more.

More and more, the shape of it is coming clear.

It's about brothers, that much I knew from the start.

Brothers who go to jail, that I just lately realized – clear as the nose on my face, but who can see in the dark?

It's about a man who tries to be a *mensch.* Again, that should have been obvious, but wasn't.

It's about a woman – what kind of a novel isn't?

It's about living your life as if heaven existed, even when you know it doesn't.

"WHAT DO YOU SAY WE TALK ABOUT this writer's block of yours today?"

"Writer's block?"

Zelda is wearing blue again today, a light blue dress with darker blue flowers, a dark blue scarf. Zan is thinking how good she looks, how much he'd like to take her to bed – if only he wasn't old enough to be her grandfather, if only he could get it up, if only he could remember how...if only...if, if, if.

"It seems to be important, it...."

"Is there a Mr. Zelda?" he interrupts.

"A Mr. Zelda?"

"A husband."

"Oh. No, I'm not married."

"A boyfriend?"

"We really shouldn't be discussing my private life, Mr. Wiseman."

"Why not? We discuss my private life. What could be more

personal than my writer's block?"

"Yes, the block..."

"So, a boyfriend or not? It's a simple question."

"No, no boyfriend."

"But you like boys?"

She smiles. "Are you flirting with me, Zan?"

"If you gotta ask, I'm not doing such a good job. If that's what I'm doing."

"It wouldn't be very professional."

"For you, maybe. I'm not the professional, I don't have to worry."

"Well, I am, so, if you don't mind, perhaps we...."

"Right. You were asking what?"

"The writer's block?"

"Oh, yes. The dreaded block. It may be over. I told you I'm working on a new novel? I do a little every day. It's...moving."

"That's wonderful. I hope it keeps up. But the block – if that's the right term – it's certainly been a problem for you over the years."

"Not *a* problem, *the* problem."

"So it bears talking about. Correct?"

"Correct. So what would you like to know?"

"Well, when did it begin?"

"Begin? Nineteen twenty-nine. There was an accident, remember? The Crash?"

"The Depression, yes."

"The Crash landed right on me. That was it. Kaput. Like a concrete block landing on Glenn Gould's hands – so long, piano."

IT HADN'T BEEN THAT SIMPLE, of course, but not that far off. *The Wise Men of Chelm* wasn't published until 1932, three years after the Depression's start – and he'd barely even begun writing it in October 1929, when the stock market took its plunge, pulling the economy down along with it. In Winnipeg, the effects weren't noticed for awhile, and, safe and secure in Luna's apartment, where he was experiencing the exhilaration – joy and frustration – of working on the novel, Zan had barely been aware of the Depression for months, and even then, and for several years afterwards, he'd been sheltered from most of the effects that rippled through the city, although he was conscious that, were it not for his brothers, whose trucking business limped along, his mother would likely have had to go on relief. Luna seemed secure at the university – if anything, the numbers of students were growing as jobs became harder to find – and the Wiseman family too wasn't all that affected, Zan's father having been ill and out of work for some time anyway, and the types of work his brothers did, cartage and under-the-table things he pretended not to know about – he was certain Saul was a bootlegger, and Abe involved with him in some way – were immune to the normal fluctuations of the economy. But the truth was, for the two years and more he worked on the novel under Luna's sponsorship, he lived as if in a cocoon, barely aware of the larger surroundings. Even his father's death, which likely would have hit him hard were he living at home, was experienced as if through a veil of gauze. When he got word, he went directly home, of course, and was by his mother's side that day and the day of the funeral. But as soon as Abe began organizing men to sit *shiva* and say the *Kaddish*, he retreated to Luna's, to the safer worlds of his novel, of Chelm. "A dutiful son I wasn't," he says now to Zelda, looking down.

By the time he'd finished the writing, Winnipeg was firmly in the Depression's grip, of course, and the condition of the city's poor very much in the minds of Zan's Communist Party comrades. He hadn't completely lost touch with them, and, with the novel done, he threw himself back into Party work, and for a year or so that became the focus of his activities, while *Wise Men*, mostly through the guidance of Luna and a friend of hers in the English Department who had published a novel himself, sought an agent in New York and eventually a publisher.

The agent and the publisher must have been aware of the dangers, but to Zan, there was no reason to connect the fate of his book, as it gradually inched toward becoming a reality and finally was published, in the fall of 1932, and the state of the world. Wall Street was far away from Winnipeg, though only blocks away from where the New York publisher had its offices. Still, there hadn't been any reason to think one thing would affect another. There was a good review – "an exceptionally good review," Luna said – almost immediately in the *New York Times*, and another a week or two later, one almost as favourable, in the *Herald*

Tribune, but by Christmas, like a shot fired by an unseen gunman, the publisher had gone bankrupt and the book had disappeared from bookstores.

"And not just bookstores," he tells Zelda. "It disappeared, period. It was like it never happened." Indeed, Olafson, the English professor who years later single-handedly brought the novel back to life, would tell Zan there were no copies to be found in Winnipeg, and Nick, the young writer he would befriend in Toronto, told him how he had became the sole reader of the sole copy in that city's public library.

Disappeared was only a slight exaggeration. There were a scattering of other reviews, mixed, and finally, a few months later, a devastating one in the *New Masses*, the Communist magazine from New York; but there was no Canadian edition of the novel, no clamour for autographs, no speaking tours, no royalties, no demand for a second book. Nothing, really.

"It doesn't matter," Luna had said. "We know the novel's wonderful, and so does anybody else who reads it. When the economy comes around, we'll find another publisher for it. In the meantime, you'll write other wonderful novels." That was before the *New Masses* review, and her optimism seemed reasonable.

He was already well into the second one, a sequel to *Wise Men*, taking the boy whom the first novel revolved around and his family a few years further along, and, based on the review in the *Times* and a sample he sent to the New York editor Maxwell Perkins at Scribner's, he'd received a contract for it and a $1,000 advance, so it was easy to think that maybe she was right. But the second novel didn't come as easily as the first had, "and there were too many butt-in-skis," he told Jack years later. Bill O'Connor, who was one of the Communist Party leaders in Winnipeg, in particular had wanted to see the manuscript chapter by chapter, would have looked over Zan's shoulder as he wrote if he could have.

"And you let him?" Jack sounded incredulous.

"Why not? It wasn't my private property. When it's published, everybody can look, so why be so secretive when you're writing it?"

"This is you talking, or this O'Connor fellow?"

Zan shrugged. "He wasn't the only one who said it."

"And you believed that?"

"It was the Party," he said after a moment. "What's that they say? You had to be there? You had to be there."

He remembered well the feeling that the novel was, in a sense, the Party's property or, no, that it belonged to them all. They'd sit endlessly at the café on Albert Street, after meetings, or in the lounge at the Union Hall, just around the corner on Market Square, talking about writing and art as often as they did politics. There didn't seem to be a line, really. "Art belongs to the people," Stanley Rueben said, and who could argue with that? Who would want to?

Rueben was a colleague of Luna's at the university, and the man the Party in Winnipeg most relied on when it came to matters of literature and art – when Rueben pontificated, O'Connor would nod his head as if giving an official imprimatur. It was Rueben who had elevated Zan to the position of "Important Writer" in the eyes of his comrades.

"And that means the making of the art belongs to anybody who wants to get a leg in?" This was David Cahann, a poet who often read his work at the café. He was a thin, bony man who always seemed to be withdrawing into himself, but when he read his poems, or drank too much wine, as he had now, his face would perspire and get shiny.

"Why not?" Zan said. "The more legs the better, especially if they're ladies' legs, in stockings."

"This is serious," Cahann insisted.

"I'm being serious. You got something against legs, David? About ladies?"

They would argue endlessly, but one thing was clear to everyone in the room but Zan: *Wise Men*, for all its virtues, hadn't gone far enough in depicting life as it should be. "It's suffocated by its own dark view," Rueben said.

"The humour doesn't leaven it?" Zan argued. In his view, *Wise Men* was funny as hell.

"Of course it does. I'm not saying the novel is airless, you know I don't believe that, Wiseman. But not enough. And humour can be misinterpreted."

And on they would go. Zan was already losing heart about the sequel and, shortly after the *New Masses* review, he radically changed the storyline and his whole concept of the novel, which meant putting his contract with Scribner's and the advance in jeopardy. The novel, which he called *Nineteen-Nineteen*, began to spin in the currents the Union Hall arguments stirred up. It was about the Winnipeg General Strike, about a family not all that different from the Wisemans, brothers, sisters, father and mother all caught up in the ferment of the strike, and another family, Irish, father and son policemen. The son believed in the strike, the father had a family to support, a job to do.

"Sounds very...deliberate," Jack said.

"You might say that."

"Almost...pedantic?"

"You might say that too."

"And that's what you wanted?"

Zan paused. "It was."

"You actually believed in all that socialist realism stuff?"

"I'd like your question better without the word 'actually.'"

"You're right. I'm sorry. You believed in social realism?"

"I did. You had to be there."

Nineteen-Nineteen was turning out to be very different from *Wise Men*, although it hadn't started out that way. The first novel, as Zan described it to Jack, was "nothing more than a simple tale about a boy and his daydreams," although by the time he was seeing Jack the novel was back on bookstore shelves, in paperback, and Jack was able to see for himself. The new novel, which Zan had begun thinking about even before he'd finished the first, was really supposed to be a sequel, following his boy character into his teenage years. The ferment of the General Strike was intended to be background, no more. But, gradually, the boy's father and elder brothers took on more importance, as did the strike.

The sequel hit another roadblock when he realized it echoed the title of the latest novel by John Dos Passos, *1919*, actually published the same year as *Wise Men*. Like Zan, Dos Passos, an American he admired, was a leftist who had run afoul of the Left. That aside, the similarity in titles forced him to change his to *Strike!*, which, as it happened, the Union Hall brain trust preferred.

He'd worked on the new novel all through the fall and winter of 1932 and into 1933, spending every morning at the fine oak desk Luna had bought, set up in the dining room, pecking away at the typewriter, or, when the words wouldn't come, staring at the wall or through the window, which looked out on the Assiniboine River, shouldering its way through the ice, then stalled, then moving again, running free, grass and flowers erupting on its banks, then turning brown, snow falling, piling up, the river sluggish again, the rhythms of his writing following pace, sluggish, stalled, moving, rapiding white with froth, sluggish, stalled, frozen.

"I think I have to get out of here," he told Luna.

"You mean Winnipeg, this apartment or this relationship?" she asked. "For the weekend, the week, a month or for good?"

"I don't mean you, I mean this place. More than a fucking weekend, but not for good. Something in between. How's that?"

He had heard about the Yaddo and McDowell colonies and yearned to spend time at one or both of them.

"Not good enough, but go ahead if you want," Luna said with a laugh, a laugh that rang in Zan's ears as cruel, something he hadn't heard from her before. "You really think you'll be able to write better somewhere else?"

"Not better. Just write."

"This is your own idea?"

"Yes, it's my own idea. What do you think?"

"Your darling Billy O'Connor didn't put a little word in your ear?"

"Bill did say there might be a job for me in Toronto. With the Party or arranged by the Party, I'm not sure. That's all. But that's not what I'm thinking of, really."

"He'd love that, wouldn't he."

"What?"

"To break us up."

"He doesn't want to fuck you, if that's what you're thinking."

"It wasn't me I was thinking of."

"Oh, for Christ's sake, Luna...."

"He could have you all to himself."

"Don't start."

"You and him and your precious Party."

"Don't start that again, Luna. Please."

But she had, over and over, ignoring the irony that she had been in the Party first, that it was she who had urged him to join, and eventually he'd left, though not till well into 1933 and not intentionally moving out, leaving many of his clothes and books in Luna's apartment, continuing to think of it as his permanent address. He would be back and forth between Toronto and Winnipeg, staying at Luna's the first few times, then gradually seeing less and less of her, over the next two years, until his brothers were arrested for robbery, bringing him back to the city for an extended period, and, it seemed, his life turned upside down.

"This isn't goodbye," he said when he did go. "I'll be back."

"No you won't," Luna said. "Even if you don't know that, I do."

As usual, she knew better than he, knew *him* better than he knew himself.

BUT HOW WAS IT, IF ZELDA WAS ASKING about writer's block, that he had closed down, that he had dried up, that he had forgotten how to do what, so recently, had come so naturally to him?

How did it happen, how *could* it happen, that he hadn't written a word for so long?

"Over fifty years," Zelda says. "That is a long time."

Jack had asked him the same question – the timelines appropriately shortened, as the drought had only been thirty years long then, long enough – and been so impressed with his answer that, the following week, he took him along to a class to let his students hear the answer for themselves.

"I just couldn't," he'd told Jack, using essentially the same words with the students. "There was a weight on my chest, so I couldn't breathe, weights on my wrists so I couldn't lift my hands. There was a weight on my head – rocks, boulders – to smother my brain. Weights on my thighs and feet so I couldn't get up from the typewriter – I'd spend the whole day without eating, drinking, without going to the toilet. That's how I spent years, working on the second novel, the third, the fourth. None of them finished, the third and fourth barely more than started. A white page in the typewriter like a ghost, a few black blurs smeared across it, and the weight, pressing me down. Writer's block... Twain, I think it was, said any writer lucky enough to have a block should sit down and use it as a desk. Writer's *weight* they should call it. With me, it's not so much a writer's block as a Writer's Gibraltar, a Writer's Rocky Mountains, a Writer's North American Continent."

This description came easily to Zan's lips, having spoken it almost the same way within the past year or two with Nick, his young writer friend. Nick had listened in stunned silence, shaking his head.

In Jack's classroom, the students seemed similarly stunned. "Any questions?" Jack asked and, after a suitable silence broken by shifting of chairs, one young fellow had bravely asked: "Why didn't you kill yourself?"

"Kill myself?" Zan had echoed. "To kill yourself you first have to be alive."

BEING ALIVE WAS WHAT HE HAD BEEN when he wrote, in the days before the weight, before the Party had started looking over his shoulder, clearing its throat and suggesting – no, never telling – what he should write, before his fingers had frozen. He'd been a normal enough young man, he thought, with all the requisite desires, impulses and juices, yet when Luna would come up behind him, sliding her hands down under his shirt along his chest, her tongue dipping like that of a hummingbird's into the opened heart of a flower against the back of his neck, whispering to him in French what she had planned for him, what her tongue longed to do, he would brush her aside like a mosquito, so mesmerized by the developing world materializing before him on the page, so enlivened by his own creation. All during the two years and more he'd laboured over *The Wise Men of Chelm* – writing it, rewriting, honing, polishing till he was satisfied with every action, every gesture, every word – he'd had at his availability her hot breath and cool hands, her passion along with her whispered encouragement, a muse in every sense. "When this novel's published, I should share the glory," she would joke. "A joint byline and half the royalties too, thank you very much."

"*If*," Zan would insist, "*if* it gets published, not when. If it gets published, you can have *all* the royalties, I'll take the glory."

"Oh, money means so little to you? I can stop supporting you?"

"If you want the royalties, you have to make the investment. And don't forget, you'll be able to bask in my glory. 'Was there anyone who inspired you, Mr. Wiseman?' the journalists will ask, and I'll say, 'Oh, yes, there was a certain woman, what was her name now...?'"

In bed, in the spent pool of their embrace, they'd laugh like children, he'd open himself like he had when he and Adam and Abe were children and would pit their daydreams against each others', but his limbs lay languidly on the pleated sheets and his mind would fill up with cotton batting like a pillow being stuffed at the furniture factory where his friend Bootsy had worked for awhile, bringing home bagfuls of the fluffy stuff; he'd succumb to weariness's pull at his eyes, his breath, falling into deep, satisfying sleeps in her arms. To be alive, really alive, he had to be not in her arms, not between her legs or in the ever-fascinating mysteries of her mouth, but sitting at the heavy oak desk in his study, before the typewriter, the index fingers of each hand dancing across the keys, the ferment in his mind spilling out onto the page. A normal enough man, yes, young, in love with her and himself, in love and in tune with his time and place, except for this one quirk: let her talk, let her whisper, let her sing, let her profess the greatest love, the most arching desire, yet it was his own language he loved the most, his own words and the world they were capable of creating.

"SOMETIMES, I THINK I WAS NEVER a writer at all," he told Jack once – but could that have been true? He had written as a child, yes, from ten or eleven on, wrote, thought about writing, thought of himself as a writer – but couldn't that be dismissed as childish ways, explained away? Then he'd won that contest that Luna had judged – was he sixteen then? No, seventeen – and everything he wrote for the next dozen years bore her stamp, was written for her, either her real eyes or imagined ones. Surely *The Wise Men of Chelm* had been inspired by her, informed, influenced, nagged out of him by her. She'd bring home a copy of Joyce's *Portrait of the Artist* or *Ulysses*, or Faulkner's *Sound and the Fury*, raving about them, Zan would devour them and his own style would subtly change. "For Pete's sake, she paid the bills," he said, and Jack merely smiled, his small, rueful smile, the one that seemed to say "now I've heard everything," except that he used it so often. "But it wasn't just her money," Zan protested, "I was in her thrall."

"Well, you obviously don't need me to lead you to that bit of self-illumination," Jack said. A satisfied smile. "Congratulations."

"Epiphany," Zan said.

"Pardon?"

"Epiphany. That's what we call it in the writing racket."

There was another thing as well, Zan told Jack, something even more fundamental: "It all came so easy then. Maybe that was it. When I was a kid, I didn't think, I just wrote. I sat down and the words came flooding out of me. Natural. Rewrite? Never heard the word. Revise? What for? Polish? Who polishes diamonds but a dilettante, and I sure as hell wasn't one of those, not when I was a kid."

"And the novel?" Jack asked.

"The whole thing took one year, maybe a little more, start to finish. I had the idea, although it wasn't quite the same as how it ended up, I sat right down and started in on it. Three months for the first draft – it could have been quicker still, but there's an exhaustion factor. The body can't keep up with the mind, it has to sleep. It just came, it flowed, like someone was whispering in my ear...."

"Luna?"

"That's what I say, maybe it was her. If not her own voice then some ventriloquist voice she threw at me."

"Three months for the first draft...."

"Ah, by then I'd learned some things. No matter how good it was on the first pass, it could be better. And this was a novel, don't forget, not a short story or a poem. I'd written dozens of stories, hundreds of poems, and they all came out in one piece, you could see the whole expanse of them with one glance. This was something different – not just longer, bigger, but deeper, more complicated, hills and valleys, shadows... I wrote it, then Luna said to me, 'Okay, what does it mean?' And I had to figure that out. I swear, I never noticed all the people dying in the story until Luna pointed them out to me and we counted them up."

"So the novel was about death?" Jack interrupted.

"No, about life. But that wasn't till later. First, I worked the hell out of the thing and finally got it done, thought I had it done, a little more than a year, like I said. Then Luna read it. 'No, it's not quite right,' she said. I wanted to kill her, wanted to kill myself. I sulked for a few days, then spent a day rereading it, then tossed the whole thing out and started right back in on it. She was right, of course, and I knew it."

"So Luna showed you the way?" Jack asked, incredulous.

"No, not at all. She didn't, wouldn't, couldn't. All she did was tell me when I was going wrong, getting it wrong. That's what writing's all about, don't you see? Getting it right."

"And you had it wrong."

"Well, I did. I mentioned all the dead bodies. I hadn't really noticed them before – not really noticed them – and when I did, I jumped to the wrong conclusion."

"Death."

"Of course. What else? But, you know Emily Dickinson? The American poet? She says something like this, about poetry but it's the same for fiction: 'Tell the truth, but tell it slant.'"

"Slant," Jack said.

"Slant, yes. Not death, but life, the other side of that coin. That's what it took me so long to understand. Luna poking at me. I had to figure out what that whispering in my ear had been trying to say. Rewrite. And again. Rearrange some of the jigsaw pieces that didn't quite fit. Get rid of some stuff that didn't fit in at all – and you think cutting off your arm is hard to do? A grown man circumcising himself is easier than a novelist cutting the chaff from his novel, of this I can assure you. And some new stuff, to fill the holes that developed. Another year, this to-ing and fro-ing, so two years altogether, then more time polishing, polishing. I'd be polishing still if Luna hadn't taken it away from me, said, 'Okay, it's done, we're sending this to the agent now.' But I tell you, Jack, it was easy. There was never anything easier – and never anything as easy again."

Jack avoided the logical next question – as he often, maddeningly, did, and instead posed a question more as a statement: "So Luna was your muse."

"In every sense," Zan said immediately. It was something he'd already spent over thirty years considering, continuing to be grateful to her even while he was turning away from her, even long after, even now. He had completely lost touch with her, but heard she'd gone to New York, where she'd done her graduate work, to teach at a university there, married, he didn't know what else, didn't know, really, whether she was alive or dead. She was as completely absent from his life now as once she had been the centre of it. "Except there's nothing amusing about the thought."

"So, naturally, you turned your back on her."

This time Zan was silent for a long moment, shocked at the therapist's quick mental leap. This conversation was early in their relationship, their friendship, and they were still surprising each other. "Naturally," he agreed.

HOW HAD IT HAPPENED?

"Over fifty years," Zelda says. "That is a long time."

What comes back to him now, unbidden, over all the years, is the taste of sardines. That's what he invariably ordered at Economy Drugs, one of the Main Street haunts he liked to retreat to when the demands of either Luna or the typewriter grew too intense – about halfway between the Balmoral apartment and his family's house on Flora Avenue, and open at all hours, day or night. Sometimes, he and others would be crammed into a booth toward the rear of the store, but today he was sitting at the lunch counter. Sardines from a can on pumpernickel, mustard and lettuce, pickle on the side, a glass of seltzer. The blonde waitress wrinkling her nose prettily at the very notion. Above the left breast of her yellow uniform, in script, her name, Marilou. What kind of a *shiksa* name was Marilou? With all those yellow curls, that slightly flattened nose, she must have been Polish.

Beside him at the counter, Avi Slonim was about to begin eating his usual order, eggs, scrambled with onions and peppers, rye toast smeared with chicken fat, a refill of black coffee. Day, night, early, late, it didn't matter, Slonim was always eating breakfast.

"This fellow, Slonim," he might have told Jack, if Jack had asked, or if it had seemed pertinent, "was someone I'd known practically all my life, from the neighbourhood, on Selkirk Avenue, at Aberdeen School, St. John's, one of the gang of kids Adam and Abe and I hung around with, and at university, where he studied history when I was a literature student, and now through the Party, although, being in different cells, we weren't supposed to know about each other, that was the theory," and in all those years, and the years they would know each other still to come, he couldn't remember a single other thing the man had ever said – not a conversation, not a damn-you-to-hell-anyway, not an endearment, not a word, yet so clearly could he remember what came out of his mouth this one afternoon, the smell of sardines, surely, emanating from his own: "Some review. An assassination better they should call it."

On the counter in front of Slonim lay the *New Masses*, the leftist magazine from New York, for March 14, 1933, folded open to page thirty-seven, but even if it hadn't been there Zan would have known what Slonim was referring to. *Wise Men* was clearly set in Winnipeg, but it had been published in New York, and had gone out of print so quickly he had no idea whether even a single copy had found its way to Canada. Not surprisingly, it hadn't been reviewed by any Canadian papers or magazines that he was aware of, including the *Worker*, the Communist paper from Toronto that continued to publish, even though the Party itself had been outlawed and gone underground. But many in the Party in Winnipeg read the *New Masses*, and the belated review had quickly reached a notorious status.

Zan's eyes involuntarily went to the headline, which read "Personal Celebration of the Self Sinks Ambitious Novel," although he knew it by heart, as he did the byline of Eugene Blanchard and the brief explanation at the bottom of the review that Blanchard was a professor of American literature at New York University and a frequent contributor. What it didn't say was that he was an acquaintance of Luna's, and that a letter from her had alerted him to the novel, a gesture of support that had backfired – or had it, in fact? Over the years since, Zan had asked himself innumerable times if she hadn't possibly been deliberately seeking to undermine him.

Zan had already read this review dozens of times, had memorized key phrases, which repeated themselves endlessly through his waking and sleeping thoughts, had allowed its poison to begin to pool in his blood, his urine. As Luna had repeatedly told him, the much more flattering reviews that had appeared in the *New York Times* and *Tribune* were also much more important, but this was the one that had become the most important to him. But why should Slonim be reading it, why today, why should it be there, open on the counter in full view? Afterwards, for years later, he would often wonder about that, and he expressed that wonder again to Jack.

"But you say Slonim was in the Party," Jack said.

"Yes."

"So it was natural that he might read the magazine. It was a left-wing magazine, right?"

"Yes."

"And it was the current issue."

"Yes. Well, a few weeks old already."

"It came by mail? Subscriptions?"

"Are you crazy? No. But it was easy to buy. At Elkin's National on Selkirk, or People's Books, on Arthur Street. Even Winnipeg News, downtown."

"So there wasn't anything untoward in Slonim having a copy."

"No."

"No indication of any conspiracy."

"Certainly not."

"And he was a friend, an acquaintance, at any rate, so it was only natural that he'd want to read a review of your book."

"Absolutely."

"So the fact that he was reading it this day – not an otherwise extraordinary day?"

"No."

"The fact that he was reading it that day, that it was open on the counter as you sat down beside him, that was all no more than coincidence, isn't that right?"

"Yes, except that...."

"Except what?"

"That I don't believe in coincidence."

"Oh?"

"History is what people do, not what's done to them," Zan said, with certainty.

"History?"

"What happens. History, life, the news, call it what you want. It's what we do."

"All right. So the question here is why was Slonim doing what he was doing?"

"I guess that's what I'm asking. Not asking you, just asking aloud."

"And it's not possible, as I suggest, that his actions were completely innocent? That they were a mere accretion of – we won't say coincidence – but circumstance?"

"Of course it's possible."

"But not probable?"

"Even probable. Not *provable*, Dr. Freud, not provable. Not to me."

"AND WHY WAS THAT REVIEW so important?" Zelda asks him now. Zan smiles, recalling that Jack *hadn't* asked that, hadn't needed to.

"It wasn't the review itself so much, but where it appeared. The *New Masses* was the Bible to the Communists, to all sorts of people on the Left. At least those who were readers. What it said wasn't opinion, it was *edict*. All the big names wrote for it – Hemingway, Dos Passos, Sherwood Anderson. *I* wanted to write for it – but never again after that."

"I still don't understand. It said your novel was no good?"

"Not that it was no good – that would almost have been bearable – but that it was – you'll laugh, Lady Doctor, this sounds hopelessly funny now...."

"I promise I won't laugh."

"You will. Maybe not now, in my face. Later you will. At the next psychologists' convention, you'll have your colleagues rolling in the aisles with this."

"I promise, I won't, Mr. Wiseman."

"It doesn't matter. Go ahead, laugh. *Bourgeois*, that's what he said it was. Bourgeois."

"And that's bad. *Was* bad?"

"That was bad. That was very bad. That was the worst. Who's the psychologist with the worst reputation in the world? Is it Adler? No, don't bother invoking your ethical credo and not answering, let's just say for the sake of argument it's Myron Adler from Dubuque, and someone says of you, 'That Dr. Zelda is so Adleresque.' See how that would hurt?"

"Yes, I see."

The thing was – and this was why it had nagged at him so long, the thing he had tried to explain to Jack and that he wouldn't bother to explain to this one, this Zelda, who would never be able to understand – was that he had only realized how bad it was that day, that moment in the drug store, the taste of sardine and lemon filling his mouth, his tongue swimming in salt and sour juice.

"Let the fancy-ass NYU critic have his say," Luna had said, dismissing it with a wave of her hand. "It's still a free country. He can have his opinion. It's only his. *We* know what *we* know." That had been comforting, but it *wasn't* only *his* opinion, Zan realized. Slonim, improbably, had blue eyes, and they were wide, innocent, implacable.

"Some review," he said. "An assassination better they should call it." He took a sip of coffee, a mouthful of egg and toast, another sip of coffee. The moment, Zan remembers, hung naked between them, expectant, like the sky about to break open with rain. "Still," Slonim said, "maybe he's right."

"Indulgent," that's what the critic had written. "Self-indulgent...preoccupied with self...concerned only with the individual." That was what had hurt, because the last thing Zan had been thinking of, all through the writing, was himself – he could have sworn to that. Family, the neighbourhood, that's what *Wise Men* was *about*, wasn't it? Blanchard hadn't thought so – and now, apparently, neither did Slonim. Zan already knew what O'Connor thought, not that the bastard had said anything, no it was all in what he *didn't* say, in his expression. And it was his opinion that was most important, at least as far as Zan's future in the Party was concerned, and hence his future, period. It was hardly Slonim's opinion that counted for anything, except that, according to Blanchard, at least, it was exactly his opinion, Slonim's opinion, that *did* count, that counted the most.

"Maybe he's right?" Zan echoed.

"Well, of course he's right," Slonim said. "All the good things he said, that goes without saying" – and Zan was able to remind himself that there had been good things, that the critic had praised his elegant style, the Joycean penetration of the mind of the child, the skillful manipulation of mythological elements, the humour, some of it deadpan, some slapstick – and then turned the praise on its head, using it to condemn. "*Bourgeois, self-indulgent...*" Zan had squirmed on the swivelling stool seat, the padded plastic squeaking under his buttocks. "But maybe he's also right," Slonim went on, his mouth lubricated with more coffee, "that it doesn't serve the people as well as it could" – and if, Zan realized, Slonim was no more than O'Connor's agent, sent to deliver a message, that was certainly it.

"Could, should," Zan told Jack. "*Didn't* is what he was talking about."

Dave Margoshes

"Serve the people," Jack mused. "That's what literature is about?"

"So I was learning," Zan agreed, neutrally.

"What I mean," Slonim had said, waving his yolk-stained fork like a baton, "is that you have the boy and the people on his street, and maybe the focus needs to be less on the boy, more on the street."

He remembers that he took a swallow of seltzer, that it went down his throat with a looping muscularity, as if it were all of one piece, a satin ribbon of liquid, studded with salt. It was then, he remembers, that as the waitress leaned over the counter to place the blue-rimmed plate containing his sandwich in front of him, and he caught a glimpse of the pregnant line between the tops of her breasts, just barely visible in the small opening, one button's worth, at the top of her uniform, and caught a thread of her perfume, that it came to him that he wasn't looking at her just because she was pretty, sexy, but that he could fall in love with her. Both within him and without, all around him, he could feel the subtle change in the air that comes as the barometer rises or falls, the change in the tides, the sea change that pulls along with it all the creatures of the sea both large and small. It was then too that the thought crossed his mind that Luna and this Eugene Blanchard, this friend of hers in New York, may at one time have been lovers.

"And?" Jack asked.

"And?"

"What was it?"

"What was it? What's that song on the radio, 'The Sound of Silence?' A couple of nice Jewish boys singing like girls. 'Hello, silence my old friend....'"

Silence, silence, what he'd heard then – imagined he heard – was the clamour of silence, his own silence, creeping up on little cat's feet – and now, more than twenty years after his conversations with Jack, the silence of the grave was beckoning, just over the next rim, and Zan just as mute as ever.

CHAPTER 21

February 7, 1989

Feb. 7, 1989 – I made it – eighty-three today!

Something to celebrate or something to mourn, which I'm not so sure about.

Plenty of times, I didn't think I'd get this far. But from this vantage point, it doesn't seem I've gotten all that far – eighty-three years old, but not a lot to show for it. One book with my name on it in the library, that's all. Still, older than any of my siblings got to be, Abe excepted, of course, and he's indestructible. Way older than my father when he died, but still five years to catch up with my mother. The way I feel today, that looks like an impossible task, catching up with her. But I never could keep up with Momma, so nothing new there.

How old, I wonder, is Luna, if she's alive? And where's her grave if she isn't?

Close to a hundred, probably, if she is.

And, if she is, does she ever think of me?

"YOU'RE LOOKING PLEASED WITH YOURSELF," Zelda says.

"When you're my age, every morning you wake up still alive, you're pleased with yourself," Zan says. "You beat the Ragman again. But today, especially so, because it's my birthday."

"Really. Happy birthday. And you're how old? I've forgotten. "Eighty...."

"Eighty-three. At least I think so. All year, I've been saying I was eighty-two, so, presuming I was right, that I didn't get it wrong last time, then I must be eighty-three today. Look, I've brought you a piece of birthday cake."

"That's sweet of you. Thank you. Did your brother Abe bake it?"

"Abe? No, apple pie is his specialty. We splurged last night, I splurged, that is – Hy's, big steaks, the best! And cake, of course. 'Why such a fuss?' Abe complains. 'Eighty-three's not so special.'

"But it is to me. I never thought I'd get out of the last year alive."

The therapist made a notation. "It *was* a hard year, Mr. Wiseman. Your wife's death, moving here, a lot of adjustments at a time of life when change is difficult. But, you know, I think you've done well. Eighty-three, that's a good age. And your various ailments notwith-standing, you're in pretty good shape for that age, I'd say."

"Yes, all those notwithstandings notwithstanding, you're right. I used to think, when I was a kid, I mean, that I'd live to be a hundred – that was my goal. Not that I had so many things I wanted to accom-plish that I needed all that time, but just because it appealed to me – a century, a nice round number. Actually, the number one hundred, with all those zeros, that's round, 'century,' the word, that sounds more square – a nice solid square, a cube, like a block of marble. Something substantial. Well, whichever it was, for whatever reason, that's what I hoped to live for."

"And now not any more?"

"Well, with inflation, a hundred's not what it used to be, don't you know. To get the feeling of satisfaction I thought of about a century when I was a kid, these days you'd have to live to be two hundred, maybe more. Medical science does wonders, but that much wonder, no, it hasn't kept up. So forget about that plan. But moving back here, to Canada, I mean, made me very conscious of the exchange rate. For me, with the Social Security from the States, Myrna's insurance, some royalties, that's all to the good. My income goes further here. The Canadian dollar's just worth about eighty-eight cents on the American, so that's my new goal, to live to be eighty-eight, that's how old my mother got to, and what kind of son bests his mother? That's a nice round number too – those nice curvy, sexy eights – an eight is just two zeros stacked on top of each other, so eighty-eight is twice as round as a hundred, don't you see? And eight has always been my lucky number – my first memory, believe it or not, is from when I was two, which was in 1908, and then, when I was eight I had my first sexual experience – oh, don't look so shocked, Lady Doctor, I'm just kidding. But eight, yes, I like that number, and eighty-eight twice as much, no, ten times as much, or whatever the math is. I like it. So that's my goal, and as of today, eighty-three, there are just five years to go. Not to say I have to keel over and die on the day I reach eighty-eight, but that's the age I'm aiming for and anything beyond that will be gravy.

"Abe – my brother Abe – I told you, I think, he's thirteen minutes older than me, so he says he's got a head start on me in the old-age sweepstakes, that he's closer to the end and has a clearer view of what lies ahead, although frankly I think he's too ornery to die, God, if there is a God, isn't too likely to want Abe kicking around heaven bossing all the angels around. Abe has an opinion on this, of course – he has an opinion on everything."

"And you don't?"

"Ah, touché, Dr. Zelda, you're right, I do, but I don't always deliver myself of my opinion to whoever happens to be standing next to me, interested or not. Well, maybe I do, but I'm not quite as pedantic about it as Abe, or, knock wood, let's hope not.

"Abe, he has a theory of heaven. That's one difference between him and me – I stopped believing in God and heaven a long time ago, if I ever even did, but he still does. But I give him credit for this – and it's really the CBC and Peter Gzowski I give credit to, for being a good influence on him, liberalizing, you know what I mean? He used to have set ideas on these matters, what the Bible says, what the rabbi says, that goes. Now, he's not so sure. Now, to his great credit, he has a sliver of doubt.

"So Abe says, when we die and we go to heaven – of that he has no doubt, neither that there is such a place nor that he will wind up there – and stand before God, and again, there's no doubt in his mind on that score, no doubt that there's a God, no doubt that he'll stand before Him – ah, *Him*. Here's where the doubt comes in. Abe says, 'Well, what if the Christians were right after all, that Jesus really was the son of God, the Messiah? It's not such a big stretch – we Jews believe in the Messiah, after all, just not that Jesus was the one. We believe in God's ability to perform wonders, so there's nothing in the New Testament that we don't believe *could* happen, we just don't think it did. Okay, okay, so let's say, just for the sake of argument, that we were wrong on that, all the learned rabbis were wrong, all the Jews down

Dave Margoshes

through the centuries, all wrong – yes, it's unlikely, but let's just say maybe, just *maybe* it's so and there really was a Jesus, that he really lived, really was the son of God, that he really did perform miracles as the Gospels say he did, that he really was betrayed by what's his name, Judas the disciple, that he really was judged and condemned, really crucified, really died on the cross, really said 'forgive them, Father,' really was put in a cave and really – and this is the crux here – really rose after three days, and really sits at the right hand of God. Well, when we get there, we'll know for sure, won't we? He'll either be there or He won't. If He isn't, of which I'm pretty sure, good, we'll all have the satisfaction of knowing we were right. We and God will be able to have a good laugh over it – God, are those high-and-mighty Christians ever *farmisht*, confused. You put a good one over on them, God. And' – this is Abe talking, remember, not me – 'and if He is there, this Jesus, just for the sake of argument let's say He is, okay, that's not such a big deal, so we were wrong on that small point. That I can live with, I won't lose any sleep over that – if sleep is what you do in heaven. One small error anyone can make, and I'd be very surprised if God made a big deal of it, if He rubbed it in. Maybe a bit of a raised eyebrow, a bit of a smug smile, but no more than that. Don't forget, it was God Himself who caused the confusion – telling us one thing, the Christians another.

"'But' – and here's where I give Abe credit for the open-mindedness of his thinking – 'if there's one small error, that opens the possibility of there being others. Someone on Gzowski said the other day maybe God is a woman. Can I accept that? Of course I can – why not? The Bible doesn't say God is a man, it doesn't even use the pronoun He, if you read carefully.' Abe, I should tell you, Lady Doctor, is a literal-thinking man, he doesn't have much use for metaphor, but he has an understanding of how they work just the same. 'So it says in the Bible God made man in his own likeness,' Abe says, 'but that doesn't necessarily mean down to the very last detail. So might God be a woman? I don't think so, but why not. So all right, this fellow on Gzowski says, maybe God is not just a woman but an Ethiopian woman, black as ebony, and not just an Ethiopian woman but an eighteen-year-old woman, not eighteen years old really, God is ageless, but in the form of an eighteen-year-old Ethiopian woman, with legs a mile long, with breasts out to here' – well, shaped like a figure eight, maybe a pair of them – 'what if God is not just a woman but a sexy, young black woman. Can I believe that? Why not?'

"But, and here's the tricky part, 'If God is a woman,' Abe says, 'that's one thing, even if she's a delicious, young black woman – black, yellow, red, whatever she may be – that doesn't really matter. God is God, regardless of His or Her form. Who am I to question that?' That's what Abe says, as I say, to his credit. And, Abe says, 'If Jesus is by God's side, again, who am I to question that, if it is, it is. So we were wrong on that score. But that isn't the end of it.'

"'It isn't?' I say.

" 'No,' Abe says, 'because if there *were* a Jesus, if he's sitting at God's right hand, then that means that God is a Christian. Oh ho! That God is a woman, that's one thing; that She's a Christian, not a Jew, that's another. That's a little harder to accept. Abraham's God was a Jew, Moses's God was a Jew, King David's God was a Jew – or so they thought and we thought, down through the generations, as it says in the Torah. So now all of a sudden, it turns out God is a Christian?'

"'And that's not all. If God is a Christian, and a woman – whether an eighteen-year-old Ethiopian woman or a woman of some other kind but a woman, then that means God is a *shiksa*, and a *schvartze shiksa* maybe even, if she really is Ethiopian, eighteen years old or not. That would be hard to accept, yes, that would be hard to swallow.'"

"He believes all this?" Zelda asks.

"You look incredulous. Who knows if he believes it or not? It's a delicious idea, that's the key thing. My brother Abe, you can see, is a philosopher, and, what's that expression? There's more to his philosophy than is known in heaven and on earth."

DUET 7

"So Zannie, listen, I've been thinking...."

"This is an achievement."

"...What if I go first?"

"Go?"

"Pass away."

"Die, you mean?"

"Die. Die. We're not getting any younger."

"Another inspiration. How do you do it, *Abela?*"

"We're all that's left."

"Left?"

"Saul's gone, Annie's gone, Hersh, Adam, Momma and Pop...."

"Hersh! Hersh died seventy years ago. I can barely remember him. Adam also seventy years ago. Saul fifty years ago."

"So?"

"So, they're gone is hardly news."

"I'm just saying."

"Poppa, I can't even remember when he died."

"You can't? It was 1930, just a few months after the Crash."

"Momma long after that. Still, twenty years, more."

"Thirty. No, thirty-five almost, 1964. You don't remember anything. She had the constitution of an ox, but even an ox has to go."

"Go. With you it's go."

"We all go, Zannie."

"And...?"

"Annie four years ago. And your Myrna..."

"My Myrna?"

"Gone."

"Gone? You mean like went out for a quart of milk and the paper and never came back? That kind of gone? Or real gone, man."

"Gone, I mean gone. Never coming back. Gone to meet

their maker, if there is such a thing."

"Is that a hint of doubt in the devout Abraham Wiseman? Maybe there isn't a God after all?"

"That I didn't say. I'm just saying."

"I know what you're saying, believe me. Gone. Go...going, going, gone. That's the usual order of things."

"So that means we can't live forever."

"Who says we would? Or should? Who would want to?"

"So what I'm saying...."

"What *are* you saying?"

"What I'm saying, if you'll let me, is, what if I go first?"

"Go?"

"You go first, heaven forbid...I'll say *Kaddish* for you."

"You won't!"

"I will. But what if I go first?"

"You won't, Benchy. You won't go first, and you won't say *Kaddish.*"

"I will. I mean, I will say *Kaddish,* if you go first, heaven...."

"I don't want you to say *Kaddish* for me."

"*Want* don't figure in it. It's a given."

"Even if I ask you, *Abela,* please, as a brother, I'm asking you, I'm begging you, don't say goddamn prayers over me."

"Don't ask me that, Zannie."

"I am asking. You don't hear so good?"

"I hear terrible. I don't hear a word."

"Who said anything?"

"What?"

"Your hearing's improving."

"But...."

"But?"

"But what if I go first, heaven forbid?"

"If you go first? I'll go to your funeral. You have a will? You left instructions? I'll visit Dolly. Maybe not every day, like you do, that much of a saint I ain't. Whenever I can. That I'll promise you, *Abela.* Dolly will be well looked after."

"Of course I have a will, what, you crazy? My lawyer has it, he knows what to do."

"Good. You tell me, I'll just forget."

"Thank you. Thank you for visiting Dolly. She gets lonely."

"So do we all."

"But...."

"But?"

"But will you say *Kaddish?*"

"*Kaddish?* Me, say *Kaddish?*"

"For me."

"For you?"

"For Dolly, when the time comes, God forbid."

"For Dolly? She's not even Jewish, what does she care about *Kaddish?*"

"She cares, I care. After all this time with me, you think she's not Jewish?"

"So it's settled. I'll go first, there won't be an issue. You can say *Kaddish* for me if you really want, or not. I won't be around to hear it or not hear it, either way."

"I will, Zannie, don't worry. I will. But...."

"But what?"

"If you don't go first? What if I go first?"

"You're strong as an ox, *Abela*. You won't go first. I will."

"If I ask?"

"Ask? Ask what?"

"You know."

"Don't ask me that, *Abela*. What do I know of saying *Kaddish?* Don't ask."

"I am asking, Zannie."

"Don't ask."

"I am, though."

"Don't."

CHAPTER 22

February 14, 1989

"I'D LIKE TO TALK ABOUT THIS WRITER'S BLOCK of yours some more," Zelda says. "I still don't see why it's lasted so long."

"You've been thinking about me," Zan says, with just a hint of sarcasm. "That's sweet."

"Well, I have. Compulsion is common, believe me; so is avoidance. Your situation is a little different. It's intriguing."

"That's what that other therapist I told you about said too. Jack. And that was twenty years ago, when there was still reason to think I'd be writing again any day. Not that there isn't today. I told you I started a new novel."

"Yes. You said."

"*God Blinked.* He's still blinking, I'm still writing. Four or five chapters already. Rough stuff, but it looks good."

"I'm happy to hear you sound so hopeful."

"That might be putting too fine a point on it. No, I take that back. I *am* hopeful. I've started novels before, gotten to three or four chapters before, even five or six, then...kaput. But this time feels different."

"Feels different how?"

Zan gives her a long look. "I don't know.... Maybe only another writer could understand. Writing a novel isn't like cooking a meal or even something long and complicated and ambitious like building a house – there's usually a blueprint. There's no blueprint for a novel. It's like walking across a strange country without a map. You don't really know where you're going till you get there. This one, this novel...it feels like I know where I'm going. So...I'm hopeful."

Zelda is smiling. "Hopeful is good, Mr. Wiseman. Very good."

"Hopeful is status quo for me, Ms. Freud. I'm always hopeful, ever hopeful. When you are not there yet, what choice do you have but to hope? What's the word for when your hopes are fulfilled?

That's where I haven't been yet."

"You were once. You wrote a novel, saw it published. Almost sixty years ago, yes, I know, but you were there then, regardless of what happened afterwards. Lots of writers never get published, isn't that true?"

"Yes, yes. I know, count my blessings. Thank you, *rebbe*."

Rebbe. That's what he used to call Jack, hasn't used it for this one before, this Zelda. She's tough, but Jack was tougher.

"For Christ's sake, what is the big fucking deal?" Jack exploded once. "Forgive my language, very unprofessional of me, I know, but seriously, concentrate. You finish a book, it's published. Then things don't go so well – I'm not arguing that. It's a setback. Postpartum depression, to use a popular if not exactly clinical diagnosis. But most people get over it."

"What about extenuating circumstances?" Zan protested.

"Yes, they can play a role. You had some?"

"I had my brothers in jail. I had an arranged marriage. I had myself in jail. I had a brother dead. I had a failed love affair, a new one, another marriage. Oh, and there was a war too, maybe you heard about that."

"And these were all extenuating?"

"Weren't they?"

"No, not for everyone. Some people took the war in stride, for example, even thrived on it. Some people don't let adversity knock them off course. This isn't a judgment, merely an observation."

"Well, on me they extenuated," Zan said. "All those things I mentioned. And more. Let's just leave it at that."

To Zelda, he says again: "Lots of writers never get published, yes," because he has, for the first time in years, thought about Nick.

LONG BEFORE THEY BECAME FRIENDS, Zan and the boy had been aware of each other. Zan had been the bearded, joking man who came to Nick's father's store to buy green olives and goat cheese, always on Tuesdays, usually a little after the boy got home from school at three. Even then he was aware of the boy's interest in him, curiosity, whatever it was. Then, and of much more obvious interest to the boy, Zan was The Writer Who Came to the Store – years later, when they were friends and roommates, that's how Nick described his response to Zan at the time. Nick himself was the slim, quick-moving boy who darted from shelf to shelf in response to his father's barked commands in Greek. He reminded Zan a bit of himself at that age, working at the box factory, though Zan the adult was nothing at all like the Commodore. Then Nick was the acolyte, student, apprentice, worshipper. Finally, friend. Roommate. Zan was mentor, a role he'd never played before, and relished, recalling Luna. What he would not do, he vowed, was make demands.

Nick was probably nine or ten the first time Zan wandered into the store, cool under its striped canopy and pungent with odours that called out to him with their exotic unfamiliarity that seemed, nonetheless, familiar. To his recollection, there had been only one Greek restaurant in Winnipeg, or only one he'd ever been to, at least, and that had been with Luna, linking the experience inextricably with his memories of her. So it had only been in the last few years, here in Toronto, that he and Rose had become fans, and were regulars at a series of Greek restaurants along Danforth Avenue. And only now, and by accident, walking by, noticing the store with the bold lettering spelling out Papagapolous' Dairy and Fruit on the plate glass window and on impulse going in, that it had occurred to him that he could make their own Greek dishes at home, "Greekify them," he told Rose. This was a period when Rose was still doing substitute teaching and Zan was working full-time, at a machine shop far out on the Danforth, where he was pulling a drill press for decent money, having recently graduated to a Browne & Sharpe single spindle lathe, top of the line for the time. His shift started early and was done by midafternoon. He usually rode the streetcar west on Danforth to about Woodbine or Coxwell, then walked the rest of the way to their place in the Beaches. This was soon after his first hospitalization for depression, and the doctors had urged him to get more exercise, to try harder to relax.

He was barely aware of the boy that first time in the store but, for some reason, Zan made an impression on him. Years later, Nick would remind him: "You looked the way I would have looked if I'd just walked into a candy store for the first time. You were awestruck."

"And you noticed that?" Zan was skeptical.

"I guess so. I remember it."

"I think you imagined it. That's all right."

"No, I remember. I remember it *because* of my imagination. I made up a story about you. I remember that too."

Dave Margoshes

All right, ten then, and twelve and fourteen and sixteen, growing like a Greek spiced bean, tall and stringy. Zan was certainly aware of him, but took no special notice of him. It was the boy's father, Papagapolous, with whom he was friendly.

"Let me try some of those olives, Mr. Papagapolous."

"Call me Papa, Papa, that's what everybody calls me."

This was the fourth or fifth time Zan had come in and the grocer, like his son, recognized him.

"Like Hemingway," Zan said, not really expecting a response, it just blurted out.

"The writer! That's right. *The Old Man and the Sea*." Papagapolous beamed with pride. "Papa. Me too."

Zan was surprised. "You know that story?" Actually, Hemingway's big, bearded mug had been on the cover of *Life* not long before, when the magazine ran the long story, so he shouldn't have been.

"Sure, sure. That big fish. Some fish, eh?"

"I loved that story."

"A great writer," Papa said. "You a writer too, Mister?"

"I am," Zan said, after a moment of hesitation. "What made you think so?"

It was that, Nick said later, that really caught his attention. That uncertain pause before he'd answered.

"I don't know," the boy's father said. "You look like a writer. The beard, eh? *Serious*." He puffed up his cheeks and frowned to impersonate some great eminence in his den, thinking.

Zan had laughed. He'd been wearing a beard for a year or two at that point, closer to his face than Hemingway's, black with thin streaks of grey, but hadn't thought about it doing anything for his writing – if it had, he thought, he'd have grown it long before.

"I never knew I looked like a writer, but I am one. Not a great one, though, no Hemingway. Not much of one, actually." Although it pained him to say this, he added, with a rueful smile: "I'm a writer who thinks more about writing than actually writes." That, Nick would say later, is what *really* caught his attention. He too thought of himself as a writer, but it was *all* in his head. "All I did was think about writing. I didn't have the slightest idea how to actually get any of it done."

Papagapolous laughed too, wiping his hands on his apron. "You're still young, Mister. Plenty of time to be great."

"I hope you're right, Papa," Zan had said, and, remembering the exchange on his walk home later, a bag filled with the makings of his and Rose's supper in his arms, he'd smiled wryly. A great writer! It was the mid-fifties then, and *The Wise Men of Chelm* was twenty years behind him, long enough but not yet so unreasonably long to fear there'd never be another book. He remembered with just a twinge of bitterness but the usual wellspring of regret that for one brief moment – a period of no more than three months – he'd had a contract with Scribner's, publisher of Fitzgerald and Wolfe, even Hemingway himself, writers he admired enormously, and had corresponded with the great Max Perkins, their editor, who might well have been his. Then he had thrown it all away. He'd laboured over three other novels since then, in fits and spurts separated by long periods during which he didn't even attempt to write, all the time working off and on in a succession of factories where the skills he'd acquired as a tool pusher in Winnipeg served him in good stead. A great writer! Even a good one would have been good enough – even being a writer again, period, would have been good enough.

The boy knew none of that, could not have.

But, caught up in his own dreams, his imagination seemed to settle down on the image of Zan, as lightly as a butterfly on a blossom – that's what he told Zan years later, using that very image. Then, like the butterfly, he'd begun to suck the sweet nectar.

Years later, Nick now an adult too, when they *were* friends, mentor and apprentice, Zan asked him, incredulous: "So even then you wanted to be a writer? At ten?"

"Sure. Even younger. I always made up stories."

"Well. All children make up stories. They don't all become writers. That doesn't *make* them writers."

"But I always knew they were stories I was meant to tell," Nick said, growing excited. "I wasn't making them up just for my own amusement. I knew that." He looked at Zan. "Didn't you do that, old man?"

Zan smiled at what was clearly meant as an endearment. "Make up stories? Sure."

"No. Know they were for more than you."

"Sure." Zan was silent for a moment. Was *he* the mentor or was Nick? "But I always thought I was the only one."

"Good enough for you but not for me?" Nick demanded, only half kidding behind a veil of mock petulance.

"Bad enough," Zan said. "Bad enough, not good." He didn't want to tell Nick about the agonies that might lie ahead. A hint, maybe. "You think being a writer is all roses and honey?"

"Bread and roses would be nice." Nick was grinning now.

"Bread and roses some days, crumbs and thorns other days."

Nick got up. They'd been sitting on a bench in the park they liked to walk through, East Lynn Park, not far from both the store and the apartment they shared. "You can be a prick." Now he *was* petulant.

Zan laughed. "You're just finding that out? I thought you were quicker."

He *had* been quick. But shy, and, though, as he later confessed, he longed to talk to Zan, he held his peace – this all came out when finally they became friends. "I went to the library and got your book. They didn't have it at the branch here but it was in the card catalogue so I went downtown. I was twelve, thirteen maybe. Had to convince the librarian to let me take out an adult book."

"It's about a boy," Zan objected.

"That's what I told them. I'd already read the first chapter in the reading room. Anyway, they were right – it was too hard for me and I couldn't get through it. I did finally the next time I tried, when I was fifteen. I fell in love with it when I was seventeen."

"You've read it twice?" Zan was astounded.

"Twice? I've read it a dozen times, I'm sure."

"What, that the only book the library has?" Actually, Zan was surprised to learn there had been even one copy of *Wise Men* in the Toronto Public Library in those days, amazed that anyone ever took it out, let alone actually read it. Now, the book's fortunes having changed, there was a display featuring it.

"No, but it's the only one by you. I kept waiting for you to write another."

"Me too, Sonny Boy. Me too."

"I was mad that you didn't. So I'd read that one again. I wanted to buy a copy but couldn't find one."

"But you did read other books too?"

"Sure. I read everything in our branch, everything worthwhile, anyway. But I kept coming back to you. I was your biggest fan."

"Probably my only one," Zan said.

"Maybe," Nick admitted and he told Zan how, as an experiment once, he'd put a slip of paper in the book between pages 100 and 101. "The next time I took it out, about a year later, it was still there. But I kept going back to it."

"Because?" They'd been walking, and Zan stopped in the middle of the sidewalk. People brushed past them.

"Because you were the only writer I knew. Go on, laugh if you want, it's silly, I know. But I kept looking at you, coming into the store, buying olives, cheese, bread, telling your corny jokes, laughing, don't get mad, but just an ordinary person..."

"Why should I get mad at that? That's what I am."

"Okay. But what I mean is, if you could do it, then I could too. That's what I thought."

"Do it," Zan echoed. He still hadn't gotten it.

"Be a writer," Nick said.

"Anybody can be a writer," Zan said. "All you have to do is write."

"As simple as that."

"Simple as that. Anybody can make love to Marilyn Monroe, too. Anybody can fly."

Another time, months later, in a café having Italian coffee, Nick said, "You don't know how much you can hurt me, old man."

"We're not lovers, you know."

"We might as well be," Nick said, and Zan had been catapulted back through space and time to Luna's room. He remembered the look of disdain – or was it disgust? – that flashed across her face when he'd told of her of his decision to change the story of the *Wise Men* sequel, to focus less on the family and more on the strike, the same look that had come over Rose's face almost a decade later when he told her he'd made up his mind to enlist in the army.

"Whose bright idea was that? Bill O'Connor's?" The contempt in Luna's voice was thick.

"I don't need O'Connor or anyone else telling me the obvious," he snapped. "*Wise Men* went nowhere. Neither will this one. I need to write books about the people, books that touch their lives, that show them the truth about...."

"Thank you very much, Joseph Stalin," she snapped back.

Zan could feel pinpricks of tears and he turned away, speechless.

"You're going to have to pay back that advance, you know," Luna cooed. "A thousand dollars. Don't look to me for it."

Indeed, it had taken him a couple of years to pay back the debt, but he'd left Luna's apartment long before that. More than thirty years later, he was beginning to realize he had never really left it.

NICK WAS ALMOST SIXTEEN before he finally worked up the courage to ask if he could show Zan some of his writing. And then, as so often happens with these things you've worked up a lather of fear over, he'd been completely agreeable.

"Sure," Zan said.

"You will, really?"

"It's not a thousand pages, is it?"

"No, no, just a couple. A couple poems."

"So put an extra couple olives in the order and we'll be even," Zan said with a wink.

No, that part was easy. What was immeasurably harder, what Nick hadn't expected and couldn't have, was Zan's response. "I thought you'd say you hated them," Nick told him much later, "or, an outside chance, that you loved them. That's what I was hoping for, of course."

"Of course."

"What I didn't expect was that you'd challenge me. 'Good but they could be better,' something like that. And 'Why waste your time dancing around X when what you're really after is Y.' You really took them seriously."

"That's what I said?" Zan asked. "X and Y?"

"No! I don't remember exactly. Just that you smelled out the bull-shit and wouldn't let me get away with it."

Zan laughed. "I've smelled so much of it wafting off my own type-writer over the years, I've developed a pretty good nose."

"You shouldn't do that, you know."

"What?" Zan was expecting him to say, "put yourself down," something like that. Instead, Nick said, with a hint of belligerence, "shift the conversation from me to you."

"Is that what I did?" Zan was genuinely baffled.

"Didn't you? It doesn't matter."

They were at the breakfast table, eating sausages and waffles Nick had made. This was a luxury to Zan, who for years had gotten along on toast and instant coffee and the company of the newspaper in the morning, both before and after leaving Rose. He didn't want to jeopardize that, so he held his peace. He remembered the eager face on the boy, a face he imagined mirrored a distant memory of his own. He felt a mild sense of obligation – a debt unpaid – and was more than willing enough to oblige.

"So I challenged you. And you rose to the challenge, if I remember right."

"I tried. I did something I'd never done before – rewrote. I remember you saying it took you years before you'd learned to do that."

"So you were years ahead of me." Zan smiled.

"Well, the rewrites were just as bad as the originals, but you never said that. You always found something positive to say. But you never let me get comfortable, always reminded me it could be better."

Sixteen, seventeen, eighteen, Zan was there at the store every Tuesday afternoon – after awhile, he made a point of staying away the rest of the week, even if he wanted something – and more weeks than not the boy had a few new pages for him and Zan had a few minutes to talk to him about the previous week's, poems, stories, and, chapter by chapter, a seemingly endless science fiction novel that wound its serpentine way around the farthest corners of the universe. Not very good but promising, promising, with flashes here and there, and always meticulously printed out by hand with a black pen on butcher's paper, with frequent notes in the margins in a looser hand.

Then, partly at Zan's urging, because Papagapolous would have been just as happy to have had his son grow into a younger version of himself, Nick was taking classes at the University of Toronto. And then, midway through the second semester...something – had he been expelled? Dropped out? Nick would never say what, reminding Zan of his own aborted academic career. He was back at the store for a few restless weeks and then...was gone, just disappeared.

"What do you hear from that boy of yours, Papa?" Zan would ask the grocer when he'd drop by the store, no longer careful what day it was or what time of day, and for months, over a year, always the old man would shrug his big shoulders, the straps of his apron rising around that thick bull neck, a neck twice as thick as his son's would ever be. Before he'd become a grocer, Zan had learned, Papa had been a longshoreman in Greece. "You'd think he'd take pity on his mother, drop a card in the mail, maybe put a dime in a phone booth even." Papa would shake his head, the pain on his face clear as tire ruts in a muddy road. Zan was reminded of his own mother's pain when word had come back that Hersh had been killed in the war, the first of the boys to slip permanently away into the open-mouthed world. Of his own pain, he preferred not to think, put it out of his mind.

Then, just when Zan was beginning to think the boy must be dead, lost forever, a card did come – not to the parents, but to Zan. "I'm writing!" was all it said, no signature, but the handwriting unmistakable, Zan had seen enough of it to be sure; no return address but the markings on the stamp and postmark clear enough: Greece. "Don't think about who he sent it to," Zan told Papa when he brought the card over, the next day, "just be grateful that he's alive." The broad-shouldered old man wept, unashamed of the tears streaming down his ruddy cheeks, and again Zan was reminded of his mother. Saul, her second son to disappear – though he would return – had sent a card too, from jail in Vancouver. That's when Zan had set out on his first extended voyage, Abe in tow, to visit his brother in prison, with vague romantic thoughts of rescuing him somehow, delivering him. There could be no rescue attempt this time. At least the boy was alive.

More years passed. No more cards came to Zan, but often he would hear of the boy from a beaming Papagapolous. He was writing home regularly, even phoning sometimes. This was the period when Zan was himself going through changes – the rediscovery of *Wise Men*, the chance to quit his job and stay home, throw himself into writing again, another new novel, the gradual disintegration of what was left between Rose and him – but he was able to keep track of Nick through his father: Nick was in university in Athens, so well had he mastered his parents' language. Nick was at sea, sailing across the Adriatic as a hand on a yacht owned by a rich American who had put into port on the island where Nick had been living on the beach. Nick was married – and Papa was soon to be a grandpapa! Nick was in business, exporting the very olives and oil Papa was handing over the counter into Zan's hands. Nick had left his wife and job, was adrift again. And then, again without warning, one day he was, unbelievably, behind the counter of the shop when Zan had stopped by.

"It's you!" Nick said.

"I know you?" This was no one Zan had ever seen in the store before, certainly not Papa, though there was a resemblance, and not one of the succession of helpers there'd been over the years. This was no boy, but a man, mid-twenties, slender-waisted but with a powerful chest and shoulders straining against the cloth of the white shirt he wore beneath the apron, Zan could see, but then a surprisingly slender neck, a firm jaw, a finely chiseled Greek nose... "It's you," he exclaimed. "Nick!"

"I've been looking for you. I went by your place, you're not there."

"We moved."

"I looked in the phone book."

"I don't have a phone." He didn't say he was living in a furnished room, only a few blocks away from the store. In the two years or more since his breakup with Rose, he'd fallen deeper into depression, drinking more heavily than ever, and had wound up one day at the Queen Street mental health facility, a low point from which he'd climbed and which had, happily, led him to Jack.

"My father said you haven't been by for awhile."

"I've been away. I've been busy." He didn't say he was eating in cafés, or canned soups and stews heated on a hotplate in his room – royalties from the reissued *Wise Men of Chelm* were trickling in, not yet gushing, and Zan's long-ingrained frugality continued. Today, it was just by chance that he was walking nearby and was struck by a yearning for olives and feta. There was no refrigerator in the room, but if he got just a little cup of cheese he could eat it before it spoiled.

There was an awkward silence and then, in one of those moments of synchronicity that can send shivers down spines, they both blurted out: "So, you still writing?" Actually, it was Zan who said, "So, you still writing?" and Nick said, "*Have you been* writing?" but the words blended together into one harmonious chord, and then they were laughing, and it was only a few weeks before Zan had moved into Nick's apartment on Glebeholm Boulevard, only a few blocks away from the store, neither of them thinking there was anything odd about it, just two men on their own, one young, the other not yet old, throwing in their lot together, and, as it happened, Nick often away, at his father's shop all day and often spending the night with the woman who was the reason for his return to Canada, to his home. Neither man gave much in the way of explanation of what had brought him to his present circumstances, neither asked questions.

"Better not ask," Zan said simply.

"Yes," Nick said, nodding his head. "Don't ask."

Zan was equally reticent on those circumstances themselves. Nick was not. He was in love – as madly, passionately in love as only a Greek could be, he claimed – with a young ballerina from Athens, now with the National Ballet. He wanted to marry her, but was waiting on his divorce, which had become further complicated by the physical distance between him and his wife, who was still in Greece. And he was writing, writing again, after a long time away from it, writing a novel. "Not the romantic crap I used to show you," he told Zan, "or that juvenile sci-fi shit. This is the real stuff. Richler, Mailer, Leonard Cohen – those are my gods, my models. And you, of course."

"All Jewish!" Zan laughed.

"You're right. I didn't even think of it."

"What, there are no Greek novelists?"

"Plenty in Greece, sure. Kazantzakis, Seferis, I read lots of them. In English, I don't know...."

Zan waved his hand airily. "Well, no matter." He grinned. "I don't know about me, but those others, you could do worse for models."

The novel Nick was writing – and he *didn't* want to show Zan any of it, not yet, though he was happy to tell him about it – was, no surprise, about a young Greek-Canadian writer who runs off to escape an oppressive family, a dead-end future in the family store, goes to Greece, relearns the family language, absorbs Greek culture, marries, becomes successful in business, then drops everything for love.

"With a dancer?" Zan interrupted.

"What? No." Nick looked at him blankly for a moment. "Oh, I see, you think I'm writing about myself. No. It's fiction."

Zan was laughing and reluctantly Nick began to as well.

"Well, maybe a little. About me. But, no, not a dancer. A violinist."

Zan winced, recalling Rose's precious instrument, which she hadn't played in years. What had become of it in the move, he wondered. "A good disguise."

"A child prodigy," Nick said, ignoring him. "Then she's in an automobile accident, or maybe it's a sailing accident, I haven't decided, and she hurts her hands. It looks like she'll never be able to play again."

"Is there a secret?" Zan interrupted again.

"A secret? What do you mean?"

"You know, a secret. Something somebody doesn't want somebody else to know. Or something your hero doesn't even know he doesn't know until he finds it out, and then everything makes sense all of a sudden. A secret. Most novels have them."

"Oh."

"Read Mailer and Richler again. You'll see."

"I guess there is a secret," Nick said. "I hadn't thought about it that way, that's all."

"Well, take my advice then," Zan said. "Get rid of it. It's just a prop, a trick. Get past it. Let it all out at the start."

He was laughing, but later he wondered if perhaps he wasn't actually right. *The Wise Men of Chelm* had been filled with secrets. He tried to remember if *Strike!* had one, or any of the other aborted novels, but couldn't. He would wonder about that for a long time.

Even now, another twenty years and more later, he was still pondering the question. What was the secret of this new novel he was playing with, he wondered now, of *God Blinked?* Was it a secret worth telling?

ANOTHER TIME, HE'D FOUND HIMSELF pompously lecturing the younger man on narrative strategy, as if he were an authority. This was a few years after *Wise Men*'s paperback publication and suddenly he was in demand. He had been to a conference of academics in Los Angeles, an honoured guest, in which he participated on a panel on his own novel, retelling the painful tale of the novel's failure and his own cowardice – that was the word he applied to himself – in failing to follow its path, the paralysis that followed. The other panelists had been horrified by his use of that word, insisting that, at the most, he'd been guilty of poor judgment, something one of the professors attributed to his youthfulness and the capriciousness of the times. He'd talked also about the novel's story, and had the pleasure of hearing others discuss it. He'd come home with his head filled with this rhetoric, and some of it inevitably spilled out.

"Writing *Wise Men*, I first created and introduced a happy community of buffoons to seduce the reader's amusement and trust," he told Nick. "Then I killed a few of them off – first of all, to shock the reader, to alert the reader to the menace of the plot – this would be a story in which things would *happen*, and sometimes they would happen *to* people, with unpleasant results. But secondly, I wanted to disabuse the reader of any complacency, of any trust in me as a benevolent manipulator of my characters' lives – yes, I was a god, but not a just one; rather, a vengeful god, a rapacious one, a random one. In short, just like the God so many people believe in, even though most of them might not describe him that way. Even though I had every intention of bringing us all home safely to a happy ending, I wanted the reader to experience the thrill of anticipating exactly the opposite. And, the truth is, there are no happy endings, even in stories with happy endings."

Having delivered himself of this pronouncement, Zan looked up to find an expression in Nick's face that was a combination of respect, wonder and amusement, an expression such as that which passes over the faces of fond uncles during the performances of precocious children. It was an expression he recognized immediately as one he used to wear sometimes when listening to Luna expound. His own face went red, but the beard he was wearing in those days disguised it.

Then, to disguise his discomfort, he challenged Nick: "So, young man, how's it going, your novel, how much have you written – not thought about endlessly, but actually written?" He couldn't help but notice Nick's unconscious squirm.

"I've got a beginning."

"A beginning? Don't talk to me about beginnings. Beginnings I've had plenty. That's the real Wiseman curse, not heart attacks. Talk to me when you have a middle, an end in sight. That's when you can start to call this thing you're writing a novel."

Nick looked stung, and afterwards, Zan wondered why he had spoken so harshly. Was it the boy he was admonishing, or himself?

THE DANCER'S NAME WAS IRENEÉ, Ireneé Ileana, but there was something about her that made Zan assume from the beginning she'd made that up, the "eé" at the end of Ireneé as phony as everything else about this girl who had, he was sure, reinvented herself in her own image, all eyelashes and teeth and impossibly long legs, flat-chested and thin as a rake handle, a tangle of black curls erupting from beneath her crooked blue beret, making him think of Luna, not as she'd looked when he first saw her, but as she might have looked a decade before that. Well, more power to her – reinvention was a trick Zan was on familiar terms with himself – and it was far from his duty to protect Nick from the wiles of young women; he was a grown man and could look out for himself. What could he have done anyway? The poor besotted bastard was deep in love thick as his muscular upper arm and what could you do but stand helplessly by, watching it run its dangerous course. As it would, Zan was sure of that. Everything about Ireneé was too good to be true, and already the glitter was starting to blow off the fairy tale. She and Nick fought constantly, or so he told Zan, who only rarely saw them together; in his presence, she was always on best behaviour, sweet and affectionate to Nick, respectful if somewhat condescending to Zan. "Two artists, not a good mix," Nick explained ruefully. He didn't go into details.

"Two egos, not a good mix," Zan replied dryly. "Two people, period."

One thing was genuine enough – she really could dance. Zan had been to enough ballet with Rose to be able to tell the genuine article, not that he had any reason to doubt the judgment of the National Ballet. Soon after he'd moved in with Nick, Ireneé provided them with two tickets (good downstairs, centre-of-the-theatre seats) to *Swan Lake*, with Ireneé as an ethereal, otherworldly swan queen. Zan had already made up his mind to dislike her, based on what Nick had told him about her and their one brief meeting at the apartment, where she had briefly extended a languid hand to Zan to hold, perhaps even kiss. Was this conceit the ballerina in her? The Greek? Or merely the beautiful young woman conscious of her power? At any rate, Zan wasn't the sort to change his mind easily, but as he sat transfixed by motion and colour and music, he felt himself softening. Thinking back to his first sight of Rose, at that New Year's Eve party so many years earlier, he could understand falling in love with this vision. Later, in the moment or two with her backstage – Nick had pulled him along – before she disappeared into her flower-engulfed dressing room, he was able to harden again. "Oh, Zen, how nice to see you again," she pronounced, like a princess leaning down from the back of a very tall horse to a loyal retainer, that's the impression it had on him. She treated Nick in almost as patronizing a way, Zan thought.

"God, she's amazing," Nick was saying, over and over again, on the subway ride home. Now that the season had begun, she limited him to spending the night only on those evenings when she wasn't performing.

"She's a wonderful dancer," Zan agreed, but it was clear that her abilities on the stage were only a small part of what Nick meant. He had a grin plastered on his face that would have taken a good pair of pliers and a crowbar to pry off. Ireneé struck Zan as a man-eater who changed moods as often as her earrings, a woman not altogether different from Luna, and tonight everything Nick had said and did seemed to please her. And why not? Tonight, she was a star, and Nick a vassal kept at a certain distance. A few days ago, when he had said or done something that displeased her – he claimed he didn't know what – Nick had been in her deep-freeze and Zan knew he would be again, tomorrow or the next day.

"Tell me more about your violinist," he ventured, but the last thing Nick wanted to talk about was his novel.

"What am I going to do, old man?"

They'd had such conversations before, with Nick complaining that Ireneé was too temperamental to live with. "She's handcuffing me," he said. "I'm trying to write but all I can do is think of her, how can I please her, what did I do wrong this time, that sort of thing. You know?"

"I do."

Now, as the subway car lurched and roared, he turned to Zan with tears in his eyes, and it was impossible to tell if they were of joy or pain or both.

"From me you're asking advice about women?" Zan asked. Since he'd left Rose, or she'd left him – an interpretation that varied depending on how he was feeling – he hadn't thought much about them, no further than letting his mind idly follow his eyes as a young woman walked past on the street. But that night, as he lay in the narrow bed in Nick's second bedroom, he found himself, inexplicably, thinking of Ireneé, that haughty gesture of her hand, as if expecting him to bend over and kiss it, the flash of her eyes. He shook off the thought but, when sleep came, he dreamt of her.

A FEW DAYS LATER, at his regular appointment with Jack, he told the therapist about all this, flushing a bit when he came to the dream. He'd already told Jack about Myrna, whom he'd become increasingly entangled with through letters and phone calls since their meeting a couple of years earlier. A divorced woman, about his own age, with adult children – he was wary at first, then seduced by the feeling of comfort she induced in him. Jack was supportive of that. As for his dream of the ballerina, "This is natural enough," he said, smiling. "You've been a little repressed for awhile." Zan just shook his head.

But before the soap opera with the two young Greeks got too deep, the whole thing abruptly ended. He'd come back to the apartment one evening to find Nick's closets empty and a note on the kitchen table. He was going back to Greece. He had to make a choice between his novel or the woman, he wrote. He'd decided. Zan could have the apartment if he wanted, or give notice and move out at month's end.

There was no mention of what had brought this on, and Zan couldn't help recalling how, as a late teenager, Nick had just disappeared, without even a note, bewildering his family. Zan also wondered if this was a replication of what had happened when he left Rose – had he been that deliberate? That dramatic? He didn't think so. And how much, if anything had he told the younger man? He couldn't recall.

And what about when he'd left Luna? She certainly had been handcuffing him, to use Nick's phrase. Suffocating him.

Zan did stay on in the apartment another couple of months, enjoying the luxury of being on his own again, if only briefly, but this was when he and Myrna were drawing closer and eventually, with Jack's encouragement, he'd moved to Las Vegas to be with her. He never heard from Nick again, and if he ever published his novel, Zan wasn't aware of it.

Feb. 14, 1989 – Thinking about Nick all day. Went to the library after seeing Zelda, a nice librarian helped me search. No sign of Papagapolous, Nick, Nicolas or any other, not in the Calgary Library or *Books in Print* or anywhere else she looked. What's that they say? "Another good man done gone." The Wiseman Curse maybe – get too close to Zan and your juices dry up. How's that for self-pity, Dr. Zelda?

The Wiseman Curse or the Wiseman Wager. Hard to tell which is which.

I wonder what Luna would have thought of Nick? What she would have made of him?

CHAPTER 23

February 21, 1989

"HAVE YOU EVER BEEN ARRESTED, Mr. Wiseman?"

"Arrested? Sure, lots of times. Why do you ask?"

"Just following up on a loose thread. I thought you said something about it once." Zelda glances at her notes. "Lots of times? Are you a big-time outlaw, Mr. Wiseman?"

"Me? No, that's my brother Abe you're thinking about. All my brothers were big-time outlaws, jailbirds. Me, I was a goody two-shoes."

"Now that's a role I definitely don't see you in."

"Well, I didn't rob banks or jewelry stores. That was my brothers. And I didn't ride in the tail of bombers over Germany either, that was strictly Abe. Compared to my brothers, I was a seminarian."

"But you were arrested lots of times anyway."

"Hey, it doesn't take a big-time criminal to run afoul of the law. You heard about freedom of speech? Sure, you can say anything you want, until you piss someone off, excuse my French. You can say to your boss, what a lovely ass you have, Boss, and may I kiss it, please. You say the same thing about the boss's wife and you're in jail."

"And that's what happened to you? You insulted the boss's wife?"

"No, nothing like that. You have to learn not to take me so literally."

"That's what we do, I'm afraid, Mr. Wiseman. We therapists. We ask questions, we try to make sense of the answers."

"There's your problem right there, trying to make sense of me."

"Yes, I'm learning that. So, you were arrested lots of times. And, in jail?"

"That's what arrested means. A few hours, a day or two, till someone bails you out or the judge throws the charge out. Mostly Party stuff – Communist Party stuff. I told you about that?"

"Yes."

"Leafleting without a permit, parading without a permit, being alive without a permit! Harassment, nickel-and-dime stuff, a few hours or overnight in the pokey, just to show who's the boss, as if you didn't already know."

"Ever longer?"

"Once or twice."

"Those times the judge didn't throw the charge out?"

"He threw *me* out, or in. To make an example. 'In the pokey you go, Wiseman,' he said. In I went."

"For freedom of speech? Saying something you shouldn't have?"

"Something like that. Trying to say something. Once it was a play. A play I wrote. Some friends of mine helped me put it on. The boss, the boss's wife, the judge...they didn't approve."

"And why was that?"

"Why?" Zan regards her with interest. She's persistent, this one, he gives her that. "You heard about *Eight Men Speak*, maybe? It's a play, a famous play."

"I don't think so."

"That's okay, don't feel bad."

"This was your play?"

"No, no. You heard, maybe, about Tim Buck? No? Okay, McCarthy I know you've heard of, Senator McCarthy in the States."

"Yes, the Communist witch hunts, I know something about that."

"Ah, okay, now you got it. I've got to give you a little history lesson, that okay?"

He sees her glance at the clock over his shoulder, but she seems open to it, so he pushes on.

"The Depression, you know about that. Bennett, he was prime minister. Everyone in Calgary knows Bennett – local boy makes good. This is long before McCarthy, our own homegrown witch hunts. Bennett was Red-bashing when McCarthy was still in knee pants. The Party was outlawed here even before down there, some people thrown in the clink. Buck, he was head of the Party, not the brightest coin in the pile but a street fighter, he knew some things. I heard him speak once or twice, he was okay. There was a trial, trumped up charges, something out of Kafka, almost – I don't want to bore you. Buck and seven others sent to jail, the penitentiary in Kingston. That's the eight men."

"*Eight Men Speak*, the play."

"You got it. But that's just the start. At Kingston, the guards try to kill Buck, there's a riot, shooting, somehow he comes through it, word gets out. In Toronto, some people at a theatre company write a play about the whole thing, the trial, the riot, the capitalistic system, the bosses, Bennett, the whole thing. Written by committee – you can imagine, Shakespeare, Ibsen, Eugene O'Neill it isn't. Still, it's a play, they try to put it on."

"This is when exactly?"

"Depression, I don't remember the year. I'm in Toronto then, so, '33, '34 maybe. They have a theatre, a couple of professional actors but mostly amateurs, rehearsals...and one actual performance. Then the cops shut them down. There's a lot of stink over this, you can imagine, and in Winnipeg they try to do the play too, some friends of mine, but there, the cops are smarter, they shut them down even before opening night, they threaten the theatre owner and that's that.

"Then there's this fellow named Smith, a Christian minister from Winnipeg, I knew him, he got very active in the Party. He made some speeches in defence of Tim Buck and that bunch and *he* got arrested for, what do they call it? Sedition, treason, something like that. Again, a big stink. There were big rallies all over the country for Smith. This is all ancient history, nobody remembers it these days, but back then, people got very hot under the collar about it. But all this I'm telling you, Doctor Zelda, is only the background."

"None of any of this, what you've just been telling me, has anything to do with you, right?"

"Right, it's just a history lesson – except, well, a little bit about me, because I was part of the theatre group that tried to produce the play in Toronto. Amateur theatre, you understand, just something some of us did, I was part of that. But now we come really to me. It's a few years later, '35, '36, I forget when exactly. I'm working away on a novel, in Toronto, my second novel. It's about the General Strike in Winnipeg, that you must have heard of."

"Yes. And you've told me about this novel."

"Ah, okay. So I'm working away but not getting too far, this I probably told you too, and someone says, 'why don't you make it into a play?' So I did. And it gets produced, in Winnipeg, the same group, more or less, that tried to do the other play. A few years have passed since all the fuss about Buck and Smith, but now there's an election in Winnipeg, council and mayor and school board, and a couple Communists are running for one thing or another, and Buck and Smith are both coming to speak at rallies. And I happen to be back in the city, something to do with my brothers. The timing couldn't be better. A play about the Winnipeg Strike, but almost twenty years later, the heart of the Depression, the election, all this other stuff still fresh in people's memory. What could be more natural?

"So, we're getting this play ready, and, again, the cops close us down before we get even one performance done. But we outsmart them and have a rally and get most of the play read aloud before the cops realize what we're doing. So a few of us get hauled in. We all get tossed in the clink, me for, what, three months, I think."

"Three months in jail for putting on a play!"

"I wrote the thing, so the judge makes an example of me. This shocks you, Lady Doctor? Hey, it's like I said, free speech, except sometimes you have to pay."

THE THEATRE WAS DARK, the breath of the several dozen people scattered through the hundred or so seats rising like that of one animal, an animal at rest in the dark, its eyes on the funnel of light pouring onto the stage. Zan had been in a play in high school – playing Puck in *A Midsummer's Night's Dream*, though when he tried out for a role in *The Pirates of Penzance* he was gently told he couldn't carry a tune – and he'd seen a dozen or more others, and played some small roles in Winnipeg amateur productions, but this night, for no reason he could name, he felt as if something auspicious was about to transpire. In fact, he was weary beyond mere tiredness, he was drained, empty and waiting to be filled. The house lights came on to a man and woman sitting at a table. They began to talk, their words starting to trickle into him.

He'd been in Toronto for several months and his novel was more than stalled, it was gridlocked. A full day could pass, with him sitting for hours at the typewriter, without writing a single word. Or a morning could produce a paragraph, only to be reduced through the afternoon to a sentence, or be obliterated entirely. Or, hoping to rouse himself, he would type furiously, producing a line such as this one: "Fuck shit damn cunt piss cocksuck motherfucking shit damn fuck." Beyond that, he worked sporadically at an office on St. George Street near the University of Toronto, typing reports of archaeological studies conducted by a team of professors and students who had spent several summers in Mexico and Guatemala. One of the professors was a Party member and had been helpful; the job wasn't entirely gratuitous, though, as Zan could type. That was one final gift from Luna, an irony that had not escaped him. Whether he was seated at the standard desk typewriter at work or the portable one in his rented room, the typewriter Luna had given him, he rarely placed his fingers on the keys without thinking of her, at least for a moment, but it had been weeks since they talked on the phone and their letters had become more and more infrequent.

Some nights, gripped with inspiration, he would write in a mostly unbroken spasm, stopping only to drink water and piss, until dawn, when his fingers would be too sore to type more, and then fall dazed into a dreamless sleep, waking at noon to lurch up and ready himself for work. But invariably, when he reread what he'd written that evening. he'd tear it up in frustration. He felt like a marksman inspecting his targets – the shots had felt clean and true but were far from the bull's eye. The world he created on the page, skillfully enough rendered, was nevertheless only a vague shadow of the vision in his mind.

"So you'd lost your mojo," Jack commented when Zan told him about those days.

Zan looked up, glaring. He'd forgotten that he used that word in a positive way when describing the ease with which he wrote *Wise Men*.

"Lost it, yes," he mumbled.

Some evenings, Zan would stand outside the gates of a number of factories on the west side, passing out copies of the *Worker* and attempting to engage anyone interested enough to take a copy in conversation. "Selling papers was the first job I had, when I was ten, and here I was almost twenty years later doing the same damn thing," he told Jack. "But not making a penny from it. This is progress."

"What did you do about it?" Jack wanted to know, characteristically.

"What did I do? Nothing."

"And tell me, why were you there, again?"

"I know, I know, it seems silly...."

"Silly's not the word I'd use," Jack said. "Really, tell me."

"The Party sent me."

"And you went."

"It's not as ridiculous as it sounds, but I don't expect you to understand. It's like being in the army. You believe in something, you give yourself to it completely. You take an oath. There are orders. You follow them. You might not always agree, but you don't question them."

"But you didn't always agree, is that what you said?"

"Damn it, Jack, I'm not saying I didn't agree with what the leaflets said or the idea of handing them out. But, yes, maybe I didn't think me standing in front of a factory gate handing out leaflets was the best use of my time."

"When you could have been beating your head against a typewriter."

"Now I know why you should grow a beard," Zan said. "To hide the smirk."

But it was true enough. For weeks, he'd been feeling frustration, living on a loaf of bread, a jar of peanut butter, a few hard-boiled eggs and a teabag for days on end, writing letters to Luna – and occasionally to Maxwell Perkins – that he never mailed, watching the post for mail that never came.

But still he did nothing, continuing on his daily routines as if by rote. What could he have done? The novel was a tunnel through which he was hurtling – or crawling – and from which there could be no escape but the opening at the end. But tonight, he'd been invited by some Party people to the theatre, the Toronto Progressive Arts Club, which the Party was supporting. "I really liked *The Wise Men of Chelm*," one of these people, Mike Dabbs, said. "Have you ever thought about adapting it for the theatre?" He was a short, slight man with the head of someone larger, round, bushy-haired, adorned with long ears. He was a carpenter, with the faint smell of sawdust clinging to him.

"Turning it into a play?" Zan asked, smiling. "I can't even get a novel off the ground, you want me to write a play too?"

"Just an idea," Dabbs said, and that's all it was, but that night, as he watched *The Cradle Will Rock*, a play that had caused a furor in the States, unfold in front of him, coming alive on the stage, he began to think, not so much of what he could do with *Wise Men*, but what he might be able to do with *Strike!*, the story that, as a novel, was turning to lead in his hands.

"It was really heavy with narrative," he told Jack. "Heavy, heavy, heavy – I mean, my hand, the author's hand, like a butcher's thumb on the whole works. It didn't matter how much humour there was to leaven it, it was a lead weight. I began thinking about how less narrative and more dialogue might work, not a play but a novel with less of me and more of my characters. It was thinking about the possibility of a play that led to that idea, though."

That night, he fed the pages of his manuscript into the wood stove that usually failed to keep his room warm.

"It must have gotten pretty hot that night," Jack said.

"It did," Zan said, smiling. "For a few minutes. It doesn't take very long for a novel to burn. It's just paper. Still, in those few minutes there was more heat and light from those pages than there'd been in a year or more of writing."

The next day he started again.

A FEW MONTHS LATER, the half-done manuscript was in a cardboard box on the top shelf of the closet in his room, and he was spending most of his time down at the theatre, rehearsing for his role as one of the jailed Party members in *Eight Men Speak*.

"An actor!" Jack said.

"You're telling me! The first time I was in Toronto, a dozen years before, they had to drag me to a public speaking class, had to force me with a pistol at my head to go out begging door-to-door, but it worked. Now I'm standing in the dark declaiming to whoever wants to listen. Too bad we only lasted one performance."

"That was it? No recourse?"

Zan laughed. "With the cops and a court order? No, no recourse. That was it. From a PR point of view, maybe that's even better, you make your point and retire gracefully, basking in whatever headlines you get. From an artistic point of view, disappointing."

Great as the pleasure of acting was, he explained to Jack, there had been more to it than that. This was the real stuff, agitprop, social realism, call it what you want, it was going directly to the people with the message. Everything that wasn't happening in his novel. And he kept thinking, maybe just being around it all the time, speaking lines like that out loud, maybe he'd absorb some of it. Osmosis.

"That worked?" Jack wanted to know.

"What're you, nuts?" It hadn't worked, but it had sucked him deeper into theatre. And a couple of years later, back in Winnipeg, it led him ultimately to Rose.

HE HADN'T WANTED TO BE ARRESTED, hadn't wanted to cause a stir. It hadn't even occurred to him to write the play, really. That was Bill O'Connor's idea.

Everyone knew Zan was writing a novel, that it was set during the General Strike, that it wasn't going well. He didn't make a secret of it. So he didn't take offence when O'Connor suggested it. He didn't have the highest regard for the man personally, but he was the leader of the Party group Zan was part of, so he was used to giving him at least outward shows of respect.

"Why don't you write it as a play, Wiseman?" he'd said.

Zan had come back to Winnipeg from Toronto after his brothers' arrest and, with the help of someone in the Party, found a machinist job, not at the CPR shops, where he'd worked before off and on, but for a small metalwork firm on North Main Street. With his brothers facing long terms in prison, most of his focus was on his family and his machinations to get them freed, and he'd completely shelved the novel. Then had come the disastrous marriage to Goldie. With all these distractions, he wasn't doing any writing at all.

"A play?" Zan was incredulous. "Someone else made the same suggestion about my other novel, *Wise Men*. I didn't take it seriously." Who had that been? Dabbs? He wondered if that funny little man and O'Connor had been talking.

"You know about the stink over *Eight Men Speak* here, of course," O'Connor said. The way he spoke, you could never tell if he was making statements or asking questions, and if it was a question how much of the answer he already knew. "We were thinking maybe we could have another stink as part of the election campaign. The General Strike – what better subject for Winnipeg, what better for right now."

"It seemed like a good idea – of course, why didn't I think of it?" Zan told Jack. "There I was in Winnipeg – the idea of writing *about* Winnipeg, *for* Winnipeg, was brilliant. And a play? I remembered how, for awhile, having plays in mind had loosened up the writing I'd been doing on *Strike!* But maybe that story was really meant to be a play, not a novel after all."

"A playwright now," Jack said.

"I couldn't believe how well it went, how easily. All the weights fell off my fingers, they flew. I was reborn. Well, it felt that way. Maybe this was the way, I'd been wrong all that time writing prose. I was a playwright all along! Well, why not?"

The play had come together quickly. The writing itself took him less than two months, but from the moment he agreed to write it, plans for its production began. Zan and O'Connor acted as producers, with Joe Zuken, his old friend from university days, as director. Zuken was now a full-fledged lawyer but remained active in amateur theatre and had been part of the crew that had tried to put on *Eight Men Speak*. The Walker Theatre downtown was booked for two weeks, its owner told only that the play was something with local appeal. Casting began as soon as Zan figured out all the characters. "Everything fell together like clockwork," he remembered.

"So there must be a 'But' coming," Jack said.

"Of course. What else?"

THE POLICEMAN AT THE DOOR HAD that same sort of hopeful Irish look Zan had seen a hundred times before, like a dog nosing around a table where people are eating. "You Wiseman?"

He was an ordinary-looking Joe who happened to be wearing a blue uniform, not one of the big apes Zan was accustomed to seeing when he was on a picket line or guarding the gates when he was handing out the *Worker*.

"Who wants to know?"

"I got a letter for him, champ. For you, if you're him. From the deputy chief."

"So what's the big deal? I get love notes from him all the time."

The cop's hopeful look didn't fade. "You'd do well to read this one, champ."

Dave Margoshes

He'd been half expecting something. In Toronto, *Eight Men* had played to a big crowd – fifteen hundred or more – but it was just one night, and there'd been so much noise that when they tried to do a second show, the theatre caved in to the cops and cancelled. "Ottawa had its nose out of joint," he told Jack. "Bennett himself wrote a letter about the play. You wouldn't believe the fuss. They're so dumb, just like in the States today over Vietnam, the civil rights stuff. So instead of a thousand or so people seeing it, hundreds of thousands got to read about it in the paper."

"And in Winnipeg?"

"Shut it down before it even got on stage."

"And your play?"

The note was from the deputy chief, just as the cop had said, Charles McIvor. "He wanted to see a copy of the script."

Jack shook his head. "Naturally, you sent it right over by courier."

"Right. I send him a note, tell him to stuff it. You could see what would happen. They lean on the theatre – it was the Walker, a great old vaudeville house – and they cancel, what else? You couldn't blame them – they let our show go on, their doors are padlocked for weeks maybe. Hundreds of people show up anyway, mill around, picket the theatre, yell at the cops. Hey, we sold lots of tickets in advance. We had protest meetings, a rally – first we had to cancel one after handing out thousands of leaflets because that hall cancelled on us, the Civic Auditorium – then a big one at Market Square. Everybody was there. I get up and give a speech: 'Listen, the cops say this is obscene. Does this sound obscene to you?' And then I read one of the monologues from the play. Then I introduce Rose – my wife-to-be Rose, she's in it. One of the benefits of coming back to Winnipeg is remaking her acquaintance, we become friendly. 'Keep your clothes on, for God's sake, or we'll all be in jail,' I tell her. I introduce her and ask: 'Does this sound obscene to you?' She gives one of her speeches. We run through the whole cast. Free of charge, we put on almost the whole play. Not so much action but lots of speeches and exchanges. Hundreds of tickets we'd sold, only a couple of dozen wanted their money back."

"What does all this have to do with the novel?" Jack asked.

"Do? That's exactly the point. Nothing, it has nothing to do with the novel. And everything. I'm just taking the long way round to tell you that. I thought, okay, maybe I'm not meant to be a novelist, I'm meant to be a playwright. And like I said, writing *Strike!*, the play, went like a dream after all those months of struggling with it as a novel. But then the whole thing goes to rat shit. The play never goes on, and if not in Winnipeg, where the hell is a play about a strike in Winnipeg going to play? Plus – did I mention this? The cops raid the rally, I'm in jail for contempt of court.

"'But we honoured the court order,' I tell the judge. 'We cancelled the play.'

"He's not impressed. 'And put it on anyway in public.'

"Three months in jail. I thought, okay, maybe I'll get some writing done there, but no, no chance of that. I thought about it a lot, though. I dreamed about it, and it seemed like what I was dreaming was the novel, not the play. It feels like I'm right back to where I started. So, okay, I thought, maybe the whole exercise was worthwhile after all."

"Three months in jail for putting on a play," Zelda says now, after Zan's condensed version of the story – he will never tell her as much, about this or anything else, as he used to tell Jack. "It does seem a little excessive."

"It could have been more. Unlawful assembly and intimidation. God only knows who I was supposed to have intimidated. They dropped that. The judge gave me a special lecture – what's a nice Jewish boy like you doing in a place like this? I guess he didn't know about my brothers, the kind of things *those* nice Jewish boys had been up to already. Lucky for me he couldn't read the future, didn't know what they'd be getting into next. I actually got six months, but I got out early for good behaviour. I told you I was a goody two-shoes, Lady Doctor."

CHAPTER 24

THE MORNING OF THE DAY THEY LET HIM OUT of Headingly Gaol, a Saturday in May 1937, was cool and misty, and Zan came back in from the brief exercise period with his uniform damp. But by the time he'd had his breakfast and been processed, and stepped outside the anticlimactically small door that disgorged him from the prison in his ill-fitting grey suit, the sun had burned the mist away and was blazing above him, a fierce squinting eye in a bowl of sharp electric blue that covered the treeless prairie stretching in all directions. He shaded his eyes with a hand and peered toward that unrelenting sun, squinting back. Then, feeling like a damn fool, he stood around with his thumb up his ass for almost an hour until a black spot appeared on the horizon, materializing into a car, a black, rattling Model A Ford, its windows closed against the dust, and finally into the extended hand and apologetic grin of Max Brown, who'd been dispatched to fetch him.

"A big party tonight," Brown said, "at the Labour Temple."

"What about the others?"

"That's it. You're the last. You got the longest sentence."

"They didn't tell me shit in there."

"That's the whole idea. *Incommunicado.* They strip away everything. They don't just put you *in* jail, Wiseman, they transform your life *into* a jail. You become the jail yourself."

Zan was impressed by the metaphor. "You've been inside?"

"Once or twice."

He took a closer look at Brown than he'd ever done before: the man was of that generation somewhere between Zan's own and that of his father; "nondescript" was the word he came up with after a moment, that and "brown" or "beige," medium height and build, brown hair cut in no particular style, olive skin, brown suit and shoes, thin white shirt faded grey – in short, a man ten or fifteen years older than Zan but in every other way all but identical. It occurred to him that, though he'd known the man, casually, for several years, around the Party, he knew practically nothing about him and had rarely heard his first name spoken; people generally called him Brownie or Brown, which Zan suspected he'd made up or, at least, shortened from something like Brownstein. Or perhaps it was Braun – Zan knew that little about him. "In the strike?" he asked. Within the world Zan inhabited, "the strike" referred only to the 1919 General Strike, the subject of his own novel and play, and needed no further elaboration.

"That too."

And just like me, a blabbermouth, he thought. He should talk to him about it, he supposed, but doubted Brown would cough up anything of value. "And since?"

The other man turned his head in Zan's direction and looked him over briefly. They were not friends, barely acquaintances. Brown didn't look like he might be interested in the theatre but he belonged to the same dramatics club, and he'd been part of the backstage crew for the play. There were certainly no hard feelings between them, no distrust. "You know better than to ask," he said, closing the conversation.

"I do but I don't," Zan said. "So now I know better."

He'd been in the Party for seven or eight years but many of its codes of conduct and secretive ways were still a mystery to him. He believed fervently in the Party's goals – at least in a romanticized way, since, as far as he knew, the vaunted workers' paradise had yet to materialize in the Soviet Union – with a bit of skepticism in its methods, and not at all in its – as it appeared to him – Machiavellian style. But he had learned that criticism was pointless and only brought hard feelings. Mostly he kept his own counsel and, to his own constant surprise, did as he was told.

They drove east into the city and down the long spine of Portage Avenue with Brown's metaphor of the jail still ringing in Zan's ears, shimmering behind the lids of his involuntarily closing eyes. Brown pulled the rusted car over to the shoulder once and both men took off their suit coats and laid them neatly in the back seat.

Brown took him to O'Connor's house in the Corydon Avenue area but first, at Zan's request, they took a brief detour into Wolseley and stopped at the house on Chestnut Street Rose was sharing with another young woman, Belle, an actress and a seamstress, who'd had a small part in the play too, and helped with the costumes.

Zan had seen a lot of Rose in the weeks before he was jailed – she was one of the first to be cast for *Strike!* – but nothing had come of it outside the theatre. She was a keen amateur actress, and played the violin passably well, but had no real aspirations with either; she made her living as a substitute high school English teacher, a profession that made her uncomfortably similar to Luna, in Zan's eyes, but the two women were as different as could be, he felt.

He'd been working up the courage to ask her for a dinner date when word of his marriage to Goldie got out, as Zan had hoped it wouldn't. Rose's interest in him had seemed clear enough, but now she turned cold toward him overnight. He didn't blame her for that. But she'd been on his mind a lot during his three months in jail, and he'd been so bold as to write her a letter, explaining the situation.

"Believe me," he had written, "this is something that, although I initiated the marriage, is part of a larger picture that's beyond my control. I'll be completely frank. Other than the marriage licence and the fact that we share a residence (with separate bedrooms) there is nothing between myself and this woman. At the same time, I find myself feeling more and more affection for you."

There had been no reply, but Zan was determined to see Rose as soon as possible, hopefully today, though he had no idea what to expect.

Zan got out of the car, looking up and down the street for what he didn't know, and knocked on the door. There was no answer, and Belle's little red Franklin roadster wasn't parked on the street, where Zan had seen it several times. "Why would they be hanging around on a beautiful Saturday like this?" Brown asked when he slid back in beside him.

At O'Connor's, Zan was debriefed and caught up: the stink over the play and its suppression had struck a chord with voters, and both Communist candidates had been elected – one to city council, the other to the school board. Others involved in the play who'd been jailed got lighter semtences, and, as Brown had told him, everyone else was out, most of them after only a few weeks. "A slap on the wrist, that's all," O'Connor said. "But you, six months! They're out to get you." He was grinning approvingly.

"Why should that be?" Zan asked.

"What, you're shitting me?"

"Anyway, it was only three months," Zan said. He was feeling uncomfortable in the new role of working-class hero.

Brown had been right about there being a party that night, too. "Not just to celebrate your getting out, we haven't celebrated the others," O'Connor said. "So it's an accumulation. By the way, if you're wondering, you still have a job to go to – but not till Monday."

Zan nodded his head in gratitude. "Have you seen anything of Rose?"

"Here and there, sure. Why do you ask? Never mind, forget I said that. She'll be there tonight probably."

"I'd like to see her," Zan said simply.

"It's been three months," O'Connor said, shrugging. "That reminds me." He went into another room and came back with a sealed envelope, which he handed to Zan. "To tide you over. Can't make up for income you lost, but...."

"Income," Zan laughed. "Whatever this is, it's probably more than I would have made doing anything else, ten times as much as what I'd have made writing."

They had some lunch, canned sardines and crackers and apples, Zan made a couple of phone calls and O'Connor drove him into the West End. He and Goldie had a small house on Spruce Street, close enough to Polo Park that they could hear the roar of the crowd on racing days in the summer. The house belonged to one of Goldie's brothers and they lived in it rent-free; that had been part of the bargain.

"You're home," she said when he walked in the door. She was a small woman with the plainest of features and a pear-shaped body, shallow chest and rounded hips, qualities not masked by the unflattering dresses she chose to wear. Today, it was a high-waisted blue-striped smock that seemed to accentuate her worst physical features. She peered at him through small, nearsighted eyes.

"I'm home. You're home. We're home together." Zan took off his jacket and looked around with distaste.

"Already, you're starting. I don't deserve this. Three months you're in jail, not a letter, not a card, not a message. Thank God, your friends are *mensches*, one of them let me know right away, otherwise I would have thought you were dead, or just gone."

"I knew someone would tell you. *You* didn't come to visit, so don't get on my back."

"I would have been welcome?"

"Why not? You're my wife."

"I don't deserve this," Goldie said again.

"You're right. You don't. Talk to your brothers."

"If I do that, if I stop lying to them, they'll beat the shit out of you, they'll make you a cripple. As it is, they want to kill you for getting arrested."

"So maybe we'd both be better off. I'm tired. I'm going to take a nap. We can talk later."

They didn't, of course. Zan slept till six, had a bath and shave, dressed carefully, declined an offer for dinner.

"I've got an engagement this evening. I'll grab a bite on the way."

"Is it something I could come to?"

"No, sorry."

"I haven't seen you for three months. I haven't seen my husband for three months."

Almost from the beginning, from the moment they actually met and he could tell this arrangement would not work out, Zan's strategy had been to ignore her, coming just short of treating her badly, in hopes that she would initiate a break. But as so often happened, he softened when he saw the hurt look on her face.

"So another day won't matter. We can talk tomorrow, spend the day together. Listen, we'll do whatever you like. A picnic, maybe?"

"A picnic would be wonderful." She gave him a doubtful look. Then her gaze became more hopeful.

"Okay, then, don't look so downcast. Cold chicken, some Gunn's rye bread, pickles...my mouth is watering just thinking about it. The menu at Headingly isn't exactly four star."

Pausing at the corner, he looked over his shoulder and saw her standing in the doorway watching him; he lifted his hand in a wave, even adding a half smile, though he knew she couldn't see it, then continued on his way to Portage, where he caught the streetcar. He was famished, despite the lunch at O'Connor's, and he got off at Hargrave and went into Simon's Deli, stuffed himself with corned beef.

There were dozens of people already at the hall when he arrived, way ahead of him into the schnapps and beer. "Zorro," someone called, using the nickname the theatre crowd had been calling him, and they were all around him, Zuken, Schwartz, O'Connor, Cahann, Rueben shaking his hand, slapping him on the back. He knew Rueben, who taught at the English Department with Luna, would have news of her if he asked, but he decided against it. He hadn't seen or heard from her at all since he'd come back to the city, almost a year earlier now. In his mind, his disregard for her paled in comparison to her disregard for him.

"Always you have to be last, the last word," Zuken said, grinning. He pressed a wet, cold bottle of beer into Zan's hand.

"I didn't ask to be arrested," he said. "I didn't ask to be a guest of the government. And I certainly didn't ask to overstay my welcome."

"So modest," someone said. "He didn't *ask* to be arrested."

"A printed invitation, no, that far he didn't go," someone else said. "So thoughtless."

All the others from the play, actors and production crew, were there, none the worse for wear, or so it seemed.

"So, they beat a confession out of you finally, that's what took so long?" Mary Chaney asked, always the imp.

"It's not that I didn't *want* to confess," Zan said. "I just couldn't remember what I did wrong."

At the makeshift bar, he downed a whiskey, drained his beer, had another whiskey, opened another beer. Looking around, he saw no sign of Rose but caught a glimpse of Belle. The roommate was blonde, petite, pretty, a flame around whom men circled like moths. She flashed a smile at him but it was half an hour or more before he was able to talk to her.

"So, Belle, the belle of the ball, as always." He lifted his bottle to her in a salute.

"Zorro, the swashbuckler, as always. I'm surprised to see you here."

"Swashbuckler!" He snorted. "Zorro the zero, you mean. I'm devastated that your roommate isn't here. But where else would I be?"

"Didn't you get her note?"

"Note? What note?"

"Rose is up at the lake, at her father's cabin. She wrote you a note, I delivered it to your place myself, put it in your mail slot."

"My place? What...?"

"On Flora Avenue?"

"Ah, that's my mother's. I haven't lived there for awhile."

"Oh, sorry, I asked around, nobody seemed to know *where* you lived but then someone said you'd been staying there."

"Ah, no, I was, for awhile. And I go there, of course, to see my family, but live there, no, and I haven't been over there today. I stopped at your place this morning, there was no one there, then I went to...well, to see a friend. So we missed each other."

"Yes, sorry, I just thought.... I thought you might be going there when you got out."

"It doesn't matter. What's this note?"

"Just...that she's up at the lake, that she'd like to see you, why don't you join her there? If you feel like it."

"Feel like it! There isn't anything I'd rather.... The lake, you mean Winnipeg Beach?"

"Gimli, actually. She has a cabin there, a horrible, smelly fisherman's cabin. Well, it's her dad's – he paints up there in the summer, it's full of his paintings and stuff. She goes there to commune with nature and her soul and God only knows what else. You take the train."

"How..."

"There's no phone, so she's hard to reach. She said she'd meet all the trains tonight, or you can call her at the phone booth at the station. The number's..." she smiled prettily, "...in the note. Sorry. You can probably find out at the train station here. If you're going, the last train's at ten. I remember that."

"And, Belle, tell me something, please... Do you know how inclined toward me she is?"

She laughed, her teeth glistening. "More generous than *I'd* be, quite frankly, considering everything. Beyond that I couldn't say without violating a confidence. And you wouldn't want me to do that, now, would you?"

He thought idly of calling his mother's, having Annie read him the note – there was a phone there now, but since his brothers' arrest, no one liked to answer it, he knew, fearing what new trouble a call might bring. And there wasn't enough time to get up there, unless he borrowed someone's car. Hardly worth it to retrieve this note, though the thought of holding in his hand something Rose had written with hers made his heart race faster.

He had another drink, for luck, a dance with Mary Chaney, a conversation with Zuken and two other men, another drink, for courage, a dance, another drink for luck, another for courage. At nine, feeling more than just tipsy, he called for a cab, stood impatiently in the doorway until it came and was at the CPR station with time to pace the lobby of the cavernous hall after buying his ticket.

There were only a few passengers on the train; most Saturday night beachgoers took the six o'clock Moonlight Express, which returned at midnight. These latecomers were mostly family men, he observed, tired-looking men in rumpled suits, no doubt delayed at work and now on their way to join their wives and children for a shortened weekend at family cottages or guest cabins. He watched the lights of the city fade away, then propped his forehead against the cool glass and studied the darkness as the train rushed through it, a blinkering darkness that allowed no opening, no softening, no solution to the problem he was unable to articulate to himself. Nor was there an answer to the more tractable riddles:

What if she wasn't there?

What if she was?

The station at Winnipeg Beach was noisy and crowded with people arriving to await the midnight train back to the city. As he'd guessed, most of his fellow passengers detrained, leaving just Zan and a morose-looking old man with a nose like a road map in their rattling coach for the final leg of the trip, another fifteen minutes further up the fog-shrouded lake, broken only by an occasional distant light on the water. The station at Gimli was deserted and Zan followed the old man onto the platform, then stood watching as he disappeared down a brightly lit sidewalk and into shadows of the street beyond. Miraculously, the sky had cleared and a toy-shop of constellations were flickering into focus above him.

The train had let him off a hundred yards or more from the station building, and as he turned in that direction the lights in and on it were doused, plunging the platform into darkness except for the feeble pools of pale light cast by two overhead lamps at either end, and, like a brief punctuation mark, the flickering yellow spilling from the open door of a telephone booth to the left of the station house. Those lights and that offered by the now-brilliant canopy of stars in the moonless sky above. Zan paused to allow his spinning head to clear. There was no sign of Rose, or of anyone. Had she forgotten? Had she been teasing? Had *Belle* been teasing, or gotten the message in the misdelivered note wrong?

The light from the telephone booth down the platform seemed to pulse, calling to him much the way the light across the bay did to the tortured gangster Gatsby in the Fitzgerald novel he'd recently read and been impressed with. Gradually, as his eyes adjusted to the dark, he saw a figure, still too distant for him to make out clearly, emerge from the phone booth, and he began again to walk toward the light.

ABE 5

Dolly, you wouldn't believe the weather outside. Snow, cold, wind, the steppes of Russia couldn't be as bad. I've got to just sit here and warm my hands for a minute before I kiss you – I don't want to give you a chill.

Oy, and that brother-in-law of yours, eighty-three years old and still not a *mensch*, still a little boy, a *petseleh*. You wouldn't believe the pigsty he lives in. Three months he's been there, or is it four? How anyone can accumulate so much junk in so short a time, I can't imagine. Piles of newspapers, magazines, overdue books from the library, dirty dishes, clothes everywhere, you can't find a place to sit down. He offers you a cup of coffee you wonder what might be growing in the cup – he takes one out of the sink, rinses it off, pours in the coffee. He makes good coffee, I give him that. Buys beans at the Safeway, grinds them himself with a little electric grinder, makes it strong. I can't be bothered with that – instant, teabags, that's me. The shortest distance between A and B, that's me. With Zan, it's the scenic route, with stops all along the way.

That man! All he does is talk about the past, think about it. He's always asking, "Abe, do you remember so and so? Abe, what do you think happened to so and so? Abe, do you remember when we did such and such?" Like I have all the time in the world, nothing else to think about than to keep my head up yesterday's ass, you'll excuse me, Dolly, please. The past can kiss my sweet patootie, you'll excuse me again.

This will make you laugh – the other day, he asks me, "What happened to that man Mom married after Pop died?" Like I should remember someone so forgettable. Even Mom forgot about him after a year or two. We used to say she didn't so much divorce him as overlook him, you remember, Dolly? He was a mistake, Mom was smart enough to know it after only a few weeks, but he wasn't smart enough to figure it out for months. Finally, Zan had to tell him himself – he doesn't remember that, doesn't remember the lie he told that man – Steinberg, his

Dave Margoshes

name was, now it comes back, a good German Jew – that we were being paroled, Saul and me, that we'd be back in town and we'd get him. That was all it took, Mom said – he packed his bags and was gone the next day, not just out of the house but out of Winnipeg. When she did divorce him, it took the lawyer weeks to track him down to serve the papers. Remember how we laughed when you told me – you used to come to the prison every visitor day, *every* one, *that* I remember, darling Dolly. Some things you don't forget, can't forget, other things...why would you *want* to remember? It's *better* to forget.

Zan, he's seeing this doctor – I told you? Not a real doctor, a doctor for the head, not even a real doctor, just a talker, a woman, so what would you expect? Every week, Tuesday afternoons it is, he goes, they sit, they talk. This is because he's constipated. Such a genius this head doctor is, she thinks talking will soften his shit. What she's doing, this genius, is stirring up all sorts of things in him that should be allowed to rest, poking him to remember – but he can't remember, that's why he's all the time asking me. I should go with him Tuesday afternoons, he can consult me like you look at a calendar. The head doctor will ask him a question and Zan can say, "I don't know, ask Abe," like I'm the historical record, a dig like those Dead Sea Scrolls guys I heard about on Gzowski, they dig one layer, then another, each layer comes up with something, some new surprise. That's fine in the Holy Land, but in the real world, who wants such surprises?

The other day, he asks me about the gun, the pistol we used in the robbery all those years ago, that sent us boys to prison. The gun! Like this is something I keep up front in my head along with the weather forecast, my address, people's names and faces.

"I was wondering about the gun," he says. Just like that. Like I'm supposed to know what he's talking about, what gun. It could be that guy on television, Paladin, remember him? *Have Gun, Will Travel*. It could be his gun, for all I know.

It's Friday night, he's over for supper like usual, the candles are lit, I've said a prayer – he smirks while I say the prayer, I see him, but you think that bothers me? At least he doesn't crack a joke. We have a glass of my crabapple wine, he makes a face, I tell him if you don't like it, don't drink it. He could bring a bottle from the liquor store, that would kill him? We sit down at the table, herring, rye bread, soup, then chicken, roasted just the way you taught me, just like always. Zan always says about the chicken, "ah, just like Momma, she taught you well, *Abela*," and I don't tell him it was you taught me, not her. But still, it was she who taught you, so he's not completely wrong. This is all just like always, every Friday night since he came, no surprises there. The only surprises are what he'll say.

"Eat," I say. "You think I cook just to keep in practice? Leave a little room, though, apple pie." My apple pie is too flat, he always complains, so this time I make it a little thicker.

"I was wondering about the gun," he says, there's a forkful of kasha halfway between his plate and his mouth.

"Gun? What gun?"

"The gun you had in the closet."

"Closet? There's no gun in the closet. There's no gun in this house."

"Not this house, *Abela*. The gun you and Saul had, the gun you used in the robbery."

On my mother's grave, I swear, Dolly darling, this is the first I realize what he's talking about. Gun, gun, how am I supposed to know what gun he means, like that gun after fifty years is still under my pillow when I sleep at night. And like I haven't had something to do with a few since that one. I don't even remember what make it was, what it looked like. It was a revolver, I remember that, a long barrel, like in a cowboy movie. Do they make such guns any more? Right now, as we talk, I can remember the feel of it in my hand, first cold, then hot. I don't know, maybe Zannie's right – I can feel it in my hand like I had it there an hour ago.

I ask him: "You were wondering about that gun, Zannie? Why were you wondering about that? Why were you *thinking* about that gun?"

Dave Margoshes

"I'm writing something, Abe."

"Writing something about a gun?"

"Abe, I've been writing about that gun all my life. I've written a scene involving the gun a thousand times. This time I want to get it right."

He glares at me – a look I've been getting from this *pischer* all my life.

"What I was wondering was why I didn't see it before," he says. "You must have had it. It was hidden? Was it always in the closet and I just didn't see it? Didn't notice? And when I did see it, why didn't I..."

"Didn't what, Zannie? Didn't shoot us with it? Didn't point it at us and lead us down to the police, like Hopalong Cassidy? Or Palladin? *Have Gun, Here's My Brothers*. Didn't what?"

"Didn't take it and throw it in the river." This he says with a completely straight face, believe me, Dolly, he isn't making a joke. He takes another bite of chicken.

"What, and you think that was the only gun in Winnipeg? That without it our lives of crime would have come to an end, that we would have turned into choirboys? Saul would still be alive, a judge maybe, I'd be president of the CPR and the B'nai B'rith man of the year? That you'd have won the Governor-General's Award and the Nobel Prize? That what you think?"

He looks down at his plate, I swear, just like a little boy who got yelled at, I have a flash of him sitting at the kitchen table in our house in Winnipeg, Pop yelling over something, his chin down to his Adam's apple, eyes down, mouth drooping. I must have looked the same way – maybe *he* can remember that. "I didn't mean that," he says. "I could have done something. *Should* have done something."

"Could, should, don't give me any coulds or shoulds, thank you very much. For God's sake, Zan, this was over fifty years ago, we were kids, we were different people, there was no way you could have known, and there wasn't anything you could have done if you had."

"We were all grown men," Zan says. "Not kids."

"Okay, so we were grownups."

"I should have known," he says. His lower lip is stuck out now, just like a kid's, a lip like a slice of apple in the pie we'll be eating soon if we ever get the chicken done.

"How could you?" I tell him. "We lied to you. Oh, yeah, don't look so surprised. You asked about that gun. We lied."

We did, too, Dolly. It was on the top shelf in the hall closet – God only knows why Saul put it there – under a pile of scarves and hats and mittens. Maybe he had it with him, someone was coming so he stuck it in there. But why did he have it with him at Momma's house? Did we do the job that night? The next day? No, that would have been *shabbos*, even us, we wouldn't do a robbery then. But maybe the next week. Who knows? Zannie wasn't living at home, was he shacked up with that viper, Luna, then? You'll excuse my French, Dolly. But now I'm all *farmisht*. Was he living with her then, going to university, writing his book? That was one good thing, the only good thing, he got from that woman. But no, maybe it was later, I don't remember, maybe he was writing another one, trying to, and God knows what else he was doing. He went to Toronto, came back, did this, did that, even in jail he was for awhile, nothing like the rest of us, but still, behind bars. He didn't tell us much. Why should he? Obviously, we didn't tell him much either.

But he came home some Friday evenings for *shabbos* dinner, especially after Pop, blessed be his memory, got sick and after he died. He always brought something, a bottle of wine or some fruit, and a few dollars, God only knows where he got them, from her, that Luna, maybe. At least, Mom used to say, she didn't have to worry about whether Zan had a meal on the table in front of him, didn't have to worry about him being able to pay for his classes, or his books. That woman took care of him, if nothing else.

But no, I *am* all mixed up, this was much later.

You and I, Dolly, we were living together then, remember, in that little suite on Notre Dame? Right downtown, feeling like real swells. I remember Momma spitting, 'A fine pair of sons I've got, you and Zannie, both with *shiksas!*' No, by this time we were married already, Dolly. *Ach*, of that time it's better not to think, the way my parents told me not to come to their door again. But they softened, Momma relented, I don't know why but she did. And she even came to love you, Dolly, you know she did. Were you with me that night? No, I don't think so.

Saul, I don't remember where he was living, not at home, it was just Annie there, going to teachers' college and engaged to that nice boy – ah, that was not to be, I know, you don't have to remind me, Dolly darling. But this Friday night, we were all there, not you, I don't mean, but Annie and Saul and me, and Zannie later. And that *shlupp* Steinberg was there that night too – were he and Momma married then? That I don't remember, but he was hanging around already, definitely.

On this Friday, Zannie hung his coat up in the closet, and something fell from the shelf, a scarf or a mitten. He reached down, picked it up, whatever it was, reached up, stuffed it back into the jumbled pile, under the pile, and his hand hit something hard, cold. "What's this?" we heard him call out from the hallway.

It was Friday night, I already said, so we were all there, Mom and Annie in the kitchen, Steinberg too, trying to be helpful but getting in the way, Saul and me in the parlour. We were playing cards, probably, something we did a lot when the three of us were together, but that can't be, we wouldn't have been playing cards on *shabbos*. "What's what?" one of us called back, maybe it was me.

Then Zan's standing in the doorway, the gun in his hand. "What's this?" It wasn't loaded, but the way he's waving it around it still made us all jump.

"Don't wave that thing around," Saul yells at him. "Here, gimme that." He's on his feet and grabs it out of Zan's hand, pulls out his shirt and stuffs it in his pants in case Momma or Annie should come in to see what the fuss is about, but they didn't pay much attention to us horsing around, at least Momma didn't.

"So what is it?" Zan says again. He's still standing in the doorway, his hand still outstretched, just the way it had been except the gun isn't in it any more.

"For God's sake, it's a gun, whaddya think it is," Saul says, lowering his voice.

"I can see that," Zan says. "What's it doing here?"

"What's it doing here?" Saul repeats. "It's minding its own business on the shelf in the hall closet. At least, it was. Minding its own business. You could learn from a gun."

"I could learn plenty, I'm sure," Zan says.

This conversation is not going anywhere, Dolly, they're just yelling at each other, and who knows what Saul might have said. So I jump in: "It's Izzy's gun, Izzy Arcovich. We're holding it for him, that's all."

"Izzy has a gun?" Zan asks. He doesn't sound like he believes it, but at least I can see him relax a little, and his shoulders, which had been like slabs of cement, fall down to size. "What's Izzy need a gun for?"

"It's not even his," I say. "It's his uncle's, from the States." Izzy *did* have an uncle in the States who had been in trouble, we all knew that. He was a union organizer, a Wobbly, a bit of a *shtarke*, a strong-arm man who'd come up here and stayed with the Arcovichs for awhile, "till things cooled down" in Chicago or wherever it was he was living then, Izzy would say. After a few weeks, he'd disappear. This uncle was a good guy, we all thought he was a hero, but he was no *zaddik*, excuse me, Dolly, no saint, so the idea of him having a gun anyone could believe. "Izzy is just holding it for him," I say, looking Zan right in the face, as *chutzpadik* as I could be, brazen. "His mother almost found it and he asked us to look after it."

"If he keeps it on the shelf in the coat closet, it's no wonder she almost found it," Zan says. "So could our mother, you geniuses."

"We know that," I say. "No, I just brought it over today, this afternoon, I shoved it up there when I came in because Mom was in the parlour and I didn't want to have it in my belt when I kissed her. Then..." I grin, shrug, "...I forgot about it. I'm gonna put it out in the barn, under the loose board where we used to hide stuff, remember? Now that the horse is gone, no one goes in there, no one'll find it. Saul, lemme

Dave Margoshes

have that stupid thing. I'm gonna go stash it right now."

"Geniuses," Zan says, but he comes over to the chesterfield and sits down. We grin at each other, shit-eating grins, lame grins. Zan takes out the gold watch I gave him, takes a look at it, gives it a little wind, puts it away. The band is long ago broken and he uses it like a pocket watch. He gives me a punch on the shoulder. "Genius," he says. Saul gives me the gun and I put on my boots and go outside. I go down to the barn, have a smoke, think about the old days when we used to play there in the hay with the horse, kick up the straw. I go back in the house and Mom's calling everybody to the table. I go into our room, our old room, no one's using it now, and slip the gun under one of the mattresses. That's all there is to it.

Zan doesn't say another thing about it, and I don't see him again for – what? Days? No, weeks probably, when he comes down to the jail with Momma and the lawyer to see us. Yeah, I remember now – Dolly, that brother of mine has got me so *farmisht* – Zannie's back living in Toronto then and he *shleps* all the way back to Winnipeg to try to bail us out. Anyway, by that time, the stupid gun's blown up in our faces and done all the damage it can do, but Zan doesn't ask me about Izzy, about Izzy's uncle, anything like that. The lawyer asks us where we got the gun, sure, but Zan doesn't say anything.

Now, all of a sudden, all these years later, he's filled with questions. "That gun, *Abela*," he asks me, "about that gun...." But the question itself, the questions, he can't quite get them out. It's like the ghost of that gun is too much for him, just the thought of it. He wants to know, he doesn't want to know.

"That gun is long gone, Zannie," I tell him. "That gun doesn't remember you, now you forget it."

CHAPTER 25

February 28, 1989

Feb. 28, 1989 – There was a movie, a big musical, *Seven Brides for Seven Brothers*, something like that. Rose and I saw it at that little movie house on Queen Street we used to go to, I remember that.

I've been trying to decide how many brothers in my novel, how many brides.

In my own family, there were five brothers – and how many brides? None at all for Hersh or Adam. Just one for Abe. One for Saul too – when he was dying in prison, he told me he'd married a woman when he was out in British Columbia, the first I'd ever heard of it. "No need for a divorce," he said, winking, always the joker, Saul. And me, two or three or four, depending on how you count, wives, lovers, companions. Annie, she had one almost husband, one actual one. Things aren't as straight-forward in real life as in the movies.

Even Momma had three husbands.

So I'm trying to do the math for this novel, how many brothers, how many brides, how many turns in the story? It's giving me a headache, just thinking about it. Novel writers aren't mathematicians, we're metaphysicians, turning straw into gold. And who counts the stalks of straw?

In this novel, there's a woman – well, women there are plenty, all those wives just for starters. But one woman in particular. Wife? Lover?

"WE WERE TALKING A FEW WEEKS AGO about your being or not being Jewish," Zelda says after he's gotten comfortable. "Remember?"

"To be or not to be. If I didn't know better, Dr. Zelda, I'd wonder if you weren't being anti-Semitic, harping on this subject."

"Oh, I'm sorry if I seem to be harping." She reddens just a bit. "It's certainly not anti-Semitism."

"I said, if I didn't know better."

"Still, if it makes you uncomfortable...."

"No, no, go ahead, you wanted to ask something?"

"Well, actually, it's not really about that, but about something you said when we talked about religion before, about not being a good son."

"Ah, maybe we should better talk about being a good Jew."

"And why's that?"

"Not being a good Jew bothers me not a bit. The other, well...."

"And you don't want to talk about that?"

"Have you done things you wish you hadn't, Zelda? That you're ashamed of? Don't answer, I know you have, everyone has. Even someone as shameless as Eichmann must have been ashamed of some things he did – maybe to *his* mother. Honour thy mother and father, the commandments say, Moses's commandments, the Bible we all boast we believe in so firmly. How many of us do that, live up to that – this is not even mentioning the other commandments. Just honour thy mother and father. Not many."

"I seem to have struck a nerve, Mr. Wiseman."

"I'm a bundle of nerves, Lady Doctor. Isn't that why I'm here?"

"That's what we've been trying to find out, I believe. Why you're here."

"Why I'm here? Because my mother gave birth to me, naturally. And round we go."

"Yes. Can you talk about this thing you're ashamed of? In regards to your mother?"

"Not thing. Things."

"Can you talk about some of them? One? Maybe you can honour her now, just by talking about it."

"You're sneaky. Very sneaky."

"We have our ways."

"You do, you do. How high up are we here, Miss Zelda?"

"How high?"

"What floor. I push the button on the elevator where it says mental health, I forget the number."

"Nine. Ninth floor."

"Ah."

The building he's thinking of now was at Portage and Main, one of those steel and stone towers a dozen stories tall or higher. Even in the 1930s, Winnipeg had some skyscrapers, big by the standards of the time. The office they were in, a lawyer's office, he's pretty sure, was on the top floor, the twelfth – was that Zuken's office? No, his own lawyer couldn't have been in such grand quarters, it must have been someone else's. Fox's? No, he was at the university. And what had brought him there, what piece of trouble was he then in? Something to do with him? Or was this the moment when the bribe was paid – the bribe that should have freed his brothers but worked so poorly. Or maybe it had to do with the divorce that freed him from Goldie and his obligations to her hated brothers. No, why would his mother have been there with him for that? Something to do with Saul, perhaps, his deathbed delivery into the arms of his mother. No, all of that is beyond the reach of memory. All he remembers is the whiff of trouble and the sumptuousness of the lawyer's office, if that's what it actually was, so different than what he was used to, even in Luna's apartment; the smell of expensive furniture, leather and wood polished with lemon oil; and the expanse of the city lying just outside the window, a view he'd never seen before, not from that height. But was it really the twelfth floor? Yes, he's pretty sure it was the Childs Building, that odd-shaped, shining white building at the corner of the two big streets, tallest in the city then, twelve stories high and they were on the top.

He can almost hear the ding of the elevator's bell as the car reaches that floor, the "twelve" flashes and the boy operating the elevator cracks the doors open. He can remember his mother's hand on his arm, the brief flashes of fright that had passed across her face when she entered the car, when the doors closed, and when it started its rise – was this the first time she'd been in an elevator? And then, a corresponding look of fright as a secretary in high-heeled shoes led them into a room to wait, a bright room flooded with sunlight from a large window overlooking the city.

Zan had stood at the window gazing down, beckoning to her.

"Come look out the window, *Mommela*," he said, in English, then

Dave Margoshes

switched to Yiddish. It still came easily to him in those days, though it was really only with his mother that he spoke it. "Portage and Main! A million miles from Selkirk and Salter it might as well be. But look, you can almost see the old neighbourhood."

"It's not the *old* neighbourhood," his mother replied, reasonably. "It's *my* neighbourhood, my *home*, and it should be yours."

Zan shook his head. "I don't live there any more, *Mommela*, I'm sorry."

"No." She was a small woman, his mother, no more than five feet tall. Zan was no more than half a foot taller than that himself, and she had not yet begun the inevitable shrinking process that would overtake her in old age, no, she was just around sixty on this day in spring of – what, 1937, '38, '39? – but it had not escaped him, in the many times he'd seen her since leaving home, that she was even smaller than he remembered her, when he was taller than her already but still a child. Now, and perhaps the height of the building itself had something to do with it, she seemed smaller still. But her stature aside, she still spoke with a certainty that implied weight and force. Her "no" now, as it had done when he was a child, left no opening for any meaning other than its own.

"No, Zan, you don't live there any more, and more the shame for that. You bring shame on your neighbourhood, on your home, on our house, on my head."

Had she really spoken so eloquently, his almost illiterate mother? No, surely that was memory playing tricks.

"Shame, *Mommela?* For being arrested, for being in jail for a few days? Have you forgotten about your other sons, *Mommela?* Have you forgotten that they're in prison? Not for handing out leaflets but for stealing money at gunpoint. Have you forgotten all that?"

"I don't forget anything," his mother hissed. "You think that's something a mother can forget? No, I don't forget that."

"Or forgive me for not being with them," Zan spit back. "For not being there in Abie's place, or Saul's. For not being dead and buried in Hersh's place. For not having done something to stop them...." He stopped, choked for a moment. "I know that, *Mommela*, believe me, a day doesn't go by that I don't know that. Not an hour. Not a minute."

His mother stared at him, shaking her head. She was dressed in black, the same black she'd worn without cease since Hersh's death in the war, some twenty years earlier, a shapeless black dress closed at the neck and descending almost to her ankles, a black shawl around her shoulders, a black scarf pinned to her hair. "*Dumbkopf!* My smart son, so smart he goes to college, so smart he writes books, so smart he lives with a *shiksa* professor. So smart he sells himself to the Reds! How could such a smart son be so dumb? Answer me that, smart boy!"

Zan sighed. He turned away, to the window again, and let his eyes wander across the distant cityscape, the rippled contour of street and buildings and street, then river, then street and buildings and street again, stretching toward the horizon. "What is it, *Mommela*, what is it your dumb son doesn't understand?"

"You think I'm mad at you because you're *not* in prison? I'm mad at you because I'm afraid you *will* be! My one son who is well, you throw yourself again and again in front of the streetcar."

Zan stood his ground at the window, but he turned his head. "*Mommela*," he began, but his mother's face was screwed up, her eyes nearly closed, her cheeks reddening from the energy building up like steam beneath the skin.

"Then where will I be? Is that what you want? That I should be robbed of *all* my sons? You think it isn't bad enough that when I walk down the street Mrs. Lipshitz across the street should whisper to Mrs. Goldenberg, 'Look, there goes poor Mrs. Wiseman, poor woman, husband dead, one son dead in the war, two of her sons in prison, one of them dying, but thank God, at least she has *one* son who's responsible, who's a *mensch*, who looks after her, who she can depend on....'"

"You *can't* depend on me, *Mommela*," Zan interrupted quietly, so quietly he wasn't sure the old woman could hear him. "Isn't that obvious enough?"

"That isn't bad enough? Better you want they should whisper, 'Poor woman, poor Mrs. Wiseman, *all* of her sons either in prison or dead, bad enough two of them are gangsters but one of them a Bolshevik, a Lenin's boy....'"

Fifty years later, it is this moment, his explosion that followed it, that is most clear in his memory, as clear as a slap in the face, his mother's hand hard and hot on his cheek. "A Bolshevik! Is that what

Dave Margoshes

this is about *Mommela*? Is that what you're ashamed of? That I'm a Communist? That I'm in the Party?"

"My smart son! My college boy! My book writer!"

"Maybe you're not so smart yourself, *Mommela*. This isn't the *Arbeiter Ring* we're talking about, the Workmen's Circle, I'm not just a *member* of the Party, *Mommela*, I'm part of it, I'm *married* to it. You know what that means? Did you defy Poppa ever? Did you go against his word?"

"This isn't a marriage, Zannie, this...."

"Isn't it?"

"Zannie...." Suddenly her voice dropped, softened. "I'm not asking you to come home."

"Good."

"I'm not asking you not to have a life of your own."

"That's good, *Mommela*."

"All I'm asking, Zannie, all I'm asking..."

"What? That I quit the Party?"

"...is that you not bring shame on us."

"Shame!" The thought of some of the things he had done – some of the things he *hadn't* – washed over him now with the abrupt force of a cough or sneeze. "Don't ask me that, *Mommela*."

"I'm begging you, Zannie...."

"Don't beg me, *Mommela*."

His own voice changed here, he remembers, it hardened. He turned again to the window. On the street below them, twelve stories below, figures of people walked, men or women he couldn't tell, figures so small he could barely tell they were human. "Listen, *Mommela*," he said. "Come here and look out the window. I'll open the window and you can walk out on the ledge. You can tell me you'll jump from the ledge if I don't renounce my beliefs, if I don't quit the Party, and I won't even tell you not to. Nor would I go to your funeral if it were to interfere with something the Party asked me to do that day. Do you understand that, *Mommela?*"

Fifty years later, he doesn't remember any more of the conversation, remembers his own words but not hers. What he remembers most clearly – and with most pain – is that he meant it.

"I'LL TELL YOU THIS ABOUT MY MOTHER," Zan says now, clearing his throat. "And then, with your kind permission, Lady Doctor, we can speak of something else today. Maybe another day we can speak about her, but not today. For today, I'll just say this. What she got, my mother, she didn't deserve."

"And does anyone?" Zelda asks quietly.

CHAPTER 26

March 7, 1989

"THERE WAS SOMETHING I WANTED to ask you about," Zelda says.

"Go ahead. Questions are free."

"It's about the Communist Party."

Zan looks at her hard. He remembers how interested Jack had been, how his face had lit up whenever the subject had arisen, his eyes growing more alert. "Ah. The Party. Of course. You've probably never met a real live Red before. We're a rare breed these days, in this city especially."

"I haven't, as a matter of fact. Maybe that's the problem. I mean *my* problem. I'm trying to understand some things. It wasn't quite the same as being a Liberal or a Tory, was it?"

Zan laughs. "To us it was. Looking at it from outside, maybe not."

"You told me the other day about..."

"About putting the Party ahead of my mother? Go ahead, you can say it."

"Well, you didn't actually say that. You intimated it, at any rate, that's the understanding I took away from our talk last week."

Zan considers for a moment. "You didn't misunderstand."

"Still, it's a little hard *to* understand."

"Ah. You can't believe, let alone understand, the grip the Party had, not just on me but on everybody. Like an addiction. Drink, gambling, sex, it's all the same. You have it, I don't mean the normal interest, I mean the *bite*, you're stuck. One drink, you're gone, believe me, I know all about that particular devil."

"I see."

"Maybe you see a glimmer. Here's what I mean. I'm organizing leafleters, Winnipeg, it's in the thirties sometime, when exactly, what it's about, I don't remember, but it's leaflets, must be a Saturday. I'm the captain, in charge. There's this fellow, I won't say his name, ah ha, not because I don't remember it, like you're thinking, but because, who knows, you might recognize it. This is a fellow who became something. You'd be surprised. But at this time, he's a nobody, don't worry. A young married man, with a darling young bride, a baby in the crib. They have a house in the North End, where else, I think it was Jarvis Street. A nice house they just bought, I remember that, what today you'd call a fixer-upper. I'm downtown, organizing things, getting people started, and we have a quota, so we need a certain number of hands. Someone calls, she's sick, someone else has another excuse, and this fellow just doesn't show up. So we're shorthanded. I call this fellow and the wife answers, No, so-and-so can't come to the phone, he's busy. Tell him it's Wiseman, sorry, he's busy, goodbye.

"So I hop a cab – this is not as extravagant as it sounds. It's not far, and I've got some expense money. And cabs were cheaper then too. I get to the house and sure enough, there's so-and-so, in his undershirt, up on a ladder, he's plastering the kitchen. 'Wiseman,' he says, 'what are you doing here?'

"'We're leafleting today, maybe you forgot?'

"'I did,' he says, very red-faced. He climbs down off the ladder. 'I'll finish this evening,' he tells the wife.

"She starts to harangue him, 'you bastard, you promised you'd do it today, this man means more to you, your damn *Party* means more to you, than I do.'

"He's picking up his tools, washing his hands, 'Wiseman, I'll be with you in a minute, I'll just change my clothes,' and the wife is crying, cursing.

"'You go away now,' she tells him, 'don't bother to come back.'"

"And did he? Go?"

"What do you mean, did he go? Of course, he went. He went with me, yes, we went leafleting. What happened with the wife, I don't remember, that's not the point.

"Zelda, you look a little shocked. Believe me, this is nothing. When the Party whistled, you jumped. You heard about Popoff's dogs? Pavlov, okay, okay."

"Definitely not the same as being a Liberal or a Tory."

"It's more like a Jew becoming a Catholic maybe."

She laughs. "And you did that, too, didn't you? Or tried to?"

"Not really. The idea of being a priest appealed to me, in a romantic way, but I didn't want to be a Catholic." He pauses for a moment. "Any more than I *wanted* to be a Jew, but I was stuck with that one."

"Okay, that's a good distinction. But you *did* want to become a Communist?"

"I wouldn't put it that way. I didn't *want* to become.... I just *became*. I saw the world a certain way, and I became aware that there were others with the same view. I was already a communist before I knew anything about communism, already a small-c communist before I heard about the Communist Party. Then it was just a matter of deciding to join."

Zelda doesn't pursue that, but he remembers how Jack had, remembers how he'd talked Jack down Selkirk Avenue to the Liberty Hall, Elkin's National bookstore, the back of Civkin's barber shop, where people could be found talking politics at any time, and they hadn't cared who might be listening, even a nosy kid with ears big as pitchers' handles; talked him through the 1919 strike, speeches at Market Square, the Young Pioneers, the Progressive Arts Club theatre group, the New Theatre. He hadn't *wanted*, he told Jack just as he now tells Zelda, he had just become, just *been*.

"But becoming, even *being* is one thing," Zan says, "*ending* is another."

"Getting out?" Zelda makes a note.

"Everything changes, everything ends, isn't that what they say?"

"Not so easy?"

"Not so easy. Like a marriage. You can run away, maybe, you can't just *walk* away."

"You were a member of the Party all through the thirties, through the Depression?"

"Through the thirties, through the Depression, through the Hitler pact, through the war, through the forties, through most of the fifties."

"The McCarthy period didn't shake you?"

"*Scare* me, you mean. No."

"And the...you'll have to help me here...something about Stalin...."

"Something about Stalin, you should be a diplomat, Dr. Zelda. That's putting it mildly. We all knew he was a tough guy, but we didn't know how tough. Khrushchev. You must remember him, the guy who banged his shoe at the United Nations. He started telling tales out of school. Some true, some not so true, maybe. That *did* shake people. It shook me. But it didn't scare me off. Like Nixon, say. In Las Vegas, everybody voted for him. Later, when they were sick of the war, Vietnam, when they found out he was a crook and everything else, when you talked, it turned out *nobody* had voted for him. How he got elected, it was a miracle! A regular virgin birth. But my point is, sickened though people may have been, they didn't stop being Republicans or whatever they were, Democrats remembering the butcher and liar LBJ. They were shaken, but not scared off."

Nothing had *scared* him off, really, nothing *driven* him off. That might have been better, he'd told Jack, it would have been cleaner. He'd *drifted* off, like an old man, though he was far from old, and that nagged at him, still does, some thirty years later.

"What then?" Zelda asks.

"What...I wish I could say. There wasn't any bolt of lightning, no revelation, no argument or fight...nothing you could say 'that was it.' Or, if there was, I don't remember."

Jack, as always, had been able to put it best: "A love affair cooling off," and Zan thinks to echo it now, but when he articulates the words in his mind, prepared to speak them, they seem trite, too glib, although he can't imagine a better way of expressing what had happened. There had been too much, or not enough, going on, too many tangled strands, or not enough. But he was lying – or forgetful – about there not having been a decisive moment.

What he does remember – can not forget – is a walk on the beach one early summer day in 1956 or '57, sometime not long after the Khruschev revelations. This was at Rose's father's cabin at Gimli, a place where, ironically, he had come to feel more at home than home. More than thirty years ago, but he can still remember the feel of the sand under his bare feet, the cool wind blowing off Lake Winnipeg, the never-ending horizon. The memory was still fresh in his mind in the days with Jack, but he never told Jack about that day, *too* fresh, maybe. He and Rose had been so close then, still so close, although their breakup was only eight years away, and she had taken his hand – that was it, *she* had taken *his* hand, not *he hers* – and he had looked at her with gratitude for making it easier for him. There were tears in his eyes, but they were from the wind, which whipped her brown curls into a tangle around her face and flattened her long flowered skirt against her legs. The miscarriages, brutal though they were, had spared her extended pregnancies, and her body had changed little, just a soft-ening in her face to betray the passage of years. She lifted her loose hand to brush hair from her eyes, a gesture that seemed both familiar and, somehow, foreign, as if she were becoming someone other than the woman he'd known her to be.

"What do you think I should do?" he had asked – he wasn't asking anything as profound as whether he should leave the Party or stay, but should he take a certain job – and later, it was that question more than anything else that made up his mind for him, or prevented him from making a *real* decision, the asking more than the answer that seemed to matter. Although she hadn't *answered*, any more than she ever would. Still, it seemed to him that, for that moment, her gaze shifted, from his face out to the incessant waves, the flock of gulls lofting above the surf, that something in her hardened. But his eyes were filled with wind and tears, so he couldn't be sure.

In her father's cabin, the stink of the great painter's failure still clung like fumes of spilled booze or splattered paint to the bare beams, to the rag-rope rug in front of the fireplace, to the grainy curtains hid-ing the rough symmetry of the kitchen window. He'd been dead almost twenty years and, as expected, his fame and value as a painter had soared, and his notoriety as a man had, at least somewhat, faded, though perhaps not in Rose's mind. Only one of his paintings hung there, a study of gnarled roots and rotted leaves that had doubled in value on his death and had probably quadrupled since then. Rose had sold many of the others she'd inherited – they'd lived at least partly on the income from them for more years than Zan liked to admit – but had stubbornly held onto this one and a few others hanging in the Toronto house, and was unlikely to part with them, this one par-ticularly. She never spoke of her father any more, but Zan knew well enough that his ghost inhabited the cabin, keeping her away from it for long periods, drawing her to it in others. His weaknesses, the drinking, women, gambling, and his treatment of her mother had all horrified her, but everything else about him was a magnet – all this Zan knew, even if Rose herself didn't. Now here he was matching weakness for weakness with this absent rival in a way that made the wind in off the lake feel even colder. Rose let go of his hand, shrugged, gave him a noncommittal peck on the cheek and turned up toward the cabin, leaving him on the beach in the company only of gulls. "You'll do what you always do, what's best for you," she'd said. There were tears in her eyes now, but whether from the wind or not he couldn't tell. There was an echo in that remark of an earlier accusation, made during a similar moment of indecision, over fifteen years earlier, when Zan was trying to decide whether to enlist in the army. If there was bitterness in her tone, it was drowned out by the rumble of surf on the beach, the keen of wind.

The immediate problem had been the suggestion that he go to work for the Party's insurance brokerage. It was more than a suggestion, actually, but just short of an order, so the possibility of refusing and continuing in relatively good graces existed – he had earned that much credit over the years. The man who'd put the proposal to him was Jeff Barber, the Party leader in Toronto, a man who always reminded Zan of Bill O'Connor, the leader in Winnipeg back in the old days. More than twenty years had passed, but styles hadn't changed. Both men had brush cuts – finally in fashion – and wore limp white shirts, soup-spotted dark ties, black or blue or dark brown suits, cordovan shoes that were both polished and scuffed. They spoke in the same quiet, clipped tone of voice, not giving orders so much as effortlessly persuading to their way of thinking, to the Party's decisions. Usually, Zan needed very little persuasion – he'd gone where he'd been sent, done what he'd been told, taking most of it with good cheer. But relations between him and Barber had been stretched for two or three years at least – all the betrayals and revelations leaking out of the Soviet Union had had that effect on even the best of Party relationships and friendships. Zan had done nothing to arouse the slightest suspicion, but such was the nature of suspicion that it needed no cause – this was soon after the period of the McCarthy witch hunts in the States, which had seen some middle-class intellectuals rat on their comrades to save themselves, leaving the confidence of the Party shaken. Despite Zan's persistent loyalty, he had always been considered somewhat suspect, for a variety of reasons, a taint of anti-Semitism not the least of them, Zan believed. If anything, though, it was Zan and others in the cell to which he belonged who had good cause to be suspicious of the leadership – recent world events had made that clear. Zan had struggled with that, pushing doubt aside, to Rose's increasingly spoken scorn. Her

Dave Margoshes

own flirtation with the Party had been brief – as had been Luna's – and hadn't survived their move to Toronto. For her, it was something she was neither ashamed of nor proud of, just something she associated with her youth, like the theatre and music, which she had moved beyond, out of necessity if not necessarily desire. She hadn't done any acting since leaving Winnipeg, and it had been years since she'd even picked up her violin. Teaching, she sometimes said crossly, when she was tired after a day in the classroom, was more than enough. Zan, she seemed to imply, had not yet grown up.

So he would have to make his own decision without benefit of help from her. Still – and this was what stuck in his craw, that day and later, still sticks in his craw now, another thirty years on – he had asked.

He had promised Barber he'd give him an answer the following week, as soon as he got back to Toronto, and he'd been wrestling with the problem for a week already, without any success. "You're not going to finish it, are you?" Barber had said, referring to the novel Zan was working on at the time – what he referred to, without title, simply as "the novel." Barber was that blunt, a quality Zan ordinarily admired. The novel had something to do with a working-class boy from Winnipeg who seeks his fortune in Toronto during the turbulent thirties, the riot at the Kingston penitentiary and the making of the *Eight Men Speak* play; and, as had happened with the novels that had gone before, Zan had begun it with inspiration and energy, but had eventually lost focus. There were, by then, a string of aborted, abandoned novels, like the trail of bread crumbs Hansel and Gretel had left to help find their way home.

He'd smiled bleakly. "Why would you think that?"

Barber had a practiced smile that showed a flash of teeth, then barely curving lip. "You might as well face it, Wiseman. Maybe it's not your calling."

Not his calling! Failed novels or no, that was an unthinkable thought, and this *was* a slap. Zan could feel his defences rising, feel himself closing up within himself. It *had* been almost twenty-five years since *Wise Men* was published, and everything he'd set his hand to since had been aborted, stillborn or unpublishable, the characters either wooden or transparent, the plots overblown or half-baked, the writing either stilted or florid, its flow halting, a trickle or, finally, dammed entirely. What had been an irritation, then an open wound, was now a fissure running Zan's length and breadth, a seemingly insurmountable chasm. What had once been a joke, decreasingly funny over the years, was now a mortal pain in whose grip he twisted through every waking minute, clouding his vision, plugging his hearing, blunting the feeling in his fingers, his lips.

Still, it was not as if he were a cripple, dependent on the Party or anyone else for his sustenance – though Rose had certainly been the main breadwinner of the family, willingly so, not complaining about it, at any rate. During the more than fifteen years they'd been in Toronto, he'd done occasional small writing jobs for the Party, even some commercial writing work acquired through Party connections, and worked at a variety of other odd jobs over the years when finances had been tight, mostly as a machinist, the trade in which he had developed some accumulated skill; it was fussy handwork that appealed to him, mindless but precise. Within the heat and stink and controlled danger of the metal shop, and its incessant noise, metal spinning against metal and hissing of oil, he found a certain sense of comfort.

Typically, he would spend months working on a novel, either new or an old one rekindled, until he would throw it aside in frustration and seek out a machine shop job or something else, staying away from his typewriter for months until, finally, inspiration would again seize him, he'd quit his job and the cycle would continue.

Whether writing or working at a paying job, he'd always been available for Party work – more available than most: an endless cycle of leafleting, picketing, organizing, not that he was any good at that. On the job, he quietly went about the subtle task of steering locker room and lunchroom conversations to the Left, helping to organize unions or, where they already existed, to push them into more militant positions, actions that occasionally got him fired. Zan was reliable, but he could tell from Barber's attitude that reliability was no longer enough. That, and the Party's almost perverse determination to test its members constantly, even to its own detriment. And the nagging irritation to the leadership that, whenever an assignment for Wiseman was being contemplated, the fact of his Great Unfinished Work – as he imagined they must refer to or at least think of it – needed to be considered.

"The people don't owe you a chance to prove something to yourself," Barber had said. "The Party certainly doesn't."

Dave Margoshes

That had really stung. "Prove to myself? I'm not trying to prove anything to anyone, least of all myself," he'd protested, with some vehemence, but now, in the roar of the waves and wind, his voice reverberated in his mind as a feeble squeak, barely heard. Was that what he'd been doing for the last thirty years, exercising a narcissistic streak of masturbatory vanity for the edification of no one but himself? Was he not only a fool but a vain fool?

All he had as a way of refuting that compelling notion was the simple sequence of facts surrounding *The Wise Men of Chelm*, that "lyrical," "soaring," "wickedly satiric" and "compassionate" – those were all words others had applied to it, and he had the clippings to prove it – novel of childhood, set among the legends of those otherworldly fools of the Old World, among whom he now appeared to be in good company. The fact that he'd written it, start to finish; the fact that a publisher had thought it good enough to invest in; the fact that it had been published, even if soon to disappear; the fact that, the *New Masses* notwithstanding, the handful of reviews it had received had found it worthy, even exemplary; the fact of the high opinion of a small group of people whose opinions he valued and respected; and, finally, his own high opinion – in the face of everything that had come in the wake of the novel, that had never wavered, his belief that despite any failure of talent or skill or will, despite any implied moral failure his long silence may indicate, he had been responsible for one truly fine piece of writing, something pure and fine and true, to use Hemingway's words for himself – all of this years before the book's rediscovery, its reissue and a revival of interest in its author, developments he couldn't possibly know about now though they were just a few years away. And if once, then why not again? But wasn't that belief just further proof of what a narcissistic fool he was, a *wise man* indeed?

Zan squatted in the sand, his buttocks resting lightly on his heels, letting his weight rock lightly on his toes and arches, and skipped a small, flat stone across the foaming waves. A fishing boat bobbed gently in the distance and he allowed his imagination to place him on its rolling deck, the wet planks slick and unsteady beneath his calloused feet, filled his nostrils with the smell of fish, his eyes with the silver flash of their pulsing throats. The men on the boat – the real men, not the imagined – were workers of a kind that Zan had always idealized, their work basic and hard enough, simple enough, to imbue it with a certain purity of both purpose and execution – nothing like the fussy intricacy, the contrivance, of writing. He'd done work of that sort when he was a boy and, to a certain extent, in brief stints, as a man, but it had never interested him of itself – no more than the machinist work he did so well and found oddly soothing interested him of itself. His "work" had always been his writing. Yet he had always thought of himself as a working man, part of the working class. In Toronto, except for a few friends he'd met through Rose's teaching, and a handful of other writers, most of the people he knew were workers in the factories and machine shops where he himself had worked, people who mostly lived in small Cabbagetown bungalows like the one he and Rose had rented for a few years, after they'd made the move east just at the start of the war and before they'd bought their house in the more middle-class Beaches. The cell he belonged to was made up of men, and a few women, who worked in those factories, and Zan had never thought of himself as any different from them, despite the very obvious differences in their lives. And, of course, it was people such as these – though never a fisherman – who populated the novels he struggled so mightily with, workers, their concerns and aspirations, and the forces that kept them down or at bay. Novels that failed.

He skipped another stone and found himself smiling at the thought of a cut-glass goblet filled with wine. It was one of a set that Rose had brought with her to the marriage, goblets from which her parents, in their flush times, had drunk better wine than Zan was ever able to afford, but he had taken a liking to them. Drinking wine with dinner, or at a small gathering of Rose's friends, teachers and the occasional musician, these were the glasses that would be used, and there was one in particular, with a small chip in its lip, that he was particularly fond of. But when men from work, intrigued perhaps by a foray into richer territory, or just the chance for a walk along the lakeshore, would drop by, bringing a bottle, usually of rye, or a case of beer with them, or accepting the offer of whatever Zan had to hand, it would be out of water glasses that they'd drink. That in itself was not remarkable; what *was* was the phantom feel of the cut-glass facets in his hand he always missed, its weight, the play of light along the rim. "Champagne taste, beer budget," Rose would laugh, neither extreme exactly right.

Dave Margoshes

But she was right that Zan was different from most of the men he spent time with; now, perhaps, Barber was right too.

"We really think you could make a contribution with the insurance," Barber said. "You have a good way with people, you make them trust you." Not *they trust you* but *you make them* trust you. "The Party needs the income, and it's a wonderful opportunity to make inroads."

Zan had to laugh at that. *Making inroads* had always been the rationale, as long ago as the Twenties in Winnipeg and expounded by O'Connor, for his machinist jobs. Barber had often parroted that same line – but now there was a new way to "make a contribution."

Contribution. As always, Barber's argument was persuasive. "What's more," he'd said, "it could well work to your advantage in a number of ways."

"Oh?" Zan was intrigued.

"A full-time, white-collar job would put you more in tune with your wife, don't you think? And would mean less pressure on her as wage earner."

And would take him further away from the class he meant to represent, Zan thought, but didn't say.

"More importantly," Barber went on, "the Party would demand a commitment that you'd stick with the job, for several years at least, not drift in and out of it, excuse me for being blunt, as you're prone to do with your machinist work."

"In other words, I'd have less time to write," Zan translated.

Barber's response was just a shrug, but his silence seemed to be suggesting there'd be less pressure on him *to* write. Perhaps, the suggestion seemed to be, he could drop the pretense entirely. Was that all it was, conceit?

Two kids dressed only in shorts were wandering along the beach toward where Zan squatted, a crusted and brittle clamshell in his hand. From a distance, it was impossible to tell if they were boys or girls, and even as they approached him he still couldn't tell. They were about four or five, with identical mops of tousled sandy hair, barely neck length, and dirty smears on their cheeks and mouths, as if they had recently eaten something sweet. They were holding hands, like the two children on the cover of *The Family of Man*, a book of photos that was then popular, and, as they came up to him he could see that they both had clear blue eyes, like stones fresh from the water.

"Hi, mister," the slightly taller child said. Zan guessed it was a boy, that the other was a younger sister. "Look, we got shells." The extended hand contained several shell fragments. The girl, if that's what the smaller child was, extended her hand too, but it curled only half open, so he couldn't see what was in it, just the suggestion of something mottled. The eyes of the children were smiling, filled with sun.

"I got a shell too," Zan said, showing them the clam. Inside, there were whorls of the most delicate blue and pink. He pointed: "That's where the clam lived. See, there's the living room, there's the bedroom, there's the kitchen."

The kids laughed and the girl giggled out: "Where's the bafroom?"

"Oh, clams don't have indoor plumbing," Zan said. "They have to go outside to the biffy."

They laughed again, covering their mouths, and Zan presented them with the shell, placing it carefully in the boy's hand. "But you have to share," he cautioned. "Say, are you kids twins?" He had a flash of what Saul and Hersh must have looked like as children, even more so what he and Adam might have been like. When he thought of Adam, all he could conjure up was an image of himself, but Adam was gone, replaced by the pseudo-twin Abe, slightly taller, huskier.

This brought on a new fit of giggling and the kids turned around, as if on cue, and began to trudge back the way they had come. "Goodbye, mister," the boy called over his shoulder. The thought of Rose's miscarriages floated into his mind, the children that might have been. Eventually, after three pregnancies that went awry, they'd stopped trying, it was too hard on her, and stopped talking about it. For Zan, this had been almost relief, but Rose hadn't ceased mourning, and seemed to slip deeper and deeper into a fog of regret that Zan could not penetrate.

Rose's accusation – "You'll do what you always do, what's best for you" – came back to him now, bringing with it the memory of an earlier walk along a different beach, the one just a few blocks from their house in Toronto, an earlier moment of indecision, only a couple of years after their move to Toronto. Hitler's reneging on the pact with Stalin and Germany's invasion of the Soviet Union had changed everything,

Dave Margoshes

including Zan's view of the war, as it did for most of his colleagues. He'd never really approved of the bargain with the devil he'd played a part in that sent Abe to the front lines as a trade for his life in prison, but now he was eager to go himself, the martial music playing in his head stirring up echoes of the passion and ultimate disappointment he'd felt only a few years earlier over the conflict in Spain. Already he was beginning to envision a righteous novel of workingmen setting off as part of a worldwide struggle against fascism, something along the lines of what Dos Passos had produced out of the First World War.

Zan's circumstances had changed considerably since Spain and his involvement with the detested Goldie, but again the formula that might have led him into uniform contained an X representing a woman, a wife, this time one he hated to leave as much as, the previous time, he had looked forward to getting away from. The formula was complicated further by Rose's pregnancy, her first. At least partly because of her age – like Zan, she was then in her mid-thirties – her doctor had warned Rose there could be complications with the pregnancy, that she needed to avoid stress. Now here was Zan telling her, as they strolled along the beach, that he wanted to leave, to take up arms, perhaps to be maimed or killed. "Please don't," she said. "Don't go."

"I don't really have a choice," he'd replied.

"Of course you do. A simple one. Your wife and child or the war."

"It's not that simple, Rose. The Party wants…"

"Ah, *there's* the choice, then. The Party or me. It *is* simple."

They'd talked more, for hours it seemed, over a period of days, but what he remembers most clearly was her final, bitter words, "Go, don't go, please yourself."

As it turned out, all the soul-searching and angst had been for nothing, his childhood illnesses and their lasting effect on his heart conspiring to keep him out of the service. But the fact that he'd chosen to try to enlist lingered as a wound between them.

Then had come the miscarriage, and somehow, in Rose's mind, those two facts became linked, as if the one had led to the other.

The lack of children was a darkness in their lives, a persistent sore, he knew that, and may have played some part in his extended silence of the last decade, but it hardly explained the halting work of the previous one. More to the point, those absent children had taken some part of Rose with them, turned their marriage brittle in a way it had never been before. Neither was to blame, they both knew that, but there was a liability just the same, a deficit.

Zan got to his feet, wiping sand from his pants, his palms. He watched the kids as they grew smaller and smaller, then disappeared around a bend and rise in the beach. Along with Rose's miscarriages, those missed opportunities for parenthood for them both, he thought also of Nick, the Toronto grocer's son, a teenager now, whom he'd befriended. The boy had been pressing stories on Zan to read, and a sort of tenderness was developing between them that baffled Zan. In the households where he would attempt to sell insurance, were he to take the job, there would be children like these two and like Nick, sunny-faced boys and girls to whom an insurance plan could be a blanket should their father die. Some absences can't be filled with money, consolation or comfort, but others can. He knew all that.

His hands free of the shell, he stooped now for another stone to skip across the water. In the cabin, he was certain, Rose would be brewing a pot of tea, sitting on the back porch, facing the woods, rather than the front, the lake. Whom would she be thinking of: Zan, the children that might have been, her father?

Once Rose had joked she could never love a man who didn't love the lake, the cabin, these woods, all things she'd inherited from her father and, perhaps inexplicably, taken as her own.

"I do love them," he'd said solemnly. "They're easy to love. It's as easy to love them as to love you."

What had surprised him over the years was how that love of this place had deepened: he loved the lake, the cabin, the woods, even the long train ride to get there, loved their annual summer weeks at the cabin. He always brought his little Underwood portable with him, thinking the *something* here that was so special might touch him the way it had her father, who had done his best work here. Whatever it was, though, it hadn't ever worked on Zan, but it had, he suddenly realized, given Rose one more point of comparison. Why had he never thought of that before? This very moment, the typewriter sat in its usual place on the picnic table on the front porch; he had opened its case and laid several sheets of fresh paper beside it, with a stone for a paperweight, on the first morning after their arrival, out of habit, and hadn't touched it, barely glanced at it, since. Now, he realized, it must be all but pulsing not just in its usual reproach, but in duplicate, triplicate, as a reminder to Rose not only of her husband's failure, but of her father's successes *and* failures.

As the old man had sunk deeper into his bottle, toward the end of his life, it was to the cabin that he would retreat, spending whole summers there with the young woman who had supplanted Rose's mother. The one time Zan had met him, Rose pulling him up to Gimli from the city expressly for the purpose, he'd emerged from the woods bigger than life, bald and bare-chested, Picasso-like, a brush in one hand, a bottle of rye in the other, a bandana stiff with dry paint tied around his sunburned neck. As the old man and Rose embraced, Zan, standing awkwardly, by waiting for the introduction and the scrutiny, could see the small clearing from which he'd emerged, an easel, a canvas, the woman sunbathing in shorts, halter and straw hat on a blanket spread beside the easel. She looked up from her book with a bored expression, and eyes green as grass caught Zan's for a moment before she rose to join them, a woman not much older than Rose and beautiful in a dark, Hellenic way. But later, when Zan had occasion to see the painting the old man had been working on when they arrived, he was surprised to see it was not a portrait of the woman – far from it, it was branches, leaves, lichen, light.

Rose's father had died not long after that afternoon, knocked down in his studio, brush in hand, by the force of a stroke; his passing had coincided more or less with Abe's release from prison, the last step in the puzzle Zan had so intricately assembled – his marriage to Goldie to pay the bribe for Saul's and Abe's release, on the condition that Abe enlist and Saul obligingly die. The divorce from Goldie took over two years to finalize, but, in the meantime, there seemed to be nothing holding them in Winnipeg any more and they left for Toronto. They married there the day after the divorce became final.

Coming up the stone steps leading from the beach to the cabin now, Zan could see no trace of the old man; not long after his death, Rose had spent one frantic weekend on her own erasing signs of his presence: not just taking down paintings, collecting and packing up all his supplies, chipping into kindling the homemade easel, but compulsively attacking with linseed oil and steel wool any smudge of paint on walls, furniture, fixtures, even applying a fresh coat of powder-blue latex on the outhouse, which had been decorated with hex signs, runes and other magical formulations.

All signs too of the young woman who'd been with her father when he died were gone, and what had become of her Zan had no idea.

All that remained of her father when Rose was through was the one large painting, still hanging across from the fireplace, a signature work of tangled roots and branches, a close-up view so precise it had turned the natural into abstraction.

"This won't help anything," Zan had said the following week, when they'd gone up together.

"Just shut up," Rose said back, her face darkening. "It's not your affair." Her attitude cemented the notion, easy enough for Zan to accept, that close as they had become, some things remained the sole province of each of them, a claim to privacy writ large.

They'd never mentioned it again, rarely even discussed her father, though his presence certainly continued to be felt at the cabin – a presence through absence. Now, Zan found himself wondering if Rose would some day obliterate all traces of *him* from her life, if, even at this moment, that was what she was daydreaming of over her tea. It wasn't the first time that thought had crossed his mind, but today the possibility seemed both more real and closer, and he shivered in the sudden gust of cold wind.

Standing motionlessly on the porch, he could sense Rose's presence inside, but his attention remained focused outside, on the slim wedge of lake he could see through the overgrown stand of spruce. He always wanted to trim the trees back, reclaim the view, but Rose was just as happy to let nature take its course, to allow the view to become obliterated as she had allowed so much else to be overcome, by one thing or another. Why was he asking *her* to help him with his decision? Still, she did take action, in her own peculiar way, getting up each morning, going to school, curling up in her armchair by the fireplace each evening with a bundle of marking. That too was a reproach, unspoken, but she did what was required of her. Too far from the beach, he could no longer hear the waves, even the sharp cries of the gulls, but the wind whistled disinterestedly through the spruce boughs. He didn't know what to do, couldn't decide, he did know that much. And Rose's silence in response to his question was really all the answer he needed, certainly all that would be forthcoming. Its meaning was clear enough.

The week in Manitoba ended, so did the interminable train ride back to Toronto, punctuated by long silences between him and Rose, but Zan didn't call Barber on the Monday or on any other day that week, nor did he go to his cell meeting that week, or ever again. For a few weeks, he even declined to answer the telephone. Barber phoned once or twice in the evening and left a message with Rose asking Zan to call him, but then all communication ceased.

Later, he would recall that he never had made a decision about the insurance job, and certainly never made a decision to quit the Party – he *hadn't* quit, he explained to Jack. "It wasn't that easy to quit anyway. You couldn't just say, 'That's it, I've had enough, so long.' The Party was the one that said who stayed, who left."

"You can't quit, you're fired, that it?" Jack asked, tamping his pipe.

He had thought there might be a letter, something to document his expulsion from the Party, even a knock on the door, but no, nothing. Perhaps Barber and the people he answered to were just as happy with this outcome, relieved.

"Something like that. But if the subject never comes up for discussion, they can hardly disagree."

"You...." Jack began, but he didn't finish the thought, and Zan recalls glaring at the man. He was pretty certain he could finish the sentence, but he didn't want to. He and Jack were just starting then and seemed to like each other. He didn't want to spoil it.

To Zelda, now, he adds something he never did say to Jack: "There was something else. I dropped out, just didn't go back. If they inquired after me, I never heard about it."

"But still," Zelda says after a moment, "afer all those years, you must have missed being part of that."

"I suppose." Zan frowns. *Part of that.* All of *that* – the activity, the meetings, the endless debates and the times in jail too – has merged into one long blur, like fence posts viewed from the window of a speeding train. All that Zan can really remember is the warm feeling of belonging, the unsettled feeling of being adrift when it ended.

"But pretty soon, I had my mind on other things."

"Oh?" Zelda raises her head, clearly interested.

"That was about the time my novel was rediscovered. I was expecting a call from this fellow Barber I mentioned; instead there was a call from a professor, a publisher, asking about my book. I told you about this, I think. It was the last thing in the world I'd been expecting. That call seemed to be telling me something."

FROM ZAN'S JOURNAL:

March 7, 1989 – What the hell happened to Barber anyway? He phoned a couple of times, left messages, and then nothing. Maybe Rose told him something, said I didn't want to talk to him, told him to go to hell. Never thought of that before, but I wouldn't put that past her. Maybe she helped me out then in a way I never knew about. I don't know. A whole lifetime of political fire extinguished just like that, with an unanswered phone call. Could it really have been that simple?

Why not? Wasn't everything else I ever did simple? What could be simpler than walking away?

DUET 8

"Zannie, look, tickets for the circus."

"The circus?"

"Sure, the Shriners, we bring the circus every year, it's to raise money for kids. Want to go?"

"You're a Shriner, Abe?"

"Not so much any more, but I used to be."

"They let Jews in? I didn't know that."

"Why not? They let me in, I know that."

"So good for you."

"Good, bad, the point is, I have these tickets. So let's go, it'll be fun."

"When, today?"

"Not till next month, April. Think about it."

"We went to the circus at home, remember?"

"In Winnipeg? Sure, at the Ex grounds."

"Lions, tigers, elephants...."

"...popcorn, peanuts, Cracker Jacks...."

"...candy apples, cotton candy...."

"...hot dogs on a bun...."

"We ate that *chazerai?* Did Momma know?"

"Kosher hot dogs, Zannie, perfectly all right."

"This circus here, it'll have all that stuff?"

"Lions and tigers, maybe not. Kosher hot dogs also maybe not. Everything else."

"Remember the little trapeze girl?"

"Little girl? What little girl?"

"At the circus, at home."

"There was a little girl?"

"Sure, in the trapeze act. The trapeze artists, a handsome man and a beautiful woman in tights, high up on the trapeze, then a clown comes out, he says, 'What's the big deal, anybody could do that, why any little girl could do it.' He looks around and sure enough, there's a cute little girl sitting in the stands, the spotlight goes on her. A little red dress, little white socks and black shiny shoes, patent leather, a red ribbon in her hair. The clown says, "Look, I'll hypnotize her," and he says to the little girl, "Look into my eyes, listen to my voice, you're getting sleepy, very sleepy....'"

"We saw this, Zannie? A *ketsele*, a clown?"

"Sure, you don't remember? Wait, listen. The clown goes on and sure enough, she falls asleep. Then the clown says 'Now you will go on a trapeze and perform death-defying stunts like they're nothing, come with me, little girl,' and she gets up and follows him, her arms outstretched, sleepwalking, and he takes her out into the centre of the ring where a trapeze is waiting, he puts her on it and it lifts her up – not too high, but high enough that everybody watching gasps. And sure enough, she does some tricks – nothing too fancy, this is just a little girl. Then she comes down – and then the trapeze couple come out, it turns out she's their daughter, the whole thing is a trick. You don't remember this, *Abela?*"

"I must have been looking at the tigers. I loved the tigers. The lions too."

"I loved that little girl. And you know what else I remember? The tall man and the small man."

"I remember – a giant and a midget."

"The tall man must have been seven feet, dressed in pin-striped pants and a frock coat and a top hat, remember? He looked like the top of his head must brush against the sky."

"And the little guy came not much higher than the giant's knees, but in a suit and cap, and smoking a big stogie. I remember him."

"He was black."

"Which?"

"The midget. The tall man white, the small man black. They were as different as day and night, as different as they could be."

"But together in that show."

"Just like you and me, *Abela*. Different as can be, and just the same."

Dave Margoshes

CHAPTER 27

March 14, 1989

IN THE MIDDLE OF THE NIGHT, a shot rings out.

He doesn't know, something, something has gone wrong, someone in the wrong place, something unexpected. Cries, a tussle, someone's been hurt. That's all he knows.

He doesn't hear the shot himself, of course – just the ringing of a phone, someone calling to tell him the news – but he imagines it. That shot echoes through the years in Zan's ears, asleep, awake, it doesn't matter.

And then the boys in custody again – Saul, for whom this sort of thing has become old hat; and Abe, who ought to have known better. That stupid half-embarrassed, half-proud grin he knows so well plastered over their faces – no, he isn't there, how could he be? But he sees them anyway: in the police car, roughed up, in the cell, their heads hanging down finally, waiting for morning, the cup of thin coffee, the talk with the lawyer, some of the brass finally rubbed off them.

That's the dream, but, waking, the memory isn't all that much different.

He hadn't been there, of course, over a thousand miles away in Toronto, but he knew so well what it must have looked like, what must have been said. All he really knew was his mother crying in the background, the voice of Mrs. Lipshitz, the neighbour with the phone, "You'd better get down here. Your brothers have gone and done it good now."

And they really had. Caught red-handed this time, not on the word of some rat, in a jewelry store, a gun in Saul's hand.

Zan packed his few things and closed up his apartment – he didn't figure he'd be back any time soon – and caught the train the very same day.

They had a lawyer already, of course, Joe Zuken, who had gotten Abe and Saul out of scrapes several times, and as soon as he got back to Winnipeg, Zan telephoned Adrian Fox, the law professor who had helped the boys out once before. He and Zuken conferred and afterwards had little encouragement for Zan.

"This is entirely different from the last time," Fox said. "They've got them dead to rights. A guilty plea is their best course. Frankly, they're going to prison either way." Then, noting the look of helplessness that swept across Zan's face, he added, softly: "There's really not much you can do."

Fox was tall, angular, thin, cut from the same cloth as Luna and her father, who was also a lawyer; and as the Commodore, even his friend John Archer. What was it about him that attracted these people, Zan often wondered, although he certainly didn't count Luna's father among his fans. Fox had taken an immediate liking to him when they first met, at a party at Liberty Hall Joe had dragged him to, the pale-skinned Anglo with his chiseled features so out of place among the swarthy Jews and Slavs. Soon afterwards, that had been cemented when Fox gave a talk there on how the justice system works. Liberty Hall was a left-wing split-off from the *Arbeiter Ring*, which itself had been to the left of the Peretz School, and become popular as a meeting place. Zan had been first up with his hand when the professor asked if there were any questions. "Do you agree with Lenin's proposition that there are two forms of justice, one for the rich and one for the poor?"

"Absolutely," Fox said.

"And that the cards are stacked against the poor?"

"Again, absolutely. But this is hardly news. Most poor people discover this on their own, without benefit of advice from a law professor. Or from a Russian revolutionary."

"And is their situation hopeless?" Zan pressed.

"No, never hopeless. I don't use that word. But difficult, of course."

"Good that you can maintain hope while your clients rot in jail."

A slow smile began to form on Fox's thin lips. "I think I know, but which camp are you from?"

"The poor," Zan shot back.

"Then you might as well leave right now, wouldn't you think? The situation being so hopeless." But Fox was grinning now. He had no poker face.

"Maybe I'll stick around for awhile," Zan conceded after a moment. "Just in case I ever get rich."

"Just in case," Fox echoed. "Yes, a good strategy." Strategy was something he talked about a lot, in class, according to Joe Zuken, and outside as well. He liked to hold his own style of court in a tavern near the law courts on York Avenue, and during the years Zan was taking classes he was among the handful of students, an eclectic group and definitely not all from the law school, who would be invited along. "Are you Jewish, Mr. Wiseman?" Fox asked him the first time they were seated over beers.

"Yes, does it matter?"

"To the bartender, probably. To me, no."

"But the bartender didn't ask, you did, professor."

"That's true. And from that you're inferring something other than my disclaimer."

"Not inferring, wondering."

"Is wondering something worth articulating?"

"Isn't that what you did?"

Years later, telling Jack about the bantering relationship that had developed between them, Zan had blurted out: "You remind me of him."

"Rangy, athletic, patrician...you make him sound like George Plimpton," Jack had retorted. "I'm dark, bearded, overweight...."

"I meant in personality."

"He told you what to do."

"I didn't say that. I definitely didn't say that."

"But you took his advice about your brothers."

"It wasn't just his. Joe Zuken said the same thing. There really wasn't any doubt they did it – the gun, witnesses, everything."

"And what you did?"

"What I did? I wasn't there."

"I mean afterwards. To get them out."

"I didn't do what he told me. I asked his advice, he gave it. I did what I wanted to do. I didn't get my money's worth, but that wasn't his fault."

NONE OF THIS HE TELLS ZELDA.

Once again she's been probing about the women in Zan's life, the relationships, narrowing in finally on the one woman whose name he usually professes not to remember. "Tell me about the mysterious other woman in your life, Zan," she says when he's settled himself. "The woman you say was your first wife." She riffles through her notebook. "The one you say 'doesn't really count.'"

"Goldie was her name," he acknowledges, flustered. And the sound of her name breaks open a flood of memory that only tangentially relates to her: the boys in trouble, in jail; the lawyers; the bargain with the devil.

"Yes, my first wife. Legally, but in no other way. It was loveless, a hard-bargained arrangement, a mistake but unavoidable nonetheless. It didn't last long."

"An unavoidable mistake, an arrangement. That's interesting," Zelda says. "Tell me more about this."

"No. Some things I forget, I know; but some things are best forgotten."

But she persists, just as Jack had.

NONE OF IT HAD BEEN FOX'S FAULT; that man had done everything he could, everything Zan had asked and more, taking chances he shouldn't have, he'd told Jack. It was Zan's idea, Zan who paid the price to raise the money, but it was Fox who had actually done the bribe – approached the people, broached the subject, carried the money, passed it over. It was he who would have gone to prison, been disbarred, ruined, he who had everything to lose, not Zan.

"Why would he have done that, taken that risk?" Jack had asked.

Zan shook his ahead. "I've wondered about that ever since. I think for the thrill, maybe...you know, like these people who jump out of air-planes...."

"Skydivers? With parachutes."

"Sometimes they don't open. You control the situation only so far, then it's...chance. There's the thrill."

"And this fellow, Fox, was a thrill-seeker?"

"And he got caught up, maybe, in the drama."

"One of my brothers is dying," he'd told Fox. "If he dies in prison, my mother will die too."

That was surely an exaggeration – Chaika Wiseman had already

lived through too much, was too resilient for that sort of erosion –
but there was more to it than that: Annie's engagement had been broken, irreparably it seemed, and even his mother and her suitor, the
unappealing Steinberg, were at odds. The whole family was in tumult,
though Zan had remained blameless. He'd moved back into the house
on Flora Avenue temporarily, a house he found silent in a way he had
never known it to be, as if the air had been let out of it. Even the smells
seemed thinner, the food on the table hot and steaming but somehow
tasteless, less substantial. Where there had once been so many, now
there were so few at the table – just Zan, his mother and sister, and
occasionally Steinberg, who would soon become a permanent member
of the household with his mother's marriage to him, as if, in grasping
at straws of normalcy, she hoped to set her life straight again – and
Zan came to the table without hunger, left it feeling unfilled. The only
times he could remember the house being even remotely like this were
almost twenty years earlier, when Saul had come home from the war
alone, everyone tiptoeing around the cramped rooms as if afraid to
awaken Hersh's sleeping absence; and when his father had died, just a
few years earlier, again bringing down a shroud of silence on the old
frame house. But even through those crises, the life of the house had
gone on, its noise only temporarily diminished. This time, his mother's
pain, Zan remembers, was palpable.

"And?" Fox asked pointedly. "There was a question you wished to
ask, Mr. Wiseman?" Within the domain of his office, as in his classroom, the professor adopted a formality that was absent in the tavern
or even on the street, where he would have called Zan by his first name.

"Is there something that can be done? Yes, that's the question."

"Are you asking about appeals? Pleading guilty isn't exactly the
best..."

"No," Zan interrupted. "I'm asking about something else."

"In the case of the dying brother, the premier can be asked for
clemency."

"Something like that," Zan said.

The two men appraised each other. "That's not the sort of thing a
client should ask of his lawyer," Fox said after a long silence.

Zan said nothing.

Again, a long silence, which Fox ended: "Something can always be done. Usually, it involves money. I had the impression, Mr. Wiseman, that you didn't have money."

"Money I can get."

"Oh? Not the way your brothers tried, I trust."

"Money you can always get," Zan said, although he really had no idea how. He'd thought of asking Luna for a loan, but decided against it – it was well over a year since there'd been any contact between them – and going to the Party was out of the question. The one person he had approached was his one-time mentor, the Commodore, who'd turned him down with a shrug. "I thought I taught you to be more self-reliant," he'd said. Self-reliant, yes, and now the beginning of an idea was fermenting in his head, based on a rumour he'd heard on the street, something about a woman seeking a husband – or, to be more exact, a group of men seeking a husband for their sister. He had no idea what the price would be or what he could raise, what he would be worth. "That Zan will be some catch," the neighbour ladies whom his mother had coffee with had been saying, ever since they first started seeing him wearing a sports jacket and carrying books under his arms.

"I had the impression, too," Fox said, "that you were burdened by scruples, Wiseman." Zan noted the absence of the "Mr."

"Scruples you can always put aside for the moment."

Afterwards, he remembered the burnt grain smell of the room where the deal was struck, in the rear of a warehouse just off Sutherland Avenue in Point Douglas. The street itself, he recalled, as improbably named Syndicate. The Sorroman brothers were reputed to make their moonshine there, although there was no sign of a still, just a surprisingly clean table and four wobbly chairs. Card games were said to be played in the room as well. Saul would know – the elder Sorromans had been part of the same tough crowd he and Hersh had once run with – Abe too maybe, but neither was available for consultation. Zan sat in one of the chairs, facing three brothers arrayed around the table, almost as if they were playing cards, or were about to.

"I had the good fortune – or bad fortune, depending on your point of view – of meeting some fellows who had a service they wanted to buy at a time when I needed some money badly," he explains to Zelda now.

He had approached the youngest of the brothers, Danny, whom he had gone to St. John's Tech with, on the street a week earlier. He was a wild one, with unruly red hair and a squint. "I hear you have a problem with your sister," he'd said.

It was the card table, the idea of the card game, that made him tell Jack, years later, that he'd won his first wife at poker, "that and a dowry."

"How much?"

"Two thousand dollars."

He uses the same language with Zelda, but stops there. With Jack, he'd told the whole story – that man could get anything and everything out of Zan, as far as he could remember – but to Zelda now he merely says his brothers had "debts."

"And you had to pay them?"

"They couldn't, I could," he says simply.

"So to pay your brothers' debts you married a woman you didn't love, for her dowry?"

"Love didn't enter into the picture. She was old and ugly – forgive, please, any violation of feminist sensibilities. Stupid too – the old and ugly I might have gotten used to, the stupid, no. Dowry is just a code word. I needed the money and I married her for it. In the Old World, such arranged marriages are common, in some places, the norm, you take what you get. What I did was not beyond the realm of civilized behaviour."

"I didn't suggest it was," Zelda says. Then, after a pause: "How old? How ugly?"

Zan smiles. "As old as I was, and just as ugly. No, that's not right – I was thirty, she was older than that, less than forty, I don't remember exactly. Way too old for her brothers to think anyone legitimate would come along on his own. And too ugly. Not so ugly that if you passed her on the street you'd think 'there's an ugly woman,' but ugly enough that most men wouldn't dream of holding her in their arms. Crooked teeth. A twisted upper lip."

"And how stupid?"

"Stupid enough to have let her brothers talk her into this. In that, no more stupid than I was, though I at least had reasons. Well, she did too, I know that. Stupid enough that I couldn't have a conversation with her for more than five minutes without my skin starting to crawl."

Zan was silent for a minute, the silence broken only by the scratching of Zelda's pencil.

"If you're asking me is this fair, no, it wasn't fair, Lady Doctor. Not that she looked the way she did, not that men don't find that appealing, not that she was stupid, not that I married her for money. None of it fair. Of the first three, I had no hand. Just the last."

"And you did it anyway."

"I did it."

"To pay your brothers' debts."

"To pay their debts, yes." He hesitated. "Damn it, to pay some bribes, to get them out of jail! Maybe we could change the subject now."

"I see." Zelda was silent for a moment. "Did it work?"

"Yes and no." He shrugged.

The smell of burnt grain is sharp in his nostrils – he can't remember Goldie's face, not even the sound of her voice, but he remembers that smell, that and the words of the oldest brother – was his name Sammy? – as they got up from the table: "You do the right thing or we'll kill you."

He doesn't tell Zelda that either.

OF COURSE, HIS INTENTIONS WERE LESS than honourable, far less. He was already half in love with Rose – that relationship was immediately frozen when word of the marriage got out, but she remained uppermost in his mind. And it was during this period that he went to jail.

"I told you about my play, about being arrested?"

"Yes."

"That went on after the marriage. I didn't do the play to get arrested, believe me, and I didn't get arrested to get away from that woman, but that's what happened. Three months in Headingly while still a newlywed, three blessed months apart from her. Her brothers weren't happy, but what could they do?"

Beyond that, it was 1937 and, as he explained to Jack, Europe was exploding. Around the Party, there'd been a lot of talk for months about sending volunteers to Spain, and Zan had been thinking seriously about it from the first, the thought that his health might keep him out never even crossing his mind. He was perfectly healthy, as far as he knew, in good shape from his physical work with the CPR and vigorous, and the weakness of his heart all but forgotten, not to be recalled for several more years. In the spring of 1937, the go-ahead came and units were being organized all over the world; in Canada it was the MacKenzie-Papineau brigade, with the Party in the forefront of rounding up volunteers. Now Zan's path seemed clear to him. He would sign up with the Mac-Paps and take his chances. He could honestly say that going to Spain had been his intention before the marriage, and if he'd neglected to say something about it to Goldie, or her brothers, well, it had not been deliberate. The marriage had been quickly planned and executed, without benefit of a rabbi, guests or a party, just a licence and a justice of the peace, with the three brothers as witnesses, and, the truth was, there was little time for talk between them. He would go to Spain and take his chances. If he was killed – of which, by all accounts, there was a good chance – that would be the end of the story, he would leave the woman an honourable widow and she could get on with her life. If he returned, well, it would surely be in no less than a year, perhaps two, and who knows what might have transpired in that time, what boredom might have seized the woman, what new lover might have come along to sweep her away, or what changes might have come to the fortunes and strength of the Sorroman family. At the very least, it would be a year or two away from the problem, and then he would see what he could see.

"And this didn't strike you as running away from your problems?" Jack had asked.

"I wasn't running away, I was going to war, like men have done down through the millennia."

"And it didn't strike you that you were behaving less than honourably?"

"That stupid I wasn't, even at that tender age. I knew what I was doing. I didn't like it. I tried to spend some time with that woman but I just couldn't. If you're asking me did I feel like a piece of shit, yes, I did."

Part of the arrangement was a house the Sorromans owned in the West End, on Spruce Street, a location that suited Zan fine. The house wasn't free, but the rent – $40 a month – was low enough that he could afford it from the small salary he made at a machinist job. Goldie had also brought with her some pieces of furniture, linens, dishes and kitchen utensils, enough to set up housekeeping, and she set about turning the house into a home for them.

Neither her stupidity nor her ugliness, he told Jack, was as bothersome to him as her neediness, the way she clung to him. He would go out, she would want to go with him. He would stay in, she would want to talk. She was always touching him, tucking in his collar, straightening his tie, like a child with a new pet.

"She was your wife," Jack observed. "Maybe she had some expectations."

"If she did, they were unrealistic."

"And sex?" Jack asked.

Zan just looked at him. "That dishonourable I wasn't."

"You were married, for God's sake, man."

"In name only."

"It was legal."

"It was an arrangement."

"Did she see it that way?"

"The arrangement wasn't with her, it was with the brothers."

"Tell me something, Wiseman. You and *your* brothers, and your sister. Would you have made such an arrangement for her?"

"Annie? Annie was an angel, a beautiful angel. Men were around her like flies, from when she was a teenager."

"Didn't you say her fiancé broke their engagement after the trouble?"

"Yes, but..."

"And she had to settle for someone less than she was perfectly happy with, didn't you tell me that?"

"Marvin is a fine man. He was lucky to get her, she to get him. They have a good life together. Four wonderful children."

"Fine, lucky, good.... Isn't it true that the man she loved ran out on her? Isn't that what you told me?"

"Yes."

"So fine, lucky, good, she didn't have who she wanted, what she wanted. And settled for something else, made the best of it. Isn't that what Goldie was doing?"

"What, I'm paying you to make me feel worse than I already do?

To tell me things I already know. A conscience I already have, Doctor."

"So don't bullshit me, Wiseman. Don't bullshit yourself."

With Zelda, he has no intention of being this forthcoming, even if he were able to remember nearly as well as he had with Jack. With her, he says merely that there was no love between them.

"You're sure she didn't love you?"

"How could she? I didn't treat her very well."

But he didn't desert her, not the way he intended. He had signed up for Spain, let them know at the metal shop he'd be leaving but, luckily, hadn't formally quit – had even taken the train up to Stony Mountain to tell the boys, to let them know the pardon should be coming soon, to say what he thought would be his last goodbye to Saul, who was in the prison hospital then. Done everything but tell his mother and Annie, and tell Goldie – so, as it would happen, they never knew how close they came to losing him.

O'Connor, who was part of the small group in Winnipeg recruiting men for the Mac-Paps, called and he took the streetcar up Main to Economy Drugs, where O'Connor liked to do business out of a booth toward the rear. He was expecting, he remembered, a pat on the back, the usual pep talk.

"You're not going," O'Connor said.

"Not going? What do you mean? I'm all packed, I'm almost gone."

"Unpack," O'Connor said. "There are plenty of soldiers. We need you here, Wiseman."

"Wait a minute...."

O'Connor was strict, but he was something of a friend, too. It didn't take Zan long to worm it out of him.

"Your brother-in-law was here to see me."

"My brother-in-law?"

"Samuel Sorroman. He told me about your arrangement."

"He... O'Connor, this is none of your business."

"It's the Party's business, Zan. He means to let everyone know this is how members of the Party conduct themselves." O'Connor shook his head. "You're right, Zan, it isn't my business, so don't tell me the details. I don't want to know. But I don't want others to know, either. Do you?"

"That bastard. How did...?"

"How did he find out? I don't know. He hears things, I imagine. A man like him, he's got plenty of ears."

"What does he want?"

O'Connor laughed. "What do you think? For you to live up to the bargain, to be a husband. What – he says – you agreed to be. In writing. You really signed something?" He shook his head. "Well, that means being here. Not Spain."

He remembered walking home, down Main and through the subway under the CPR tracks to Portage, vibrating with anger, resentment, disappointment, stopping once for a beer at the St. Regis Hotel, and then down Portage, past the old university campus – Manitoba College, where he had once taken some classes, had, ironically, been sold to a Catholic school, St. Paul's, run by Jesuits – all the way to Spruce, a walk of a couple of hours. Enough time for him to cool down, and come to a decision.

"Which was?" Jack asked.

"That if I was to be a husband and a civilian, then a husband and a civilian I would be. I'd make the best of it."

"You'd be a husband? A real one?"

"I'd try to be."

Does he remember that now, that resolve? Zelda asks him again, "Are you sure she didn't love you?"

"Yes. She couldn't have."

"And how long did you say it lasted?"

"How long? Lady Doctor, time doesn't mean much to me any more, you know that. I don't remember. Not long."

In fact, it had been almost two years, that long before he was no longer able to restrain himself, before finally getting together with Rose – and then many more years paying off the promissory note. "Those bastard Sorromans were sore losers," he told Jack. "They got their pound of flesh out of me, that's for sure."

Two things had happened even before Rose. The first was Saul's death. "He was just forty," Zan told Jack. "Hadn't really done anything with his life yet. Except get in trouble. Like he'd been stillborn." He winced at his own choice of words. "He had the misfortune to be born in a family of wayward brothers." The $2,000 had been enough to win his release although, as Adrian Fox had pointed out, "By the time they got around to it, he was so sick they would probably have released him anyway." After his heart attack, all his time had been served in the prison hospital anyway and they were probably just as glad to get rid of him, Fox had said. "Save the province the cost of his final days and the funeral. You didn't get your money's worth with that one, I'm sorry to say."

Nor with Abe, as far as Zan was concerned.

The boys hadn't been released, as Zan had been led to expect, or their sentences even shortened; instead, they'd been sent to the prison farm, considered easy time. When Zan went to visit, Abe had shrugged. "Don't worry about it, Zannie. This is easy time, it'll fly by."

"Too easy," Saul said. Though maybe not, as his heart had given out just weeks after that visit. "Too easy for us. People are gonna think we ratted on someone."

"Let them think," Zan said. "So what?"

Saul just shook his head, giving Abe a look. Despite everything, it had always been those two who were most alike, *they* were the twins.

Fox gave him a similar look when Zan complained. "They asked for three thousand, you gave two. They said they'd see what could be done. I told you there weren't any guarantees. This isn't the chamber of commerce."

No guarantees, that's what he told himself there were in his arrangement over Goldie as well. That was the second thing. Do right, the brother had said, and he had, by his own sights, that's what he told Jack. "For a year or more we played at being the happy couple. I was home every night, dinner together, we talked, went out, anything she wanted to do – up to a point. I tried to be what she wanted me to be even if I couldn't be what I wanted to be. But it never had a chance. I was who I was."

Then there was Rose. Something had just been beginning to develop between them, and she was furious when she heard about the marriage, rightly so, Zan thought, but later became sympathetic. He'd kept thinking about her, especially while he was in jail, daydreaming about how to get out of his predicament, which chafed all the more because of her, and be with her. An understanding developed between them. "When does romance pay attention to the necessities of life?" he asked Jack.

"And has it ever occurred to you that she, perhaps, never really forgave you?" Jack replied.

Zan was dumbstruck. "No, of course not. She said that was all past us, it was forgotten."

"Ah. And you believed her."

"Of course. Why shouldn't I?"

To Zelda he says now: "With love, the story is between your ears, not between your legs. The problem is, all my life, I kept forgetting."

"And Rose knew about your wife? She didn't mind?" It's almost the exact same question Jack had asked.

"Yes, she knew, yes, she minded. Of course she minded. I told her it didn't mean anything, she wasn't convinced. The situation was intolerable. It had to end. If I'd been killed in Spain, the woman would have been a widow, which would have been far better than a spinster. Why not a divorcee?"

"That's all it took?" Jack asked. "Was your friend Fox a divorce lawyer too?"

"You do him a disservice. Divorce lawyers there are plenty of. It took more than that."

Once again, he'd met with the brothers, though this time it was in an office. The end of the Depression seemed to be in sight, and things were getting better for many people, the Sorromans especially, it seemed. In just that short time, they'd prospered, making money in real estate as well as their earlier ventures.

For Zan, the decision to end it was sparked by Abe's release. Canada declared war on Germany December 10, 1939. Within weeks, Fox was calling Zan to tell him of the proposal he'd received: a pardon if Abe would go directly into the military. It was only months after they agreed to the terms, after Abe's departure, that Zan learned many other healthy young prisoners were given the same offer. Once again, he'd felt cheated. Still, it brought the whole thing to an end.

"It's going to happen, one way or another," he told the Sorromans. He looked straight in the eye of Samuel, the eldest, and the eye of the middle brother, but he was unable to meet the squinting gaze of Danny, the youngest. They'd never been friends but, one time, there had been some small something between them. "I've tried, I've done the best I can. But this can't work. Have you talked to your sister? You

Dave Margoshes

know how unhappy she is, unhappier than I am, probably, unhappier than she was before, probably. You have to kill me, go ahead, but killing me won't help."

The brothers looked at each other. There were conditions, one being neither an abandonment nor an annulment but a proper divorce; another being that he leave the city; and other financial ones he could accommodate. "There's the matter of interest," Samuel said.

"I don't have it all now, but I'm good for it. You know that."

"You can sell your sister," Danny said. "She should bring a few bucks." Zan let that go.

Between what he had saved and what he could borrow, he was able to raise $1,000. The note he signed was for four thousand more, each thousand due at the end of a further year. He left Winnipeg at the end of that week. Rose was already in Toronto, waiting for him. He could throw himself back into writing at last. There was already a new novel clattering around in his head, something about a marriage of convenience, about betrayal.

"That's it?" Jack asked when he was through telling the story.

"That's not enough?"

"No remorse? No regret?"

"Three thousand fucking bucks through the nose, that's not enough remorse?"

For Zelda, the question is different, as he expects: "And she *did* love you, Rose?"

"Yes," he says, bowing his head, "she did."

"You're *sure?*"

"How sure can you ever be someone loves you? That's how sure. *Now* we'll change the subject?"

"*Abela*, about that gun...."

"Again with the gun. Leave me alone with that *cockamayme* gun, for God's sake."

"I only asked you once."

"Once is enough."

"But you didn't answer."

"And this time should be different?"

"I just want to know where it was."

"Where it was? It was in the house, Momma's house, a blessing be on her memory. *Our* house."

"Where, though? Where in the house?"

"In the house, ain't that enough?"

"No. Did I see it?"

"Did you see it? You held it in your hand! You waved it around like Hopalong Cassidy."

"I did?"

"No, you didn't, Zannie. You didn't touch it, didn't see it, didn't get a whiff of its perfume."

"So which is it? I did or I didn't?"

"Forget it, Zannie. If you don't remember, it's a *mitzvah* on you. It's old wash, you don't wanna stick your nose in it."

"I do."

"You'll just get a stink up your nostrils."

"I don't care."

"He don't care. So I should help him?"

"Why not? You're my brother. I'm asking you a favour. If you passed an old man on the street and he asked you a favour, wouldn't you do it?"

"This is the street?"

"Forget the street. An old man asks you for a favour."

"Old man is right, too old to be worrying about something that doesn't concern him."

"That's just it, *Abela*, it *does* concern me."

"Fifty years ago, dead and buried, that concerns you?"

"Fifty years is yesterday, Abe. You and I aren't dead yet."

"Knock wood."

"Knock wood."

"Zannie, what can I tell you. *We* had the gun, Saul and me. Not you. *We* used it in the stickup, not you. *We're* the ones got sent away, not you. The gun was *ours*, Zannie, not yours. It's none of your business, not then, not now."

"That's just it, *Abela*, it *was* my business...."

"Believe me, Zannie, baby brother, it wasn't."

"*Abela*, you're giving me a headache. Just tell me...."

"*You've* got a headache? What's this I got in *my* head? An ice cream sundae?"

"Just tell me where the gun was, for God's sake."

"Oh ho, now God enters the picture!"

"Forget God. Just tell me where the gun was."

"Forget God, I don't do, Zannie. You forget God maybe, I don't. God doesn't forget you."

"The gun, *Abela*, just tell me about the gun. Please."

"The gun? It was in the house, that's all. Who remembers where? In the sock drawer, in the cupboard with Momma's pickles, in the coal bin. Who knows? In the house, that's all you gotta know. Ain't that bad enough?"

"Abe, please!"

"Where the gun was, you *schlemiel*, it was right under your nose. There, you satisfied?"

CHAPTER 28

March 21, 1989

IT ASTONISHES ZAN THE EASE with which Zelda brings their sessions to an end.

"I don't think you need to be seeing me any more, Zan."

A simple statement, no buildup, no rhetorical flourishes or throat clearings, no looking away.

He never knew what she might bring up, so never entered her office with any specific expectations. The subject was always *him*, his past, his present, even to a certain extent his future. Within those narrow parameters, anything was fair game, and over the six months he'd been seeing her – has it really been that long? – she'd never surprised him. But now he is surprised.

"I don't?"

"I've enjoyed getting to know you, Zan, our chats, as you called them once. But we really don't need to see each other any more, I don't think."

"You don't? We don't?"

"You weren't feeling well when we started, remember? You'd been in hospital? Your wife had died? You were in shock?"

"You're asking me or telling me, Lady Doctor?"

"Just refreshing your memory."

"My memory could always use refreshing, so thank you for that, but all this is old news."

"And the *new* news is that you've come through all that, Zan. You're fine now. For an eighty-three-year-old man, you're remarkably healthy, well-adjusted. You really don't need me any more."

She's right, he knows that. Still, he feels numb. It crosses his mind that his reluctance to discuss Goldie the previous week might have had something to do with her decision. Maybe not.

"You seem surprised, Zan. Are you all right?"

"I'm fine. But I am surprised...just didn't expect it. Was there something I said?"

"No, nothing like that. I've been thinking about it for a few weeks. This will be our last session. Our conversations have been useful to you, I think, but it's not to your benefit if we allow them to be a crutch."

"A crutch?"

"I'm not saying that's what they are. But they could easily become that. Don't you agree?"

"Isn't that my question?"

"Is it? Maybe it is. At any rate, you had a lot to talk about when we started, there was a lot of emotion blocked up, you were having trouble handling it all...."

"And not any more?"

"No one ever comes completely to terms with his past, but I think you've come a long way, Zan. This novel you're working on, it's proof of that, don't you think?"

"Yes, you're right about that."

"And how's it coming, by the way?"

"Coming? It's coming. And that's not just making conversation. It really is. Seven, eight chapters. Not to tempt fate, but that's more than I've been able to do before."

"And you feel good about that?"

"Good? Of course I do."

"Well, then. I think you're okay."

"Okay?"

"Yes, okay."

"And okay is good?"

Zelda gives him a parting gift, one of her rare smiles, teeth and lips, even gums, the kind of smile from a woman like her that a man might crawl into, even a man like him.

"Yes, okay is good. It's good enough."

Maybe it was, maybe *he* was, but he's shaken nonetheless as he leaves her office, knowing it's for the last time. The rest of their brief conversation after her pronouncement was – and perhaps he only imagined it – somewhat more formal than usual, more clinical, less cordial, as if she had already withdrawn from what he thought of as a special relationship. And as he went out her door, there was no cheery "Let me hear from you from time to time," or "Keep in touch." Riding down the elevator, he has to remind himself, they aren't friends, their relationship has been strictly professional.

Yet, although it pains him to admit it, and he certainly wouldn't have said this to her, in the last few months she had become the most important person in the world to him, not that there were too many other important people in his life, just Abe and, by default, Dolly, whom he'd been to see a few times, sitting awkwardly in the aura of silence she cast. No, Dolly didn't count, just Abe, but even he, his own brother, the man closest and dearest to him in all the world, even he was eclipsed in importance by Zelda.

Why? "Because she listened." He actually says these words aloud now, moving his lips as if whispering them to a lover as he lurches down Eleventh Street toward Seventeenth Avenue. But there is no lover, and most certainly not Zelda, just a handful of passersby who pay him no mind, another elderly man talking to himself as he shuffles along, no cause for either alarm or interest.

Were he to drop dead in the street, or die in his apartment – that is to say, were his dead body to be found – it wouldn't be she who would find it or even be notified, she is no next of kin, no kin at all. Perhaps she would hear of it at some later point – his Medicare card would be cancelled surely, and there might be some conveyance of this information from one low-level bureaucrat to another and somehow, someone, might mention it to her.

"Wiseman...wasn't he a patient of yours?"

"Yes, what's that irascible fellow up to now?"

"Nothing, he's dead."

"Dead? That's a shame. Well, he was eighty-three...."

Zan smiles – and this, rather than his mutterings, does alarm a passerby, a stout woman of indeterminant age in a heavy maroon coat who seems to take offence to strange men smiling at her. She makes a sour face back at him and mutters something herself, just under her breath and beyond the capture of his hearing.

He passes a café he's stopped in for coffee once or twice, slows, stops, turns around. Midafternoon, the place is almost empty. He asks the waitress for a coffee and an orange-cranberry muffin and sits down at a table for two with a copy of the *Calgary Herald*.

Flipping through the pages, he smiles grimly at the thought that his death might even warrant a small item in the paper: "Minor

Novelist Remaindered." Zelda might come across it in the paper over her morning coffee. "Oh, no, Zan. Who will say *Kaddish* over you?"

Indeed.

I'm a free man, he thinks, sipping his coffee. The improbably named Zelda has given me my walking papers. Dusky-skinned, long-lashed Zelda, object of my erotic fantasies, such as they are – she and I are through. Now I'll never find out the mysteries of her miscegenation, the origins of her unfashionable name.

We she says – *we* really don't need, like all along it's been a mutual exchange society, her telling him a secret for every one of his. No, *we* don't need to see each other any more, he grants her that.

No, he doesn't need her - but he'll miss the audience, he thinks, almost saying it aloud. Did she think about that? Was he consulted? No.

But what was he complaining about? He doesn't have better things to do with his Tuesday afternoons?

CHAPTER 29

April 4, 1989

ZAN WAKENS IN PREDAWN DARKNESS. No more reliable alarm clock than the bladder of an aging man. It takes a moment for the synapses to whirr and fall into place, bringing him sharply back to this time and place, 557 Eighteenth Avenue S.W., Calgary, Alberta, Canada, April 4, 1989, here and now. Any significance to that date? No, not really, just another day alive. And to the place? No, you have to be somewhere, so why not where you are, wherever that is? Someone once said that. Maybe Zan wrote it.

Okay, good, another day, still alive, the Ragman nowhere in sight. He has an aversion to the image of himself being found dead in his bed, perhaps in a puddle of his own waste – a terrible legacy to leave to Abe and whomever else might be privy to it. Better to go fully dressed, on your feet, perhaps run down by a truck, or squashed by a two-ton safe falling from a building, as in those Road Runner cartoons, obliterated.

These are the thoughts of an eighty-three-year-old man upon waking. You were expecting philosophy maybe? Theology? How about string theory, chaos theory, abstract expressionism? Zan smiles in the darkness, amused by the thoughts of an old man, shakes his head. *Old man!*

Always a surprise, that. He's been an old man for – what? – ten years, fifteen? But every day, facing himself in the mirror, facing the thought in his mind, it's a surprise. Now, another one: like a cat creeping up on him, Nick Papagapolous slips again into his mind – he was always calling him "old man," and that was more than twenty years ago.

Damn, what had happened to Nick? After he'd disappeared from Toronto, Zan had assumed he'd hear from him at some point, as he had after the boy's first disappearance. And had assumed – well, hoped – that someday he'd see his photograph smiling out at him from a bookstore window. But no, not a word, and no book. Another victim of the Wiseman curse?

He gets up and pads through darkened rooms, drawn by the dim glow of a night light in the bathroom, sits on the toilet and lets the urine splash out. Okay again, good, plumbing still working. One less thing to worry about today.

Nick couldn't finish, didn't anyway. Yes, the Wiseman curse, or Wiseman syndrome! Now there was a mouthful. Something, whatever you called it, to be devoutly avoided.

He flushes the toilet and, turning around, is arrested for a moment by his image in the medicine chest mirror – even in the feeble light cast by the small bulb near the toilet, he can see the ghost of a face, that of an old man, bent, white-haired, gaunt, and that misshapen nose, the weak chin, those small eyes, too close together for comfort, qualities that have nothing to do with age, features he's had all or, in the case of the nose, most of, his life. He shakes his head to ward off that ghost and lurches back through the living room toward bed, no light to guide this return trip, just the well-worn rhythm of habit. There's no clock with an illuminated face in the suite, and the streetscape outside the uncurtained window is completely dark – it could be one o'clock, two, closer to when he retreated to bed than when he should venture out of it, three, four... Fitzgerald was right, it's always three in the morning in the darkened soul – and what soul isn't darkened? Even the muffled, unsteady throb of traffic from Seventeenth Avenue, a block away, which he knows is constant throughout the night, gives no clue. Certainly worth the effort to try to fall asleep again, though that will be uncertain. He had been in the arms of a dream, wisps of which now flicker tauntingly through his mind, and it would be good to sink back into its embrace.

It occurs to him that when he went to bed, whenever that was, as little as an hour ago, or as long ago as four or five hours, it was Monday, which means it is likely Tuesday now, certainly will be when he wakes up again, should he be able to get back to sleep. Tuesday, and no session with Zelda awaiting him, the second full week he will have gone without her company. He is a graduate. He smiles at this thought – so many times in the loony bin or on the couch of a head-shrinker, surely he's a grad student by now, a PhD, a post-doc. But, no, the metaphor is wrong – he is an addict, being weaned from his drug. Two weeks and counting without the comfort of conversation.

He closes his eyes and within moments hears the imagined strains of a brass band, fading into the jaunty pneumatic tune of a calliope, smells the pungent aroma of sawdust and manure. For weeks, since Abe had first mentioned the circus, he'd been experiencing intermittent dreams of various sorts, always involving the circus in some way, always involving him, sometimes Abe as well, even, sometimes Adam, the three of them as boys, as young men, as old men, and it surprises Zan on waking that he's been able, within the dream, to recognize Adam as an adult, even as an old man. But why shouldn't he? Adam's face, at any age, is his own. Also in these dreams often would abruptly appear the tall man and the small man, the giant and the midget, he remembered so vividly from the circus of his childhood. And through the dream, swinging above it, as if to remove herself from the worldly cares of mortal man, a little girl with a red ribbon in her hair, alone and live on a trapeze. But they have absented themselves from this particular dream, the silent girl and the two silent men, leaving lions and tigers and Siberian bears to roam unmolested through the dreamscape, harmlessly hunting clowns and brightly dressed acrobats to the brassy choruses of a disembodied band.

Nor was there any sign of them, the girl, the tall man, the small man, at the actual circus the two brothers had attended the previous afternoon.

"No giant, no midget," Zan said.

"Who said there would be?" Abe replied.

They mock-whispered to each other, leaning into each other's ear, so as not to disturb the people sitting all around them, but at a higher pitch than normal to be heard over the general din of chatter, laughter and music.

"Nobody said, somebody – me – had hopes."

"Hopes! Look at the posters. Did you see any giants? Any midgets?"

"Always the realist, you."

"Always the optimist, *you*."

"Is that the difference between us, *Abela?* I'm one kind of *ist*, you're another?"

Abe laughed. "Sure, that's how Mom told us apart. Like different coloured ribbons."

"I thought it was *Adam* and me who had to be told apart."

"Nobody could ever tell *you* anything." Now Abe was grinning, a gap-toothed sight that always brought Zan inexplicable joy.

They were in a huge arena, somewhere in the massive Stampede Park – Abe had expertly led the way – in good seats only ten rows above the ring around which the troupe of performers was parading, handsome young men and women in spangled, form-fitting costumes, clowns in red bulbous noses packed into an impossibly tiny car, splendid white horses, a sinuous tiger on a leash held by a man with a formidable moustache, even a solitary elephant, being ridden by a woman slender as a child and trailed by a vague scent of dung. But no giants, no midgets, no other freaks of nature. Zan looked around him; the section where they sat was mostly filled, mostly with children and their harried-looking escorts, relaxed now that their charges' attention was riveted. No, no freaks of nature in the audience either, present company included. Just two old men – coming through the concourse on their way to their seats, Zan had caught a glimpse of their reflection in a window, two old men, one with a full head of white hair, the other almost bald, both bent, shrunken, limping along in a comic caricature of dance – nothing freakish about that.

"There's just one ring," Zan said.

"Ring?"

"You know, the ring." He pointed to the spectacle before them. A large ring, like the rubber stopper on a thermos bottle, separated the first row of spectators from the action, no more than two feet high, painted white.

"So?"

"So there used to be three. At home, at the Exhibition, three rings."

"Who remembers such things?"

"What, you don't remember Ringling Brothers, Barnum and Bailey's famous three-ring circus?"

"Ringling Brothers we didn't get in Winnipeg. Who it was, that I don't remember, but it wasn't Ringling."

"But three rings, whoever they were. This is only one."

"Three, one, what's the difference? You can only look at one at a time anyway. Would you have three TV sets in your living room, going at the same time?"

"That's not the point, Abie, three rings, circus, that's the way it used to be."

"*Used* to be, there, you explained it yourself," Abe told him. "That was then, this is now."

"So you've told me before, on more than one occasion."

"Even that, it's *then* you're more interested in, not *now*."

The argument, if that's what it was, rumbled on, amiable and comfortable. The arena went dark, then spotlights pinpointed trapezes being lowered from the impenetrable heights. A beautiful woman and a handsome man were lifted high above the crowd, hurling themselves through the air with supernatural skill. But no sign of a daughter.

"There's no little girl," Zan whispered.

"What?"

"You know, the little girl...."

"What? I can't hear you."

"Little girl, on the trapeze. Red ribbon. Remember?"

"What?"

Zan stood up abruptly, grabbing onto the back of the seat in front of him for balance.

"Where you going?" Abe demanded

"Nature calls."

"Now? You'll miss the trapeze."

"It's okay, there'll be more."

He made his way carefully along the row of knees and elbows to the aisle, taking the time to orient himself for the return trip, then down to the bottom and through a doorway that led him into a tunnel and then to a concourse, jammed with people as they had passed through it less than half an hour earlier but now all but deserted, with food booths and washrooms. He visited one of the latter, avoiding his reflection as he washed his hands, and then made a stop at one of the former for a hot dog, which he lathered first with bright mustard, then piled on onions and sauerkraut. Abe had been right, the hot dog wasn't kosher, but it was firm and chewy, the mouthfuls it produced a mixture of sweet and sour. He found a bench and chewed slowly, taking sips from a root beer and listening to the passing hubbub. Gradually he became aware of a rising whine, like that of an electric saw, growing louder. Only when it stopped did it register that he'd been listening to a siren drawing closer. Now, a set of doors at the end of the concourse that was in his line of vision flung open and two men in black pants and white shirts pushing a stretcher on wheels burst through. One of the men was black, short and wiry, the other white, tall and gangly. A security guard in a blue uniform met them a few steps from the door and gestured for them to follow him. They sped across the concourse and disappeared into the same tunnel Zan had emerged from only a few minutes earlier. Unbidden, the image of Abe sprang into his mind.

Zan got to his feet, placed the remains of his hot dog and drink in the already overflowing trash can beside the bench and began to move, heading in the direction the paramedics had gone. As he entered the passageway, he felt as much as he saw the narrowing of the slightly rounded walls, as if he had entered a funnel and was being swept along toward an inevitable exit. He was walking as fast as he could, aware that it was still absurdly slow, and his heart had begun to ricochet against his ribs, adding to the growing clamour that loomed at the end of the tunnel. Then he was out in the open again, at the fringe of the arena. An usher, a teenaged girl with a ponytail and a toothy smile, blocked his way. "Can I help you to your seat, sir?"

"No, I'm..." He moved his hand in a vague gesture. "Where did they go, the..." he began, but the word "paramedics" eluded him. He looked around, grasping for the miniature sight of Abe's face in the distance. He spotted the pillar emblazoned with the letter "W" that he had used to orient himself, and brushed past the usher, heading toward it. Ahead of him now, he saw the blue uniform of the guard. He tried to move faster, but people were blocking his path, on their feet, clogging the aisle. An indecipherable murmur swam above their heads like a low-lying cloud.

Zan pushed his way forward, stumbling, his hand darting out to the top of the low wall defining the ring, righting himself. He saw a flash of white, then the shape of broad shoulders of one of the paramedics. Then both men swam into view, he saw them bending over someone lying in the aisle between banks of seats several rows above him. Is that where they'd been sitting? He tried to move forward again but his way was blocked by a large man and an even larger woman standing motionless, planted. "Excuse me...." Zan began, then, "Zannie," someone said, and he stumbled around to find himself face to face with a face almost his own.

"Abe."

"You."

"I thought...."

"*You* thought? That's what *I* thought."

"*Me?* Why would you...?"

"Why would *you* think *me?*"

"Right. A young man like you."

"You gave me a scare," Abe said. Zan could see that the skin around his brother's eyes had grown taut and white.

"*You?* You gave *me* a scare."

Abe didn't reply. He stepped forward, around the feet of a teenager sprawled in his seat with legs extended, and took Zan in his arms.

There was no mirror, no plate glass window to hurl their reflection back at them, but Zan knew well enough what they looked like, the spectacle they presented, two old men, twins not twins, caught in a bearclutch, in a clownish dance on their own graves.

ZAN STIRS. SOMEONE, SOMEWHERE, IS CRYING. A baby? Someone in pain? His eyes spring open, his head lifting from the pillow. No, just the blaring of a car horn outside his window. He blinks, his eyes adjusting to the full assault of daylight, lies back, closes his eyes, reaches for the hem of the dream that, just moments ago, he'd been wrapped in. Already the cloth of the dream was turning to lace, dancing out of his reach. The circus, music, clowns, strangely unmenacing tigers, a flash of light on the trapeze. Yes, the circus, dreamed of again. But then, as dream shifts to memory, the slow machinery of memory begins to move, the gears of narrative, like currents of muscular water beneath the transparent skin of ice.

Dave Margoshes

CHAPTER 30

APRIL 7, 1989 – NOTES TOWARD A NOVEL – and no, this isn't a late April fool's joke. This is as serious as can be. This is a beginning.

Many pages done, over two hundred now, but every day, a new beginning.

Given my age, how weary I am, it's not likely there will be an end to this novel, but that's okay. I've written novels without ends before. But this will be different. It won't be failure of will that will stand in the way but failure of flesh. That will be easier to live with. Ha ha.

HE'S TYPING FOR THE FIRST TIME on the new computer, Abe's surprise gift to him yesterday.

Its keyboard is familiar enough, close enough to a typewriter's, but the screen is still a puzzlement, the words so mysteriously appearing and just as easily disappearing if he wants them to. Still getting used to it, but he has to admit it makes the mechanics of writing easier. Not the writing itself, just the mechanics. But the writing itself has been easier these last few weeks too. He can see where he's going.

"What am I supposed to do with this?" he asked after Abe, still strong, had lugged it up the stairs, wrestled it out of its box and onto the kitchen table, shoving Zan's old Underwood aside.

"Do? It's a writing machine, Zannie. You write on it. Write!"

They stood gazing at the computer. "How do you turn it on?"

"I should know? Figure it out. Here, there's a booklet, it tells you everything."

Again they stood in silence, admiring, puzzling.

"You know, I could have bought this myself, *Abela*. I've got more money than you."

"But would you have? Did you? No, and no. So say thank you, Zannie, and figure out how it works. And write. Write."

THIS IS A BEGINNING. And isn't that something, after all this time? All this silence?

NICK. ALL THAT TALENT, all that waste. What had become of him, of the novel *he* was struggling with. Had he, Zan, somehow failed the boy? Failed to be the proper example he needed? Like Pascal's gamble, better to take a chance on a failed writer who might yet just produce another book than on a successful one who just might never write another word. Something like that. Zan smiles at this mishmash of metaphor. And which was it that Nick had wagered on, the successful Zan or the failure? Maybe that wasn't clear, maybe the final roll of the dice had yet to be thrown.

Again, the notion of the wager rises to the surface of his mind. Pascal had it easy, his bet a sure thing. Bet for God, and if you lose you never know it. Bet against, and if you win you never know, but a loss could mean eternal damnation – or perhaps just a key to a house in a rundown district of heaven, if God's more benevolent than the Bible lets on. But Wiseman's Wager is tougher to suss out. Bet against a failed novelist and you have the grim satisfaction of being right if he stumbles yet again and the pleasure of being wrong if he doesn't; bet against him, and he comes through, well no real harm there, no loss for you, just a pleasant surprise, and if he doesn't, again that grim satisfaction.

Yes, better to bet on a novel you think you can finish than give up on one you fear you can't. When the Ragman knocks on the door, I'll be holding one more draft.

THIS IS A BEGINNING. I think I know what this novel will be about, is about. What could it be but about me? And *Abela* a little. The spaces between us. Well, and maybe about a woman. Maybe more than one, two or even three. I know this material well. Well, I think I do. What I need to find, as the creative writing teachers say, is a shape for the story, an arc. All right, how hard could that be? A robbery, maybe, a robbery gone bad, some violence, intrigue, conflict. A mystery, that's the ticket.

Dave Margoshes

THIS IS A BEGINNING. I know, I know, I keep saying that, but you have no idea how good it is to type that: This, Is, A, Beginning. Four words, like God's: Let, There, Be, Light. Even God needed a beginning, on that first day, before He created the sky and the firmament or whatever it was, even before there was A Plan, God had to have a beginning. Do you suppose He had a shape, an arc? An ending in sight? Not on your life. Just a beginning: "In the beginning...." I can do that. On that day when He created man and woman, there in the Garden, could He possibly have known how that would all turn out? Did He know about the serpent? Had He already blocked out Cain and Abel, Abraham, Moses, David, all the others, all the generations? Had He already conceived Sodom and Gomorrah – yes, a brilliant stroke! *The story turns here*, God exclaims to the angels, attentive and jotting down His every word on stone tablets with quills from their own wings. The Flood? The Plagues of Egypt? All the betrayals? No. How could He have and gone on? If He had seen where it would lead, how could He possibly have gone on?

No, "this is a beginning," God thought, "and let's see where it goes."

THIS IS A BEGINNING. The plot I'm still hazy on, but character is strong. A strong personality, a bit idiosyncratic, cantankerous even. Godlike – yes, that flawed. And there's a brother, of course. A sidekick, a Sancho Panza. Can there be a hero without his other side? And a woman, of course, a woman, some Adam's rib. Some Eve, before the serpent, the apple, the temptation, the sin. Some Luna.

I don't expect redemption, epiphany. No blinding flash of light. No, no illumination of any sort. This will be a story without resolution, a mystery without a solution, a mystery *about* mystery. Yes, I like that.

Nick, this one's for you.

A beginning, a couple of good strong characters, what more do I need than that? Put them in a room somewhere, get them talking....

YES. A BEGINNING. And, yes and yes and yes, a middle too. And even an end in sight.

FOUR FORTY-FIVE. The Earth wobbles on its axis like a gyroscope beginning to run down and the motion shoves him fully awake, jerking him upright in the dark like a puppet. Through the open door to the living room, he can see the ghostly glow of the computer screen, pulsing like a heart. Fitzgerald was both right and wrong. It *is* always night in the soul, but not always three in the morning.

But what kind of a *cockamayme* believes in the soul, anyway? What kind of a *cockamayme* believes in God, any god?

He gives his head a shake.

ACKNOWLEDGEMENTS

This novel had a long journey from start to finish, not even counting the gestation period. Along the way, it was the beneficiary of writing time supported by a number of agencies and institutions, for which I am exceedingly grateful.

Work on the novel began on New Year's Day, 1996, while I was living in Winnipeg as part of a writer-in-residency program funded by the two provincial arts agencies that also brought Sandra Birdsell to Saskatoon. (I had the additional benefit of living in Sandra's Winnipeg home during that nine-month period.) The residency was also supported in part by the Manitoba Writers' Guild and the University of Winnipeg. Over the subsequent dozen or so years, I worked on the novel, between stints with other projects, during a residency at the Saskatoon Public Library funded by the Canada Council, a month's residency at Toronto Artscape's Gibraltar Point studio on Toronto Island, and a similar residency at the Vermont Studio Center in Johnson, Vermont. (My travel to Toronto and Vermont was assisted by small grants from the Canada Council and the Saskatchewan Arts Board.)

In addition, I worked on the novel at home in Regina and on the farm where I now live west of Saskatoon, at the Wallace Stegner House residence for artists in East End, Saskatchewan, and at colonies organized by the Saskatchewan Writers Guild at Emma Lake, Christopher Lake and St. Peter's Abbey, all in Saskatchewan. In addition to the funding already cited, I was able to write for unbroken periods of time in 1996-97 with the assistance of a Canada Council grant, and in 2009 with the help of one from the Saskatchewan Arts Board.

My thanks to all the people and agencies involved. Funders of the arts – be they private or public, individual or corporate – help to make art happen.

Thanks also to the terrific team at Coteau Books (which itself is the beneficiary of funding from the Saskatchewan Arts Board, as well as Sask Culture, Canadian Heritage and the City of Regina) led by Nik Burton; to my sharp-eyed editor, David Homel; and my equally sharp-eyed "pre-editor," David Carpenter. Between them, those two Davids conspired to bring out the best from this one.

Wiseman's Wager was the recipient of the City of Regina Writing Award in 2004, when it was still in draft form. A short excerpt from it appeared in *A/Cross Sections: New Manitoba Writing*, edited by Katherine Bitney and Andrew Taskans, Manitoba Writers' Guild, 2007.

As I wrote, I read a lot, about Winnipeg in the '20s and '30s, and about Jewish immigrant life in the first half of the twentieth century. I'm particularly indebted to these authors and books:

James H. Gray, *The Boy from Winnipeg*
Harry Gutkin, with Mildred Gutkin,
    The Worst of Times, the Best of Times
Irving Howe, *World of Our Fathers*
Alfred Kazin, *A Walker in the City*
Julius Israel Kohsen, *Memories of My Life*
Norman Podhoertz, *Making It*
Doug Smith, *Joe Zuken: Citizen and Socialist.*

ABOUT THE AUTHOR

DAVE MARGOSHES has published more than a dozen books of fiction, poetry, and nonfiction. His collection of stories, *Bix's Trumpet and Other Stories*, was Saskatchewan Book of the Year, won the Regina Book Award and was a finalist in the ReLit Awards in 2007. His three previous novels are *Drowning Man, I Am Frankie Stern*, and *We Who Seek: A Love Story*. He has published seven story collections, including *A Book of Great Worth* – which was one of Amazon.ca's Top Hundred Books of 2012 – five volumes of poetry and several non-fiction works, including a biography of Tommy Douglas.

He has had stories and poems published in dozens of magazines and anthologies in Canada and the United States (including six times in *Best Canadian Stories*), had work broadcast on CBC, and given readings across the country. His awards include the Stephen Leacock Prize for Poetry. He was also a finalist for the Journey Prize.

Some of his stories and poems spring from his days as an itinerant journalist. Margoshes worked for daily newspapers in eight cities, including San Francisco, New York, Calgary and Vancouver, covering everything from politics to murder to cat shows. He's also taught journalism. He currently lives near Saskatoon.

ENVIRONMENTAL BENEFITS STATEMENT

Coteau Books saved the following resources by printing the pages of this book on chlorine free paper made with 100% post-consumer waste.

TREES	WATER	SOLID WASTE	GREENHOUSE GASES
14	**6125**	**678**	**1334**
FULLY GROWN	GALLONS	POUNDS	POUNDS

 Calculation based on the methodological framework of Paper Calculator 2.0 - EDF

MIX
Paper from responsible sources
FSC® C103214

FSC® is not responsible for any calculations on saving resources by choosing this paper.